THE

MARQUIS OF DALEWOOD:

THE HISTORY OF A FAMILY SECRET.

By the Author of

"RANKLEY GRANGE," "PAUL'S PERILS," "THE KNIGHTRIDERS," &C., &C.

LONDON:

E. & H. BENNETT, BEDFORD HOUSE, MAIDEN LANE, STRAND.

PREFACE.

THE success which has attended the publication of the "MARQUIS OF DALEWOOD" has fully confirmed the Publishers in their belief that a story of romantic interest would be welcome to a large portion of the reading public, who are surfeited with the realistic novels of the day; and they have, therefore, much pleasure in announcing that another romance, of domestic and dramatic interest, by the Author of the "Marquis of Dalewood," entitled "RANKLEY GRANGE," will appear immediately upon the conclusion of the present work.

The scene of the new story is laid partly in York and partly in London; and the period—the latter portion of the last century—will afford the Author a wealth of picturesque material, and give ample scope for the exercise of those powers of invention, skilfulness of construction, and graphic delineation of character, for which he is so eminent. The reader will follow, with unabating interest, the fortunes of Miranda, the beautiful heiress of Rankley Grange; the vicissitudes of her lover, Rowland Percy; the villainous schemes of Bernard Varley and his accomplice, Twitter; and the hair-breadth escapes and chivalrous devotion of that strange compound of good and evil, Dick Palmer, whose influence upon all the dramatis personæ is so remarkable and irresistible.

THE
MARQUIS OF DALEWOOD.

THE ATTACK UPON THE MARQUIS IN COVENT GARDEN.

CHAPTER I.

FIRE.—AN ALARM.—THE FUGITIVE NOBLE, AND THE WIFE'S LOVE.—THE GUARD.

FIRE!—A dull, red glare shoots up into the clear night sky. Fire!—A million sparks, each glowing like an eye of flame, spring upwards, and then amid the glare of their own wild beauty, instantly expire.

Fire! fire!—The hoarse rattle of wheels on the ill-paved streets of London, comes like thunder on the silence of the night. Fire!—A thousand tongues take up the appalling cry, and from every street, court, and alley of the great city there rush forth throngs of excited people, upon whose faces the red glare looks down with coppery refulgence.

The opera-house is on fire, and it is the first

day of May, in the year 1788. London—mighty London, then but a pigmy in comparison to what it is now, had slept for two hours before from the roof of the then Italian opera, in the Haymarket, there arose the lurid light of a column of flame, which was soon a hundred feet in height.

Fire! fire! fire!—The flames roared—the horses attached to the engines dashed along, maddened by the goading of their drivers, and the glare of the flames—the pumps clanked monotonously; and over a huge space the red-hot sparks fell in a fiery rain.

*   *   *   *   *

"Wife—wife, I say!" cried old Jacob Ardent, waterman-fireman, and husband for many a long year of Mrs. Ardent, bouquet-maker to the court and the opera. "Wife, I say! Good Heavens! wife, will you not awaken—and such a racket in the market as never was known?"

"Geraniums? No, my lord, hardly yet," said Mrs. Ardent, talking in her sleep, and, no doubt, fancying some customer was bargaining with her for a rare bouquet.

"Wife—wife, I say!"

"Oh, gracious! Jacob, whatever is the matter?"

"Are you awake now?"

"Yes - oh, yes! But you have quite frightened me, Jacob. Hush! There is a noise in the street."

"Yes, wife, you are right. There is, indeed, a noise in the street, and if you look up you will soon see what it is about."

"It's fire!"

"Yes, there is not much mistake about that."

A violent knocking at the door of the chamber now attracted the attention of old Jacob Ardent and his wife, and the former called out:

"Coming—coming! I know I am wanted. I'm a waterman-fireman, and I know I ought to come out; only have patience a moment."

"Uncle! uncle! aunt!" cried a sweet voice from the other side of the door.

"Why, it's Jane," said Mrs. Ardent; "it's our niece, Jane, and the noise in the street and all over the market has roused up the child. Go to bed again, Jane—it's a fire, and we know all about it."

"Where is my coat?" cried Jacob Ardent, who had succeeded in putting on the rest of his apparel. "Where can my coat be? Dear me!"

"Fire! fire! fire!" shouted some twenty or thirty voices in the market of old Covent Garden, where Mrs. Ardent carried on the business of bouquet-maker. "Fire! fire!"

With a roar and a crash that was like the fall of some great building, an engine with four horses harnessed to it, tore past the old house of the Ardents.

"Oh, Heaven!" said Mrs. Ardent, "this must be an awful fire! Jacob!—Jacob!"

"Yes? My coat—where is my coat?"

"But, Jacob, you must not go out."

"Not go out?"

"No—oh, no!"

"But I'm a waterman-fireman, wife, and as well known as old London Bridge, and they will all say, to-morrow, 'Where was Jacob Ardent?' It's in my license that I am to go out at the cry of fire. Where can my coat be? They would say that I skulked—they would say that old Ardent no longer was fit to wear his badge as a waterman-fireman. Confound it!—where is my coat? Don't you hear them? Fire! Ah, some one calls me by name. They all know that I come up from the old boat-house by the Tower here of a-night. Hark! Fire! fire!"

"Aunt—oh, aunt!" said Jane, from the other side of the door, "the sky is so red, and the people rush through the market like a drove of cattle. I can hear the roaring of the flames. Aunt! aunt! I am terrified! Open the door, and let me be with you."

"Poor child!" said old Ardent, as he opened the chamber door, and admitted his niece Jane, who flung herself upon her knees by the side of the bed, and hid her eyes in the coverlet, while she sobbed aloud in the terror of the moment. "Poor child, she is frightened out of her wits at this fire. Why, Jane, my dear, you should have seen the fires that your old uncle has seen when he was a young man, and thought no more of going up a four-story ladder than you do of making up a bouquet from your basket of flowers. You should have seen—— Hilloa! what is that? Why, they will have the door down."

Bang—bang—bang! came a succession of fierce blows at the door of Jacob Ardent's house.

The old man ran to the window, and, dashing aside the curtains that shaded it, flung it open; but the red glare of the sky, the wild roar of many voices, more and more distinct, and the monotonous clank, clank of the engines, and many other accidental sounds, that all conspired to make up an awful tumult, came so suddenly upon his senses, that he recoiled a step or two.

Mrs. Ardent, who had just hastily thrown on some apparel, screamed with fright, for the glare of red light in the sky was so great that she could not convince herself but that the whole of the rickety stands and houses in and about old Covent Garden market were in a blaze; and Jane was in such a state of terror, that she fell upon the floor of the room, half-fainting.

Bang!—bang!—bang! came at the door again.

Jacob Ardent recovered from the first shock of the approach to the window, and, leaning out from it, he saw, by the light that the angry-looking sky reflected down upon the earth, a sedan-chair, and a couple of stout chairmen, one of whom, with the end of one of the poles of the chair, was just commencing an attack upon the rather frail door of the little dwelling.

"Hold!" cried Jacob Ardent. "In the name of all that's good, what do you want?"

Upon this a lady looked out from the window of the sedan-chair, and called out:

"Jacob Ardent, is that you? Oh, yes—yes! Thank God!—thank God!"

"The Lord be good to us!" said Jacob. "Is that you, my lady?"

"Hush! Come down, and open the door. I wish to speak to you."

"Yes—yes! in a moment. Oh, dear! am I on my head, or on my heels? My coat—my coat! Why, bless me! I have got it on all the while! Coming, my lady—coming."

With great celerity the old man descended the rickety and creaking stairs that led from the upper part of his dwelling to the straggling, irregular sort of shop below; and unbarring the outer door, he rushed out, saying:

"Come in, my lady, and the blessing of Heaven be upon you! Come in—oh, come in at once—and welcome to the poor abode of Jacob Ardent, for whom you have done so much."

An elegantly-dressed lady, whose face was covered by a black veil, alighted from the sedan-chair; and as she grasped the arm of Jacob Ardent for support, she said to the men who had the care of the conveyance:

"Go now—I shall not want you! Go; you are well paid already!—Go at once, and forget me!"

"Good night, ma'am," said one of the men. "We don't mean to say that we are not paid."

"Ay, and well paid, too," said the other. "Good night, ma'am."

The lady pushed Jacob Ardent before her into the house, and then she closed the door, although she trembled so excessively that she could scarcely do so; and then, in quite a shrieking tone of voice, she called out:

"Jacob Ardent, I have tried to be kind to you and yours, God knows, and now I implore you to save the Marquis!"

"The Marquis?"

"Yes, the Marquis of Dalewood!—my husband!—the husband who has scorned me, and who has left me to misery and to want, with my child! Oh, save him! I have no friend in all the world to apply to, but yourself, Jacob Ardent, and you will not refuse me!"

"My lady, if you ask me for my life, it is yours."

"Thanks!—oh, thanks! I think I am nearly mad, and know not what I say. This tumult, too—this dreadful fire!"

"Ah, my lady, it is dreadful."

"It's enough," said Mrs. Ardent, who had come downstairs, and now appeared with a light, for the shutters of the shop prevented the glare of the flames from coming into it— "it's enough to take away a body's wits. My service to your ladyship, and God bless you! This is my niece, my lady."

"Yes, my lady," said Jane, curtseying.

"Yes, yes—I thank you all," said the half-distracted Lady Dalewood, clasping her hands together, and looking wildly about her. "But save him!—oh, save him from the block!"

"The block?"

"Yes: they will execute him for high treason—my husband, the Marquis of Dalewood. Heaven knows if he be as guilty as they say he is! But, by an accident, I found out that to-night he is to be arrested, and conveyed to the Tower."

"The Tower?"

"Yes. The Government has found out a plot in which some of the most discontented of the Irish nobility are implicated, and they will be sacrificed. Save him—oh, save him!"

"But, my lady, what can I do? I don't know where he is. I am but a poor, weak old man."

"You know him when you see him?"

"Oh, yes, my lady. He comes often to the market."

"Yes," said Mrs. Ardent, "he comes for a bouquet for—for—for——"

"Do not name her," said the Marchioness; "do not name her to me, I implore you! I know whom you mean. It is she who has usurped a wife's rights, and who reigns in the wayward affections of my husband. I can tell you, Jacob Ardent, where to find him, and where to save him, by warning him of his danger, and assisting him to escape."

"Yes, in my boat on the river, I will take him clear off," said the old man. "Will that do, my lady?"

"Yes—oh, yes!"

"But, my lady," said Mrs. Ardent, "why did you not warn him yourself? Nothing could have touched his heart more than that."

The Marchioness shook her head.

"I dare not risk going to the house where the first person I might see would possibly be the—the woman who usurps my place. No —no! I wish to save him, but I do not wish that he should know the succour comes through me."

"All's right, my lady—all's right!" cried the old man. "I am ready—only you tell me where to go."

"Yes—yes! Take this paper. It contains the direction. There is a house standing alone, close to the fields at the back of Montague House, and there you will find the Marquis, and, perhaps, others. Warn them all, but save him, by bringing him away with you. I will wait the success of your mission here. Tell him it is instant flight—or the Tower!"

CHAPTER II.

THE PLOT.—THE HOUR OF REPENTANCE.
THE DISGUISE.

Now, all this took place when George the Third was but young upon the throne, and when not only that throne, but the stability of the British Empire was threatened by the insurrectionary plots in which the Irish nobility were extensively implicated.

It was determined by the Government, by a bold stroke, to crush the incipient civil war which had been all but produced; and as, by some means, information was given to the Secretary of State, that at the Marquis of Dalewood's house, in the fields at the back of

Montague House—the same house that was afterwards the British Museum—there would be a meeting of some of the Irish nobility disaffected to the Government, an order was issued to arrest them all at three o'clock in the morning, when the streets would be quiet and deserted ; or earlier, if they should show a disposition to separate before that hour.

It had been ascertained, though, that when the disaffected nobles held a secret council, it usually terminated in a grand claret drinking, and the next day dawned and grew into broad light before they thought of separating; so the executive thought it had them quite secure.

How the Marchioness of Dalewood had got her information of what was intended, will shortly appear; but there must have been a strong feeling of kindness and longing love for one who had treated her as badly as it was possible a husband could treat a wife, to induce her to trouble herself about the Marquis's fate.

The fact was that, when a very young man, some sixteen years before the eventful night upon which our story opens, the Marquis of Dalewood had fallen in love with a poor, but accomplished girl, named Cecil Burton ; and, finding all his attempts to turn her from the paths of virtue fruitless, and unable to conquer his passion for her, he married her, and made her his Marchioness.

The old Duke of Lorton, his father, who resided in a wild, barbaric sort of magnificence on a feudal estate in the county of Galway, on the west coast of Ireland, was infuriated at the match his son had made, and from that moment declined all intercourse with him.

The Marquis, himself, too, soon got tired of the calm, domestic virtues of his young wife ; and, twelve months after their marriage, he deserted her and her newly-born infant, and plunged into all the dissipation of London, with scarcely a thought of her forlorn condition.

A scanty pittance forwarded to her through some confidential and, no doubt, rascally agent of the Marquis's, sufficed just for the support of the Marchioness and her babe ; and such was the state of things that had gone on for many a long year antecedent to the date of the commencement of our story.

During the brief time that the Marchioness resided with her husband, and had the means to do so, she had been an angel of goodness to all around her; and among others she had lifted the family of the Ardents from a complication of circumstances that would otherwise have been their ruin.

No wonder that, in her hour of distress and affliction, she and they often met with pleasant feelings upon both sides, and that they were ever ready to do anything to serve her.

With this brief explanation, we will now follow old Jacob Ardent upon his somewhat perilous expedition.

Upon emerging from his house he found the market alive with throngs of people, hurrying to the scene of the fire, which, by the glare in the sky, appeared to be raging more fiercely than ever. He had had the precaution not to go out wearing his coat and badge, or he might well have been questioned for taking a route so opposite to the locality in which his services as a waterman-fireman were required.

No one questioned the old man; and as he got farther and farther from the scene of the conflagration, he found less and less difficulty in proceeding, until at last, as he diverged from the main thoroughfare of old Tottenham Court Road, the streets began to present quite a deserted appearance.

Afar off, though, there came upon his ears the roar and the hum of the crowds about the fire, and with hasty steps the old man passed the corner of what is now Great Russell Street.

Tramp—tramp—tramp !

"What is that ?"

Old Jacob Ardent slunk into the depths of a dark doorway, and in another minute a captain's guard of the foot-soldiers passed him at ordinary time.

"Silence, my men !" said an officer, who with his drawn sword was at the head of the party, "silence—silence !—forward !"

Old Jacob Ardent looked after them. They crossed the road, and made for the front of Montague House, past which there was a regular path that led rather circuitously, but still sufficiently direct, to the house of the Marquis of Dalewood, to leave very little doubt upon the mind of Jacob Ardent as to their destination.

"They are after the Marquis," gasped the old man. "They are after the Marquis. There can be no doubt at all about it. I must save him, bad as he is, or his poor wife will go mad. For her sake, if not for his, I must try to save him."

The imminence of the danger of the Marquis of Dalewood was so apparent to Jacob Ardent, that he seemed to forget his age, and that for some time past he had been accustomed to move about with a deliberation that he would have laughed at in his younger days. He ran round the side of Montague House, opposite to that which the soldiers had taken, crossed a stile, jumped a ditch, and got into a meadow, with a celerity that was truly surprising.

It was the field way to the mansion which Jacob Ardent was taking.

Upon that field stands now a portion of Bedford Square, and the adjoining streets.

The rain, though, had made the grass heavy and slippery, and in places where the herbage was rather scanty the clay soil was on the surface, so that more than once Jacob had the greatest difficulty in making any progress at all.

Where there is a will, though, there is a way, and the old man soon found himself by a dwarf wall, that enclosed a portion of the orchard belonging to Dalewood House.

"Who goes there ?" cried a sharp voice.

Jacob Ardent paused.

"Who goes there ?" cried the voice again. "If you don't speak, I'll have a shot at you."

"It's me!" cried Jacob.

"Who is me?"

"Well, I hardly know."

"Don't be a fool!"

"The same to you, sir, whoever you are."

A man darted from the shadow of a sycamore tree that was close at hand, and suddenly clutched Jacob by the collar, as he said:

"So, my fine fellow, I have you, have I?"

"You had better be quiet," said Jacob.

"Indeed! and why had I better be quiet?"

"Because I do not like a stranger's hand on my collar, that is all, and I am not a hasty man; so say at once if you belong to the house or not."

"What house?"

"Dalewood."

"I do belong to Dalewood. I am in the service of the Marquis; and as he is afraid that the pheasants will be stolen that he keeps in the aviary, he puts me on guard here, you see."

"I comprehend," said Jacob; "and I see that you have my lord's livery on:—but they are not pheasants that you are looking after. Is the Marquis in the house, or is he not?"

"Well, what if he is?"

"If he is, go to him and tell him that a captain's guard of soldiers will, in a few minutes more, be at the front door of his house, and that if he would rather not have an interview with them, he had better get out by the back door, and escape over the fields."

"The devil——"

"Come, come, sir, don't go on swearing in that stupid way, but give my lord the warning of his danger."

"I will, by Jove! You stay here, my friend, and I will take good care that you are rewarded for your kindness."

Without another word, the seeming lackey vaulted over the dwarf wall, which was only four feet in height, and disappeared in the distance, in the direction of the house, the lofty walls of which loomed dark and dull-looking against the night sky.

That this man was in league with the Marquis of Dalewood and his associate plotters, Jacob Ardent had not the least doubt; and, although he had on one of the livery coats of the Marquis, there was a something about his manner which convinced Jacob that he was not a servant. In fact, Jacob Ardent guessed what was the truth, namely, that he was one of the plotters, whose duty it was on that night to keep watch at the back of the house.

Old Ardent had not to wait many minutes for the success of his mission. Before he could think it possible that the warning could be given, there appeared over the wall about six persons, and one of them said, in a muffled tone of voice:

"Where is the man who brought the information?"

"Here, my lord," said Jacob.

"Ah, you know me?"

"Yes, my lord, I do know you, even in the dark, by your voice; you are the Marquis of Dalewood."

"I am; and be you whom you may, I am indebted to you for my life. I rather think your information is true."

"No doubt of that, my lord."

"Gentlemen," said the Marquis, turning to the others, "you have each of you the means of providing for his own safety?"

"We have."

"Let me hope, then, that, although this interruption may delay our plans, it will not ultimately severely damage them."

"It will damage them," said one.

"Do you think so, Sir George?"

"Yes, Dalewood, yes; it is all over. The Government has now, by some means, information of what we are about, and, therefore, it will be quite impossible to go on; I shall leave England at once for France."

"And I," said another. "And I;" "And I," said two more.

"Then all is over," said the Marquis. "I have an act of justice to do in London, and when that is done, I will take the first vessel I can find, for Galway, and remain on my father's estate. It is large enough to shelter me, even if he should not receive me at the castle."

"Hark!" said one. "What is that?"

"The tramp of armed men in the garden," said the Marquis. "The soldiers are in the grounds, gentlemen. Let each take care of himself."

———

CHAPTER III.

THE MARQUIS MAKES REPARATION FOR A GREAT WRONG.

WHEN the Marquis of Dalewood uttered these last words, he hastily shook hands with the gentlemen around him, and then they all fled across the dark fields, leaving him alone with Jacob Ardent.

The Marquis turned to him, and said, in a voice of emotion:

"I do not know you; but take this packet, and when you get to your home, open it, and obey the instructions you will find therein. As for me, I know not where to go at present; but I will take my chance."

"My lord—my lord——"

"Say no more. Good-night—yet, no—I had forgotten; take this purse—you will find an ample reward in it."

"Reward? For what?"

"For giving me this timely notice to-night."

"Oh, no—no. I won't take it; but, after all, my Lord Dalewood, is it possible that you don't recollect me?"

"Indeed, I do not. But I have not another moment to spare to you, whoever you may be. Farewell."

"My lord," said the old man, as he took the Marquis by the arm, "you have just said that you don't know very well where to go at once, so I will charge myself with taking you to a place of safety. My house is a humble one, but it is all the safer on that account. You can stay in it till you have made up your mind what to do."

"I accept your offer with thanks, and trust you implicitly."

Arm-in-arm, then, the old waterman-fireman and the desolate noble went rapidly across the field and into the high road, towards the house in Covent Garden.

"Now, tell me," said the Marquis, as they emerged from the field, "who are you?".

"My name is Ardent."

"Ardent? Ardent? Ah, I have a recollection, now. You knew the Marchioness of Dalewood, before her ill-starred marriage with me?"

"I did, my lord; and good and kind she was to me and mine after that marriage, while—while——"

"While what?"

"While your love lasted, and gave her the means of being so: and after that we have been good and kind to her—that is to say, I mean, we have in our poor way tried to be grateful to her."

The Marquis uttered a deep sigh,

"Jacob Ardent," he said, "I well know you now: and time was, when I dreaded to hear your name, for the Marchioness, before our separation, used to speak of you with so much friendly feeling, that her words sounded like a reproach to me."

"Did they, my lord?"

"They did, my good friend; but different thoughts have come over me within the last few days. I don't know how it was, but a sort of film seemed to be lifted off my eyes—a cloud, or mist of vanity and pride, and error, appeared to roll away from my soul, and I am not the man I was."

"Oh, my lord! how happy you make me, by saying so! And do you, indeed, love the poor Marchioness?"

"Love her? Oh, Heaven! yes, with all my heart. But well I know and feel that she can never forgive me!"

"Oh, indeed! Ah!"

"No—no! She is a suffering angel, but I have sinned against her, past all forgiveness. Jacob Ardent, the packet that I gave you, and which I hope you have safe——"

"Oh, yes, here it is."

"Well, that packet contains a sum of two hundred pounds in gold. It is for my wife and child, for I—I—have heard—that I have a son."

"You have, my lord."

"Jacob Ardent, have you seen my—my boy?"

"I have."

"And I have not! Oh, Heaven! what devil was it that for so long took possession of my heart and brain?"

"Be of good cheer, my lord."

"No—no! I wish I were dead, before the sun of another day should rise!"

"Don't say that, my lord marquis. You have done wrong: there is no doubt about that at all. You went astray. Well—well! it is poor human nature to do that, ever so

often; but you see it all now, and you will repair the past."

"Can it be repaired? No—no!"

"But I say yes, my lord."

"Do not think so, Jacob Ardent. When I am gone from England, you will find out my wife and son, and tell them all that has passed this night. When they read the contents of the packet that you have, they will see that this repentance of mine did not arise from any sudden impulse upon meeting with you, for it is there written. I have only one deep regret."

"And what is that, my lord?"

"That in the hurry of to-night I had not time to bring away my will from Dalewood House. It is there, made in favour of my wife and child; but at your house, Jacob Ardent, I will draw up another."

"To be sure you can, my lord—to be sure. And now I have some news to tell you."

"News? What news?"

"Why, I will tell you how it was I came to know of your danger to-night, my lord."

"Oh, yes—yes! tell me that?"

"There came to me through the streets, in the midst of danger and difficulty—for do you not see that the sky is red with a terrible fire that is not far off my house?—one who had found out your danger, and who roused me up to come and warn you."

"What dear friend was that?"

"Your wife!"

"My wife?"

"Yes, your innocent, loving wife, my lord. Your wife, Cecil, who loves you well still, and who, at the slightest word of repentance and returning fondness from you, will fall upon your breast, and forget and forgive all but that you are her husband—her first, last, and only love. God bless her—God bless her!"

The Marquis staggered against the shutter of a shop, and clasping both his hands over his eyes, burst into tears.

"Hilloa!" cried Jacob; "don't do that, my lord. Why—why, you will make me cry too. Don't, my lord, don't. It's all right, you know, now. You will escape, and the Marchioness will follow you, you know, and—and—stand clear—here's an engine!"

"Fire! fire!" came the loud cry of alarm, and an engine with six horses, that had come from a considerable distance, roared and dashed past the Marquis and old Ardent, at a mad gallop.

"By Heaven!" said the old man, "this must be a fire indeed, for they have not got it under yet. Come, my lord, look up!"

"Where am I?"

"Why, close to my house, to be sure, my lord. Come on, and you will soon be under shelter. Don't be down-hearted, now. Why, this should be quite a happy night to you."

"My wife—my son! Oh, Heaven! how can I face them? How can I look on them?"

"Never mind that—only come on. Egad!" thought the old man, "if I tell him the Marchioness is at my house, he will be afraid to come to it, so I won't say a word about it."

At a turning they now took, and which brought them into the open area of the market, they came not only within sight of Ardent's house, but in full view of the effect of the still raging fire upon the night sky.

The Marquis shrank back, as well he might, feeling that he was a fugitive, from the glare of light.

"Good Heavens!" he said; "there is indeed a fearful fire!"

"It is the opera-house." said a man, as he passed them rapidly. "They thought the engines had got it under; but it has broken out afresh, and caught the next buildings."

"Come on, my lord," said Jacob Ardent, as he took the arm of the Marquis, and led him rapidly among the old ruinous-looking sheds of the market. "Come this way, and we can get round to my house without observation, I hope?"

"Yes—yes; if I should be recognized now, all would be lost. It is not that I fear so much for myself; but I do not wish to die now, till I have made my peace with my poor forsaken wife, and seen my boy."

"You will, I trust, have ample time, my lord, to do both," said the old waterman-fireman; "and as for dying, I hope it will be time enough to think of that, a long while hence."

They had now got quite out of the common thoroughfares, in which throngs of persons from a distance were flocking to the scene of the conflagration. The local knowledge that Jacob Ardent had of the old market enabled him to take a course among the old fruit and flower sheds, and rickety-looking buildings, that no one else, with any prospect of getting along at all, could have ventured upon—at least, no stranger would have stood any chance of finding the way in such a maze.

Maze as it was, though, it enabled them rapidly to near the house of Mrs. Ardent, which, by the respectability of its customers, was a place of some pretensions, compared with the majority of buildings in old Covent Garden market.

"Now, my lord," said Jacob Ardent, "in another moment we shall be in the house, and in safety."

"Hold!" said a voice: and a couple of men darting out from behind a shed, interposed themselves in the way of the fugitive Marquis. "Hold, my lord! You are our prisoner!"

"Prisoner?"

"Yes. Here is our warrant from the Secretary of State."

"You had better yield," said the other. "Resistance is useless."

"Never!"

"Down with him! Stun him! Down with him!"

One of the men with an iron club made a desperate blow at the Marquis; but he dexterously avoided it, and drew his sword, just as old Jacob made a dash at the fellow, and grappling with him, threw him by a trick of wrestling on to his back.

"Take the consequences of your resistance,"

said the other, as he drew a cutlass and made a blow at the Marquis, who parried it, and then, with all the ease of a practiced swordsman, made a feint or two, and finally ran the officer through the body.

"Help!—Oh!—God!—Ah!" cried the wounded officer, and he fell to the ground, writhing with pain.

CHAPTER IV.

THE MARQUIS'S DANGER, AND THE DEATH OF THE GOVERNMENT SPY.

THE man who had been thrown by old Jacob had come with the back of his head in rather close proximity to a round stone. The stone sustained the shock without damage; but the more fragile skull suffered, and the man lay perfectly insensible to the world and all its affairs.

"I regret this," said the Marquis, as he stood with his drawn sword in his hand, eyeing the man whom he had run through. "I regret this, deeply; but what could I do?"

"Nothing," said Ardent. "Come on—come on! Their cries may bring the watch upon us."

The ominous springing of a rattle, at that moment, added point to the remark of the old man.

The Marquis returned his sword to its scabbard.

"Take me where you will, old friend," he said. "This night's terrors and escapes, I fear, are not over yet."

The Marquis hardly guessed how truly he spoke.

Jacob Ardent took him by the arm, and came with him to the door of his house, which, on the moment, was opened by Jane, who, at sight of her uncle, cried out:

"Oh, we are so glad you have come home! The Marchioness is very ill indeed."

"The Marchioness, say you?" cried the Marquis.

"Don't ask any questions, my lord," said Ardent, "but come in at once to where no one will be more welcome."

"Yes—yes! But I must ask one question. Is my wife here, or is she not?"

"She is."

"Heaven, I thank thee!"

The Marquis followed Jane and her uncle into the house. The door was barred and bolted; and while Jane kept curtseying every time that the Marquis's eye was upon her, the old waterman called aloud to his wife:

"Mary!—Mary, my dear! Here I am, and somebody with me; so you had better prepare somebody else, for fear, you know, that somebody else should be taken too much by surprise."

"Yes, Jacob—yes."

"Follow me, my lord."

Jane went first, and then the old man, and then the Marquis, into the parlour, or common living room, at the back of the bouquet-shop; and the moment they got there, the Marchioness, who was kneeling by a chair, sprang to her feet, and, rushing forward, exclaimed:

"'Tis he! Oh, God be thanked!—'tis he! Felix, my husband! My long lost, but still loved Felix, I am here! You know me? I am your Cecil, whom you once loved. Why did you cast me from you? But you are saved, my Felix—you are saved, and I am happy!"

With a burst of hysterical tears and laughter she fell on the breast of the Marquis, and clung to him, even as the wrecked mariner might cling to the last frail plank that was between him and eternity.

The Marquis was deeply affected.

So, indeed, was the whole of the Ardent family, for they looked on the scene with surprise, and yet with a mixture of joy, for even by the dim light of the one candle that was on the table there was no mistaking the expression that was upon the face of the Marquis.

Old Ardent stepped up to his wife, and whispered in her ear:

"It is all right. Leave them together. It is not fair that there should be any witnesses of their mutual forgiveness of the past, if he has anything to forgive, which I very much doubt. Come, come."

The old couple left the room, and Jane followed them on the moment.

The Marquis and the Marchioness of Dale-wood were alone, and for the first time for fifteen years.

"Cecil — Cecil!" said the Marquis, in tremulous accents. "My poor Cecil!"

"Yes, Felix, yes!"

"Is it possible—— ?"

"That I am here, Felix?"

"No—no! That is like you; but, my poor girl, is it really possible that, after all I have made you suffer, you can forgive me?"

"Forgive you?" Oh, yes—yes, from my heart!"

"You really can?"

"I can—and do."

"Oh, just Heaven! where are your light-nings to scorch out the heart of him who cast from him this treasure that you, in your bounty, bestowed upon him? Cecil—wife! you ought to curse me—indeed you ought."

"Oh, no, Felix! Here at your feet—here, looking upward at the dear, well-remembered face I love so well, I could die and be happy."

"No—no! it is I who ought to kneel to you."

"Not to me, Felix."

"Yes—yes, Cecil, I have so deeply wronged you."

He sank upon his knees close to her, and then, folding him in her arms, she sobbed like a child upon his breast. Then she looked up through all her tears, and smiled as she had not smiled for fifteen long years.

"Felix, my Felix! our boy, our dear Gerald, grows so like you."

The Marquis tried to say something, but he seemed to be half choked in the effort.

"And he is so handsome, and so good—so brave, and yet so gentle—so all that you

would wish him. You will not blame your poor simple Cecil, if she has spoiled him some-what?"

"You are an angel," gasped the Marquis, "and I—the more a devil!"

"Hush—oh, hush!"

She placed one of her hands—it was still small and white—upon his mouth.

"My Felix, I have one favour to ask of you," she said.

"Ask my life, and it is yours."

"No—no! your life is my life, Felix; it is only that the past shall be all forgotten like a dream, and that, for the time to come, you and I shall live but for each other, and for the sake of our dear child."

"Cecil, I—I would ask you one thing, but that I know I do not deserve a quick and ready answer to it."

"Oh, what is it?"

"Is—is our boy here?"

"No."

"Oh, do not tell me no! I want to hold him in my arms—I want to hold him to my heart—to hear him say 'father.' I implore you to let me see him!"

"Oh, be calm, Felix! He is not here; but I can take you to him. You see, I got in-formation, in a strange way, of your danger, and to have brought him with me would have unfitted me for what I had to do. This good and honest family of the Ardents I knew would aid you; so, on the very wings of fear, I came to them. But our dear Gerald is safe and well, and he nightly prays for his father, whom he supposes far away on the sea, or anywhere where he could not, if he would, come home to bless him."

"Hilloa! House!—house! Open the door!" cried hoarse voices at the outer door of Jacob Ardent's dwelling.

The Marquis sprang to his feet.

"Hush! hush!" he cried; "they hunt me yet."

"Oh, no! no!" said the Marchioness, as she clung to him; "they shall not tear you from my arms."

"Unhand me! I must fight for you and for myself."

"Open! open!" cried the voices. "House here! House! house!"

The Marquis tore his sword from its scab-bard, and placing his left arm round the waist of his wife, faced the door of the room, pale and white as a statue.

"Open doors in the name of the law!" cried a voice that had not sounded before.

Jacob Ardent at this moment rushed into the room in which were the Marquis and Marchioness. The old man looked pale and alarmed, but yet resolute. His wife stood on the threshold with a light in her hand.

"My lord," said Jacob, "this is no place for you."

"I know it; but let them come."

"No—no! You must escape with me in disguise."

"But what disguise?"

Old Ardent made but a couple of steps to

an ancient wardrobe that was in a recess in the room, and then he began to tumble out various articles of apparel, saying, as he did so:

"Marquis, you must put on this suit of clothes, which will disguise you as a waterman-fireman. It is a lucky thing that I have two suits. As for me, you see, I have nothing to do but to put on my coat and badge, and I am all right. In a similar dress you and I can sally out into the street, and make our way, unsuspected, to my boat, and I will row you down the Thames. The fire at the opera-house, no doubt, has brought up so many waterman-firemen from the banks of the river that we shall scarcely be looked at."

"It is a good thought," said the Marquis.

"A most happy thought!" cried the Marchioness. "Oh, be quick, Felix!—be quick! I will help you."

The people at the door of old Ardent's house began now to batter at it with a vigour that threatened its speedy destruction, and poor Mrs. Ardent stood trembling in the passage, while the Marquis, by the aid of his wife and the old man, was attired in the complete dress of a waterman-fireman.

"Come, now, out by the back way," said old Ardent, "and I will answer for your safety. Wife!—wife!"

"Yes, Jacob."

"Place the Marquis's clothes somewhere where they won't be seen. Up the chimney, or anywhere, so that they are out of the way."

"Yes, Jacob."

The Marchioness flew into the arms of her husband, and gave him one frantic kiss, and then she said:

"Go—go!"

He tore himself away; but he could not speak. Old Ardent let him out by a door at the back of the house, just as the front door was battered in by the officers. The Marchioness, pale as a corpse, sat upon a low stool; and, as she sat there, something seemed to whisper to her with a terrible significance.

CHAPTER V.

THE PROGRESS AND END OF THE FIRE, AND THE FATE OF THE MARQUIS.

WE need not detail how, when the outer door of the waterman-fireman's house was dashed open, and when those who so dashed it open rushed in and explained their errand, it was found that they were not in pursuit of the Marquis of Dalewood at all, but were merely bringing in a nearly dying man for shelter.

The reader, when informed that that dying man had been run through the body, will guess who and what he was, namely, the officer who had made the fruitless attempt to arrest the Marquis in the market.

We will now follow old Jacob Ardent and the Marquis of Dalewood in their progress from Covent Garden.

The disguise of the Marquis was tolerably perfect, and no one, especially at that time of night, and amid the confusion of that fire,

which occupied so exclusively the thoughts of everybody, could have taken him for other than what he seemed to be.

The dress of the waterman-firemen of London was then the same which may be seen now at any civic pageant. The double fustian of waterman-firemen has gone from the river; but many of them still retain the old full-breasted coat, with the badge of their company upon the arm of it.

With the little difference that that dress was at the period of our story, a little more outrageous in its amplitude of broad cloth, it differed not from what now may be seen on Lord Mayor's day, when the great king of the city goes in state to Westminster Hall.

The route which old Ardent took was towards the Strand, hoping that by so doing he would be able to get down some of the streets near to Charing Cross, and so obtain a boat, and conduct the Marquis down the river.

But Fate had decreed otherwise, as we shall soon see.

Hardly had the pair reached the end of the first narrow street leading into the Strand, when a terrible crowd of people, in company with an old fire-engine from one of the city halls, came dashing and tearing towards them in mad career for the burning opera-house.

"What is all this, Jacob?" said the Marquis.

"Another engine, my lord. For Heaven's sake, stand aside. Let us get into this doorway, or we shall be seen."

"But am I not safe in this disguise?"

"Yes, safe enough from being thought a marquis; But not at all safe from being thought a fireman, my lord."

"Ah, yes, I comprehend."

"Fire!—fire!" shrieked the mob. "Clear the way there! Way for the engine! Fire—fire! Hurrah!—here's more help!"

"Confound you! let me alone," said Jacob Ardent, as a man caught hold of the ample skirts of his coat.

"Hands off, villain!" cried the Marquis, as he put his hand mechanically to his side for his sword; but he had left it at the house in Covent Garden, and it was a fortunate thing that he had.

"Why, what's this?" cried a man, who appeared to be in some authority. "Two waterman-firemen of the City of London, skulking in a doorway, when there is such a conflagration as hardly ever was known in London before?"

"No—no, you are wrong, Master Warden," said Jacob Ardent, "we are not skulking."

"Oh, I know you, now."

"You ought to know me, sir."

"You are Jacob Ardent, and if you are skulking, it is the first time you ever did such a thing in all your life, I will take my oath of that, my good fellow. But, come, jump on the engine. We just want a man of your experience."

"Then," whispered Ardent to the Marquis, "I cannot accompany you, you see. It is very unlucky; but we must part now!"

"Not so."

"Nay, I must go with the engine to the fire, and so cannot accompany you."

"But we need not part on that account, my good friend, for I can go with you."

As he spoke, the Marquis sprang on to the engine.

"Hurrah!" cried the mob. "On—on! Forward to the fire! Fire—fire! Way for the engine!"

Jacob Ardent had just time only to take his place by the side of the Marquis, when on tore the whole assemblage, with the engine, at a furious gallop.

And now, as they neared the seat of the fire, the roar of the flames, the hoarse shouts of the people, and the blood-red reflection of the burning houses in the sky, all became more and more terribly awful and distinct.

Jacob Ardent and the Marquis caught some of the enthusiasm of the people who were with the engine, and the old man was soon standing up, and giving directions what to do.

The Marquis, as he looked at the sea of heads around him, felt a strange and growing interest in the scene.

"For once in my life," he said to himself, "I may really be of some service to my fellow-creatures."

"Way for the engine! Give way—give way!"

The crowd parted like the waves of the sea cut by the hull of some great ship; and the engine, with Jacob Ardent and the Marquis upon it, dashed on towards the fire.

It was a terrific and a grand sight that met their gaze, as they reached the corner of the Haymarket.

The opera-house was one sheet of flames, and several houses in the Haymarket and Pall Mall had shared the same fate. The engines that were there seemed to make no sort of impression upon such a body of flame.

Indeed, it was likely enough that the scanty supply of water they had been able to throw upon it had rather the effect of adding to its fury.

The heat from the burning mass was so great, that those who conducted the engine were compelled to pause at a respectful distance; and the horses got so alarmed, that the people, to save them from more mischief, were compelled to cut their traces, and allow them to gallop off where they chose to go.

The clank of the pumps—the shouts of the people—the wild roar of the flames, all made up such a scene of unearthly din and grandeur, that the Marquis stood upon the engine, looking aghast, yet undaunted.

"It's all in vain!" cried Jacob Ardent.

"What is all in vain?" said the Marquis.

"To try to quench the fire."

"Water! water!" shouted a thousand voices. "Water! There is no more water!"

The dull, heavy clank of the engine pumps, which had formed so remarkably distinct a sound above all others, abruptly ceased.

The fire took its own course, and roared and shot up its tall columns of flame and its millions of sparks into the night air, unchecked by human agency.

The roof of the opera-house fell in.

Oh, what a crash was that! Sublimely awful! It was as if some funeral pall had been dropped from the clouds upon the burning pile, and for a moment had extinguished it.

But it was only for a moment.

With a sullen roar the flames shot up again from the fresh material that had fallen upon them to feed them.

"This is an awful sight!" said the Marquis.

"It is!" gasped Jacob Ardent. "What cry is that?"

"Hush!—hush!"

"Save her! Oh, God! save her!"

"Hush! There, again! A child is at the topmost window of yonder house. Behold how she holds out her little hands, and shrieks for aid! Oh, Heaven! this is too terrible!—Oh, my lord, what are you about? You are mad—mad! The front of the house already rocks to and fro."

"Unhand me, Jacob Ardent."

"No—no! For your life's sake, do not venture!"

The Marquis broke away from the old man, and seizing a tall ladder that was in the hands of several men, he, with all but superhuman force—men on such occasions have superhuman force—placed it against the blazing house.

The ladder came at its extreme length to within a foot of the window at which the child appeared.

Black clouds of smoke enveloped the form of the young girl who at that window shrieked for aid. The flames had not yet reached the room, but the smoke was rapidly changing in colour, and proclaiming that they were near at hand. The fact of the child leaning from the window was the only thing that saved it from suffocation, and it did that from instinct.

Heavens! what a cheer burst from the multitude! The Marquis commenced the ascent of the ladder.

Another cheer.

Then all was still as the grave, save the roar of the wildly carousing flames, and the crackle of the charred timbers, as they gave way one by one.

The Marquis slowly ascended.

The wall of the front of the house rocked to and fro; the people swayed from side to side in sympathy with it, and some held out their hands, as if they could stay its fall.

The Marquis ascended still.

A suffocating volley of smoke from a window that he had to pass hid him for a moment, and everybody thought he was lost.

"No—no! There he is again—on—on still."

The child shrieked for mercy. The wall rocked to and fro more than before, and a tall flame, like the hot, scorching tongue of some hideous serpent, shot up above the house. Jacob Ardent sank on to his knees, and hid his face with his hands.

A shriek arose from a thousand voices, and

the wall of the house fell, carrying with it the ladder, the Marquis, and the child, in one common destruction!

* * * *

One hour after that the flames subsided, and a melancholy procession, headed by old Jacob Ardent, carried something from the ruins of the house—the wall of which had fallen in—covered with a sheet borrowed from a neighbour.

The sheet fell to the proportions and shape of the dead body that lay beneath it. It was the body of the Marquis of Dalewood.

CHAPTER VI.

THE WIFE AND THE DEAD HUSBAND.—CAPTAIN GAY OFFERS HIS SYMPATHY.

THE pale gray light of early morning was now creeping over the scene of the conflagration. The raging fire had only ceased by a house being pulled down in the way that the wind carried the flames, and so, finding nothing more to feed the flames on, went out of itself.

The crowds of people still lingered about the charred and blackened ruins, and Jacob Ardent, as he walked at the head of the four men who, on a shutter, carried the dead body of the Marquis, motioned to the people with his hand to give him a free passage.

The mob fell back in silent sympathy.

"It is one of the firemen," said one.

"Yes, don't you see his coat and badge shining from under the corner of the sheet?" said another.

"It was the one that tried to save the child," said a woman.

"God bless him, then!" said a man.

This man took off his hat as the body was borne past him, and the example was followed by others in the crowd, till you might have heard a pin drop, so intense was the silence; and it was a strange thing to see everyone so reverently uncovered as the dead passed on.

Poor old Jacob Ardent then turned to the people, and in a voice of deep emotion, he said :

"I thank you all from my heart—I do, indeed. This man died a noble death. May his soul find rest in Heaven!"

"Amen !" said many voices.

"Is he much hurt?" said one.

"Hurt? He is dead."

"Are you sure of that, old man? Let a surgeon see him before you take him any further."

"Be it so. Where is there such a one?"

"Here—here!" cried many voices, and a little man in a powdered wig was hustled forward to the side of the temporary bier, on which lay the body of the Marquis.

"Come—come! good people," cried the little man, "don't be violent. I will look at him; but don't push and drive in this way."

Jacob Ardent uncovered the face of the corpse. There was no sort of disfigurement upon it. The Marquis looked as if he were in a deep and calm sleep, with a faint smile upon the half-parted lips.

The little doctor placed his hand and then his ear over the region of the heart. He shook his head.

"Dead?" said Ardent.

"Quite dead, and has been for some time!"

"Poor fellow!" cried a man, who had hustled forward, and now stood close to the head of the corpse. "Poor fellow, what a sad thing! Let me help to carry him! Upon my reputation and life, this is a sad sight! Here, good people, get something to drink!"

He threw some small coins among the crowd.

"Upon my life, and by Jove, as I am a gentleman, I pity this poor fellow, I do, indeed! Come, I will help to carry him!—Oh, stuff! don't mention it; you must be tired, some of you!"

This individual, who now hustled away one of the bearers of the bier, and took his place, deserves a little description. He was about—or we may say, a trifle above—the middle size, and rather good looking. His apparel was decidedly flashy, and had about it a half military, half man-upon-town sort of cut and appearance. His tone and gait were both of the easy-going, impertinent, swaggering order, and there could be no doubt in the world but that this man was what now would have been called a "Toff," and who then was known as one of those adventurers who drink the best of wine, keep the best of company, ride good horses, and seem to be in want of none of the luxuries of life, and yet to have no legitimate source of income.

How such men live, and there are thousands of them living in London at the present day, is a mystery that no one can fathom; but they do live, and live well, too.

"Sir," said Jacob Ardent, after eyeing this man for some few minutes, "I don't think we will trouble you."

"It's no trouble at all."

"Yes, it is, sir. Be so good as to let us carry the body ourselves, if you please."

"Oh, you are too modest by far."

"No, sir, I am not; but we don't want you."

"I know you don't, but it is requisite for us all to take a lesson in humility now and then, so I intend to help to carry the dead body of this poor man."

Jacob Ardent looked him full in the face.

"Sir, I don't like you."

"Nor do I you," said the stranger; "but I shouldn't wonder, now, if we were to become contented with each other upon further acquaintance. You seem a nice hearty old man. Any family—eh?"

"Sir, this is too bad. What right have you to force yourself upon me and my comrades?"

"What right?"

"Yes, sir; what right have you to force us to accept your services to carry this dead body, whether we will or no?"

"And what right have you to carry it?"

"Every right. He is, as you see, one of my fraternity, a waterman-fireman. That constitutes my right."

"Oh, dear, no. A word in your ear, Master What's-your-name. He is, or, I should say, as he is dead and gone now, was one of my fraternity."

"Eh?"

"Oh, you start? But I know him."

"You know—him?"

"Yes. The Marquis of Dalewood! Traitor to the Government—a price upon his head—son of the old Duke of Lorton, of county Galway. But I am a friend—mum is the word! All's right! Hem! How do you feel now, old ample-skirts—eh? You don't seem happy!"

"Happy?"

"No. Cheer up! Let's be jogging. Come on. I'll help to carry him. I was an old friend."

"Then, perhaps you—you were at Dalewood House to-night?"

"To be sure."

"And you were one of the little party—who—who——"

"Exactly. That's it."

"You will keep the secret, then, of the identity of this poor piece of clay, sir? There is one who would not like it torn from her——"

"To be sure. You mean his wife?"

"I do. Oh, yes, I do."

"Oh, I know all about it—you needn't tell me anything. I am very anxious about the poor Marquis; but this is a sad end for him to come to."

"He might have come to a much sadder one."

"Why, yes, old what's-your-name, so he might."

"My name is Jacob Ardent."

"Your servant, sir, and mine is Gay—Captain Gay, at your service; so, now, let us be off. Where are you going to take the cold meat—dear me—dear me!—I mean the sad remains of my dear friend?"

"To my humble home."

"Oh, well, he won't object to it. Come on—come on."

Jacob Ardent did not much like either the looks or the manner of his new acquaintance; but he found it now more difficult than ever to shake him off; so he let him accompany him with the corpse to Covent Garden market, where the old man trembled to think of the effect that it might have upon the poor bereaved Marchioness.

It was sad, indeed, that he should be thus torn from her by a violent and terrible death, almost within the very hour that he had called up his better nature in her behalf, and when she was looking forward to something like a return of her long lost happiness.

When the old waterman-fireman came within sight of his abode he paused, and turning to Captain Gay, he said:

"Sir, may I trespass upon your kindness by asking you to wait here for a few minutes while I carry the dismal tidings, which the sight of the corpse would convey too roughly and suddenly, to one who little thinks what has occurred?"

"To be sure, yes; I will go with you."

"Nay, I intend you to take care of the corpse."

"My dear sir—now, that is too good, as if a corpse were in any danger! You may depend it will remain here till we come back for it."

"Well—well——"

"And as for breaking the sad news to anybody, you will find me a perfect paragon at such an affair. From what you say, I suppose, the poor dear Marchioness is in the house?"

"She is—alas! she is."

"Ah, dear me, so I thought! Well, I will break it to her. It is a melancholy duty I owe to my deceased friend. Come along; and, as we go, I will think of what to say."

Jacob Ardent found it impossible, without absolute violence, to shake off Captain Gay, who took him by the arm, and walked with him to the house, putting on quite a sympathetic look as he did so.

"And so the Marchioness is here," he said; "and the dear son of the Marchioness, too? Ah, how I long to embrace that boy!"

"No—no! He is not here."

"But the Marquis has a son?"

"Oh, yes; but he is not here."

A shade of disappointment passed over the face of Captain Gay; but it was only for a moment, and then he said:

"Do you know, my good friend, that it will be necessary to get that boy, who is now Marquis of Dalewood, out of the way?"

"Out of the way?"

"Yes—of danger to himself. His father has so many enemies, that there is no knowing what they might do."

"The Marchioness—his poor widowed mother—must decide about all that. But here we are at my door. I thank you, sir, for your sympathy and attention thus far, but must not trouble you further."

"Oh, it is no trouble."

"Yes, sir; but it is. Good morning."

"Good morning as often as you like, my good friend; but still I have a duty to perform."

"What duty, sir?"

"The duty of alleviating the distress of the Marchioness to the extent of my power; that is all. The duty which all good men ought to feel under such painful circumstances as this."

It was difficult for old Jacob Ardent to say anything in opposition to this statement of Captain Gay's, or so far to show coldness to him as to prevent him from entering the house; so the old man, with a trembling hand, knocked at the door of his dwelling.

CHAPTER VII.

THE PROCEEDINGS OF CAPTAIN GAY BECOME MORE MYSTERIOUS STILL.

JANE, the niece of old Ardent, opened the door.

"Oh, uncle, how glad I am that you have come."

"Glad, my dear? Why so?"

"Because the lady is so ill," answered his niece.

"Alas—alas! I fear that the tidings I bring her will not in the least tend to make her better."

"Oh, uncle, what say you?"

"Hush! my dear—hush! Do not ask me any questions, I beg of you. Where is the Marchioness?"

"Lying on the sofa in the parlour, uncle."

The old waterman-fireman advanced in the direction of the room; but he had not gone above two steps, when he heard Jane cry out:

"Sir, I will not suffer this!"

"What is the matter?" said Jacob, turning; and then he saw that Jane's face was flushed, and that Captain Gay appeared to be attentively examining the ceiling.

"What did you say, Jane?" said her uncle.

"Nothing—oh, nothing, uncle! Let it pass. Do not vex yourself now. It will not happen again."

"I suspect," said the old man, casting a stern glance at Captain Gay, "that you were rude to my niece."

"Rude! I rude?"

"It is true," said Jane.

"Nay," added Captain Gay, "allow me to apologize, if I have done wrong. I come from a part of the country where it is considered the very height of rudeness if you do not kiss, in a friendly way, a pretty girl when you see her; and all I attempted to do was that civility, as regarded your niece here; but now that I find it to be unacceptable, why, you will look long for one who will be as demure and quiet as I shall."

"Was that all?" said the old man.

"Ye—yes," said Jane, hesitatingly.

"Don't let it occur again in my house, sir," added the old man, "or I shall be compelled to show you the door, in rather a rough manner."

"Oh, my dear sir!"

"Say no more about it."

"Nay, I am only going to add, that your natural grace of manner and politeness of style make it impossible you could show anyone to the door in a rough manner."

Jacob Ardent made no reply to this ironical speech; but he heartily wished that he had never permitted Captain Gay to enter the house.

Traversing the shop, the old man reached the parlour, where he found his wife kneeling by the side of a couch, and bathing the temples of the Marchioness with vinegar and water.

"Dear lady, are you better?" said Mrs. Ardent. "Oh, here is my husband, returned with the Marquis."

With a cry of joy, the Marchioness sprang from the couch; but when the person who was with old Jacob Ardent came within the sphere of the light, and both Mrs. Ardent and the Marchioness saw that it was not the Marquis, she sank back again, trembling.

"My dear lady," said Ardent, "compose yourself."

With difficulty, the Marchioness spoke.

"He—he—my husband—he—is safe?"

"Yes, safe."

"Oh, thank God! Tell me all—tell me how he escaped, good old friend?"

"I cannot—I cannot!" said Jacob Ardent, as he turned aside, and then said to Captain Gay, in a whisper: "You offered to break this terrible news to the Marchioness; do so now."

"Have I your kind permission?"

"Ah, yes, yes."

"Then I will do it in my best style—— Have I the honour of addressing the Marchioness of Dalewood?"

"Yes, sir."

"Then I have to inform you——"

"Of what, sir?"

"That the Marquis is dead. He has been killed by the fall, it appears, of part of the wall of a house on fire, and his mangled and mutilated body is now lying on an apology for a bier, at the corner of the street."

"Villain!" cried Jacob Ardent, "do you call that breaking the matter gently to her?"

"Patience—patience!" said Captain Gay, as he took a pinch of snuff. "How hasty you are, old friend!"

The Marchioness looked in the cold, impassible face of Captain Gay for a few moments in silence, and then, after several efforts to speak, she uttered a shriek of terror, and with one rush, bounded past everyone, and through the shop into the street.

"Good Heavens, she will go mad!" cried Mrs. Ardent.

"She is mad!" said Jacob, as he followed her.

"Hem!" said Gay. "This is really quite a domestic drama, and I may as well go and see how it ends."

The poor Marchioness had just sense left to take in the words—"And his body is lying upon a bier at the corner of the street;" and so, with these words ringing in her ears, she flew into the open air; and seeing the throng of persons that had by this time assembled round the dead body of the Marquis, she, with piercing screams, rushed forward, and kneeling by the side of the corpse, tore from the face the sheet that was laid over it.

"'Tis he! Oh, God, 'tis he!" she cried. "Dead! dead! killed! murdered! Ha, ha, ha! Oh, Heaven, my child—my son! Help! Mercy!"

She fell across the dead body of the Marquis; but when they lifted her up, they found that the poor, suffering spirit had fled, and that, although parted in life from the husband she adored, she was not so parted in death.

"Dead!" said a man who lifted the body of the Marchioness from that of the Marquis. "This is very terrible."

Jacob Ardent at that moment reached the spot, crying out:

"Oh, madam—madam! Heaven will aid you to bear up against this affliction. Remember, I pray you, that you have still a son to live for."

"She remembers nothing now in this world," said one of the men who had helped to carry the bier.

"Remembers nothing?"

"Nothing at all."

"Why, then, that is a mercy. She has fainted! Help me to take her back to my house."

"That I will do, Mr. Ardent. But it is a faint that will last till the Day of Judgment. She is dead!"

Poor old Ardent staggered back, and had to lean for support upon the arm of the first person who tendered it to him.

"Dead! dead?"

"Even so. Look in her face."

"Oh, this is terrible! No—no! All this night's work must be some terrible dream. The Marquis and the Marchioness both dead —both dead! Oh, Heaven! it is too dreadful for belief!"

"So it is," said the person upon whose arm the old man leant, and who was no other than Captain Gay—"so it is. But you and I, Jacob Ardent, must look after the orphan Marquis now."

"Fiend!" cried the old man, as he sprang from the supporting arm of Captain Gay: "this is your work!"

"My work?"

"Yes. You it was who, with all the aggravation of detail that you could cram into a sentence, told this poor, heart-broken creature that her husband was dead. Had the sad news been broken gently to her, she would have lived for the sake of her boy, at all events. You villain—you devil in human guise—it is your work!"

"Bravo!—bravo!" cried Captain Gay. "Go it! Upon my life, old man, you are a good actor. Say it was me, oh, do!—say it was me! That's right. Of course I did it all."

"Behold that man!" said Jacob Ardent to the crowd that had collected. "You all know me, and that I would not lie to you. I see the faces of friends and neighbours about me now, and you all know Jacob Ardent."

"Ay—ay, we do."

"Well, then, I tell you that that man— that bold, bad man, under pretence of breaking the intelligence of the death of her husband to this poor lady, broke her heart at one blow."

"Shame!—shame!"

"Good again!" said Captain Gay, as he took a pinch of snuff with all the *nonchalance* in the world. "Ha—ha! Good again!"

"I ought to have turned him from the house when he insulted my niece, Jane, even in my own presence, poor girl!"

"Oh, dear!" said Captain Gay, "what folks will say! I only paid the little chit the compliment of kissing her, and——"

"This is the result," said a voice behind Captain Gay. "How do you feel now—eh?"

The owner of the voice was in the undress uniform of a Corporal in the Guards, and the action with which he accompanied the word he uttered consisted of lifting up his foot, and with one kick sending Captain Gay sprawling into the midst of a heap of decayed cabbage leaves, that formed part of the refuse of the market.

"Bravo!—bravo!" cried the mob. "Capital —oh, capital! Serve him right! Ha, ha, ha!"

"What!" said Jacob Ardent. "Is that you, Corporal Budd?"

"Present!" said the Corporal, as he gave a military salute to old Ardent. "How is dear Jane, uncle-in-law that I hope is to be?"

"Very well, Corporal: but we are all in distress."

"Distress! Hem! How much?"

"Much what? Why, bless you, you don't suppose it is money we want?"

"Look out!—look out!" cried the mob.

The Corporal turned hastily, and then he saw that Captain Gay, having risen to his feet, had drawn his sword, and was in the act of springing forward to run him through the body.

"Oh, indeed!" said the Corporal, as he seized a broom that was close at hand, and parried the attack with great skill; then, thrusting the broom right into the face of Captain Gay, he flung him upon his back again into the refuse of the market produce, amid the cheers of the people.

CHAPTER VIII.

CORPORAL BUDD MAKES HIMSELF AS USEFUL AS POSSIBLE.

By this time most of the market people had begun to assemble, and as Jacob Ardent and Corporal Budd were well known to them all, and Captain Gay, with his dirty, faded finery, was not, they without further inquiry took the side of the question that pleased them the most.

The Corporal, upon this second time defeating the Captain, laid hold of his sword, and broke it over his knee, saying, as he did so:

"At all events, this shall be no further good in a rogue's hand against the life of an honest man."

"The pump!" cried a voice.

"Harrah! The pump!" shouted everybody.

A tall man, with a profusion of hair about his face, and who was well known in the market for his great personal strength, stooped for a moment over the prostrate form of Captain Gay, and getting then a firm hold of him, he lifted him up in one hand, and holding him with ease, he said:

"Did any lady or gentleman mention the pump?"

"Yes, yes—oh, yes!"

"Then come along."

The mob raised a shout of gratification, for, to tell the truth, they were not very particular who was pumped upon, provided that someone for their especial amusement underwent that process.

The men who had hold of Captain Gay carried him to the pump of the market; and in three minutes Captain Gay was so drenched that he had not a dry thread about him, and scarcely strength enough to draw a single breath.

He crawled from the market, muttering to

himself the most diabolical threats of future vengeance.

The enmity of such a man was not to be despised, as will be seen as we proceed.

A little reflection would have induced Jacob Ardent to do all he could to save Captain Gay from the punishment he received at the hands of the market people; but he really, at the time, was so irritated against him for the part he had acted in the night's proceedings, that he did not say a word.

"Come," said the Corporal, "uncle-in-law that is to be, tell me all about this affair?"

In a few words Jacob Ardent told him all, and then directed that both the dead bodies should be brought to his house; but it was some time before the mob dispersed, and the old man was able to close his door, and sit down to think upon what was to be done next.

The Corporal was taken into the family consultation; and scarcely had Jacob begun to say something, than a violent knocking at the door summoned him to it.

A party of police, with a warrant from the Secretary of State for the delivery to them of both the bodies, rushed into the house.

When the warrant was exhibited to him, Jacob Ardent took the principal officer aside, saying:

"I will inter them, to the best of my means, decently, if that is the object."

"I don't know anything about the object," said the officer; "but I must execute my warrant. A couple of shells will be here directly; and you may think yourself well off you are out of the scrape, for the Government is now aware that you were aiding the Marquis of Dalewood to escape in disguise."

There was no saying anything against this, so the officers took away the two bodies in coffins that were brought for them. What became of them Jacob Ardent never knew; but the probability is, that the prompt means adopted was for the purpose of searching the Marquis and Marchioness's clothing for papers relating to the conspiracy said to exist; for the feeling, no doubt, would be, under the circumstances, that she, too, was implicated in it.

A gleam of sunlight now burst into the old-fashioned parlour in which Jacob Ardent sat with his family after the removal of the bodies, and the old man, as he held his aching head with both hands, cried out:

"Will any of you assure me that this is nothing but a dream—nothing but a kind of nightmare? for, on my life, I cannot think it to be anything else."

"All right and true," said the Corporal. "Stand at ease!"

"Yes, uncle, it is all real," said Jane. "Don't you see Corporal Budd here, dear uncle?"

"Ah," added the Corporal. "I'm real enough."

"What shall I do?"

"My dear Jacob," said his wife, "what can you do?"

"Nothing," said the Corporal, "but stand at ease."

The old man rose and paced the room, and then suddenly he paused and took from his pocket the packet that the Marquis had given him, and cried out—

"This may explain something—yet—no—no——"

"What is it, uncle?" said Jane.

The old man appeared to be lost in thought for some few moments, and then he left the room, saying as he went—

"Do not interrupt me, any of you: I must consult my own thoughts."

Now, Jacob Ardent was a man among a thousand for prudence; and although he knew and felt that the interest of the now orphan son of the Marquis and Marchioness of Dalewood would be dear to all his family, yet he did not think it prudent even to say to them that a packet had been entrusted to his care by the Marquis, until he had himself looked at it, and seen what it contained.

Shutting himself up, then, in one of the three rooms which comprised the upstairs portion of the dwelling, Jacob set to work with trembling fingers undoing the packet that the poor Marquis had given him.

"Alas—alas!" said Jacob, "what a sad thing it is to think that at the very time when he began to see the error of his ways, and when, as regarded the time to come, he would have been such a different man, he should be snatched away from the world. Well—well, there is no certainty of anything in this world, that's a fact; and, after all, the few hours of better feeling that the Marquis had before his death, may stand him in good stead in the world to come."

The old man wiped a tear from his eyes as he thus spoke.

With reverent fingers, for it seemed as if he were almost about to converse with the dead, Jacob Ardent opened the packet; and within it the first thing that met his eyes was a something hard and oval, carefully tied with silk.

Upon opening this inner inclosure, Jacob saw that it was a miniature case, and contained a portrait of a youth of about sixteen or seventeen years of age, apparently of an engaging and ingenuous aspect of countenance.

The old man looked at it in silence for some few moments, and then he said:

"How like! It is the very model of the Marquis himself when he was young, and yet the hair is not exactly the same colour that his was. Ah! I know now who it is. It is the portrait of his son, the Marquis that now is. Poor lad!—poor lad! To lose in one night both father and mother! It is very, very sad, indeed!"

There was a letter in the parcel; but, as it was open, Jacob Ardent spread it before him to read it.

As he did so another letter fell from it, and then another; and one of the inclosures was addressed:

"To the MARCHIONESS OF DALEWOOD, from her loving and repentant husband, the Marquis of Dalewood."

The other inclosure was addressed:

"*To the HONOURABLE GERALD DALEWOOD, from his loving father, the Marquis of Dalewood.*"

Both of the letters were carefully sealed with the broad seal of the family, on an oval shield, with many quarterings.

"Alas!—alas!" said old Jacob, "one will never receive the letter addressed to her; but it will be the duty of myself to take care that both the letters, as they are, and untouched, are delivered into the hands of the young Marquis."

The old man was so deeply affected by all this, that a little long square packet, drawn up with thin cord, in brown paper, which had been about the first object in the parcel, almost escaped his attention; but now he weighed it in his hand, and said to himself:

"Money!—money! Yes, this is the money that the Marquis spoke of. Poor Marquis!—poor Marchioness!—poor son! Alas, for all of you, this has been a sad night!"

The old man's tears now fell one by one upon the open letter, which it seemed to him that he ought to read, because it was open; but it was some time before he could make out the following words:

"Dalewood House.

"*To any kind friend into whose hands this packet may fall.*

"With a presentiment that I shall not live long, I write these words in the hope that human nature is at least sufficiently sound and good, that they and the accompanying packet will have all the effect that I would wish them to have."

"Sixteen years ago I married Cecil Burton. In one year, or, indeed, rather less, pride—satiety—the remonstrances of a father, who considered that I had cast a stigma upon his ancient name by allying myself to one so much beneath it in rank, induced me to abandon my wife. My life during that period has been one of riot, in which I have endeavoured, but all in vain, to drown the stings of conscience.

"Something seems to tell me that the packet in which are contained these lines will not be opened by anyone while I live; and so, whoever reads this letter, I implore them, by their faith in Heaven, and their hope of joy in a better world than this, to carry out my instructions.

"Seek out my wife and son, and deliver to each of them the inclosed letters: and the money, two hundred pounds, which is in the small corded parcel, deliver to my wife if living—and my son, if she should be no more.

"My will, which leaves the whole of my property to my son, will be found in a black escritoire in Dalewood House. Enclosed in that will, too, is a certificate of my marriage, and a full acknowledgment of the legitimacy of my son. These will be important documents for him to possess; for my father, the Duke of Lorton, threatened to attack the validity of the marriage if I did not leave all the property I possess to him, as the head of the family.

"Carry out the instructions of this letter, be you whom you may, and the blessing of the dead and of the living, and of God, will attend you.   DALEWOOD."

"P.S.—Another portrait is at the back of the portrait of my son, which his poor mother sent to me some six months ago, with the hope that it would soften my heart."

Old Jacob Ardent clasped his hands on his face after reading this letter, and for more than a quarter of an hour remained as still as a statue.

CHAPTER IX.

JACOB FINDS IT DIFFICULT TO CARRY OUT THE INJUNCTIONS OF THE MARQUIS.

KNOWING so much as he did of all the people, except one, and that one was the young orphan Marquis, and feeling so great an interest in them, Jacob Ardent may well be supposed to have been deeply affected by the perusal of the Marquis's letter.

The brief conversation Jacob had had with the Marquis, as they came from Dalewood House, had now an absorbing interest: and the old man remembered with remarkable pleasure every word and accent of affection with which the Marquis had spoken of his wife and child.

He felt that he ought to remember all that had been said and done, in order that he might report it, word for word, to the young orphan Marquis of Dalewood.

"Yes," said old Ardent, as he firmly clasped his hands, "I will, so aid me Heaven, carry out the wishes of the dead, as they are contained in the letter—I will devote my life to do so!"

"Jacob! Jacob!" cried Mrs. Ardent, at this moment tapping at the door of the room, which the old man had had the precaution to lock.

"Yes, wife—yes!"

"Are you coming downstairs?"

"Yes, soon—soon."

"Open the door."

"In a minute—in a minute. What shall I do? Shall I tell her all? Might I? Is it my own secret? No—no; not till I have carried out the Marquis's wishes, ought I, even to my wife, to speak of this matter. It is too sacred."

Hastily collecting the money and the letters, Jacob, after glancing about the room for a hiding-place for them, placed them on the top of the old-fashioned bedstead, and then he opened the door.

"Why, what are you about, old man?" said Mrs. Ardent. "You look half-scared."

"I am thinking about the poor Marchioness, wife."

"Ah, dear, it is sad—very, very sad."

"IDIOT!" CRIED CAPTAIN GAY, "TAKE THE REWARD OF YOUR TREACHERY AND FOLLY!"

"But what will the boy say?"

"The boy?"

"Yes; the young Marquis of Dalewood that is now, by the death of his father. What will he say when he hears all?"

"Ah, what, indeed?"

"Well, wife, you and I must try to soothe him. We must speak to him calmly and quietly, and break the matter gently to him."

"Yes, Jacob," said Mrs. Ardent, sobbing.

"Shall we go to him, and bring him home here for a day or two?"

"What! Jacob, bring a marquis here? What will he think of our poor place? Oh, dear, that will never do."

"But you forget, wife, that he has been living in great obscurity with his poor mother."

"Ah, to be sure! Then, bless him! he shall come here; and, as far as anyone but his own real mother can be a mother to him, that will I be."

"I am sure of that. But then, you know, there will be Dalewood House for him to go to; for now that the poor Marquis is dead, there is an end of all his plots and all his quarrels with the Government, and they can't blame Gerald for any of it."

"Of course not, Jacob."

"Well, so I thought. Where does he live?"

No. 2.—(MARQUIS.)

"Where does he what?"

"Live?—reside?"

"Who?"

"Why, the young Marquis, to be sure."

"Lor! Jacob, how should I know?"

Old Jacob sank back into his seat with a deep groan.

"Why—why, do you mean to say that after all that has happened, and with all the necessity of seeing him as soon as possible, you don't know where to find the poor lad?"

"Alas! no!"

"Good gracious!"

"His poor mother never told me where she lived. It is true that now and then she used to come here to see us all, and to talk over old times; but as she never said where she lived with her son, of course I could not ask her, for I thought she did not like that anyone should know where the Marchioness of Dalewood and her son were forced by poverty to hide their heads."

"Yes—yes! Too true! Oh, too true!"

"Then, you see, they had but a scanty subsistence, after all; and so, Jacob, it was a pardonable kind of pride."

"Yes—yes! Alas—alas! But you can find out? Surely you have some idea?

"Not the least."

"You must find out. I—I shall go mad if you don't find out. Wife, I say, what is to become of the lad? Fancy him waiting, and waiting, and waiting for his mother—and she never coming to him! Fancy his tears, his destitution, his hunger! Oh, God! what shall I do?"

Mrs. Ardent was so affected at this picture drawn by the imagination of her husband, that she sat down on the side of the bed, and wept bitterly, and her tears had the effect of calming old Ardent a little.

"Come—come!" he said; "I am an old fool. Surely, large as London is, we shall find him. We will make it our business to look for him. We will inquire for him everywhere, and the name will find him."

"The name?"

"Yes, the name. Surely there are not so many Marchionesses of Dalewood, but that it will soon be found out by a little public inquiry where she lived. Eh?"

"Yes; but she had altered her name."

"Altered her name?"

"Yes, Jacob. She called herself Madame something; but what it was I really don't know; and it was only the last time she was here, that she told me she intended, as soon as her son was eighteen years of age, to tell him who and what he was."

"And he doesn't know his name?"

"No—no!"

"Nor his rank?"

"Oh, dear, no; as I understood it, he does not."

"Nor who was his father?"

"Dear me, Jacob, how is it possible he could know that?"

"Gracious goodness! The plot thickens. The lad, then, is lost indeed; and if we met

him even in the very streets, and asked him a question, he would answer it like any stranger. Lost—lost—lost! Oh, this is very sad, indeed! Why, we shall be haunted by the ghost of the Marquis and the Marchioness, who will call to us to find their son."

"Oh, Jacob, don't say that!"

"But it is true."

"Then, from this moment I am frightened out of my wits. If the ghosts do come, they may as well put it all to rights by saying at once where he is, and not coming and frightening a body for nothing. I'm all of a shake."

"Don't do that."

"What—oh, what?"

"Don't shake the old bedstead in that way, wife; you will bring down the—the——"

"The what?"

"The old hangings from the top of it," said Jacob, who really was afraid that the packet would have tumbled down. "Come—come; it is of no use our distressing ourselves. We can but do what we can, and we may be favoured by fortune and by Providence in our endeavours to find the young Marquis. You must try and recollect everything you have heard the Marchioness say about her son, and about where she lived. How did she come, yesterday, to this house?"

"In a sedan-chair."

"Well, that is something. Should you know the chairmen again, do you think, wife?"

"Well, really, now, I do think I should know one of them. He was so dreadfully ugly."

"That is something."

"Yes, with a squint that was enough to make anyone's eyes ache to look at him."

"Then you and I will try all we can to find him out; and, who knows, but for a crown piece, which he shall have with all my heart, he may say to us at once where he brought the lady from—eh? Why—why, I begin to think we shall find the young Marquis yet; and when we do, I have something for him, as well as something to say to him, poor boy —poor boy!"

"Poor boy, indeed. But where are you going, Jacob?"

"Out for an hour. I have somewhere to go to. The will—the will!"

"What will?"

"Eh? Did I say will?"

"Yes, Jacob, you did."

"Then I didn't mean it—that is to say, I only said I had all the will in the world to go out. Ah! My Sunday coat, wife. I am not going far—ah! oh, dear no."

Mrs. Ardent tried in vain to get from the old man where he was going, but he would not tell her; and soon he sallied forth at as quick a pace as he could go in the direction of Dalewood House.

The intention of old Jacob Ardent was, if possible, to get possession of the will of the Marquis of Dalewood, which was described in the letter to be of so much importance to the orphan child of the Marchioness and Marquis.

The old man had but one hope of getting possession of the document, and that hope lay in his acquaintance with one Grubby Wills, a coachman, who had been in the service of the Marquis of Dalewood for a considerable time, and who was about one of the most dissipated of his class, although, in the main, not a very bad-hearted man.

"If I can but get hold of Wills," thought old Jacob Ardent, " he will, for a pint of pearl, or a bottle of wine, let me into the house; and, as far as he is concerned, I might, if I could, carry off the old black escritoire altogether."

The distance was not very great to Dalewood House; but Jacob Ardent now took the nearest way past Montague House, and he had just got to within sight of the place of his destination, when he saw a man coming along with a box upon his shoulder, whom he recognized to be no other than his acquaintance, Grubby Wills, the coachman.

The heart of poor old Jacob failed him as he saw Wills with the box, for, to all appearance, it looked as if he had left his place, and was carrying his luggage along with him.

"That chance is gone, I fear," said Ardent. "Well—well, I won't despair yet. He can perhaps tell me how to get into the house, for all that."

Old Jacob Ardent was not aware that an old looking man, in a tattered great coat, was dogging his footsteps as he went; and that a glance at the face of that old looking man would have revealed the rascally features of Captain Gay.

CHAPTER X.

CAPTAIN GAY RESOLVES UPON A VERY BOLD
MOVE TO OBTAIN THE WILL.

"Cuss the box!" cried Grubby Wills, as he suddenly flung it to the ground with a crash, and then sat upon it, and wiped his brow. "I won't carry it no further, I'll be hanged if I do. Oh, dear!"

" Hilloa!" said Jacob Ardent.

"Eh?"

" Hilloa, Wills!"

"Who says 'Hilloa, Wills?' I ain't Wills."

"Why, I do. Don't you know me, Wills? Jacob Ardent, the waterman-fireman—eh? Why, what is the matter with you, now?"

"Oh, dear me! nothing. Only, that is, you gave me a kind of a slight turn, you see, that's all."

"A turn?"

"Yes, a sort of a fright. But it's nothing now. Do you know, I was just thinking that, suppose you were a police-officer, and that you—you—Oh, gracious!"

"Why, what on earth do you mean, man? You seem all of a tremble."

"I is—I is."

"And what for, pray?"

"Why, a—a—that is—how I should relish something to drink."

"You shall have something, if you will tell me, first of all, what frightened you; and, next, if you will, do me a favour."

"Of course I will, Master Ardent. I will do you any favour in my power, for I will say this of you, that, let me meet you where I would, either down by the river, or up by Covent Garden market, where your worthy and most respectable wife sells the what's-its-name,—the *bowquet*——"

"The what ?"

"Why, in plain English, they are nothing more nor less than nosegays; only as plain English is vulgar, you see, they calls them, in high life, *bowquets*."

"Bouquets, you mean?"

"Oh, ah! I knew it was something of the sort. But what on earth was I talking about ?"

"Something to drink, as usual, Grubby Wills."

"Ha—ha! Why, you are as good as a conjurer."

It was just at this moment that Captain Gay, disguised in the old ragged coat we have made mention of, slipped behind one of the columns of the front entrance to Montague House, and was effectually concealed from the observation of Jacob Ardent and the coachman; while, at the same time, he had no difficulty in overhearing every word they said to each other.

"Come—come," added Ardent, "I don't mind giving you a crown to drink, or even going the length of a bottle of choice wine, or anything you like, if you will serve me in what I shall ask of you."

"Serve you? Oh, my friend—my, my more than friend! The man who offers me a crown to drink is a—a—I don't know what he isn't, so I can't say what he is."

"Well, then, to begin."

"Yes—yes!"

"What put you in such a fright when I spoke to you just now?"

"Oh, what put me in——"

"Such a fright?"

"Well, then, I'll tell you. You see I have left the service of the Marquis of Dalewood, yonder."

"Yes?"

"Oh, my friend, it was such a service!— lots of eating—lots of drinking—lots of wages, and such perquisites! Oh! oh! such a kitchen! But it is all over now. Oh, dear!—oh, dear! I feel it in my stomach!"

"Go on."

"Well, I have left his service; and this is my box."

"Yes?"

"Well, when you spoke, I thought you might be a police-officer, who, as they are all dreadfully suspicious, might think I had a dozen of the old thick silver spoons belonging to the family, in this very box; and the idea of being even suspected put me into quite a twitter."

"I don't wonder at it."

"No, I thought you wouldn't."

"But why did you leave your place ?"

"Why, in a way of speaking, it left me."

"Indeed!"

"Yes, Mister Ardent. The Marquis is gone; and they say he will have his head chopped off on Tower Hill when he is found; and some king's messengers are now in Dalewood House, sealing up all the papers, to take them away, I suppose, to read 'em."

"This is sad news."

"It were; and so, when I saw that, and found that the kitchen chimney was cold, and the cellar not come-atable, I said to myself— 'Grubby Wills,' said I, 'you may as well go with what you can lay hold of, for it is all up with this blessed establishment.'"

"And do you mean to say that the house is in the possession of the officers and messengers of the Government now?"

"It were."

"Then all is lost!"

"Well, I should say it was. But it's no use a-grieving."

"Grubby Wills?"

"Yes—yes! Oh, dear, why did you make a fellow jump in that way for? What's the row?"

"Do you know if, in Dalewood House, there is an old black escritoire anywhere?"

"Yes."

"Where?"

"In master's study, to be sure. It's atween the two windows; and they do say as he keeps all his odds-and-ends of papers in it; but I don't know, as my department was principally in the kitchen and the cellar."

"Grubby Wills, you are out of place?"

"I were."

"You want money?"

"I were."

"Don't keep saying, 'I were.'"

"I weren't."

"Silence, for Heaven's sake, and attend to me! I want to get something out of that black escritoire."

"You don't."

"I do, I tell you. The Marquis is dead. His will is there. It is of the greatest importance to his son. It is, in fact, of very great importance to him. Tell me how I can get at it?"

"Eh?"

"Tell me, I say, how I can get to that escritoire, and then you may name your own reward?"

"Name my own reward! Oh, it's easy to name it; but I don't know how you are to get at the old black escritoire, not I."

"Oh, think—think!"

"I were."

"Man—man, you will drive me mad!"

"I tell you what it is, Mr. Ardent, if you go on in this-a-ways, you will have to be fastened with a snaffle, you will. How can I tell you how to get into the black what's-its-name? I can't. Don't bother me about it. I can't. You took my breath away by saying as the Markis is gone dead—you know you have; and as for something to drink, I shall want a lot of somethings afore I feels myself again, I shall. Oh, dear!"

"But you know the house?"

"Reether?"

"You know the situation of the escritoire —you know all the rooms—all the staircases —all the doors?"

"I were."

"Villain! will you attend to me? I must have that will—I tell you I must have it, and you must aid me to get it."

"Master Ardent!"

"Well—well!"

"I tells you what it is. Go and knock at the door, and satisfy yourself, if you ain't satisfied with what I tell you. There's about a dozen fellows with red waistcoats on, and little knobby bits of brass with a crown at the end of each of 'em, in the house; and there's one with a voice like a great drum, as calls himself a king's messenger, and as comes from the Secretary of State; and if you or I go and say in the civilest way in the world: 'Just allow me to get a trifle out of the old black escritoire,' they would walk us off to Newgate, and no mistake."

"True—oh, true!"

"Oh, it's true, is it?"

"It is, Wills—it is."

"Thank you—thank you!"

"For what?"

"The something to drink."

"There's a crown—go and get what you like. I must go home and think over this matter further. I see now how useless it would be to attempt to go to the house. Farewell, Grubby—farewell!"

"A-doo—a-doo! Master Ardent, as the gentlefolks say. A-doo!"

"A what?"

"A-doo! That means good-day to you."

"Oh, does it?"

"It were."

Jacob Ardent, at the sound of the eternal "It were" of the coachman, walked off at a rapid pace, leaving him seated on his box.

"I'm very much afraid," said Wills, with what he, no doubt, thought was a very sagacious shake of his head, "I'm very much afraid as that old fellow is a little beside hisself. Well, I can't help it; and the sooner I am off the better. Only to think, now, of the Markis being dead. Oh, dear!—oh, dear! We is here to-day, and gone to-morrow—I mean yesterday—no, I don't, I mean—oh, lor!"

A hand was placed upon the shoulder of Grubby Wills, and upon turning round he saw a tallish figure, as it seemed to him, standing by his side, and a pair of dark, sinister eyes fixed upon him.

Captain Gay had thrown off the tattered great coat, and appeared in his own proper person before Grubby Wills.

"Hold!" he said.

"Eh? Oh, dear! Hold what?"

"Be still."

"Ye—e—es."

"I have something to say to you."

"To—to me?"

"Yes, to you. Be quiet, and hear me."

"In course, sir. But—but——"

"But what?"

"I feel rather thirsty."

"You always do."

"Well, I—I do generally, more or less, sir."

"I know it. Your name is Grubby Wills, late coachman to the Marquis of Dalewood, who is now no more. His house is in possession of the Government officers, and you have just got away from it with this box, containing——"

"My clothes!"

"And a dozen tablespoons of rather massive silver, with the crest of the Dalewood family upon them."

"The Lord have mercy upon us! You are the dev——no, I don't mean that, your majesty, I——"

"Silence!"

"Yes—yes, I will. Oh, anything you like."

"You are out of a place, and you want another?"

"I do—I——"

"Silence! I will take you."

"Oh, no—no!"

"Into my service, I mean. What wages do you want? Twenty pounds? Will that suffice?"

"Oh, lor, yes! Twenty pounds a year

"A year? Pooh! I mean a day!"

"A day!"

"Yes, to be sure, a day. But you must be faithful, discreet, cunning, and all that sort of thing."

"Twenty pounds a day! Twenty pounds!"

"Oh, I see, you doubt it. I will pay you in advance. There is a guinea to begin with."

"One guinea?"

"Yes, to be sure; that one pays you for the first hour. I will settle with you as we go on. Short reckonings make long friends. Now we understand each other."

CHAPTER XI.

CAPTAIN GAY FINDS OUT AN INTERESTING TRAIT IN HUMAN NATURE.

GRUBBY WILLS was so confounded by the rapidity and coolness with which his new friend fathomed his very soul, that he kept looking first at the guinea, and then in the face of Captain Gay, and then at the guinea again, as if he could hardly bring himself to believe in the reality of either.

"Now, Wills," added the Captain, "you are in my service."

"Yes, sir."

"At nightfall you must show me how to get into Dalewood House."

"Dalewood House, sir? Oh, lor!"

"What do you look in that odd way for?"

"Why, sir, it ain't possible. There's all the police, sir, and——"

"Hush! Be still! Here they come!"

"Who, sir?"

"The police. Humph! ten of them!"

A party of ten police-officers strolled past Captain Gay and the coachman, and making their way past Montague House towards Tottenham Court Road, were soon out of sight.

"Do you recognize those as the men who were at Dalewood House?" asked Gay of the coachman.

"Lor, bless you, sir, yes."

"Well, the danger of going there, then, is over."

"Oh, dear, no, sir; they have left a couple of 'em there, and—and——"

"Hush!"

A tall man, in a half military uniform, walked hastily past them; and when he was gone out of earshot, the coachman said:

"Sir, that is the king's messenger, with the voice like a drum."

"Then there are but two officers in the house?"

"That's all, sir, I take it, and old Philip."

"Who is he?"

"The hall porter, sir."

"Lucky."

"Eh, sir, what did you say?"

"I say, that is lucky. You know this Philip, of course. Now, you will get from him a full account of what the officers have done, and what they are going to do; and come and let me know. I will sit here on this box till you come back."

"Will you, though?"

"Be off. Remember the spoons."

"Oh—oh, yes, I do! I will! Them spoons —them spoons! They feel as if they was all on my chest, instead of in my box! I'm going, sir, if you please!"

"Be quick."

"Yes, sir."

"This fool," said Captain Gay, when he was alone, "and who I verily believe takes me for the devil, may be of great service to me. What a strange thing, that just at the time when I should be sent over from Galway by the old Duke of Lorton, to try to ascertain what his son was doing in London, as regarded this wife and child of his, they should both— that is, the Marquis and his reputed wife, whom the old Duke would like to discover and leave to starve—should both die. I must get the will, and take it to the Duke, and ten thousand pounds will be my reward for that. Not a bad stroke of fortune. I am well advised that the orphan marquis, Gerald, as they call him, lies in obscurity somewhere, without knowing his origin, name, or rank. Let him rot in that obscurity. It will be all the better. I hope to get possession of the will, and then my bribe; then I will come back to London, and see after revenge upon that old rascal, Ardent, and his dear friends who pumped upon me in the market. Oh, that frolic shall cost them dear! Ah! here comes the coachman back. Well, Wills?"

"Yes, sir."

"What news?"

"Why, sir, old Philip tells me that they have sealed up all the papers, sir."

"Yes—yes!'

"And left two officers to take care of them till a king's messenger comes to-night at ten o'clock to take them away."

"Good."

"And they expect every moment a *pursi-wont*."

"A what?"

"Well, it was something like that, sir."

"Ah, I know! A pursuivant."

"Yes, sir, that's the sort of chap, sir. They expect every moment one of them to come and stay in the house till the messenger comes, so I don't think, sir, as there is a great deal of chance of getting at the escritoire, sir, I can tell you.'

"Let me think."

"Oh, yes, sir, with all my heart."

"Silence!"

"Hem! Sir—sir! look at that old gentleman on the gray nag, coming this-a-ways."

Captain Gay looked up just as an elderly man alighted from a gray horse, midway between Montague House and Dalewood House. A boy in a sober suit of brown livery had been running by the side of the horse, and now took charge of it.

"Now, Robert," said the old gentleman, "be careful."

"Yes, sir."

"Give the horse his feed, Robert."

"Yes, sir."

"And—and, Robert!"

"Yes, sir?"

"Your mistress is going to dine with her uncle, you know, Robert."

"Yes, sir."

"Well, you—you are a good boy, Robert, and so you will take care to see—eh?—that your mistress does go to her uncle's, and not to her cousin Charles, the young officer of dragoons, Robert."

"No, sir."

"Oh, dear—oh, dear! Mind, Robert, I am not jealous, but—but a man cannot be too cautious when he has a pretty young wife. Here is sixpence for you, and—and Robert!"

"Yes, sir?"

"If, Robert, you should find—but I know you won't: I am quite sure you won't—that your mistress does not go to her uncle, but does go to her cousin, you will come and tell me, Robert, that's a good lad. You will come and tell me?"

"Yes, sir."

"And—and in that case, my boy, I will give you another sixpence. Think of that—another sixpence!"

"Yes, sir."

"Oh, I am an old fool—an old fool!"

"Yes, sir."

"Eh? How dare you say, 'yes, sir?' Be off with you, and do as I have told you, boy. Be faithful to me—be intelligent, sharp, active, and secret, and there is no knowing the amount of sixpences I will give you, my good Robert. I trust to you."

"All right, master."

Away went Robert with the gray nag; and the old gentleman, after casting several longing looks after him, with a groan, stepped on towards Dalewood House.

"Grubby Wills?" said Captain Gay.

"Your servant, sir."

"Go and get a hackney-coach, and bring it to the corner of Russell Street. Make the driver drunk. You know how to do that?"

"Oh, lor, yes, sir!"

"You can then mount the box yourself, and when this old lawyer or government messenger is inside the vehicle, drive him as far as you can; and when he gets out of all patience, and will go no further, upset the whole concern in a ditch."

"Yes, sir, I'll do it; but where shall I find your honour after that?"

"Here, upon this spot, at the hour of eight this evening, when you shall have the remainder of your day's wages."

"I'll be punctual to the minute," said Grubby Wills, rushing off to get the hackney-coach.

Captain Gay went after the old government messenger with rapid strides, and called out to him:

"Sir—sir! If you please, sir—sir!"

"Eh?—what is it?"

"I arrest you, sir."

"Arrest me? You—arrest me?"

"Yes, even you."

"My good sir, you had better mind what you are about. It appears to me that you don't know me. It is my business to arrest other people; and as for your arresting me, that is too absurd, and if you mean it for a joke it is a very bad one, and if persevered in, may lead you into some trouble."

"I know you well."

"Indeed?"

"Yes; you are a treasury messenger, and you are going to Dalewood House, the property of the late Marquis of Dalewood, for the purpose of placing seals upon all the papers."

"That is true; but, pray, my young friend, what has that to do with you; and in what way does that make your arresting me any other than a very indifferent joke, indeed?"

"Sir, I only meant to arrest your progress for a few moments, that was all, upon my honour."

"Oh!"

"And for your own good, too, my dear sir, upon my honour."

"Oh!"

"Sir, I am a friend to virtue; and you are a married man."

"Eh?"

"I say you are a married man, and as such, no doubt, a friend to virtue, likewise. Your wife is young and handsome."

"She is—she is."

"While you are old, and about as ugly as you very well can be, without frightening horses as you pass along the street."

"Sir!"

"Oh, my dear sir, it is true. Don't get in a passion. It is quite true, I assure you. Hear me out now, before you make any remark upon the matter."

"But—but——"

"Nay, I know what you would say. You would insinuate that you are not quite so ugly as I have said; but you know you are apt to be partial, as we all are to our looks, so don't say another word about it, but make up your mind that I am in the right."

"Well—well, good gracious, go on! It was my wife you were speaking of just now."

"True. Your wife is going out to dinner."

"Yes, with her uncle."

"No—with her cousin."

"Her cousin?"

"Even so. Her cousin in the dragoons. They love each other! They adore each other! They laugh at you behind your back, and call you an old guy. It is all very well for you to be impressed with an idea that she is gone to dine with her highly respectable uncle, but that is not the case. It is to her anything but respectable cousin that she is gone."

"The devil!"

"No, the dragoon."

"It's all the same!"

"Well, it doesn't make much difference, I grant. I was married once myself, so I have a sympathy with husbands. Poor creatures! somebody ought to sympathize with them, at all events. I tell you what I have told you, in order that you may make your mind easy and tranquil about your wife."

"Confusion and brimstone!"

"Go on—go on!"

"Fire and fury!"

"Capital—capital! Don't mind me."

"I'll kill them both! I'll have blood—blood!"

"I would."

"Revenge—revenge!"

"Bravo—bravo!"

"Oh—oh, what shall I do? I have sent away my horse, too, and I can't walk far, for the corns and the bunions. Oh, what shall I do?"

"My dear sir, I will lend you my coach. I have a hackney-coach waiting for me in Tottenham Court Road, and here comes the driver to know if I wish him to stay for me any longer. Get into that coach, and go home as fast as you can, or rather go to your wife's cousin's, and there you will perhaps see what will make you miserable for life."

"I will—I will. Oh, how shall I thank you?"

"Not at all. Don't mention it. I am willing to do anything in the cause of virtue."

CHAPTER XII.

CAPTAIN GAY FINDS THE WILL, BUT HAS RATHER A NARROW ESCAPE.

EVEN while Captain Gay was thus talking to the old government messenger, there came stalking towards them Grubby Wills, with a coachman's great coat on, for he had carried out the instructions of his master to the letter, and made the driver of the hackney-coach drunk, and taken possession of his vehicle, his whip, and his coat.

"Hilloa, coachman!" cried Gay. "Have you your coach at hand?"

"Yes, sir."

"Then take this gentleman where he will direct you."

"Yes, sir."

"Oh, my friend—my dear friend!" cried the jealous old official, "I feel that I can never be sufficiently grateful to you."

"Don't speak of it; but go at once."

"Yes—yes, I will go at once. Oh, dear! oh, dear! that I should live to see this day—this dreadful day! You must drive fast, coachman."

"Yes, sir."

"Drive slow, and attend to what I told you," whispered Captain Gay to Grubby Wills. "You will find me here when you come back."

"All's right."

The old messenger sprang into the coach, and in another moment Captain Gay had the satisfaction of hearing it drive off at as rapid a rate as the old worn-out hacks harnessed to it could go; but he knew well that he could depend upon Grubby Wills, who, by-the-by, had taken good care to carry off his box on his shoulder, and at the same time to carry out his instructions regarding the jealous old man.

"So," said Captain Gay, when he was alone, "the coast is clear, at all events. How ready men are to believe anything wrong about their wives. You have but to hint it, and there is an end of all caution and reserve in the matter. Well, now for Dalewood House, after I have put myself in an attire fit for the purpose; and it is well that in London I happen to know where to get such accommodation. Thanks to the numerous court masques, there is no want of shops where any dress can be procured, if you are but willing to pay for it."

We need not follow Captain Gay in his pursuit of suitable costume. Suffice it to say, that he found no difficulty in procuring what he wanted, for he was well supplied with money, no doubt by the savage old Duke of Lorton, who let his barbarous pride of birth stand before any other consideration, and who had sent this rascally adventurer, Captain Gay, to London, for the express purpose of tampering with his son's happiness, and trying further to wean him from all connection with his much-injured wife and child.

Captain Gay, within half-an-hour of the departure of the old jealous government messenger in the coach driven by Grubby Wills, found himself at the gate of Dalewood House.

The countenance of Captain Gay was an official-looking and highly legal one; and round his neck, hanging by a ribbon, he wore a little silver greyhound, which was the badge of a government messenger, as well he knew.

"Now," said Captain Gay, "impudence assist me! It never failed me yet, and I should hardly think it is going to do so now."

With these words, he rang a peal at the gate of Dalewood House, that echoed throughout the whole building.

No one answered the summons.

"I'll try the knocker," said Captain Gay.

The startling knock that he gave was

enough to alarm the whole neighbourhood, and this time someone attended to the demand for admission to the old mansion.

"Who is there?" said a voice.

"Open in the name of the law!" was the rejoinder of Captain Gay.

"Well, but the law has got hold of the house already," replied the voice; "for the officers of justice are here."

"I know it—open the door."

"Yes; but who are you?"

"A government messenger. I have come to place seals upon certain papers and drawers in this house. Refuse to admit me at your peril!"

The door was opened in a moment, and old Philip, the porter, who was the only member of the Marquis's establishment left on the premises, made a low bow to Captain Gay.

"Sir," he said, "you will find the two officers in the dining-room, drinking the best claret; and I am glad you have come, sir."

"The rascals!"

"Yes, sir, that's true, sir; and I am glad you have the same opinion of them as I have, sir."

"I have, indeed. But how comes it, sirrah, that you are here, and in the livery of the Dalewood family?"

"Oh, sir, you know it was I that gave the information to the Government that the Marquis was in the habit of meeting in the house of a night with some of the disaffected of the Irish nobles in London; and so, you see, sir, I was asked to stay."

"Oh, indeed?"

"Yes, sir, of course, I don't mind telling you, as you belong to the Government and the police, and all that sort of thing."

"Certainly—certainly! But you expect a reward?"

"I believe you, sir, and a good one, too. A hundred pounds, sir, as I'm a sinner!"

"If the one hundred pounds comes as safe as that you are a sinner, I feel quite sure you will get them."

"Oh, sir, how funny you are."

"Very. I always was. And now show me to the officers."

"Here they are, sir."

The two officers, hearing voices in the hall, had thought it not inconsistent with their duty to come and see who and what it was that occasioned them. Captain Gay saw, at one glance, that the fine old wine from the cellar of the Marquis of Dalewood had done its work; and that, although not quite intoxicated, the officers had got a long way towards that, to them, delightful condition.

Before they could speak a word in the way of questioning him, Captain Gay took the initiative by saying:

"Why, you rascals, you have been drinking! What would the Secretary of State say, if I were to report as much to him?"

"Oh, dear, no, sir."

"No? But I say yes."

"Only a little drop, sir."

"Hark, you scoundrels! Do you see this silver greyhound? It is a proof of who and what I am. Now, if I say only half a word about the condition that I found you in, you will lose your appointments, and that you know as well as I."

"Oh, but, sir—don't!—don't!"

"I will—I will!"

"Oh, sir, be so good as to say nothing about it. We—we only took a little drop, sir, for fear——"

"For fear of what?"

"For fear the Irish rebels had put something in it; and then if a gentleman like your worship had chanced to take any of it, you might have been poisoned."

Captain Gay shook his head.

"You rascals!" he said, "you are good at an excuse; and so, I fear, good at nothing else. But I never like to make mischief; so I will say nothing about it if you are quick and attentive to me."

"Oh, lor! yes, sir. Only say what we are to do, and we will do it in a moment."

"Lead me to the room in which there is an old black escritoire. The Secretary of State requires some papers that are in it."

"Yes, sir. This way—this way. It is a little room off the library, sir, if you please. This way, sir."

If the officers had not been excessively muddled by the quantity of wine they had taken, it is very unlikely that they would have been so easily deceived by Captain Gay; but when the wine is in, the wit is out; so they led him at once towards the room he wished to enter.

On the route to it they had to pass through the dining-room; and then, from the array of long-necked bottles, Captain Gay could see very well that the officers had anything but stinted the use of the claret of the Marquis of Dalewood.

"I must get them to take a little more," thought Gay, "before I leave the house, and then I shall be safe."

"This is the little room, sir," said one of the men; "and here is the old black escritoire, sir."

"Thank you; that will do."

"Many thanks to you, sir."

"Shall we help you, sir?" said the other, who was more overcome than his companion, and who had to hold by the back of a chair to keep himself up.

"No—no. Go back to the dining-room, and wait for me there."

"Yes, sir—we will, sir."

Thinking, then, that they had really got off very cheaply from the offence of drinking wine, when they ought to have been vigilantly watching the house, they betook themselves back to the claret, and to a bottle of brandy, which was more to their taste, and in which they drank to the health of the very good-natured king's messenger, who was scrutinizing the papers in the old black escritoire.

The moment Captain Gay found himself alone, he made such a dash at the escritoire, that the papers began to tumble out wholesale. With the greatest eagerness he looked for the important document that he wanted, and at length a legal-looking packet, tied with a piece of red tape, fell at his feet.

"'Tis here!—'tis here!" he cried.

Even as the packet lay upon the floor, Captain Gay could see the important words:

"Last Will and Testament."

Those words were enough for him. He lifted the paper, and two minutes' examination of it convinced him that he held in his hand the important will, with its inclosure, upon which the fortune of the orphan son of the Marquis of Dalewood so much, if not, indeed, wholly depended.

"Ha—ha!' laughed Gay, "the ten thousand pounds are mine now! The old Duke, who has by robbery and plunder amassed an enormous fortune, will gladly pay me such a sum for this document. At length, then, my fortune is made; and if I continue in the practice of a life of roguery, it may be upon a larger scale now. Ha—ha! This is a bold move, and boldly executed."

Leaving the papers about which he did not care, lying upon the floor of the room, in the greatest disorder, Captain Gay, with the will carefully buttoned up in the breast-pocket of his inner coat, strode into the dining-room again.

The officers made a desperate attempt to rise to their feet.

"Oh! be seated—be seated," said Gay. "Is this claret?"

"Ye—e—s, sir."

"Then I drink it to your promotion, and bid you good-day."

He tossed off a bumper of claret, and then walked to the door of the dining-room, followed by the drowsy looks of the two officers, who, if they had had any secret suspicion concerning him, had not now strength to follow him.

"Idiots!" muttered Gay. "And these are the foolish tools that the Government works with!"

CHAPTER XIII.

CAPTAIN GAY MAKES HIS ESCAPE, AND LEAVES ALL HIS FRIENDS IN DESPAIR.

BEFORE Captain Gay could cross the marble-paved hall that separated the dining-room of Dalewood House from the outer door, there came the rattling sound of carriage wheels in the street, and then a thundering knock at the door, which echoed through the house.

Gay paused a moment.

"Oh, lor! who can that be?" said Philip, the porter, who was half asleep in the hall chair.

Captain Gay stepped aside, half behind a column, on which was the statue of a Grecian nymph.

"I may as well see who it is," he muttered, "before they see me."

Whoever was at the door seemed to be rather impatient; for in a moment or two the knock was repeated with, if possible, greater vehemence than before.

"Curses on them! Who can they be?" said Gay.

"Coming—coming!" cried Philip, rousing himself up from the chair, and running to the door. "Who is there?"

"Open in the name of the law!" cried a voice from without.

"The law?"

"Yes. Open the door!"

"Well, but the law is here already. It has been opened once in the name of the law a little while ago. I hope it is all right now."

"Open—open!"

"Well—well, then, there it is open."

Philip opened the door, and the first person who rushed into the hall was the old messenger who had been sent by Captain Gay on such a fool's errand concerning his wife.

"I have been deceived," he cried. "I have been made a fool of!"

"Lor, sir," said Philip, "you don't say so?"

"Yes, I do say so—I do say so. I have been grossly taken in and done for. My wife has not gone to her cousin. She has gone to her uncle, as I thought she would. Where is the villain, I wonder, who told me otherwise? Oh, if I could but find him! But, no doubt, he is far enough away by this time. Ah! Well, it's no use making a fuss. Come in, gentlemen—come in. I have brought a couple more officers with me. And now for the papers."

"The what, sir?" said Philip.

"The papers, fool."

"Well, sir, it's all very well, but are you in the law as well as the other gentleman?"

"What other gentleman?"

"The gentleman that came here a little while ago to look at the papers, sir, if you please."

"Good gracious, you don't mean to say that you have let anyone into the house?"

"Yes, sir, he came in the name of the law."

"Where is he?—where is he? Oh, I begin to smell a rat!"

"Oh, dear, no, sir, there hasn't been a rat in the place, sir, for I don't know how long."

"Don't be a fool!"

"No, sir."

"Where are the two officers who were left here in charge of the premises?"

"In the dining-room, sir. I took a slight look in at them just now, sir, and I'm rather afraid they are not very well."

"Not very well?"

"No, sir. The claret seems to have gone the wrong way, and got into their heads, sir."

"Oh, dear! oh, dear! here's a pretty affair! Why, we shall all get into the Tower for this. Follow me, gentlemen—follow me. We must seize whoever is in the house, for my mind misgives me that something wrong is taking place."

Captain Gay wedged himself in so closely behind the column on which was the statue, that he was completely out of sight, especially as that part of the hall was rather dark; and the king's messenger, with the couple of constables he had brought with him, rushed past the spot without suspecting that he, Gay, was so near to the outer door of the house.

"Oh, here's a row!" said Philip, when he thought himself alone. "I only wish they would pay me my hundred pounds, I would be off at once, and have nothing further to do with it. I begin to think that I might as well not have given any information to the Government at all, for they seem rather backward in coming forward with the reward they promised me. What could the old gentleman mean by saying that he smelt a rat?"

"He meant me!" said Captain Gay, as he emerged from behind the column, and took two strides towards the door.

"Murder! Help!"

"Silence—on your life!"

"Oh, must I? I have him—I have him! Help—help! Murder! This way! I have got him!"

Philip clung to Captain Gay by the skirts of his coat, while the Captain opened the outer door.

"Let me go, fool!"

"No, I won't! Ha—ha! I have him! Help—help!"

Captain Gay drew his sword in a moment, and being just able to turn, as Philip had hold of his skirts, he shortened his arm, and exclaiming:

"Idiot, take the reward both of your treachery to your master, and your folly in attempting to detain me!" he plunged the sword through his chest.

With such force was the thrust given, and so close were they together, that the sword went right through the body of the wretched man, and the hilt struck against his breast.

With a wild shriek Philip flung up his arms, and then Captain Gay raised his foot, and sent him to the farther end of the hall with one violent thrust from the sword blade.

There was a rush of feet now towards the hall; but before the king's messenger and the two officers he had brought with him could reach it, Captain Gay was gone; and the only proof they had that something serious had taken place, was the fact that the dead body of Philip, the porter, lay there in a pool of blood.

Captain Gay sheathed his blood-stained sword in a moment, and then ran up Great Russell Street to Tottenham Court Road; where, hailing the first coach he met, he ordered the driver to take him to the river side.

When there, the Captain hired a boat, and directed the couple of watermen whom he took with it to put him on shore at the first quay, some distance up the river, which was near any place where he could get post-horses quickly.

They landed him at Chelsea Reach; and there, at an inn which has long since disappeared, but which at that time was celebrated as a posting-house, he hired a post-chaise; and naming a town to the west of London, and about fifty miles off, he went rapidly in that direction.

The London mission of Captain Gay was over. Indeed, he had accomplished much more than his iniquitous employer, the old Duke of Lorton, ever thought he could accomplish.

A combination of circumstances, though, had tended to bring about such a result; and thus it was that, instead of going back to the Duke with the news that he had found out where the wife and child of the Marquis were staying, he took a much more comprehensive piece of intelligence, in the fact that both the Marquis and the Marchioness were dead, and the orphan son knew not even his own name.

It happened that the property belonging to the Lorton family was, to a great extent, settled upon the Marquisate of Dalewood, which was the title borne by the eldest son of the Duke of Lorton; and the object of the old Duke, whose cupidity was awful, was to prevent his son from disposing of that property to his wife and child; and there is very little doubt but that, if circumstances had not turned out as they did, some plan, with the assistance of Gay, would have been got up for probably the kidnapping, and possibly the death of both the Marchioness and her son.

As it was, though, Captain Gay considered that the orphan son of the Marquis and the Marchioness was not worth the looking for, as he had the will in his possession, which could alone reinstate him in his rights, and proclaim to the world who and what he was.

The object of Captain Gay now was to reach the western coast of England, and from there take a passage in some vessel bound for Ireland, to any port of which he was willing to go, although, of course, he would have preferred getting round to Galway at once; and fully intended to do so, if he could find a vessel to take him.

Travelling was by no means so easy in those days as it is now, and therefore the journey across England to a western port took Captain Gay some days to accomplish.

When he reached that coast of England, he found, to his great joy, that a ship was about to sail for the west coast of Ireland in three or four days; so he resolved to wait for it. And there we leave him for the present, exulting over the unlooked-for success of his rascally mission to London, and almost forgetting in that exultation the feelings of vengeance that he had entertained against Jacob Ardent, and the people of the market in Covent Garden.

The Government, incensed at the escape of the Marquis, although it was an escape to the grave, sequestered his estates with all the rapidity in their power, and in the course of a few days the whole of the costly effects were removed from Dalewood House, which was shut up, and left to the dominion of the rats and mice, and to the dust that settled thickly upon its floors, its walls, and upon the once gay fittings of its banqueting-rooms, which were, in some cases, left entire.

What happened to Captain Gay in his voyage to Galway, and who were his fellow-passengers, will form other chapters in this most strange and eventful history.

We must now request the reader's kind attention to the bouquet-shop in Covent Garden market, kept by the Ardent family, connected with which some very tragic and singular circumstances were upon the eve of taking place.

It will probably be more deeply interesting to notice and to record the sayings and the doings of these poor, but honest, people, than to follow the villainous career of Captain Gay; but it will be necessary to the progress of our eventful story to pay considerable attention to that personage's proceedings, inasmuch as he exercises a great control over the destinies of better people than himself.

To the pages, however, which now follow this first and striking episode in our story we would request the deepest attention, inasmuch as the revelations they contain are such as will come home to every heart, and find an echo in every fancy.

The reader will likewise bear in mind that the particular epoch of our tale was one in which the manners and habits, domestic as well as public, of the inhabitants of this country were very different from what they are now.

CHAPTER XIV.

CORPORAL BUDD MAKES A DECLARATION, AND GETS HIS ANSWER.

THE secret of who it was that had let poor Lady Dalewood know of the danger that threatened her husband, the Marquis, previous to the attack by the party of soldiery upon Dalewood House, soon oozed out.

It will be recollected that Corporal Budd, of the Guards, was, or appeared to be, on very intimate and amicable terms with the Ardent family, and particularly with Jane, the niece of the old folks; so, after hearing Jacob Ardent several times say how much he wished to know who had given that information to the poor Marchioness, the Corporal took him aside, and said to him in a mysterious tone:

"Uncle-in-law that is to be, I hope that all will be right with the orphan Marquis—eh?"

"My good friend, how can I say?"

"Humph! I'll find him out if I can; but, uncle-in-law, I don't think—eh? that—eh?"

"Good gracious, Corporal Budd, what do you mean?"

"Why, I was going to say that I don't think Jane seems to care so much for me as I would wish—eh? And yet I thought I had done a something that would have had the effect—eh?—of making her think more of me than ever."

"What was that, Corporal Budd?"

"Why, I don't mind telling you; but the fact is, it was I who gave information to the Marchioness that the Marquis was going to be arrested."

"You, Corporal?"

"Yes. All's right. Stand at ease. I did it."

"But—but——"

"I know. You would say, how came I to know it? And I will tell you. An order came to the barracks in the Birdcage Walk, where my regiment is posted, and I heard an Adjutant and a Captain of a company talking of it; and says the Captain to the Adjutant: 'I know the house very well; it is close to Montague House,' says he. 'But do you believe it?' says he. 'Yes,' said the Adjutant, 'I do,' says he; 'and, what's more,' says he, 'the Marquis of Dalewood,' says he, 'will lose his head, as sure as fate!' says he."

"You overheard that?"

"I did, uncle-in-law that is to be; so I said to myself, says I, 'Why, that must be the husband of the lady I have heard those good and worthy people, the Ardents, talk about.'"

"Yes—yes."

"'Well,' says I, 'it would be a good thing,' says I, 'to let her know all about it,' for I guessed that something was amiss that night, and I went to my own room, and wrote a letter to you."

"To me?"

"Yes. All's right. Stand at ease."

"But I got no letter."

"I know that."

"But explain, Corporal."

"I will. I wrote a letter to you, saying that I thought, and, in fact, that I knew the Marquis's house would be beleaguered, for I heard still more about it after the Adjutant and the Captain had spoken; and with the letter in my hand, I went out by the barrack gate to get someone for a groat or so to carry it to you, for I was afraid to trust any of the lads in the regiment, you see."

"True; yes, yes—Well?"

"Well, you know I saw the poor Marchioness once in this house, and went and fetched a chair for her."

"You did."

"And so I knew her; and what should I see, just down by Westminster, while I was waiting with the letter in my hand, but the Marchioness stepping into a sedan-chair; so, though it was addressed to you, I thought the best thing I could do was to give the letter to her."

"You did right."

"Well, I broke it open, so that she might have no sort of scruple about doing so; and I gave it to one of the men carrying the chair, and told him to hand it to the lady, and I had hardly time to do that, for I saw one of our officers coming down George Street, and if he had seen me give the Marchioness a letter, and had found out who she was, I should have got into a scrape."

"I quite understand, Corporal Budd."

"Glad you do. Well, that's all about it; and so, you see, she got notice, and came to you, poor thing."

"Yes—yes! now I understand it all."

"Stand at ease!"

"Alas! I wish I could feel at ease. But,

although this affair has turned out to be very calamitous, I feel much obliged to you, Corporal, for your effort to do good."

"Don't mention it. But, uncle-in-law that is to be, do you think—Eh—eh ?"

"What—what ? Speak out !"

"Well, then, do you think that your niece, Jane, will look at a fellow a little kinder ? I thought she really did seem to like me a little this morning, and that it was all but settled."

"I cannot interfere to control her inclination, Corporal. You know as well as I do that Peter Bolt is a favoured suitor."

"Peter Bolt !"

"Yes, you know him."

"The tailor ! Cannon balls and bombshells ! The idea of a tailor interfering with a Corporal !"

"It's a matter of taste, Mr. Budd."

"I'll go to Jane at once ! I'll ask her at once to be Mrs. Corporal Budd ! A tailor ! Fough ! Snip ! The ninth part of a man ! A thing of cabbage and hot goose ! A tailor ! Fuff—fuff !"

"Dear me," said old Ardent, "don't be in a passion, I beg of you, Corporal."

"A passion ? Me in a passion ? Oh, dear no ! I—I am not in a passion. Fire and brimstone, no ! I—am calm and cool, and—a tailor—a tailor preferred to me ! I'll go to her at once !"

"Stop a bit."

"What for, uncle-in-law that is to be ?"

"There is one thing, Corporal, which I may as well mention to you, as, in fact, being the one thing that of all others is likely to stand in the way of your successful suit to my pretty little niece, Jane."

"What—is—it ?" gasped the Corporal.

"We are all aware, Corporal Budd, that when my dear daughter Millicent was at home—who is now in Devonshire with her aunt—that it was to her you paid your attention."

The Corporal looked like a military man in a fix.

And old Ardent continued:

"But Millicent made you comprehend that she did not want you, and you stayed away from the house for some time; and when you came again, Millicent had gone on a visit to her aunt; and Jane, my orphan niece, had come to live with us."

"Yes ?" gasped the Corporal.

"And then you fell in love with Jane."

"Yes ?"

"Now, my dear friend, girls and women don't like that sort of thing, let me tell you."

"Yes ?"

"Don't say yes, for it's no. I thought it but right to say this much to you, for I think it will weigh more with Jane than anything else."

"I'm a lost Corporal !"

"Not so. You will, no doubt, see someone else whom you can love; but if you really wish to ask what Jane thinks of the affair, you have my free leave to do so, for I respect you very much."

The Corporal could not speak just then, but he shook the old man by the hand, and then, with rapid strides, went into the back parlour, where Jane was at work sewing. Mrs. Ardent was in the front shop. And old Ardent strolled about the doorway to calm his mind, if he could, after the startling events of the preceding night and early morning.

The Corporal had certainly made up his mind that he would know the sentiments of Jane, "Ay, or No," upon the subject of his attentions to her.

There was an expression upon Jane's face after she had taken one sidelong look at the Corporal, which evidently showed that she was a sufficient judge of physiognomy to know what the Corporal meant to say to her.

She went on at her sewing, though, as if nothing were amiss.

"Jane," said the Corporal; "Janey !"

"Did you speak, Corporal Budd ?"

"I did."

"Well, I thought you did."

"Oh, Jane ! oh, Janey !"

"Dear me ! Aren't you well ?"

"No—no—no !"

"Then I recommend you to go to some apothecary, Corporal Budd."

"But, Jane—Janey, it is all along of you. Look at me—oh, look at me ! I love you, Jane—I love you. I am but a Corporal; but I have a heart in my bosom for all that, as big as a General's, I assure you, and it's all yours, Jane—it's all yours. Here I am on my knees to you, Jane, to tell you that I love you. I am but a Corporal; but marry me now, and you will be Mrs. Corporal Budd. In time, though, I am pretty sure of being a Sergeant, and then you will be Mrs. Sergeant Budd. Oh, Jane—Janey ! only say yes, and you will make me happier than a Field-marshal. Here I am—here I am !"

The enamoured Corporal plumped down upon his knees at the feet of Jane, and looked imploringly in her face.

Jane went on with her sewing.

"Jane—oh, Janey, look at me ! speak to me !"

"Well, I am looking."

"Speak !—oh, speak !"

"I will, then. If anybody were to come into this room just now, what do you suppose they would think of you ?"

"I don't know—I don't care. I love you !"

"Stop !"

"Yes, I will for ever. Oh, Jane, you will have me ?"

"No."

"N—o ?"

"Just so. Corporal Budd, my cousin Millicent told me, that before she went to Devonshire, there was a Corporal who in this very fashion knelt at her foot, and told her he loved her, and that if she married him she would be Mrs. Corporal Budd; and that when he was a Sergeant, she would be Mrs. Sergeant Budd. Now, are you that Corporal ?"

"Geese and gridirons !" shouted a voice: and there rushed into the room, in a state of terrible agitation, Peter Bolt, the tailor.

CHAPTER XV.

THE CORPORAL RECEIVES HIS DISMISSAL, AND THE TAILOR TRIUMPHS.

"'SDEATH, cried the Corporal, springing to his feet, what is the meaning of this?"

"Keep off! keep off!" cried Peter, as he sprang to the other side of a table. "Keep off, or dread my vengeance!"

"Your vengeance, you contemptible wretch? I'll smother you!"

"Corporal Budd," said Jane, "there is the door."

"The—a—a—door?"

"Yes, the door."

"But, Jane—Janey!"

"Hold your row!" cried Peter, the tailor, as he threw himself into a theatrical attitude, "I feed upon love, where'er I rove. Jane is my darling. And she sings like a starling. Where'er I am, where'er I be, in country or in town, my heart is hers; my thoughts so free, to sweet Jane back have flown—There, you great brick-dust and pipe-clay looking animal, make some poetry like that, if you can!"

"I'll make you into mince-meat, if I can't make poetry," said the Corporal.

"No, you won't—no, you won't. You don't known the spirit of a tailor! To arms —to arms! Caitiff, come on, and take your doom! The lovely Jane, with eyes so blue, will now be mine, and get rid of you!"

Peter seized a pair of bellows which were by the fireside, in one hand, and the tongs in the other, and there he stood in a terrible attitude of offence or defence.

The Corporal drew himself up, and pointing to the tailor, said to Jane, in what he intended should be a tone of withering sarcasm——

"Miss Jane, do you prefer that being to me?"

"Yes," said Jane.

"Oh!"

"Ah!" said Peter Bolt.

"Then—I—that is—you—a—Miss Jane, would rather have a tailor, than a military man?"

"Oh, dear, yes."

"Oh!"

"Ah!" said Peter Bolt.

"And you may go," said Jane to the Corporal, "as soon as ever you like, and the sooner the better. Peter Bolt may be little, and he may be a tailor; but he has a good heart, and is kind and industrious, and supports his poor old mother in her old age; and I know of many kind acts he has done, and besides all that, I don't think he ever loved anybody else but me in all his life, and I don't think he ever will."

"Ye gods and little fishes!" cried Peter, "grant me all my wishes. Jane is the fairest of the fair, in sea, on earth, or in the air. I love her more than I can tell—and she her Peter loves as well!"

The Corporal made a spring over the table; Jane screamed; the tailor swore—yes, the tailor swore! The Corporal got hold of him by the back of the neck, and in one moment put his head up the chimney, placed his feet on the fire-grate—in which, luckily, there was no fire—and then, just as Jacob Ardent and Mrs. Ardent rushed into the room, the Corporal strode out of it.

Peter Bolt fell from the chimney, bringing with him a deluge of soot; and as Mr. and Mrs. Ardent saw the action, it appeared as if it were by that rather eccentric mode he had made his way into the house.

"Oh, gracious!" cried Mrs. Ardent.

"Why, bless me!" said Jacob, "what is this?"

"Murder!" said the tailor.

"It's the Corporal," said Jane.

"Fuffle—fluff! a-chew! a-a-chew!" sneezed Peter, as he strove to rid his eyes, mouth, and nose of the soot with which he had come into such close contact. "Oh, lor! what a horrid state I is in!"

"Never mind, Peter," said Jane.

"Oh, it's all very well to say—a—a-chew! —never mind; but the idea of being laid hold of like a wild beast, and poked up the—a— a-chew!—chimbley in this-a-ways, is enough to make a man—a-chew!—a—a-chew!'

"But what did you do in the chimney, man alive?" said old Jacob Ardent.

"Nothing," said Peter.

"But how came you there?" said Mrs. Ardent.

"I didn't come there, mum; I was put there —I was."

"In at the top?"

"No, mum; at this end. The Corporal wanted me to go, I think, while he murdered Jane, and he took it into his stupid head that this was the way out; but I'll have revenge— I'll have—oh, gracious!—a—a-chew!—a-chew!—a-chew!—a—a—no, I do think that's the last of it, as I'm a sinner."

"My dear Jane," said Mrs. Ardent, "what is all this about, child? Can you tell me?"

"Yes, aunt. Corporal Budd chose to quarrel with Peter, and then pushed him up the chimney; and so I will never speak to Corporal Budd again, aunt, if I can help it."

"Oh, dear me," said old Ardent, "that's the way! I suppose, Jane, you told the Corporal you would not have him, and in the midst of it in comes Peter Bolt?"

"Yes, uncle."

"Ah, I thought as much. Well, well, you have given the Corporal an answer, and there's an end of it. I daresay he will be very sorry that he interfered with Peter; but it was done in the anger of the moment, for I know that Corporal Budd has a good heart."

"Yes," said Peter, "he may have, and he's got a terrible hard fist, too."

"Never mind, Peter."

"Oh, it's all very well to say, 'Never mind,' when a man will smell like a chimbley sweep for a week."

"But I," said Jane, "ask you to never mind."

"Oh, Jane, if you ask me, I won't. It

shall never be said that, though Peter was put right up the chimbley along with the soot, that his Jane said to him, with a smile, 'Never mind,' and he cared for the smother before or behind,—a-chew—a-chew! We'll live and we'll love for each other, dear Jane; our lives shall be pleasure without any pain; and when we grow old, we will still love each other, in spite of the world and of all sorts of bother; and then—oh, dear! a—a-chew!—a-chew!"

"Well, Peter Bolt," said Mrs. Ardent, "I will say that, to my mind, you are a genius."

"Thank you, mum. I always thought so myself, if you please, Mrs. Ardent."

"You do make such beautiful poetry."

"Yes, mum. I feel very much put out just now, though, Mrs. Ardent, after what has happened. But I do hope as that horrid sojer won't come here any more."

"I cannot promise you that, Peter," said old Jacob Ardent. "I feel much friendly obligation to Corporal Budd, and I cannot deny him access to my house; but I have no doubt in the world, that his own better thoughts will make him very sorry for what has taken place here to-day."

"He can't possibly be more sorry than I am," said Peter, as he smeared the soot all over his face with the skirt of his coat. "A pretty figure I am!"

"Never mind about your figure," said Jane. "Have not I as good as said I would have you?"

"No. Have you, though?"

"Oh, you stupid! When a girl has two lovers, and she gets rid of one, of course that means well to the other."

"It does—it does! Come to your Peter's arms—come to my breast!"

"Not just now, Peter. You must get rid of the soot first, I think."

"To be sure," said Mrs. Ardent; "and, what's more, I won't have any coming to arms in my house, I can tell you, Mr. Peter Bolt, till such time as my niece is married to you; so don't say anything so improper again, I beg of you."

"I won't, mum. But I'll compose the sweetest poem ever you heard, about Jane; and I do think that, beautiful as she is, she owes it to belonging to your family, Mrs. Ardent, for I believe she come of your side of the house."

"She does, Mr. Bolt. She comes from the Slumkinses, which was my family name."

"Yes, mum; and I've often heard that they were famous for beauty—that I have!"

"They were, Mr. Bolt—they were!" cried Mrs. Ardent, with a toss of her head; "and I will say this of you—that, though you are a tailor, you are about the most sensible man that I know, and I am sure that, feeling as you do about the Slumkinses, you will make a capital husband."

Jane shook her head at Peter Bolt, in disapprobation of the rather profuse dose of flattery to which he treated her aunt; but Peter made up a comical face in reply, which said as plainly as possible:

"Oh, my dear Jane, all is fair in love and in war, and it is only for your dear sake that I say what I do say to your highly respectable, but rather prejudiced aunt."

Thus, then, was Peter Bolt, in a way of speaking, the accredited, and devoted, and accepted lover of Jane, the niece of the Ardents; and we shall soon see how the Corporal conducted himself.

The probability is that, but for the fickle character which the Corporal had at the establishment in Covent Garden market, Jane might have preferred him to the tailor; but he had committed the capital offence of falling in love with someone else first, and only turning his vacillating attention to Jane when that someone else was away; and that was a course of proceeding which Jane did not approve of.

To tell the truth, too, both Mrs. Ardent and old Jacob Ardent were much better pleased at the prospect of their lovely and pretty little niece becoming the wife of the tailor than the Corporal; for if she had yoked herself to the fortunes of the latter, there is no knowing what dangers or hardships might have been her lot.

With the tailor, however, if he were but industrious—and there was no reason to suppose that he would be otherwise—she was likely enough to glide through life in comfort and peace, and respectability, which were all very desirable conditions in their way.

CHAPTER XVI.

JACOB ARDENT HIDES THE MARQUIS'S MONEY FOR THE ORPHAN NOBLE.

AFTER all that had happened within the short space of four-and-twenty hours, and after the active part the old man had had to play in those events, we can easily imagine that the mind of old Jacob Ardent was a little bewildered, and that at times he looked about him at the old and well-remembered bouquet shop, in order to be quite sure that he was not in some sort of dream.

But there were too many rational points, so to speak, concerning what had happened for him long to doubt the truth of it, and among them none pressed more heavily upon the mind of the old man than the responsibility he felt concerning the last wishes of the unhappy Marquis of Dalewood.

To a simple-minded man like Jacob Ardent, the letters and their inclosures that the Marquis had put into his hands, would at any time have been absolutely inviolable; but now that death had disposed of two of the parties interested in them, he felt that they and the riches they contained were sacred things.

The sum of money, too, which accompanied the packet of written papers was one that to Jacob Ardent seemed very large; for, although the amount of two hundred pounds may sound but little for the Marquis of Dalewood to send to his distressed wife and child, yet we must consider that it was only intended to put them into funds until they could claim their inheritance.

Besides, two hundred pounds in those days was a much larger sum, in respect of its purchasing powers, than it is now.

To Jacob Ardent it was like some miser's deposit, that all the thieves in London, if they did but suspect its existence, would be after.

Can we wonder, then, that that gold, metaphorically speaking, lay heavily upon the soul of the old man?

Now, between old Jacob Ardent and his wife there had for many years existed the greatest confidence; and in any affair that concerned himself only, he would not have hesitated for a moment to consult her; but in this case he trembled and doubted whether he ought to say anything to a living soul about the contents of the Marquis's packet, until he could place it securely in the hands of the young son.

Agitated by many conflicting thoughts and feelings, the old man passed an evening of anxiety and terror upon the subject.

"Who knows," he said, "what may happen? We are pretty well off now, it is true; but we are not rich—sickness may come into our dwelling—business may get bad. I am each day becoming more and more incapable of working and bringing in any money; and if distress should enter our humble home, who knows but my wife might yield to the temptation of having so much money in the place, and take some of it; and then what could I say to the young Marquis when I saw him? Oh, that would kill me! That, indeed, would kill me! Could I say to him, 'Noble sir, your father trusted me with a sum of money for you, but I have spent it?' Oh, no—no—no!"

This feeling so grew upon the old man, that he, at length, made the indiscreet determination to hide the money from his wife entirely, and to keep secret the fact that he had it at all in his possession.

Jacob Ardent little knew what a store of misery he was laying up both for himself and his wife by this want of confidence in her; but he did it for what he thought the best; and much higher folks than the old waterman-fireman make quite as serious mistakes upon that head.

After having come to this resolve, the old man felt his mind to be a little easier, although the mode of carrying it out was a source of deep thought.

Sometimes he thought he would take the money, well secured in a box or bag, out into the open country somewhere, and bury it beneath the shadow of some old tree, which he would be sure to know again. Then, again, he thought he would take it, and hide it in his boat; but both of these schemes were open to many objections. And, at length, he made up his mind that the house in the market in which he and his family had resided for so many years should still continue to hold the money.

The back parlour, in which the family usually sat, and where they all took their meals, was paved with a sort of red tile—then in common use for the kitchen and domestic offices of London dwellings—and it struck Jacob that beneath one of these tiles he could make a little excavation that would just hold the money, and that then he should feel sure that it was safe.

It was with this determination that old Jacob Ardent returned to it on the eventful night following that on which the poor unfortunate Marquis of Dalewood had met his death at the great fire at the opera-house.

Mrs. Ardent had noticed the abstraction of her husband during the evening; and when they were alone she questioned him about it.

"Dear me, Jacob," she said, "I don't know what has come over you. You seem quite melancholy."

"No—no; and yet I might well be, after what has happened. Alas—alas! that we should have no trace of the young lord!"

"It is a sad thing; yet who knows but something may turn up to get us out of that difficulty? Surely he must be somewhere?"

"Oh, yes, that is true."

"And you know we have quite a clue to one of the men who came with the sedan-chair?"

"Yes, he was ugly."

"To be sure he was."

"But don't you think that there may be a great many of the same sort of men?"

"Well, Jacob, perhaps there may be; but, after all, the best way in the world is to hope for the best. And there is one thing that I have many great hopes for."

"Indeed!"

"Oh, yes. Can't you guess, Jacob?"

"Not I. But you may as well tell me at once."

"Well, then, I am quite certain to dream something about it. There, now, I feel quite certain of that."

"Oh, pho! pho!"

"What?"

"Stuff, wife—stuff!"

"Mr. Ardent, it's all very well for you to say stuff, but I can tell you that I always dream something, and that it always means something; and as a proof that it does, I can tell you that only last week I dreamt that I saw a white cat with a live lobster on her back, walking through the market, mewing out as she went: 'Any fresh fish to-day?' And now you see what has happened."

"What—what?"

"What, do you ask me? Why, hasn't the Marquis of Dalewood been killed? Hasn't the poor Marchioness died of grief? and yet, you unfeeling monster, you ask me what has happened? Oh, Jacob, I did not expect this of you."

"But, my dear, what has all that to do with a lobster and a cat on his back?"

"It wasn't a lobster with a cat on his back. It was the cat that had the lobster."

"Well—well, it doesn't matter; but I would just ask you now what possible connection there can be between that and the Marquis of Dalewood and his affairs?"

"Everything. There, now—you have got your answer, and I hope you are convinced; but this I know, that when people are determined to be obstinate, you might as well speak to the market pump, that you might. Oh, gracious!"

"What's the matter?"

"There's the watchman calling past eleven and a cloudy night, as I'm a sinner. Don't go on chattering any more, but go to sleep at once."

"I devoutly wish you would," thought Jacob to himself.

There was a deep silence in the dwelling of the bouquet-maker now for about an hour, and everyone seemed to sleep. Old Jacob Ardent, however, was wide awake. The thoughts of the Marquis's money were upon his mind, and effectually prevented him from closing his eyes.

What he intended to do was to rise from his bed when he should be assured that Mrs. Ardent slept, and complete the process of hiding the two hundred pounds, which he had already securely fastened up in a small leathern bag, and placed conveniently between the mattress and the bedstead.

The watchman of the market called the hour of twelve, and signified that the night was still cloudy, when Jacob Ardent, by the regular breathing of his wife, concluded that she slept; but he was resolved to be quite certain about it, so he said in a low tone:

"Wife—wife?"

There was no reply, so the old man made up his mind that she was in a deep sleep, and he gently left the bed, and took the leathern bag of money from the place in which he had concealed it.

Poor old Jacob shook like an aspen leaf as he proceeded from his bedroom; and if he had been intent upon some highly nefarious and direful transaction, instead of one of a totally different character, he could not have been more agitated than he was.

Creeping down the old rickety staircase, which now seemed to utter so many odd sounds in the shape of groans and squeaks, the old man reached the shop; and then, by the aid of some embers that still smouldered in the fire, he got a light, and shading it with his hand looked carefully about him.

All was still as the grave.

"Yes—yes!" he said, in a whisper, "I will hide the money. It will be quite safe here, and no living soul but myself will know anything about it. It is too large a sum—oh, much too large to trust even my wife with the knowledge of."

With trembling and stealthy steps, then, he took his way to the common living room of the family, and then he stopped to listen again, for he thought that a slight noise came upon the still night air.

"What—what is that?"

Jacob's hair almost stood on end as something touched his foot.

"No—no!" he said. "Oh, dear—I—I—oh, dear, it's—it's only the cat. Oh—oh, what a turn it gave me!"

A large favourite cat of the Ardents, who was accustomed to sleep in that room when the family retired for the night, had been roused by Jacob's appearance with a light, and had testified her pleasure at the visit by rubbing her head against his legs.

"Oh, pussy," said the old man, "you have given me such a fright.; but I am glad it is only you. I didn't think that any eyes that had life in them would see me put away this money; but you shall, for I know you won't tell."

The cat set up a great purring, and seemed deeply interested in what its master was about.

Jacob now placed the light upon the floor, and by the aid of his large pocket-knife, which he had brought with him for the purpose, he soon got up one of the square tiles of the floor.

The ground beneath the tile was very hard and compact, so that Jacob had no little difficulty in digging it out with the point of his knife. Nevertheless, he soon removed enough of it to make an excavation that would hold the little leathern bag of gold, and then he placed it in.

"There—there," said Jacob, "that will do. It will be quite safe there, I feel assured."

The cat sneezed.

Jacob put the tile on the spot, and made it lie quite flat, and filled up the interstices and edges with the mould, and scattered dirt from the floor over the whole, so that there was no appearance of it having been at all disturbed.

"I am easier in my mind now," said Jacob, as he rose from his work. "I am much easier, for I shall now feel that, come what may, this secret hoard of wealth is in my own keeping."

The cat sneezed again.

CHAPTER XVII.

THE ARDENT FAMILY RECEIVE RATHER AN IMPORTANT EPISTLE.

JACOB did not much like the sneezing of the cat. It really sounded so significant of the opinion of that feline individual that he was reckoning in some way without his host; but he took no notice of it, being, at all events, satisfied that he had done his best.

As he turned to leave the room, though, he thought he heard a movement of something in the shop, and his blood ran cold at the idea that there might be thieves there.

With a sudden rush Jacob made his way into the shop, and, holding the light above his head, he said in a whisper:

"Who is there—who is there?"

All was still.

"Speak!" said Jacob Ardent again, in the same subdued tone. "Speak!"

No one replied to him.

Jacob was afraid to utter a word above a whisper, lest he himself should be the cause

"WHAT DO YOU MEAN FELLOWS? AM I TO BE JOLTED IN THIS WAY?"

of creating the alarm that he dreaded, when otherwise there might be none at all; so, after standing for a few moments with the light in his hand, raised as high above his head as he could raise it, for the purpose of scattering its beams as far as possible, he became partially satisfied that he was alone, and that it must have been some noise in the market which had fallen upon his ears, and in his then excited state induced him to believe there was someone in the shop.

"It is nothing—it is nothing!" he said. "I only frighten myself into all sorts of delusions because I am apprehensive—that is all. The money is safe—quite safe, I think. Indeed, I may say, I know that it is; so I can sleep now in peace."

He put out the light, for his long familiarity with the old house easily enabled him to reach the staircase in the dark; and having done so, he crept cautiously and slowly up to his own chamber, and entered it with the stealthy step of one who might have come with the worst, instead of the best motives.

Old Jacob slipped into bed again, and the calm and quiet breathing of his wife reassured him that she had slept securely while he was hiding the Marquis's money.

"All is well!" he thought; "all is well! That great anxiety is now off my mind."

No. 3.—(MARQUIS.)

Yes, Jacob thought all was well; but as there is no occasion for keeping up a mystery which involves nothing but itself in its disclosure, we may state that, in his acceptation of the phrase, all was not well.

Mrs. Ardent knew too well the habits and modes of thought of her husband, not to be well aware that all the evening there had been a something upon his mind which he was struggling to keep from her, and although she had abstained from letting him know precisely that she had such an idea, she had resolved to find out what it was, if possible.

Hence, then—when Jacob, in so low a tone of voice, that if she really slept it would not disturb her—called to her before he went to hide the money, she had feigned sleep, and when, to her surprise, he rose from his bed, and went to the lower part of the house, she followed him.

Thus was it, then, that she saw him dig the hole in the floor of the common living room, and hide the bag of money; and it will be noticed that, unfortunately, in all his whispered words to himself while he was so hiding it, Jacob said nothing that could in any way enlighten his wife as to the real facts of the case; and Mrs. Ardent, consequently, retired to bed again with the firm and fixed conclusion that the little bag of money was Jacob's own.

How he had become possessed of it she had many different ideas; but it was possible that the sum might be the long saved-up overplus of his earnings as a waterman; or some lucky chance, of which he did not think proper to apprise her, might have thrown it in his way.

At all events, Mrs. Ardent felt no doubt about its being his own; and from that moment a feeling of coolness and estrangement arose in her mind towards him, for she felt herself aggrieved at the fact of his hiding his money from her.

Alas! what countless evils has not money to answer for! Hence we find that the mere fact of two hundred pounds of someone else's property being hidden beneath the roof of the honest couple who before that event had lived in perfect harmony together, was sufficient to engender bitterness and strife!

Both Mrs. Ardent and her husband were now in rather a painful position. He, after not having taken her into his confidence at once regarding the Marquis's money, could hardly do so with a very good grace afterwards.

She, too, could not ask a question, or institute any inquiry into a circumstance of which she only knew something by having adopted a system of espionage upon her husband which in itself was an offence; and so, although they both felt that they were not towards each other what they once had been, they neither could overstep the seeming difficulties in the way of an adjustment or understanding of the unexpressed difference.

Beware of secrets! They are the bane of domestic peace, as much as they are the destruction of right policy in states.

But there were other events that soon had the effect of, for a time, withdrawing the attention of both Mrs. Ardent and her husband from what had happened to the Marquis of Dalewood and his unhappy lady.

The dismissal of the Corporal from all chance of establishing himself in the good graces of Jane, enabled Peter Bolt to make himself much more attentive to the Ardents; and hence was it that, at quite an early hour in the morning, the gallant Peter appeared before the house of his betrothed.

"Hilloa! Jacob Ardent—Jacob Ardent!" he cried. "Peter is as grateful as his betters, and so he has come to take down the shutters. How is Jane this lovely day, which looks like the smiling first of May?"

"Hoi!" cried old Ardent, from the window, "is that you, Peter?"

"It used to was," said Peter. "Is Jane arising like the sun, before the dickey birds have begun to sing on every branch a lay, to welcome in the early day?"

"Well, Peter, I don't know; but I'll be down directly. Why, you look quite cold."

Old Ardent soon descended, and the shop was opened by the joint exertions of himself and Peter; and then Mrs. Ardent made her appearance; and just because she was terribly angry with her husband, she appeared to be in high spirits.

"Well, I'm sure, Jacob," she said, "how young you do look this morning old man. One would think you had taken quite a new lease of life, and some day intended to save up a lot of money, and go into the country, and be a squire."

"Money!" said Jacob. "Money! Oh, you are always thinking of money, wife."

"Ha! ha! ha! Deary me, am I indeed? Well, I do wish I was like some folks that think nothing of it at all; or, what is more, I wish I was like Mrs. Wheezle of the 'Dolphin' in Drury Lane."

"Mrs. Wheezle be—hem!" said Jacob. "Well, never mind, I don't care about her."

"Hoity toity! What has Mrs. Wheezle done to you?"

"Oh, nothing; but for goodness gracious sake don't say you wish you were like her! If you were, I should go out of my mind, that is all."

"Marry come up! I wish I was like her in one thing."

"And what is that?"

"Why, didn't she get a prize in the lottery?"

"A prize in the fiddlestick!"

"Oh, it's all very well to call it a prize in the fiddlestick; but she got the money."

"Money! money! money! that is all your cry. Didn't she drink herself into a madhouse with it! Don't think so much about money, wife, I beg of you."

Mrs. Ardent held up her hands, and turned up her eyes to Heaven, as much as to say: "Oh, the hypocrisy of human nature! Here is this man pretending to me not to think so much of money; and he gets up in the night to hide his in a hole in the kitchen floor!"

At this moment, though, the discussion was cut short by the entrance of Jane, looking as fresh as a rose; and the enamoured Peter Bolt made such a rush to fall at her feet, that he tore the skirt of Mrs. Ardent's dress; whereupon, as that much-injured lady wanted somebody to vent her indignation upon, she dealt Peter a hearty box on the ear, saying:

"Take that, stupid! Now you have got it."

"Oh, lor!—oh! Why, mother-in-law, what a hand you have got, to be sure."

"Never mind, Peter," whispered Jane. "Never mind."

"I won't mind."

"No, my boy," added old Ardent. "Never mind, Peter. Mrs. A. is a little out of sorts this morning."

"Oh, indeed—fiddle-dee-de!" cried Mrs. Ardent, at the top of her voice. "I'd have you know, Mr. Jacob Ardent, waterman-fireman, and all that sort of thing, that——"

"Fifteen-pence-halfpenny!" said a voice at the door; and the general postman made his appearance with a letter.

Mrs. Ardent sat upon a low chair by the fire, and wiped her face, and old Ardent paid for the letter. Peter Bolt, who had seen that a domestic storm was what he called "a-brewing," had pretended to be looking at the ceiling, and an expression of distress had come over the face of the pretty Jane.

"My dear," said old Jacob Ardent, as with the letter in his hand he advanced towards his wife, "this is from our dear child, Millicent; so do not let us quarrel, with her dear handwriting before our eyes."

Mrs Ardent began to cry.

"It's next thing to having her here herself, bless her pretty face and her sweet looks!" added the old man; "so now we will all be friends."

Mrs. Ardent showed symptoms of being a little hysterical.

"Jane," said the old man.

"Yes, uncle."

"Get your mother the cordial-water bottle."

"Yes, uncle."

A glass of the cordial-water restored Mrs. Ardent; and she wiped her eyes, and looked much as usual, as she said:

"Come, now, Jacob, read the letter, and let us know what our poor dear child is about."

"I will—I will! Where are my—Eh? Dear me, where did I put my—Eh?"

"What is it now, Jacob? What is the man muttering about?"

"My spectacles!"

"Why, you always lose them."

"Eh? so I do—so I do; somehow or another, they always get into the wrong place."

"Why, uncle, they are on your nose!" screamed Jane.

"My nose?"

"Yes."

"Oh, lor, so they are! Well, I never! The idea, now! He—he! Oh! that they should be on my nose, and I looking for them

all the while. But come, now, attend—all of you."

"But, Mister Ardent——" said Peter.

"Well, what now?"

"Shall I go? I don't feel, you see, as I ought to stay here, and cabbage the family secrets, you understand, in this here sort o' way; and if you think I ought to go, why you have but to say, 'Peter, there is the door,' and away I am."

"No, Peter, my boy, you will soon, I hope, be one of the family, by your union with our niece, Jane—so you may stay. I hate secrets, and thank God, I may say, that I have—Hem! I—I—that is—well, I will read the letter."

Jacob's heart smote him as he was going to say he had no secrets from his family, for he thought of the money he had with such care secreted in that very room—and Mrs. Ardent thought of the same thing.

CHAPTER XVIII.

CONTAINS IMPORTANT NEWS FROM MILLICENT ARDENT.

MRS. ARDENT sat on one side of the fire, and the old man on the other. Jane sat upon a small stool about the centre of the old chimney-piece, and Peter Bolt doubled up his lower extremities and squatted upon the floor at her feet.

"Now," said the old man, "listen."

He opened the letter, and after some adjustment of his spectacles, read as follows:

"'DEAREST DEAR FATHER AND MOTHER, I ought to have written to you last week, but I had not the heart to do so: and, now that I do write, the first words I must put into this epistle must consist of a hope that you will forgive your own poor Millicent. All our friends here in Devonshire have been very kind to me, indeed, and I have been very happy—so very happy that I cannot hope to express to you how happy.

"'Dear mother and father, I have a secret now to tell you, and it is in consequence of that secret that I have to ask your forgiveness and your blessing for what I have done.'"

"A secret?" said Mrs. Ardent.

"Yes, a—a—secret, it says."

"Well, but what can it be?"

"I—I don't know; but—but—let me go on, wife; I don't like secrets in families."

"Nor I, Jacob; but go on."

"'Dear father and mother, do not be surprised or shocked at what you now read; but I am married!'"

Mrs. Ardent uttered a shriek, and dropped her toast and tea into the ashes. The letter fell from the hands of old Ardent, and he could only repeat the word:

"Married—married!"

Jane, and Peter Bolt looked quite confused.

"Oh, dear—oh, dear," said Mrs. Ardent. "The idea of my child going from me and getting married!"

"Yes, and in this clandestine sort of way, too," said old Ardent. "I will not forgive her!"

"Nor I—nor I. Oh, my poor heart!"

"Well, but bless me," said Peter Bolt, "where's the odds! People must get married, you know, some day or another. It's the most natural thing in the world."

"It is not!" cried Mrs. Ardent, "and you are a fool!"

"Oh, lor! but my dear mum——"

"Oh, don't 'dear mum' me."

"But didn't you get married?"

"No—that is to say, yes; but that is not the question."

Old Jacob Ardent had clasped his hands over his eyes for a few moments in deep thought, and then, looking up, he said:

"My dear, do not let us be hasty in condemning Millicent. Let us read all the letter before we say anything further about it. We may be too hasty."

"Oh, go on—go on; but I have no patience with her. All the girls think of now—the moment they fancy themselves old enough to leave off their pinafores—is marrying; and it doesn't matter to them one straw whether it is Tom Stiles or Jack Nokes, as long as he is a man."

"There—there!" said old Ardent. "Don't say any more just now. Let me see. Where was I? Oh, here I was.

"'Dear father and mother, I know that the last words that I have written will startle you, and, perhaps, alarm you for the happiness of your child; but I know that you both love your Millicent too well to be angry with her.'

"There, wife, there—what do you say to that?"

"Go on—go on."

"'I will now proceed to let you know who it is that has won the affections of your daughter; and I do not think that you will, when you come to know all, disapprove of the step that I have taken.

"'I had not been long with Aunt Sarah, when there came to the village a young gentleman named George Drayton. He is young, and he is handsome, and he is a gentleman. He came for his health's sake, and he is not very strong; but he saw me and he loved me. I could not possibly mistake the pure love and devotion he had for me; and he was so frank, so sincere, and so ingenuous in all he said, that I could not help loving him.

"'Well, day by day we met, and he got so well—he said it was with the joy of seeing me, but I suppose the air of Devonshire agreed with him as well—that, at last, he told me how he was dependent upon his own exertions entirely for support; that he had but one relation in the world—a brother of his mother's, in Ireland, who was very rich; and he proposed that he should go to him and tell him how much he loved me, and get from him, if possible, such assistance as would set us comfortably going in the world.'"

"What a sensible young man," said Peter Bolt.

"Be quiet," said Jane.

"'This was George Drayton's idea; but the thought of leaving me was dreadful to him, and so he asked me to be his wife before he went to Ireland, on the venture of finding his rich relative kind to him. Oh, father and mother, what could I say to him?'"

The letter dropped upon the knees of old Jacob Ardent at this juncture, and he repeated the last words again:

"'What could I say to him?' Poor girl—poor girl! The heart soon gives in, doesn't it, wife?"

"No, it does not. It's the head that gives in when the heart tells it."

"Well—well, I meant something of that sort, and I suppose that is it. What could she say?"

"You go on with the letter, Jacob. Perhaps she said 'No.'"

"Oh, dear, no. But I will go on."

"'I consented to be his, and we were married a week ago, and to-day he left me for Ireland. I feel very lonely, and very unhappy; and so, dear father and mother, I think I should like to come back to you both, instead of remaining here; and I told George that when he comes from Ireland again, to look for me at the house of my dear parents, to whom I long to introduce him; so expect me soon, for I feel that I shall be much happier beneath your roof; and believe me to be still your dear child,   MILLICENT.'"

"That's all," said old Ardent, as he took off his spectacles, and wiped the glasses on the skirt of his coat.

"And enough, too," cried Mrs. Ardent, who evidently had a strong inclination to cry.

"Well, but aunt," said Jane, "only think of Millicent coming back again to us. How glad I am!"

"And I, too," said old Ardent. "God bless her!"

"She is a disobedient, good-for-nothing girl," sobbed Mrs. Ardent, "and I won't forgive her for marrying in such a way, without speaking to me about it. Why, goodness gracious, if she had married properly here in the market, there would have been no end of fuss. Such bouquets!"

"Such fireworks!" said Peter Bolt.

"Such ribbons!" said Jane.

"Such a supper!" continued Mrs. Ardent.

"Such a dance!" said Jane.

"Such punch!" said Peter.

"Pho!" cried old Ardent; "it's as well as it is; and if the girl has married a kind and good-hearted young man, it's a good job over, that's all."

"But how do you know, Jacob, that he is such? Girls are so stupid, and so easily deceived."

"Oh, aunt, I don't think that," said Jane, with a sly glance at Peter Bolt. "Indeed, I don't think that."

"Oh, you are a little goose, and don't know what you are talking about."

"But, Mrs. Ardent," began Peter Bolt, allow me to say, my dear madam, that——"

"Hold your tongue. Nobody asked you for an opinion. It's no business of yours. You are not one of the family yet, thank Heaven! But I knew it would be this way. Oh, I was well aware that something would come to pass; for only last Thursday week I was dreaming all the night long of cream-coloured coach-horses."

"But what has dreaming of cream-coloured coach-horses, my dear," said old Ardent, "to do with our child's marriage?"

"Oh, yes, do!" screamed Mrs. Ardent, "flout at me!—jeer at me!—make game of me, do!—Oh, you wretch!"

With this, the good lady—for she was a good lady, notwithstanding some little peculiarities of temper—flounced out of the room, and shut herself upstairs in her own chamber.

"Well," said old Ardent, "women are—but never mind. It doesn't matter a bit."

The old man strutted out into the market to spread the news of his daughter's marriage and expected arrival at the old house, so that Peter Bolt found himself alone with his beloved Jane, and had an opportunity of pleading his passion in the most flowery language that his vocabulary furnished him with; but Jane would not fix the wedding-day.

"No, Peter," she said, "you must not ask me yet; I feel as if something were going to happen in my uncle's family that may require all my attention. They have been very kind to me, and until I see how Millicent is settled with her husband, I will make no promises."

"But, Jane, allow me to say that you should not say nay when I mention the day, in the sweet month of May——"

"Go along," said Jane, "and don't plague me, there's a good Peter, or else I shall hate you. What's that?"

"Eh? What?"

"It's aunt coming."

"Oh, lor!"

Peter tried to escape; but Mrs. Ardent caught him just as he was going out of the room, and seizing him by the hair of his head, whispered in his ear—"Come to-night at ten."

"Dear me, aunt," said Jane, "what were you saying to Peter?"

"Never you mind."

"Well, but, aunt, I——"

"Oh, do be quiet. Who would be plagued with girls!"

Upon this, Jane was fain to ask no more questions; but she made up her mind that the very next time she saw Peter, she would ask him what mysterious secret it was that her aunt had whispered into his ear upon his departure.

And here we see how poor Peter got into a kind of maze, and was placed, as it were, between two fires: the confidence of Mrs. Ardent, and the entreaties of Jane; and how he is very much to be pitied for being made the confidant of Mrs. Ardent, in a matter that that lady had better have left alone.

CHAPTER XIX.

JACOB ARDENT CAN GET NO NEWS OF THE YOUNG NOBLEMAN.

THE darling wish of old Jacob Ardent's heart was now, as may naturally be supposed, to find out the orphan son of the late Marquis of Dalewood.

The more the waterman-fireman thought of the probably destitute condition of this lad, the more his heart bled for the possibilities of distress that might assail him; and various were the modes that he thought of, in the simplicity of his nature, for discovering his whereabouts.

"Surely," thought old Ardent, "they will not punish the son, who is innocent, for the faults of the father? That would be too monstrous and cruel for a moment to be thought of. I have a good mind to call upon some great man now, and speak to him about it; and yet what can I say, if questions are asked of me? Can I, or dare I say, 'Sir,' or 'My lord,' as the case may be, 'I am in possession of money, documents, and information regarding the son of the late Marquis, with which I will not trust you?' No—no, that will not do certainly; and yet how very hopeless and helpless I am, to be sure. What if I call upon some lawyer, and speak to him about it? Yet no. He will just want me to give up everything to him. Oh, that I could see a very ugly chairman! Ah! gracious, there is one, and ugly enough he is in all conscience, too."

A couple of men, with a sedan chair, trotted past old Ardent; but he did not like to stop them, as they evidently had a fare; so he followed them closely.

"Fellows! wretches!" said a voice from the chair, and the powdered head of a gaily-dressed fop was projected from the window.

"Yes, your honour," said the chairmen.

"Demme, fellows! what do you mean, demme? Am I to be jolted in this way, till there isn't a nerve in my exquisite and highly sensitive corporeality that is not on the a—the a—quiver—yes—the a—quiver, demme?"

"Beg pardon, yer honour, but the ways are so rough. We will go as quietly as we can."

"You may go to the a—the a——demme!"

The exquisite withdrew his head into the sedan chair again, and the chairmen trotted on, grinning at each other as they went.

"Bless me!" thought old Jacob, "that must be some very great man. Now, I wonder who he is?"

By following the sedan chair, Jacob Ardent found out that it went to St. James's Street, and set down its exquisite fare at a large house there; and then, turning to one of the chairmen, the fop handed him a note, saying, as he did so:

"Wretch! you will take this to its direction, and there is a crown for you. Be off!—be off!"

"All's right, your honour: it shall go."

The fop lounged into his house, and the chairmen laid their heads together, to read the address on the letter, which seemed to be too great a task for their learning; so old Jacob Ardent thought it a good opportunity to get into conversation with them, and he lounged up to them, and said:

"Shall I read it for you?"

"Thank you—thank you!" said the one who had the letter in his hand. "What does it say?"

When Jacob Ardent took the letter in his hand, what was his surprise to see, as the direction upon it, the words:

"*To Mrs. ARDENT, Bouquet Maker, Covent Garden.*"

"Why, villain!" said Jacob, "what does this mean?"

"That's what we want to know," said the chairman. "Can't you read it?"

"Oh, yes; but it is addressed to my wife."

"Your wife?"

"To be sure."

"Ha—ha! ho—ho! Oh, that is good!"

"Well, it may be good; but I will take the liberty of opening it, if it's all the same to you?"

"Stop—stop!"

Jacob had the letter open, although the chairmen thought that they were not quite safe in letting him, as he was a stranger to them, do so; and then he read in it:

"Lord Coldross will thank Mrs. Ardent to send him two of her best bouquets this evening, as the Italian Company play to-night at the palace."

"Oh, that's all right," said Jacob. "Thank you."

"But what is it all about?" said the chairmen.

"Why, my name is Jacob Ardent, and this is a letter to my wife, who is a bouquet maker in Covent Garden, to send a couple of bouquets to Lord Coldross, who, I suppose, is the very fine gentleman who went into this house."

"Well, that may be."

"It is, you may depend. Here is a lackey coming out, and you can ask him."

"Is this Lord Coldross's?"

"Yes," said the lackey. "He has just come home."

"All's right."

"Well," said Jacob, "I will give you a pint of purl if you will answer me a question I am going to put to both of you belonging to this chair."

"What is it, master?"

"Did you bring a lady to my house in Covent Garden market last evening, while the opera house was on fire?"

"A lady in black, with a lace veil?"

"Yes—yes! the same!"

"To be sure we did, and she paid us well. To be sure. Don't you remember her, Bob?"

"Ay, that do I," said the other man, "and, poor lady, she did seem in a flurry, surely. Something was on her mind, I take it."

"No doubt of that."

"Oh," said Jacob Ardent, "I am so glad I have met you. Can you now tell me at once where you took her up?"

"To be sure. At Whitehall."

"Whitehall? From a house?"

"Oh, dear, no. She hired us in the street, and got into the sedan-chair, and offered us double fare to take her to Covent Garden as quickly as we could. And we did, and that's all we know about her."

"That hope is lost!" said Jacob Ardent, with a deep sigh. "There, my good fellows, there is something to get the purl with, that I promised you; but I was in hopes that by your aid I could have traced where the lady lived, poor thing."

"We wish we could tell you, master; but that is all we know about it, I assure you."

"I do not doubt you for a moment—good evening—good evening. Alas! poor orphan Marquis! Unless Heaven, by some special act of its own grace, casts you in my way, I fear I may look for you in vain. Oh, if I could only for a moment look in his face, how happy I should be."

"Is this the way to Bloomsbury, sir?" said a lad, addressing old Ardent.

"Yes—yes, go on, and keep to the right."

"Sir, I thank you."

Old Jacob looked abstractedly after the lad till he got out of sight, and then he said:

"Where have I seen that face before? How familiar it did seem to me, to be sure; and there was something about the voice, too, that seemed as if he had been speaking to me before, very lately. Oh, God—oh, God! if it should be he—if it should be the young Marquis? And I have let him go. Oh, I am mad—mad! Stop—oh, stop! Yes, it was his father's voice, and his father's expression of face. And I have let him leave me! I prayed to Heaven to throw him in my way; and when it did so, I let him go again. Stop—stop! Help! Stop him!"

The old man darted off in the direction the lad had taken, and in the rapidly darkening streets he took turning after turning, until he was too much knocked up by fatigue to go further, and then he was compelled to give up the pursuit in despair.

"If I live for a hundred years," gasped old Ardent, "I shall always think that that was the Marquis's son. When—oh! when—will such another chance throw him in my way? Never!—oh, never! And so all is lost, indeed!"

With weary feet and a sorrowful look the old man took his route home; but he made up his mind to say nothing about his real or supposed encounter with the young Marquis to his wife, for he was afraid that it might turn into a subject of after repentance to him; but he handed her the letter, and told her it had come into his possession in the street, through a chairman asking him to read the address.

"Gracious me!" exclaimed Mrs. Ardent; "it's from that real gentleman as never was—Lord Coldross."

"Oh, you know him, then?"

"Know him? To be sure I do. Isn't he the pink of all the court gallants that come here to buy bouquets? Isn't he so kind, and so affable, and so complimentary? And didn't he say only the last time he was here that he thought Jane was my younger sister?'

"Oh—oh!"

"And pray, Mr. A., what are you taken so bad about all of a sudden, that you must cry out: 'Oh—oh?'"

"Nothing—nothing! Never mind me."

"Well, Mr. A., if it is any consolation to you to know it, sir, I don't mind you."

"There—there! that will do!"

"No, Mr. A., that won't do, and I——"

Old Ardent rushed out of the house again; for he knew full well that, when once his wife's vanity was touched, she did not know very well when to leave off speaking about it, and that the shortest way out of the scrape was for him to leave the house for an hour or two.

"Hoity-toity, indeed! Marry come up!" said Mrs. Ardent. "A pretty thing, indeed, that people are to cry 'Oh!' when a real gentleman pays me a little compliment. Well, I never! things have come to a fine pass, I do think, in Covent Garden. Jane!—Jane! I say!"

"Yes, aunt."

"Put on your best bonnet and cloak, and take a couple of the No. 1 bouquets to Lord Coldross's house in St. James's Street."

"Yes, aunt."

"And don't be loitering and flirting on the way."

"Why, aunt, did you ever know me to do so?"

"Come, now, don't plague; but be off at once—do!"

"Yes, aunt, I'm going."

Jane took the bouquets in two little boxes, something like epaulette cases, that were expressly made for their reception, and set off to St. James's Street with them; and then, as Mrs. Ardent had the whole premises to herself, she sat upon a little basket-chair in a corner of the shop, and, resting her face upon her hands, gave herself up to strange thoughts.

If ever the evil one presented false allurements to the imagination of a human being, he certainly did so to poor Mrs. Ardent at that period of time.

"Why, they are all out but me," said Mrs. Ardent, and her eyes fell upon the little square tile in the kitchen floor, beneath which she had seen her husband hide the money. "They are all out. I am alone in the place, and I think I shall be alone for some time, too. How very odd I feel, and how very odd it was that Jacob should hide his money under the floor of the kitchen, and get up at night to do it, too, without consulting me about it."

Mrs. Ardent approached nearer to the little tile in the floor, beneath which she knew there was the precious deposit.

"It was very wrong of him," she added, "to fancy that I was not to be trusted with the secret of this wealth. Have I become extravagant in any way? Have I mismanaged his income in any way, that I should not be trusted with the secret that there was some money laid aside for a rainy day? Oh, it is too bad. I suppose it is a comfort to him to think that he has it; but why should it not likewise be a comfort to me? Oh, that I had money of my own! If I had, I would hide it from Jacob; yes, that I would, as he has hidden his from me.

CHAPTER XX.

MRS. ARDENT REASONS HERSELF INTO THE COMMISSION OF A GREAT FAULT.

POOR Mrs. Ardent was getting into a very fatal train of reasoning indeed. She considered that her husband had done something that he ought not to have done, and, therefore, she declared her intention, if she had the opportunity, of doing something that she ought not to do.

How common is such a course of reasoning, or rather, no reasoning, and yet how fatally mistaken it is!

The darkness of the night thickened around Mrs. Ardent, so she lit a candle, and then crept to the door of the shop, and fastened it. She did not know very well why she fastened it, or why it was that she dreaded any one coming in at unawares; but she did so.

Then she crept slowly to the kitchen again, and drawing a low three-legged stool close to the spot beneath which was hidden the money, she rocked herself to and fro, and still fancied that she was reasoning upon the subject.

"Why did he hide it? Where did he get it? Did he get it in such a way that he is ashamed to tell me, and, therefore, is forced to hide it for fear of my inquiries?"

This was a new supposition, and not the least distressing of the many others that had occurred to the mind of Mrs. Ardent upon the subject of that fatal money.

"Well," she added; "but suppose he did, he ought to tell me all about it. Why don't he trust me? Oh, that I had money of my own!—I did dream that the number 4747 came up a £30,000 prize in the lottery—I wonder if one can put any faith now in such a dream? They do say that the numbers people dream of three times in succession are sure to come right; but why in succession? I don't see that at all. I have dreamt of 4747 three times; but I dreamt of the cream-coloured carriage-horses in between, and that puts me in mind of Millicent and her marriage, and her husband going to Ireland, to try and get some money—all the world is trying to get money."

Mrs. Ardent was silent now for some time, and her thoughts ran back to the childish days of her daughter, Millicent, and then to her own youth, when she was first courted by Jacob Ardent, who then was a handsome lad.

With a deep sigh, she wiped the tears from her eyes, and shook her head as she said:

"I wish I could give Millicent some money, for something seems to tell me that her young husband will fail in his attempt to get any from the relation he has gone to seek in Ireland. Let me see—let me see!"

She took a folded paper from the breast of her apparel, and unfolded it. It was one of the alluring advertisements of the lottery offices which in former times were so frequent in London.

"Let me see—let me see. The first grand prize of thirty thousand pounds, divided into sixteenths—each sixteenth only twenty-six pounds—oh, that I had twenty-six pounds! The sixteenth again divided into thirteen parts of two pounds two shillings each. Alas! that would not be much, even if one won it. Let me consider. Oh!—ah!—well, I don't feel equal to making it up just now; but it would be a great help to me, no doubt, in the winter time. What can Jacob mean by hiding his money from me? What is his, is mine; and what is mine, is his. Of course, nobody in the world can possibly dispute that."

Mrs. Ardent looked about her with a triumphantly argumentive expression; and as there was no one but the cat washing her face in the room, the good lady had it all her own way, and seemed satisfied with the manner in which she had stated the case.

After a few moments of deep silence, she said:

"It is true I have two pound two, and it is true that I intended to get Peter Bolt, whom I saw at ten to-night, to take the money and place it in the lottery for me on the number 4747; but what is two pound two? Oh, dear! oh, dear! if I could only buy a whole sixteenth now, that would be something worth the having. Now, what could possibly hinder Jacob, with all the money that he has got, from taking a chance of a sixteenth if he liked? I don't mean to say that he would, or that he ought, but he might! To be sure he might: and what's mine is my husband's, and what's his is mine. I suppose so—eh?"

The cat still winked and washed her face, and let the argument go all in Mrs. Ardent's favour.

"Well," added Mrs. Ardent, "if that is the case—and, I suppose, nobody will say 'Nay' to that, eh?—Jacob has only been hiding my money."

This was a proposition, to all appearance, exceedingly consequential upon the former statement; but still it was quite clear that Mrs. Ardent was anything but satisfied with the line of reasoning.

"Oh, dear me!" she said, after the pause of a few moments. "What a thing it would be now, if I could win the prize of thirty thousand pounds! If I could, by just taking the necessary money from Jacob's hiding-place, get so much by it; and what would be easier? Why, he would never know it, for, of course, when I get the prize, I could replace the money, and there would be no difficulty in the matter at all. What the eye sees not, the heart grieves not; and, therefore, I might take upon myself to say that, even if I were to lift up the tile and take some money, there is no harm done."

Someone rattled at the shop door.

Mrs. Ardent sprang to her feet.

"No, no! I have not touched it!" she said. "Not yet, oh, not yet! I, as yet, have not touched it!"

Tap! tap! tap! came someone on the glass half of the shop door.

"Oh, what a fool I was, to be sure," said Mrs. Ardent. "After all, it is only someone to buy something. Coming—coming! I'm a coming. Don't be impatient, whoever you are."

Mrs. Ardent opened the shop door, and Peter Bolt walked in, saying as he did so:

"It's only me, mum—it's only me."

"Oh, you wretch!"

"Eh? Oh, lor, what have I done, Mrs. Ardent? I just called to say that as you wanted me at ten o'clock, mum, I would be sure to come, for I am going now in to the city."

"Stop—oh, stop."

"Yes mum."

"I think, Peter, that—that—even now you can be useful."

"You don't say so, mum?"

"Yes, Peter, come in, and shoot the bolt of the door. I want to speak to you, Peter; and as you will, I suppose, soon be one of the family, I suppose I may do so—eh, Peter?"

"Yes mum, you may—you may depend, mum."

"Then, Peter, I just wish to ask you what you think of the great lottery that is to be drawn soon?"

"What I think, mum?"

"Yes, what do you think."

"Well, then, I haven't thought about it. It's not the easiest thing in the world to make both ends meet, and that's a fact, as things go, so I haven't got any money for lotteries; and, besides, they seem to me rather a sort of a swindle."

"You don't mean that, Peter?"

"Yes, mum, I do."

"Oh, you are wrong—you are wrong. Now, Peter, I have had three dreams, you must know."

"Yes, mum, and from all that I have heard, I should say you have had about three thousand."

"Silence, and listen to me. I am not superstitious, but when a person dreams three times of 4747, there must be something in it."

"Oh!"

"Now, don't say—'Oh,' but let me at once tell you what I want you to do. I wish you, Peter, without letting a living soul know anything about it, Peter—I—that is——"

"Compose yourself, mum. How you do shake and shiver, to be sure."

"No, I don't. No—no, why should I shake and shiver? People may shake and shiver who are about to do something wrong, but there is no reason on earth why I should shake and shiver, is there—is there, I say?"

"Oh, lor, no. Not as I knows of, mum, you may depend."

"Then don't be foolish. I wish you to take the money, and buy me a sixteenth in the thirty-thousand pound prize, do you comprehend?"

"Oh, lor!"

"Silence. And you are to promise me upon your word not to tell a living soul about it?"

"Yes, I will."

"You mean, you won't?"

"I mean, mum, that I will promise, and that I won't tell."

"As you hope to be saved?"

"As I hope to—to be shaved."

Poor Mrs. Ardent was by far too much occupied with her own feelings to take too accurate notice of the fact that Peter used the word shaved, instead of saved; but she drew a long breath, and considered the matter so far settled.

"Stay here," she said, and she shook now more than ever as she spoke. "You stay here, Peter, while I get you the money. If anybody comes to the door of the shop, cry out: "Hem!" or make any noise that will let me know, do you comprehend?"

"I do, mum; you may depend upon me."

Mrs. Ardent left him.

With trembling hands she moved the table, one leg of which was just on the little tile, beneath which she had seen her husband place the bag of money. She made fast the door leading from the shop to the kitchen; she took a strong pronged fork from the cupboard, and placing the light upon the floor, she knelt down beside the spot where Jacob fondly imagined he had placed the Marquis's money free from all chance of its ever being molested.

Never had the face of poor Mrs. Ardent worn such an expression as it did now. She was to be pitied as well as blamed, was that poor woman, who was holding so severe a struggle in her own mind between right and wrong.

And now as she looked at the little tile, which was the only obstruction to her getting the money, with which she hoped to make a fortune, she shook so that she had not strength sufficient to use the fork to raise it.

"What am I about to do?" she said. "Oh, what is it that I am about to do? After all, have I a right to touch this money? Is it not my husband's money? Has he not a right to place it where he may think fit, from the house-top to the lowest cellar, and no one ought to say him nay? What will he say to me, should he discover that I have risen in the night to watch him—that I, the wife of his bosom, have been the thief that, taking advantage of his absence, has rifled the hiding-place that he fixed upon for his gold? Oh, God! No—no! I cannot do it!—I cannot do it!"

She clasped her hands over her face, and rocked to and fro in an agony of grief and apprehension; but, even as she did so, the little clock that hung upon the wall of the kitchen struck the hour of nine, and as it did so, the sounds seemed to say to the distracted brain of Mrs. Ardent:

"Four-seven—four-seven—four-seven!" and so on till the sounds ceased with the word: "four!"

She looked up.

"Oh, can this be true? Is it possible?"

All was still.

"I may make a fortune for my child, Millicent, and then surely Jacob would forgive me. He might blame, but along with the blame would come the smile of forgiveness, if I had thousands of pounds to show as the result of what I did. I—I think I am right to do it; and, besides, when I get the prize, what so easy as to replace the money here? The exact sum that I take I can put back. Ah! it will be a much happier thing for me to raise this little tile to replace the gold than to take it. It is not for myself I do it. Oh, no—no! It is for my child, Millicent—and possibly to make the declining years of my husband all the happier. I will do it. Why not?—Eh? Why not? I have a right to do it. What is his is mine, and I will do it!"

CHAPTER XXI.

MRS. ARDENT PASSES THE LINE BETWEEN INNOCENCE AND GUILT.

POOR Mrs. Ardent had made up her mind. She moved the light a little on one side; and although her hand shook at the unholy work, she commenced with the fork to raise the tile.

Now, the tile was very loose. In fact, it merely stayed well in its place since Jacob Ardent had taken it up by its own weight; and, therefore, Mrs. Ardent had no difficulty at all in the matter. It yielded to a touch.

When the tile was removed there was nothing to interfere with her grasping the little bag of gold. What a thrill came through her heart and brain as she did so!

She spoke in a strange whisper.

"Yes—yes, it is here! Oh, where could he get all this gold? What a quantity there is of it, to be sure. How strange—how very strange that Jacob should have so much money. I wonder if he knows himself how much of it there is here? I shall never know, for I would not stop to count it for the world. Gold—bright and beautiful gold! I never saw so much of it at once before."

She dipped her hand into the bag, brought out as many of the old gold pieces as she could grasp, and let them run through her fingers with delight at the sight, and the pleasant jingle that they made.

But time was precious. Who could say that Jacob might not return, or that Jane might not come back from her errand to St. James's Street, while she, Mrs. Ardent, was engaged in so nefarious a transaction? Although she might truly keep them out of the kitchen, yet, in her husband's case, that very fact would beget suspicion.

Hastily she counted out the necessary amount to give to Peter Bolt, to buy the sixteenth in the lottery, and then replaced the bag in the little excavation beneath the tile.

"Hem!" cried Peter Bolt.

Mrs. Ardent uttered a scream, and upset the candle.

"Hem!" cried Peter, again.

"What is it? Oh, what is it?"

"Somebody wants to come in, mum."

"No—no! Keep the shop-door fast. That is, I—I don't know—yes, do! Oh, what shall I do?"

There was a rattling noise at the front door of the house.

"Oh, mum, it's Mr. Ardent!"

"Mercy! Oh, God, have mercy!"

Mrs. Ardent rushed to the fire with the candle that she had extinguished, and made several abortive attempts to light it, for the embers were very low. At length, by the aid of her breath, she got a flame, and lit the candle.

The rattling at the door continued.

"I say, mum, he will have the door down. Shall I open it?"

"Not yet. Oh, no—no—no, not yet!"

With the haste of despair, she replaced the tile in its place, and stamped it down flat. She drew the table over the spot, and then, opening the door of the kitchen, she cried out:

"Let Mr. Ardent in, Peter, now. I—I am a little better."

With the money she had taken from the secret hoard of Jacob tied in a little handkerchief, and hidden in her bosom, poor Mrs. Ardent staggered back, till she came to a chair, upon which she sank, nearly fainting.

Peter opened the door.

"What the deuce is the meaning of all this?" said old Ardent. "Why was the door fast? Or, if fast, why so long in being opened, I should like to know? Oh, so you are here, Peter? Ah—ah! I suspect."

"Oh, lor! what, Mr. A.?"

"Why, you villain! you and Jane have been talking some lovers' nonsense to each other, I suppose, and so you did not hear me. Eh?—is that it?"

"Well, I never!"

"Come—come! don't deny it, Peter. Well—well, it's natural enough. I did the same when I was young. Lor, bless you! Peter, when I was courting Mrs. A., which is a matter of forty years ago now, if you had fired great guns close to my ears, I don't suppose I should have paid any attention to them—that's a fact."

"You don't say so, sir?"

"Yes, Peter, I do; but where is Mrs. Ardent?"

"In the kitchen, sir, if you please."

"And where is Jane?"

"Why a—why a—you see a——"

"Ha—ha! The little minx is hiding from her uncle, I know, in some nook or corner. Well—well, be a good husband to her, Peter, and you will never want a friend in old Jacob Ardent while you live, boy!"

"Thank you, sir.—It strikes me," said Peter to himself, "that old Jacob has been to the Blue Lion."

Peter was, to a slight degree, right. A couple of glasses of the old ale at the Blue Lion had had the effect of banishing all animosities from the mind of Jacob Ardent, and he had come home in the best of humours.

Upon going into the kitchen, he was struck with dismay to see his wife half-reclining upon a chair, and looking pale and ill.

"Why, what's this—what's this?" he cried. "Good Heavens! are you ill? Help!—oh, help!"

"No—no! I am better—much better!"

"But you have been ill?"

"A little faint, that was all. I didn't feel quite myself. I am very much better now."

Old Jacob shook his head.

"My poor old wife," he said, "you work too hard, indeed you do. You are ever at something from morning till night. I have often thought that you work too hard, and it has often brought the tears into my eyes to think that in all these years, though I have worked hard, too, I have never been able to lay by a little for your comforts in your old age."

"What do you say, Jacob?"

"I say, my old woman, if I could only have laid by a few pounds just for your good, I should have been a much happier man than I am now."

"A few pounds?"

"Yes, only a few. They would go a long way."

"The horrid old hypocrite!" thought Mrs. Ardent; "why, there must be a couple of hundred, at least, in the bag underneath the tile!"

"But, cheer up," added the old man. "Who knows but that some day some good luck may come across me; and even yet before we get past work, wife, something may happen to make us comfortable?"

"Yes, I shouldn't wonder."

"Are you better now?"

"Oh, dear, yes. Bless me, I don't know whatever could have come over me, but I'm better, there is no doubt about that, Jacob, and I'm very much obliged to you indeed."

"Dear heart, for what?"

"Why, for wishing you had a few pounds to lay by."

"I wish, indeed, I had, and, what is more, at this particular time of all others, I wish it more than ever."

"And why at this time in particular?" cried Mrs. Ardent, rather sharply, for she was getting terribly provoked at Jacob.

"Why, because of the marriage of our dear child, Millicent."

"Oh, ah! Dear me!"

"It would be such a joy to be able to say to her: 'Here, my darling, you shall not come portionless to your husband. Here is some money, although small in amount, that your old father can give you.'"

"Jacob!"

"Yes!" cried Jacob, springing to his feet, "what is it?"

"You are an old——no, I won't say what; but I'm an injured woman. Oh, I hate you!"

"Why—why, what is this?"

"Nothing. I am mad!"

"I think you are. But something has happened. I feel certain that something has happened. There is a something on your mind, I feel assured of. What in the name of all that is righteous is it?"

"Nothing—nothing. Ha—ha—ha! I am only joking. What could it be?—what can it be? It is nothing—nothing, I tell you; so now let us have some supper, and forget it all."

Jacob looked at his wife in surprise. He had never before seen her in so strange and flighty a mood, and yet it troubled him to conjecture what could have happened. Strange to say, the truth that she had discovered the money never for a single moment dawned upon his mind.

"Oh, there's nothing the matter," said Mrs. Ardent, replying rather to the looks of her husband than to his words. "Come, Jacob, sit down by the fire, and it will soon burn up. Well, I declare, I quite forgot that Peter was in the shop all this time. Peter—Peter!"

"Here, mum."

Peter Bolt would have entered the back room, but that was not the object of Mrs. Ardent; so, when she had seated old Jacob by the fire, she went to Peter, and thrusting into his hand the money, wrapped up in the handkerchief as it was, she said to him:

"Remember your oath, and remember the number 4747—get a sixteenth in the lottery, and bring the number to me to-morrow, and take care to give it to me when no one is by, for I do not wish anyone but you and myself to know a word of this matter till I get the prize."

"Yes—no."

"Be off."

"No—yes."

"Don't be a fool, but go at once, and remember your oath and 4747. Now get along with you."

Mrs. Ardent pushed Peter out of the shop, and then returned to her husband in the parlour, who was not disposed to make a commotion by inquiring more curiously with regard to the extraordinary state of mind that his wife had been in, for he was more inclined to think that either she had applied once too often to the cordial bottle, or that old age was making some ravage in her intellect, than anything else.

In the darkness that the place was enveloped in, it was not at all likely that he should notice the displacement of the tile. If he had been able to take a good look at it, he must have seen that it had been tampered with; but he never thought of doing so. On the contrary, he rather avoided it, for fear of attracting attention to it; and no man ever thought a secret more secure than Jacob thought that of the place in which he had hidden the Marquis's money.

As for poor Peter, he felt anything but well

pleased with the confidential mission that Mrs. Ardent had sent him upon; but he was committed to it, and he did not very well see his way out of it without sorely offending Mrs. Ardent.

"Oh, dear—oh, dear!" he said, "I only wish she would get the lottery ticket herself, and not bother me about it. Let me see, what did she say the number was? Oh, 4747. Well, I mustn't forget that, at all events, or there will be a row."

It was a great disappointment to Peter not to see Jane; but he was compelled to put up with it, although he certainly would not have done so so easily had he known that Jane was in danger, as in truth she was. But that requires another chapter.

CHAPTER XXII.

JANE RESISTS THE FASCINATIONS OF MY LORD COLDROSS.

JANE had all this time been upon her errand to Lord Coldross's mansion in St. James's Street, with the bouquets, and had not returned yet. This was strange, to say the least of it.

It was not very often that Jane had to go at all upon such errands, for when bouquets were wanted, those who required them usually sent their own servants for them, who took them home at once; and it was only in the event of something very special being ordered, as in the present instance, that the Ardents found it necessary to send a messenger to the house of one of their customers.

But there was a special reason why Jane did not come home, and that special reason is the one which we are now about to treat of.

Since she was quite a child—and, by-the-by, she had not long emerged from that condition of existence—Jane had been in the habit of making long visits at the house of her uncle and aunt, in Covent Garden market, and of going such errands for them as the present one. When, upon the death of Jane's parents, she became altogether destitute, but for the kindness of Mr. and Mrs. Ardent, she always lived with them and always carried bouquets home, and never had any cross accident occurred to her before.

It was reserved for my Lord Coldross to have the unenviable occupation of showing in the first instance to a young girl that her virtue and her innocence were not sufficient to protect her from insult.

But to our story.

Jane tripped along quickly towards St. James's Street, with the two little boxes containing the bouquets, dreaming of no harm and of no danger in the world. To be sure, she now and then, we may say, gave a thought to Peter Bolt; but then there was neither harm nor danger in Peter, and so that did not disturb, in the smallest degree, the serenity of her mind.

Upon reaching the top of St. James's Street she was just turning the corner hastily, when she came against someone, who immediately cried out:

"It's her—it's her!"

Upon glancing at the individual, Jane saw that it was no other than Corporal Budd.

Wishing to avoid him, for Jane felt some degree of resentment for the way in which he had treated Peter Bolt, she pretended not to recognize him, and swerved to the edge of the pavement to get past him, but this the Corporal would not permit.

"Jane," he said, "I only wish to say four words to you, and all of them words of one syllable—that is to say, coming in single file, except one."

"No—no," said Jane.

"Oh, but do. I know you don't care a piece of an old cartridge for me, and I know you never will. I know you are offended with me, and I daresay it is quite right and proper that you should be so, Jane; but I respect the old people in the market, and your uncle and I have been friends for a long time, so, Jane, for their sake, I do hope——"

"What do you hope?"

"That you will forget and forgive the past, and, although all is over as regards you ever being more to me than a friend, I should like to see you quite happy. I wish to be able to come to the house so much, Jane."

"Corporal Budd!"

"'Tention!"

"Corporal Budd, I think that—that if you will be sensible enough to see that I don't want you as a lover, but that I admire and respect you very much as a friend, you will be always very welcome to call upon us."

"That's it. Stand at ease!"

"Well, then, there is my hand."

The Corporal let the little soft, child-like hand lie upon his own, so hard and rough, for a moment or two in silence, and then he said:

"God bless you! Jane. And may you be as happy as I know you deserve to be—and that is very happy, indeed."

"Thank you from my heart, Corporal Budd, and I will make peace between you and Peter."

"Hem!"

The Corporal made a wry face at the idea of coming into contact with Peter, in any sort of way; and then Jane, with a laugh, said:

"But what were the four mysterious words you had to say to me, Corporal?"

"Oh, I have said them."

"Indeed?"

"Yes, they were—'Will you forgive me?' that was all; and now you have forgiven me, let me carry for you those two little boxes?"

"Oh, no, I am at my destination."

"Why, where are you going?"

"To Lord Coldross's."

"Hem! Jane, he is a bad one, they tell me, so I would rather you went anywhere else. Don't you bring home any more bouquets to this house, my dear Jane."

"But why not?"

"Ah, that I cannot very well tell you; but

you see that the hall porter in his establishment is an old soldier, and so I pop in and sit by him for half-an-hour, at times, and have a kind of gossip about the wars in Flanders, in which he was engaged, and he has told me——"

"What, Corporal?"

"Oh, nothing particular, only quite enough to make me sorry to see you go in at that door."

"Then I will only give in the bouquets, and come away at once; and if you will wait for me, I will get you to walk home with me."

"Will you, though?"

"Yes, to be sure. I know you are a sincere and good friend to me and all the family."

"Ah, Jane! that I am—that I am! But won't the—a—the a—I mean Peter Bolt, be jealous?"

"I should like to see him dare to be jealous," said Jane; "oh, I'd soon let him know. Don't you mind about that, Corporal. I'll soon come out, I promise you."

Jane rang at the door-bell of my Lord Coldross's house, and was speedily admitted, while the Corporal marched to and fro, on the opposite side of the way, like a sentinel. The house was all dark in front, with the exception of one faint light at a window, that seemed to belong to a little room adjoining the drawing-room; and, as if with a strange sort of fascination, the Corporal could not keep his eyes off that window.

"Now, young woman, what is it?" growled the old hall-porter, as Jane tripped into the hall, for he was soured by old painful wounds and by rheumatism, caught in the Flemish marshes. "Now, young woman, what do you want?"

"I have brought some bouquets for my lord."

"Eugh! you have brought some bouquets for my lord, have you? Eugh! Bah!"

"Where shall I place them?"

"Oh, I don't care! Be off!"

With a noiseless tread, a lackey out of livery stepped into the hall, and advancing towards Jane, he said:

"His lordship wishes, if you come from Mrs. Ardent, the bouquet maker, to give you an order for some flowers he wishes for his table. He gives a dinner party to-morrow."

"What flowers does he wish?" said Jane.

"If you will follow me he will let you know. This way, if you please."

Jane hesitated for a moment as she thought of the undefined danger which the Corporal had hinted at with regard to her visit to that house, and then she followed the valet.

"Eugh!" growled the old porter. "Pikes and bomb-shells! if I didn't think as much. That's another of 'em. Eugh! Fine doings—fine doings! If it wasn't that I am such a worn-out old gun-stock as I am, I wouldn't stay here for love nor money; but I can't help it—I can't help it! Eugh!"

The lackey led Jane up the grand staircase,

GEORGE DRAYTON TAKES PASSAGE ON BOARD "THE SHANNON."

in the niches of which were statues—which to Jane's unsophisticated nature would have been all the better for a little drapery—and then conducted her to the drawing-room, where he paused, saying:

"I will go and let my lord know that you are here."

"Yes," said Jane, "and if you ask him at once what it is he wants, it will save trouble."

A slight smile passed across the face of the valet, and he left the room without replying.

Jane, when she found herself alone in the magnificent drawing-room at Coldross House, could not help looking about her with awe and admiration at the real splendour of the place.

The walls were covered with gold-coloured satin, and the roof was painted with some allegorical subject, that Jane, after one glance at, decided was not proper to look at. The furniture was white-and-gold, and, in fact, take it for all in all, there were few drawing-rooms in London more magnificently furnished than that into which Jane had been shown, no doubt for the express purpose of dazzling her eyes, and so subverting her judgment through her imagination.

"This way, if you please," said the valet, as he made his appearance again in the room, and held open a concealed door in the wall. "This way, if you please."

The danger she ran in the house of Lord Coldross was of too undefined a character to enable Jane to hesitate about going into any room that she was ordered to enter, so she obeyed the summons, and passing through the concealed door, which closed again behind her, she found herself in a small room, with a little glass chandelier suspended from the roof, and the fittings of which were all of crimson and gold.

On a couch, in a rich *robe de chambre*, reclined his Lordship of Coldross, while on a small, richly-inlaid table before him was wine, together with choice fruits.

Jane made her best curtsey.

"Oh!—ah!" said his lordship, "you come with the bouquets?"

"Yes, my lord."

"From—Mrs. Ardent's?"

"Yes, my lord."

"Very good. Place them on yonder buffet, my dear. Do you know the price of them?"

"Yes, my lord. A crown the two."

"A crown? Come now: hold out that pretty little soft hand of yours, which, by the way, I may say would make a Duchess die of envy, and let me place the money in it."

She held out her hand, and his lordship placed one guinea in the little soft palm, and then he looked in the face of Jane, and said:

"One!"

"My lord?"

"Two—three—four—five!"

As he spoke, Lord Coldross placed five guineas, one after another, in Jane's hand, and then he looked at her again, and she looked at him, and then his lordship smiled; but Jane did not smile, so they looked at each other for the space of about half-a-minute in silence, till his lordship said:

"Well, my little dear, why do you look so surprised? Are you considering what a sweet dress five guineas will purchase you?"

———

CHAPTER XXIII.

CORPORAL BUDD ASTONISHES MY LORD COLDROSS AND HIS VALET.

"My lord!" said Jane.

"Well, my dear?"

"I do not comprehend you."

"Oh, you don't? Well, that is good! If I really did think, now, that you did not comprehend me, and that you were such a piece of unsophisticated innocence as you pretend to be, I would make those guineas ten."

"But the bouquets are only a crown."

"Ha—ha! Well, you can pay the highly respectable Mrs. Ardent her crown for the bouquets, and keep the remainder of the money yourself, you know."

"Oh, no—no!"

"Pshaw! Stuff! Come closer to me, my little dear, and let me kiss those cherry lips. By Jove! There is not such a bouquet in all the world, nor ever will be, as that mouth!"

Jane dropped the gold to the floor of the room, and shrank back a pace or two with fear.

"My lord," she said, "if you have any orders to give me for my aunt, give them to me at once, and let me go. I have already been too long upon my errand."

"Pho—pho! Do you think, now, that I wanted bouquets? Do you think that I would have taken all this trouble about a few inanimate flowers, for which, to tell the truth, I have no taste at all?"

"I do not know, my lord. I only know that I must go home now at once."

"No, beautiful what's-your-name. By-the-by, what is your name, my dear?"

"It is of no consequence, my lord. Where is the door?"

"Ha—ha! Never you mind the door. What was I saying? Oh, I was about to say that—that it was the richest flower of all flowers—your own sweet self—that I wished to see. Come, now, be kind and good, and name your own reward. I am rich, and I am liberal."

"My lord, this is an insult."

"Oh, stuff! Don't play the prude here, I beg of you. We are quite alone, and no one is within earshot but the discreetest of valets; so now you may as well be civil."

Lord Coldross rose — and his little, debauched-looking eyes glared like hot coals.

Jane flew to the wall of the room in which she knew there was the door; but so closely concealed was it by the deep gilt mouldings that she could not find it. Terror took possession of her, and she trembled like a leaf in autumn.

"It is of no use for you to try to escape me," said Lord Coldross. "You are here, and that is enough. I love you."

"Oh, no—no!"

"I say I love you. I saw you as I passed through the market, and from that moment I loved you in my way, and all your opposition only adds a kind of piquancy to my feeling for you. You shall be rich. The most elegant lodging in town shall be yours. An equipage that shall rival royalty — rich dresses — diamonds— servants——"

"And infamy!" said Jane.

"Eh?"

"I say, and infamy to crown the whole. Is it not so, my lord?"

"Oh, dear, no—stuff! That is all old fashioned now, my love, and is never thought of now."

"My Lord Coldross?"

"Your most obedient."

"I demand my liberty. Where is the door of this room? I demand that it should be opened, and that I be permitted at once to leave this house. Upon no other terms will I consent to look over the insults I have received within its walls."

"Insults! Upon my life you have a strange idea of what an insult is. Why, here have I for the last quarter of an hour been paying you all the most handsome compliments I could think of, and you, all of a sudden, graciously promise me upon what terms you will look over my insults! Why, the girl doesn't know what she is talking about."

"I did not know, but now I think I do. Lord Coldross, beware! I say to you, beware!"

"Of what?"

"Of your danger."

"My danger? Well, that is good. Come, my little Lucretia, what is the danger? What hidden plot is about to break out? What danger awaits me?"

"Your danger consists, my lord, in the possibility of my informing those who would avenge me, that you have insulted me."

"Ha—ha—ha! Ho—ho! The—the—bouquet-maker! The good folks of the market—the sellers of cabbages and potatoes—oh, that is good! So they would avenge you, would they?"

"They would."

"Well, I must take the dreadful consequences of their vengeance. I must be called out, I suppose, by some itinerant vendor of vegetables, if I so much as kiss a pretty girl! But enough of this. It is folly—it is worse than folly, for it is scandalous waste of time. I tell you, girl, that you are in my power."

"Oh, no—no!"

"It is so, and nothing can save you."

"Heaven help me!"

"Ah, the age of miracles is past; and if it be not, they certainly don't happen in St. James's Street."

"My lord, are you a gentleman? Have you any heart at all—any one feeling of goodness left?"

"Oh, don't—don't preach, whatever you do. Really that is too bad, my dear. You may say what you like; but don't give me, at second-hand, a sermon on morality, for that will be too bad, upon my soul."

He advanced a pace or two towards her.

"Help—help!" cried Jane.

"Oh, stuff! You will only aggravate that pretty little voice till you make it hoarse, that is all, if you cry out in that way. Come to my arms, and to my heart, dear girl, for there is no one in all the world, or in all London—and that is my world—to compare with you."

"Help! No—no! Ah, there is hope yet!"

Lying upon a side-table was a steel-hilted elegant court sword, that his lordship had placed there upon coming home to keep the self-made engagement with Jane. She grasped it in a moment, and the scabbard, catching in the rich covering of the table, remained there, leaving the bright blade in her hands.

"Villain!" she exclaimed, "I will defend myself now, and Heaven has graciously placed the means in my hands with which to do so."

The bright blade flashed in the eyes of my Lord Coldross, and he staggered back till he was brought up, so to speak, by the opposite wall of the room.

"Why—why—what does the girl mean? Are you mad?"

"No—no! But I should have gone mad, I think, if Providence had not placed this weapon in my way."

"Well, but, I—a——"

"Stand off, sir, or dread the consequences."

"Good Heaven, girl! you do not mean for a moment to say that you would attempt to do one a mischief with the sword?"

"I would."

"But it is madness!"

"I care not."

"Oh, come—come! You are only joking, after all—I am quite sure you are only joking. This has gone quite far enough now, and if you will only have the goodness to say what will satisfy you, all may yet be well."

"My liberty."

"Your liberty?"

"Yes, liberty to leave this house at once, to which I never will return."

"Oh! but only consider, now. Why, your hand trembles so that you can hardly hold the sword at all, and, believe me, it doesn't look well in your possession. Give it to me, and let us talk over this little matter quietly."

"No—no!"

The Lord Coldross was a coward as well as a villain; but that was what was to be expected—so long as he saw that Jane was firm and resolute, he took good care to keep out of reach of the sword; but when he observed, as he soon did, that the sudden nervous energy that had supported her was giving way, and that the sword shook in her grasp, he made a dash forward and caught it by the blade.

"Ha—ha!" my pretty little heroine!" he cried. "So you thought you had it all your own way, did you?"

"Help—oh, help!" cried Jane; and she drew the sword-blade right out of his grasp, and made a pass at him, wounding him in the arm, and then, as she withdrew the sword again, she dashed a pane of glass in the window to atoms with the point of it.

"Curses!" cried Lord Coldross, "you have wounded me! You are mad! I say, girl, that you are mad, and know not what you do!"

"No—no! I am not mad; but I will defend myself, and if you come by death, it is your own fault."

A violent knocking at the street door of the house now came upon both their ears.

In another moment the valet of Lord Coldross popped his head into the room, and said:

"If you please, my lord, there is a man, dressed like a soldier, and almost mad, in the hall."

"Ah, it is my friend," cried Jane.

"Your friend be—well, well!" added Lord Coldross, "never mind that. Don't let him come upstairs, Stephen; use any means to prevent him."

"Yes, my lord."

"But I will go to him," said Jane. "I now

see the door of this room, that was so artfully hidden from me, and I will leave you, my lord, with the contempt you deserve."

"Stop her, Stephen!"

"All's right, my lord. Not so fast, if you please, my girl. You don't pass out of this room without his lordship's order, I can tell you."

"Clear the way!" said Jane, as she made a dash at the valet with the sword, which he only avoided by flinging himself on his back in the doorway.

"Stop her!" cried Lord Coldross. "That will do. Cling to her, Stephen. I have hold of the sword now, and she cannot use it. Now, my little spitfire, I rather think you are a captive. What have you now to say for yourself?"

"It doesn't matter, since I am here to say something for her," cried Corporal Budd, as, with one spring, he darted towards the little door from the large drawing-room, and, standing upon the prostrate valet, seized Lord Coldross by the collar, and flung him with such force to the farther end of the small room, that, after striking against the wall, his lordship fell to the floor insensible. "What's all this about, Jane?" said the Corporal, as he clasped one arm round her, and took the sword in the other hand.

"Oh, do not ask me; but take me away from this dreadful house! Heaven has sent you to save me!"

"Murder!" cried the valet.

"Hilloa! Who are you?"

"Murder! Don't be standing upon me in this way. I give in. I am half dead already."

"Serves you right, too!" said the Corporal, as he gave him a parting kick. "I don't know who you are; but I have no doubt you are as great a rogue as your master."

"No—no! Oh, dear—oh, dear! you have broken my ribs, I do think, and I'm a lost man! Oh, lor—oh, lor! Have you killed his lordship, do you think?"

"I don't know, and I don't care," said the Corporal.

CHAPTER XXIV.

THE CORPORAL ESCORTS JANE HOME, AND RECEIVES THE THANKS OF PETER BOLT.

JANE clung to Corporal Budd so tenaciously that it would have been quite out of his power to defend himself with anything like effect had he been suddenly attacked by either the valet or Lord Coldross.

Luckily, however, neither of those persons happened to be in very good trim for doing him any mischief.

By the dim light in the large drawing-room, all that could be seen was the valet, crouching down in the doorway leading to the small apartment, and rubbing his sides, upon which the Corporal had trodden, and groaning as he did so.

Lord Coldross, though, was recovering from the shock he had sustained in consequence of

the throw that the Corporal had given him; and just as Jane entreated her defender again to leave the house at once, his lordship, blind and maddened with rage and disappointment, caught up a brace of pistols, which he opened a drawer in the buffet to get at, and, springing forward, he cried:

"Wretch! be you whom you may, your vile life shall pay the penalty of this interference!"

With the utterance of these words, then, which he gave forth in a yelling tone of voice, that echoed through the room, he made a rush forward, and not noticing the valet, rolled over him with such a vengeance that he could not stop himself, but was dashed right under a large round table, and off went both the pistols, to the irreparable injury of a mirror of great size and cost, which both the bullets hit and smashed to pieces.

"Curse you!" roared the valet, who was exasperated to a degree of frenzy by the way in which his master had knocked him over. "Where were your eyes, that you didn't see me in your way, you idiot?"

The Lord Coldross swore dreadfully.

"Oh, you may call me what names you like," said the valet; "but I won't stay in your infernal service any longer—so here goes to square accounts with you."

With this, the valet sprang at his master, and commenced such a pummelling at his head and face, that Lord Coldross grew wild and furious, and fought with desperation; and they both rolled over each other on the floor like two madmen.

"Bravo!" cried the Corporal, "that's the way to do it. That is just the thing!"

"Oh, come away—come away!" said Jane.

"Yes, Jane, all's right. Come away at once."

Poor Jane's feet trembled so that the Corporal soon found she was unequal to any rapid movement; so, without a word, he took her up in his arms, as he would have done some child, and, with the utmost care and tenderness, ran down the grand staircase, and into the hall.

"Hilloa—hilloa!" cried the porter, "what is it all about?"

"I'll tell you another time," said Corporal Budd. "Open the door, old friend, at once. —Thank you."

The old soldier guessed pretty well what was amiss, and flung the door open for the Corporal, who, with Jane still in his arms, sallied out into the street.

"All's well, dear Jane," he said; "don't take on about it. Here you are, as safe as possible. God bless me, do you mean it? Do you really love me so? Oh, no—no! She has fainted, poor girl."

Jane's head had fallen upon the breast of the Corporal, so as to give rise to the mistake he had made only for a moment that she had willingly placed it there; but, in good truth, the excitement of the scene she had gone through, now that it was over, and she felt herself in safety, was too much for her, and she had fainted in the arms of the gallant Corporal.

At a rapid pace, for there was just a possibility (and with the insensible Jane in his arms) that the Corporal might have been taken at rather a disadvantage, he ran up St. James's Street; and, at the top of it, the first thing he saw was a sedan-chair, and a couple of men waiting for hire.

"Hilloa!" he cried. "Do you want a job?"

"Yes, master."

"Then open the chair."

"Is she dead?"

"No—no! She has only fainted; that's all. Open the chair, and let me place her in it."

"But she will fall," said one of the men. "Look! she doubles about all manner of ways, like a limp collar."

"Then you must take me, too," said the Corporal, as he stepped into the chair, and took Jane upon his lap. "Now, get on to Covent Garden market as quickly as you can."

"All's right."

"Oh, Heaven!" said Jane. "What has happened?"

"Stop—stop!" cried the Corporal. "She is recovering. Jane, speak to me. Oh, speak to me!"

"To whom—to whom?"

"To Corporal Budd.'

"Is it a dream?"

"No, it isn't. But only tell me one thing, and that is, have you strength to sit upright in the sedan-chair while they take you home to your aunt and uncle?"

"Oh, yes—yes; but—but——"

"But what?"

"You must not leave me. If you do, they will seize me again. Oh, do not—do not leave me!"

"I will not. I will place my hand upon the window-frame of the chair all the way we go."

"Will you, indeed?"

"You shall see. Don't you cry, now, Jane, or you will make my poor heart swell to such a size, that my waistcoat will be too small to hold it. There now, will that do?"

"Yes—oh, yes!"

The Corporal got out of the chair, and placed his hand upon the window-ledge of it, and so, by keeping accurate step with the chairmen, which his military training enabled him to do with ease, he was always in the same relative position with the sedan-chair.

As for poor Jane, she held his hand in both of hers all the way; and never had the Corporal been so happy, although he could not flatter himself that all this in any way was likely to advance his own rejected suit, to the detriment of Peter Bolt.

The chairmen trotted along at a good pace, and, as they went, Jane became more and more composed, and conscious that she was quite safe from any further attacks from Lord Coldross; so she said to Corporal Budd, in a timid whisper:

"I recollect now all that has happened."

"That's right."

"But there is one thing I do not know, and cannot at all comprehend, my dear friend."

"What is that, Jane?"

"It is how it happened that you came to my rescue."

"Why, you see, I was waiting for you."

"Waiting for me?"

"Yes, don't you remember I met you, and agreed to wait for you, and see you home?"

"Oh, yes—yes. How confused my head is, to be sure! Now I do, indeed, recollect all about it. But how did you know that I was in any danger?"

"I will tell you. I went to the other side of the way to wait for you, so as not to appear to be watching the house, and then, as I looked up at it, I thought it very odd that there was no light anywhere but at one small window."

"But there was a faint light in the large drawing-room."

"Yes, so I found afterwards; but it was too faint to show at all through the blinds, and I saw it not. Well, then, Jane, as I was just thinking that you were a long time selling a couple of bouquets, what should I see but a pane of glass suddenly broken in the window of the room in which the light was.'

"Yes—yes."

"You did that?"

"I did."

"Then it was a lucky thought of you, for you might be sure, of course, that I was watching the house, and would, upon that, guess that all was not well."

"Alas! it was an accident, merely. I did it with the point of the sword, which I seized to defend myself in my despair at finding myself exposed to the persecutions of Lord Coldross."

"Well, accident or no accident, it gave me a hint; so, over the way I went, and spoke to the old soldier in the hall, and then I heard a kind of cry for help upstairs; and up I flew, I don't know really how, and you know the rest, Jane."

"I do—I do, and what do I not owe to your gallant conduct, Corporal Budd? Oh, if ever I have said one unkind thing to you, will you forgive it now?"

"Don't think of it. I only hope——"

"What—what?"

"That his lordship and his valet have eaten each other up by this time, and that there is nothing left of either of them. But here we are close upon home, and, by Jove! there is your uncle and Peter Bolt both at the door looking out for you. I'll be bound, they little expect to see you come home, like a lady, in a sedan-chair. Look—look, do you see them?"

"I do—I do, and that I do see them once again is all owing to you, Corporal Budd."

"Oh, well, never mind that. I do think that when a dear, good, pretty girl like you is in any danger from a villain, that Heaven keeps a kind of an eye on the whole campaign, and sends some good fellow with a strong arm to take her part—and the only thing is, that it's quite a piece of good luck to be picked out, and ordered to march on such a service, you see, so that's all about it."

Jane was too much affected at the kind Corporal's mode of trying to eclipse what he had done for her, to make any reply to him just then, and as the sedan-chair reached the door of the Ardents, the Corporal drew himself up, and called out to the men:

"Halt!"

The sedan-chair came to a standstill.

"Right about face! Open the door!"

"Why, what is all this?" exclaimed old Ardent. "Is this you, Corporal Budd?"

"Yes. All's right. And here's Jane in the chair!"

"Jane in a chair!" cried Peter Bolt, as he cut such a caper as was wonderful to see. "Jane in a chair, and you with her. You, Corporal Budd, with my Jane! Oh—oh, I die—I expire! No—no, it cannot be. Fidelity is thy name, Jane, or am I insane? Have you been in a chair, with your beauty so rare, along with this military man, who is born to be my bane?"

"Don't be a fool," said the Corporal. "Here she is, as sound as a bullet, and quite safe. There, Mr. Ardent! My service to you, old friend. I have brought her home to you all safe! How do, Mrs. A.? Here she is—and I think that you will see she is your own Jane, and, that after all, there is no harm done. What the deuce is this?"

"Villain—wretch!" screamed Peter Bolt, as he suddenly made a rush at the Corporal, and clung to the skirts of his coat. "I will fight you with a needle—I mean a goose—no, I mean a gun or a cannon—or a sleeve-board —or a thimble—or a bayonet—I'm an undone tailor! Oh, despair—despair! where has Jane been, and where shall I go?"

"Go to the deuce, if you like," said the Corporal; "but let go of the skirts of my coat, whatever you do."

"I won't—I can't—I shan't. Oh, my heart is broke to small pieces! My Jane is false, and yet the world goes round, and I am undone."

"Come—come," said old Ardent, as he released the Corporal from the grasp of the infuriated tailor, "I am quite sure that there is something that only has to be explained in all this, to set your mind at ease, Peter Bolt, so come in-doors all of you, for you are actually collecting a crowd of all the dirty little boys of the market about you. Come in —come in."

CHAPTER XXV.

THE ARDENTS RECEIVE A HANDSOME AND MUCH LOVED VISITOR.

PETER BOLT had an immense respect for the judgment of old Jacob Ardent; so, when he heard him speak in this sort of way, he began to think that, after all, there might be something to explain, that possibly might place a new complexion upon the whole affair.

"Well," he said, "I feel just now as if I didn't care whether anybody murdered me with my own goose or not, but if there can be anything explained, Mr. Corporal, I shall listen to it, of course, and make good the damage."

"What damage?" said the Corporal. "I don't know of any particular damage you have got to make good."

"I allude to the tails."

"To the who?"

"It isn't a who—I mean the tails of your coat. They are both nearly off—one, of course, is quite off, and here it is in my hand, and the other only hangs by a thread or two; but if so be as you can explain all about how it is that you came home with my Jane in a sedan-chair, I will set to work and sew 'em both on again in a jiffy."

"A plague upon you!" said the Corporal, "for pulling them off."

They all went into the house after old Ardent had well satisfied the chairmen, which, by the way, was in those days almost as difficult as satisfying a cabman of the present era. We don't say it was quite so difficult, but very nearly.

Now, Jane, when she found herself in perfect safety in her uncle's house, gave way to a flood of tears, and it was some time before she could say a word. The Corporal, however, gave his version of the story; and although that was far from being complete in all its particulars, it was still amply sufficient to let Ardent and his wife know the danger that Jane had run.

Peter, too, began to get enlightened upon the subject, and springing to his feet, he cried out:

"Revenge! revenge and despair! The revenge of a tailor is dreadful. Thunder and lightning, and shears and thimbles, and earthquakes, and storms, and sleeve-boards! Oh, what will the world come to?"

"Nothing," said the Corporal, "I suppose. But do be quiet, will you?"

"Quiet? Did you say quiet?"

"Yes, I did."

"Then I won't! I'll annihilate Lord Coldross! I'll smother him in cabbage. I'll——"

"Don't be a fool!" said Mrs. Ardent—"don't be making such a noise here, or you must go out of the house."

"Mum, I bows to you, I does; but as for Lord Coldross, I'll—I'll——Well, I don't know what I'll do, quite; but yet only let him beware!"

"Come—come, Jane," said old Ardent— "let us rather rejoice that you are in safety with us again."

"Yes," added Mrs. Ardent, "and let my Lord Coldross only venture into the market, that is all."

"Well, I don't know about that, my dear," said Ardent. "You know that Jane is not as yet received into the market as one of the members of the kind of society into which you market women and florists have made yourselves."

"Yes, that's true. She has not yet received that honour; but she will, you may depend upon it, Jacob, soon. I intend to propose her; and, as my niece, and brought up under my eyes, I don't think that anyone will be exactly bold enough to make any objection to her. She will be an ornament to the market."

"But I don't want her to belong to the market," said Peter Bolt. "I think, if I can get plenty of work, that I would rather she didn't."

"You don't want her, you half-starved, miserable wretch—part of an individual!" screamed Mrs. Ardent; "and who in the name of goodness cares what you want and what you don't?"

"Why, I thought that——"

"And who gave you leave to think?"

"Well, but I had an idea——"

"And how dare you have an idea?"

"Oh, well, I——"

"It isn't well, wretch. Oh, dear! oh, dear! but this is ever and always the way I'm threatened, just because I am too indulgent and quiet, and let everybody put upon me!"

"My love," said old Ardent, "I think you are put out because Jane has been in danger, so you had better be quiet: and as for Lord Coldross, leave him alone. He is a powerful nobleman, and may do us more injury in an hour, than we can do him in all our lives."

"But he is a wretch!"

"Yes, my dear, he is; but, so far, you see we have the advantage of him—we who can lay our hands upon our hearts, and say that we are unconscious of wrong-doing; we are honest, and that is more than he is; we are poor, but with all our poverty we have kept our integrity. You know that he is a gentleman, my dear; and it was only the other day that I heard he is mixed up with all the lotteries!"

"The—the lotteries!" gasped Mrs. Ardent, as she darted a glance at Peter Bolt.

"Hem!" said Peter.

"Yes, the lotteries, my dear—those pests of society which bring so much misery and so many tears into many a poor man's house. The lotteries! Oh, I hate the word!"

"I don't feel very well," said Mrs. Ardent.

"No, more do I," said Peter Bolt.

"Oh, you are an idiot!"

"Yes, mum, I know I am——47——"

"Silence! Oh, what is that?"

A sharp knock came upon the shop door, and the whole party was silent in a moment.

Rat! tat! tat! came the knock again.

"It strikes me," said the Corporal, "that someone is there. Let me go and see."

"No—no," said old Ardent, "I'll go."

"Nay, let me go, Mr. Ardent. It may be no friend; and, if so, I will take upon myself to say, that it will be a little disappointment to find me in the doorway, for I can stand a brush with most people. I'll go."

"Or—shall—I?" said Peter Bolt, almost in a whisper.

"Fuff!" said Mrs. Ardent, as she hit him a knock on the head with the snuffers. "You sit still."

"Yes, mum. Anything you like, for peace and quietness. I'll go and sit next my Jane."

"No," said Jane; "I don't like you."

"Not like me? Oh, I——"

"Hush!" said old Ardent. "Let me listen who is at the door."

Just as another tap sounded at the door, the Corporal strode to it, and flung it open, when they all heard him utter an exclamation of surprise, and then a soft, gentle voice said:

"I think that now, Corporal Budd, we may be very good friends, indeed, may we not?"

What the Corporal replied to this no one heard, if, indeed, he made any reply at all; but Mrs. Ardent uttered a scream, and old Ardent sprang into the shop, crying out:

"That is the voice of my child, Millicent, or some dear angel in her likeness."

It was Millicent, and in another moment she was in her father's arms. Poor Mrs. Ardent was so affected, that she sobbed aloud, and when Millicent came into the parlour, and flung herself upon her knees at her mother's feet, the good lady could only half smother her with kisses.

"My Milly!—my own child! And so you have come back to me—back to the old place again? Oh, bless you, you dear one—bless you!"

"And do you forgive me, mother?"

"Forgive you?"

"Yes; and you, father, do you forgive me?"

"For what?—for what?"

"Why, for marrying without your consent."

"God bless me! I had forgotten all about that. Dear me, yes, you are married; of course you said so in the letter, my child. Yes—yes! I forgive you with all my heart!"

"And so do I, if he is an honest, kind-hearted lad," said Mrs. Ardent; "but yet I should have liked to see him."

"You will see him, mother and father, and you will all see him; and then you will see that your child is the wife of a man who can be respected and honoured. Oh, he is so good, and so clever, and so handsome, and such a gentleman!"

"A gentleman?"

"Yes, he is a gentleman. He has been educated by someone—that is to say, his education has been paid for by someone, whom he never knew, at some great school; and he speaks, and thinks, and looks like a gentleman, does my husband."

"Milly," said Jane, "you have not spoken to me."

"Ah, dear Jane, forgive me!"

They were in each other's arms in a moment, and the tailor made a movement, then, to embrace them both, but Mrs. Ardent put a stop to his enthusiasm by dragging him back into his seat again, and giving him such a crack on the top of the head with a thimble she had on, that his attention for a few moments was fully taken up in rubbing it.

"And so you all expected me?" said Mrs. Drayton, for such is the name by which we ought to call Millicent.

"No, my dear," replied her father, "not so soon."

"But I wrote to say I would be here to-night."

"Then we never got that letter at all; but never mind about that, as we have got the dear delight of seeing you."

"Certainly," said Mrs. Ardent. "Ah, my child, how handsome you do look—you grow more and more like my family every day!"

"Do I, mother?"

"Yes, my dear; but come now, tell us all about your husband, and what he is going to do, and when he is coming here?"

"I will—I will; but first, what news is there here? I suppose Peter Bolt and Jane are going to be married?"

"Yes," said Peter, "yes, we——"

"No, we are not," said Jane.

"Eh?"

"Go along—stupid."

"Come—come, Jane," said Millicent, "if you love Peter, do not pain him by saying you do not—if you intend that he should be your husband, and to link your fate with his, do not give him the pang that I can see your words have even now inflicted upon his heart. He is true and faithful to you, no doubt, and we have all of us long known him for an honest, truth-telling lad. Why, father and mother have known him since he was a child. Come—come, Jane, you must not say nay with your tongue, to Peter, when your heart says yes."

"Oh, what a *hangel* she is!" said Peter.

Jane began to cry.

"There, now, I have pained you, dear Jane," said Millicent.

"No—no! But Peter does say such ridiculous things."

"Yes, out of love for you, Jane, perhaps."

"Just so," sobbed Peter. "It's all out of love for you, Jane. You know that I think as there's nobody in all the world half so beautiful—half so dear—half so good as you are."

Jane smiled.

"Well, Peter, then I forgive you," said Jane.

"Oh, do you, though?" exclaimed Peter Bolt.

"Yes, and I won't vex you any more; and I begin to think that, after all, there is nothing like a nice little tailor."

They all laughed at this, and Millicent sighed, as she said:

"If my George were but here, we should all be happy."

"Ah, yes," said Jane; "and I can tell you what, Milly, when I am married I shan't let my husband leave me. Why, one might as well not be married at all, as be in one country, and one's husband in another. Eh, Peter, what do you say to that?"

CHAPTER XXVI.

CORPORAL BUDD RETURNS TO HIS OLD AFFECTION.

WHEN Jane said they would all be happy if Millicent's husband were but there to join the family party, she made a slight mistake. Poor Corporal Budd was anything but happy.

It will be recollected that one of Jane's objections to the Corporal—although it would not have stood in the way a moment if her inclination had sided with his proposals, only it was a good objection to state, and one that he could not very well find an answer to—was, that he had, before speaking to her of his affection, fallen in love with Millicent.

Now, this was true; for before Millicent had gone to Devonshire, the Corporal had doted upon her, and tried every possible means to win her heart, but without success.

After she had been gone, though, for some time, and he had called at the Ardents, and seen the pretty sylph-like Jane flitting about the old house, and heard her merry laugh, he had thought less and less of Millicent, and finally he had, as we have seen, attempted to rival Peter Bolt in his affection, with what success, or rather, with what want of success, we have seen.

Now, strange to say, one glance at Millicent —one tone of her voice—had had the effect of returning the Corporal to his original allegiance, and his love for Millicent was as strong as ever it had been before her departure for Devonshire.

The poor Corporal, however, knew now that all hope in that quarter was cut off by her marriage, and with a heart full of affection he had remained in the shop by himself, while all that we have related took place in the parlour.

So intent were the Ardents upon giving a reception to their dear Millicent, and so full of attention were they to her, that they quite forgot that such a person as Corporal Budd was in existence, till old Ardent suddenly said:

"By the way, where is Budd?"

"Ah, where is he?" said Mrs. Ardent.

"He let me in," said Millicent. "Surely he has not left on my account? I hope not."

"Oh, no—no."

"Nor on mine?" said Peter. "Perhaps he is getting a little afraid of me."

"Oh, surely not," said Millicent, with a smile, "I do hope that now he will continue his friendly visits to us all."

"Yes," said old Ardent, "and I can tell you, Milly, that we are bound to the noble-hearted fellow by a still stronger tie of gratitude, for only this evening he saved our Jane, poor girl, from the attacks of a villain."

"Indeed?"

"Yes, my dear, your mother will tell you all about it; and I will say that a more courageous, noble-hearted fellow than Corporal Budd doesn't exist in the world."

"Yes—yes," said Peter; "the fact is—I —a—that is, I wasn't by at the moment, to punish the rascal that assailed Jane, so the Corporal acted as my deputy—as my deputy, that's all—that's all."

"Good-evening to you all," said the Corporal, as he popped his head into the parlour from the shop, "I oughtn't to stay here and hear myself talked about; but I was afraid if I left without speaking to you, and you heard the street-door go, you might be wondering who it was."

"Come in—come in," cried Ardent, "don't go."

"Oh, yes—I'd better."

"No—oh, no," said Millicent, as she rose and took the Corporal by the hand, "do not go, old friend. Recollect how long it is since I saw you last."

The Corporal turned red and white by turns, and tried to speak, but his words died away in his throat, and so he sat down in the nearest chair.

"Come—come," said old Ardent, "I shall make a little mulled wine for us all. Ah, wife, you recollect who gave us that wine."

"Yes, Jacob. It was poor Lady Dalewood, who is dead and gone. Bless her!"

"Lady Dalewood—dead?" said Milly. "You do not mean that?"

"Yes, my dear," said her father, "and the Marquis, too. It is quite a long story, but I will tell it all to you, to-morrow; but now you must let me know who and what this George Drayton, your husband, is, and what he has left you, to try after. Come, we are all friends, and we will listen to the story with all the attention in the world."

"Oh, father, it is surely no story; but I can tell it to you in a few words."

"That's right, my child. The truth, some-how, never does take long in telling."

"No," said Peter; "and while she is telling of it, I'll sew on the Corporal's tails, if you will lend me a needle and thread, Mrs. A."

"That I will, Peter."

"Then you ain't in a rage with me, mum?"

"Me in a rage with you, Peter? Certainly not. You need not mind what I say when I am put out of my way a little, for all the world knows that I am apt to say a great deal more than I mean."

"Oh, well, that is a comfort," said Peter. "Give us your coat, Corporal Budd, and we will soon put it to rights, and I daresay Jane will thread the needles for me, won't you, Jane?"

"That I will."

The Corporal sighed as he took off his coat, and handed it over to Peter. He seemed then about to say something to Jane; but, upon second thoughts, he left it unsaid. And so, while Peter stitched away at the coat, Millicent began her story about her husband, young Drayton.

"You must know then, dear father and mother," she said, "that he is very hand-some."

"Ah," said old Ardent, "every girl thinks her lover the handsomest man in the world; but go on—go on; it is but natural, after all."

"But he is handsome," persisted Millicent, "and it would be quite impossible for anyone to see him, without prejudice, and not to own that he was so. Well, he had been fairly brought up, quite like a young gentleman, it appears, by somebody, who had paid for his schooling, but kept secret who he was."

"How very odd!"

"It is odd, father."

"Yes," said Peter Bolt; "but my own case is odder still, I can tell you."

"How so?—How so, Peter?"

"Why, my schooling was kept secret, as well as the person who paid, or who ought to have paid for it, and the consequence was, I got none at all."

A general laugh ensued upon this comical way that Peter found of drawing a comparison, and it was some time before Millicent could go on with her story. When she did, however, she made short work of it, for she merely added:

"Seeing that he was handsome, and feeling certain that he was kind and good, I gave him my heart, and when I had given him my heart, I thought it was foolish not to give him my hand, too, and so we were married."

"Oh, how nice!" said Jane.

"But, my dear," said Mrs. Ardent, "I want to hear about his going away and leaving you."

"Oh, don't call it leaving me," said Millicent, with a shudder; "that has such a strange sound. He had an old relation in Ireland, and it was to go and get money to keep me like a lady, as he said I ought to be kept, that he went, and he will soon be back."

"But—but," said old Ardent, as he took his daughter's hand in his, "if he don't get the money he goes for?"

"Then, father, he will come back without it; that is all. And he will work for me, and keep me as best he can, and I will help him, and I don't think we shall be much less happy, notwithstanding."

The old man drew a long breath, as he said:

"No—no, my love! That will do. If he comes back, and loves you well, and—and if he does——"

"If, father? Oh, do not say if! But I ought not to blame you. You do not know him as I know him. Oh, father, he is all truth and honour! Do not doubt him—oh, do not doubt him, I implore you!"

"I won't—I won't!"

"It will break my heart if you do."

"I won't, my dear; nor will any of us doubt him. And when he comes back, whether it be with the money, or without it, he will find a welcome in this house, for your dear sake. Why, come now, we will celebrate your wedding, after all, when your husband comes back, and have yet a dance at it."

"Yes," said Peter, "and who knows but by that time Jane and I may make up our minds to—oh, dear!"

"Don't be foolish!" said Jane, as she gave Peter a hint with the point of one of the needles she was threading for him. "Don't be foolish! That is no business of yours."

"Oh, I thought it was."

"Then you thought wrong."

"Well—a—I—a—ha—ha! I did think that I might have some little to do with it."

"Then you haven't. When I intend to marry, I will let you know."

"Oh!"

"So don't you trouble your stupid little head any further about it, I beg; and, when I do marry, you may make up your mind to one thing."

"Ye—e—es. What is that?"

"Why, that I will let you know where the broomstick hangs, if you don't behave yourself."

Everybody laughed at this, and the Corporal even smiled faintly, as he rose, and said:

"Come, Peter, have you done my coat?"

"Yes—yes, in a minute. But you ain't going, really—are you, now?"

"Yes, I am."

"You don't say so? How sorry I am, to be sure, to lose your company. Here's the coat! Let me help you on with it. There, now, upon my life! the skirts fit better than they did before—don't they, everybody? Only look at him. There's a figure for you! Good night, Corporal—good night. Mind how you go."

"Good night to you all," said the Corporal. "I wish you all the joy in the world."

They all bade the Corporal a kind and friendly good night, if we except Peter Bolt, who, although rather profuse in his expressions of friendship towards the gallant son of Mars, yet managed to throw sufficient sarcasm into what he said to let everybody know that he was not at all sorry to see him gone.

The fact was, that the jealousy of Peter Bolt had been so thoroughly awakened with reference to the Corporal, that he could not get rid of the feeling.

The Ardent family now rose to retire for the night, so that Peter, too, was forced to go; and having received a box on the ears from Jane, for trying to salute her before leaving, he crept to the outer door.

Mrs. Ardent managed to follow him, and to whisper to him:

"Be sure you get the lottery ticket."

"Oh, lor, yes."

"Remember the number—4747."

"Yes, I shan't forget it; but, oh, Mrs. A., if you would but, in your quiet way, tell Jane that she might as well be a little civil to a fellow."

"I will—I will."

"Will you, though?"

"You may depend upon it I will. Only you be faithful and discreet, and you may depend upon my interest in your favour."

CHAPTER XXVII.

FOLLOWS THE ADVENTUROUS CAREER OF CAPTAIN GAY.

It has been necessary that, thus far, we should devote our attention to the proceedings of the Ardent family; but now we can turn our attention to the darker phases of our story, in depicting the career, to some extent, of the villainous Captain Gay, who, it will be remembered, was *en route* for Galway, with the will of the deceased Marquis of Dalewood in his possession, full of hope and exultation at the prospect of receiving from the old Duke of Lorton the reward of his villainous services.

That Captain Gay had various revenges yet to gratify in England, we are well aware, but he thought that they would keep for a time, for he knew, as well as most people, that revenge is a commodity that seldom grows weaker by being stored up in such minds as his.

The great object of the rascal, was to get to Galway as quickly as possible, to detail to the old Duke of Lorton the complete success of his nefarious mission to London; and, having ample funds for all such purposes at his disposal, Captain Gay did not spare horse or man to expedite his travelling.

In this way, then, Captain Gay soon reached a port that was on the western coast of England. His idea had been to get to the nearest possible port in Ireland, and then go across the country to Galway, which a glance at the map of Ireland will let the reader see is on the western coast of the island; but fortune, which disposes as she pleases of the propositions of humanity, disposed it otherwise, as will soon be seen.

Upon reaching the port from which he had contemplated taking his departure, Captain Gay found that there was a large merchant ship actually going to Galway; and, although the voyage was long and perilous, yet the temptation of going all the way by one conveyance, and so effectually getting rid of the risk of crossing so many miles of country with the will that was of such importance to him in his possession, prevailed, and he made up his mind to accept a passage in the vessel.

The reader will, therefore, please to imagine himself at the port from which the ship was about to start, on a rather raw and gusty evening, just as the sun was about to set, and that Captain Gay, well wrapped up, is stepping on board the vessel.

"This way, sir," said the Captain; "this way, if you please, sir. Your cabin is all ready for you."

"Thank you," said Gay, as he reached the deck of the vessel, and glanced about him with a not unobservant eye, for what was there in all the world that Captain Gay did not know something of?

"All right and taut, sir?" asked the Captain.

"Why, yes, as regards the ship, yes; but I was looking at the weather, Captain."

"Well, sir, it is, as one may say, doubtful."

"More than doubtful."

"Perhaps, sir, a little more than doubtful."

"Hilloa!" cried a voice.

"What's that?" said the Captain.

A travel-worn and dusty-looking young man stood on the quay. A knapsack was at his back, and a travelling-cap upon his head; but yet, despite the wear and tear that his apparel had undergone, there was that about his face which bespoke the culture of a gentleman.

"Are you the Captain of this vessel?" said the stranger.

"I am, sir; my service to you."

"And you are going to Ireland?"

"Yes, sir, right away to Galway."

"I don't want to go so far; but if you can put me on shore anywhere near to Bantry Bay, I will take a passage with you, always provided we can agree upon terms."

"No doubt about that, sir. Come on board; and as for putting you on shore at Bantry Bay, sir, there is no doubt about that either, for as we pass that part of the coast, we are sure to fall in with plenty of fishing boats, any one of which will take you on shore."

The young stranger leaped on board the vessel, and holding out some money in his hand, he said:

"If that will suffice, take it. If not, I leave you."

"Humph! It isn't much, sir; but perhaps some other time your honour will make it more?"

"If I live, I will."

"Agreed. All's right then. Look alive there, my men!"

"Ay—ay, sir."

The usual bustle of a ship's departure now commenced in earnest. Ropes were cast loose, and made fast, and orders apparently of the most opposite description were given. A crowd of idlers assembled on the quay to see the ship clear the harbour; and finally, under her stay-sails only, she slipped from her moorings, and stood out to the St. George's Channel.

The heavy swell of the Atlantic set in from the south-west; and in that quarter of the heavens the sky looked black as midnight. There was a long streak of crimson red, too, in the west, which had a stormy aspect.

The ship surged through the hissing sea.

"Make all taut, forward there!" roared the Captain.

"Ay—ay, sir!"

"Keep her head west by north."

"Ay—ay, sir!"

The foresail was hoisted; but the Captain, after a brief consultation with his mate, did not think it wise, in the doubtful state of the weather, to touch his main sheet, and so on went the good ship *Shannon* through the hissing water, and the dim outline of the English coast grew more and more indistinct each passing moment of time.

The strange effect of the recession of the land from the vessel, instead of the vessel from the land, struck the young traveller, as he stood about midships, holding on by the main shrouds; and he might have quoted, had the age not been one far anterior to the existence of the poem, the eloquent description from the *Ancient Mariner*:

"The ship was cheered—the harbour cleared,
    Merrily down we drop
Below the channel—below the hill—
    Below the lighthouse top;"

for such seemed to be the slow, down-hill like progress of the vessel, as it stood out to sea.

The young stranger sat down not far from Captain Gay, who had been regarding him with the sort of interest that such an adventurer was sure to regard any human being with whom he was brought into contact.

There was a very engaging air and manner about the young man; and when he removed his travelling cap for a moment or two, the masses of rich auburn air that floated to the wind gave his countenance a very graceful look indeed. His age could not be above two or three-and-twenty at the most; and, after a time, Captain Gay was full of curiosity to know who and what he was.

Under these circumstances, to address a fellow-passenger, and the only one, too, was far from being difficult for a man of the world like Gay; so, putting on his most captivating look, he sat down by the young stranger.

"We seem likely, sir," he said, "to commence our passage under rather doubtful auspices."

"You allude to the weather?" said the other.

"I do, sir."

"It does look threatening; but those who cross the Irish Sea, I suppose, must make up their minds to a little knocking about."

"True, sir—true. I believe we are the only passengers on board the vessel."

"Indeed! Is it so?"

"So I believe."

"Then, how can it be worth the while of the Captain to start upon his voyage?"

"Oh, he is a trader, sir, and is allowed by his owners, as I understand it, to take a few passengers, if he can get them on his own account entirely."

"I comprehend. Well, sir, I hope that we shall have the good fortune to make ourselves mutually agreeable during the time that we are thus thrown together."

"One half of that hope, sir," said Captain Gay, as he slightly bowed, and lifted his hat, "is already accomplished."

"Indeed?"

"Yes, sir, for you have made yourself quite agreeable to me."

The young traveller laughed, as he said:

"Sir, you must be a courtier—you pay a compliment with so much grace."

"I might retort upon you the same expression, since, after all, yours is the greater compliment of the two."

"Well, sir, a truce to compliments, for, at the best, they are exaggerated truths, when they are truths at all, and so I don't much like them under any circumstances. How long shall we be in making our voyage's end, think you?"

"You go to Bantry, and may, if the wind hold good for us, reach your destination by to-morrow night; but I go on to Galway, and when I get there, is uncertain as yet; but at all events, it will be a three days and two nights' voyage, I am sorry to say."

"Yes, I go to Bantry," said the young man, abstractedly.

Captain Gay saw that his mind was occupied by his own thoughts, and he forbore to be intrusive, although, to tell the truth, his curiosity was strongly excited by the tone and manner of his young fellow-voyager in the *Shannon.*

"There is time enough," thought Gay, "to find out all about him before we separate. Of one thing I am quite sure, and that is, that he does not know me, and I will take good care that he does not either, or else he will be a more clever fellow than I take him to be."

As the night deepened, contrary to expectation, the weather did not get in any respect worse. To be sure, it was very dark, and black clouds seemed to be piling themselves up in huge masses everywhere; but the wind was but moderate, after all, and the ship sped on its way in safety.

What wind there was, too, was favourable for the progress of the vessel to its destination; so that when the gray light of the early dawn broke over the face of the deep, the ship had made good progress on its route.

The morning was squally, with dashing showers of rain, and now and then a little sleet. The decks looked as if they had been well drenched by a few seas that had swept over the ship from the weather-bow; and the waves were more boisterous than they had been.

Captain Gay looked rather pale as he slipped out of his cabin, and clinging to the shrouds, cast a long look about him.

"Curses on all sea voyages!" he said. "I hate them; and yet one must endure them."

"You don't like the sea, sir," said a cheerful voice close to him; and, upon turning rapidly, Gay saw his fellow-passenger looking much as he had done the night before.

"Good morning, sir," said Gay.

"Good morning."

"You seem to be a good sailor, sir."

"Pretty well. I have been a voyage or two, for the pleasure of the thing. I slept on deck all night."

"Oh, on deck; and how did you like it?"

"Very much, indeed."

"But you don't seem wet."

"Oh, no, they accommodated me with some tarpaulin, and with that and a hen-coop I kept myself dry and comfortable."

CHAPTER XXVIII.

DETAILS HOW THE SHIP WAS WRECKED ON THE COAST OF GALWAY.

CAPTAIN GAY looked in the face of his fellow passenger for a moment or two in silence, and then he said:

"Sir, did you say that you jammed yourself into a hen-coop, or did I misunderstand you?"

"You certainly did misunderstand me, my friend."

"Then how was it, sir?"

"Why, I put my head in the hen-coop, after placing it on one side, and stuffed a couple of pillows into it, and then I covered a tarpaulin all over it, just leaving a space for fresh air, and so I slept quite cosily."

"Oh!"

"Yes; and seeing that I had no cabin—for the Captain politely informed me that what I had paid only entitled me to the smallest amount of accommodation he could possibly give me, which was just leave to be upon the deck—I think I managed pretty well. What do you think, sir?"

"I can only think one thing," said Captain Gay, with a look of intense vexation; "and that is, that I must have been too mad last night to think of anything or of anybody, or I should have offered you the use of my cabin."

"Oh, it doesn't matter a bit."

"But I am vexed about it."

"Pray forget it. What a squally sort of morning this is."

"It is, indeed."

"It strikes me now, that before we get to the end of either of our voyages, we shall find out the seaworthy, or otherwise, qualities of this ship."

"Do you think, then, that we shall have a storm?"

"I do, indeed."

Captain Gay gave a long whistle.

"Who is that?" roared the Captain of the ship. "What infernal lubber is that—eh? Who whistled?"

"Whistled?" said Gay; "why, I did."

"Then, the devil take you, sir."

"The same to you, sir," said Captain Gay, lifting his hat with much mock politeness, "and many of them, sir."

"Don't be whistling here, sir!" roared the Captain. "We have quite wind enough without that."

"Well," said Gay, "of all the extraordinary fools that ever stepped, this fellow is the worst. What on earth can I add to the wind, by merely whistling? Why, my good man, if I were to whistle till I was black in the face, I couldn't so much as stir the lightest rope in the ship."

"But you make the wind come, by whistling, you know that well enough."

"Oh, you are mad."

"I tell you what, sir, I am Captain of this ship, and if anybody says I am mad, or does

GEORGE DRAYTON AT THE WRECKER'S MERCY.

not obey my orders, I will soon let him know what I can and will do."

"My dear sir," said Gay, "I am, while I have the honour and the intense satisfaction of being on board your ship, your very humble servant, indeed. But when we get on shore——"

"Well, what then?"

"Oh, nothing at all."

The Captain went forward, muttering his dissatisfaction of Gay as he did so; and then Gay, turning to his young fellow-passenger, said:

"What an extraordinary thing it is now, that the captains of ships, when they get out to sea, and everything does not happen to go exactly to suit them, get into the most terrible temper that can be conceived."

"It is an old superstition, sir, of all sailors, that, to whistle, provokes the wind to blow, and just now, I suppose, they think they have enough of that commodity. Don't you hear it among the cordage?"

"I hear a strange sighing, whistling noise."

"That is the wind."

"Well," said Gay, with a look of satisfaction, "the captain of the ship may prevent me from whistling, probably, as he has some ten or twelve ruffians here in his pay, but he can't prevent the wind from doing so, that's clear."

No. 5.—(MARQUIS.)

The young passenger laughed, as he walked to the front of the vessel.

Although the bad weather still kept threatening, yet nothing of importance in the way of a storm took place as yet, and the day passed with that terrible monotony which can only be possibly experienced on ship-board, in a dungeon, or in London on a wet Sunday.

As the sunset approached, Captain Gay rather congratulated himself than otherwise; for the fact was, that the ship, owing to the wind having been very favourable, had made immense progress on her voyage, and the sky looked more calm and light.

The Captain had got over his little tiff with Gay, and was on quite affable terms with him.

"Well," said Gay, "when shall we see Cape Clear, captain?"

"We shall pass it soon, but not before sunset; so that you will only see the light."

"It is getting very dark."

"It is, indeed; and I don't at all like this rather suspicious lull."

"Nor I," said the young passenger. "I hope, Captain, you will not run past Bantry Bay, in the night."

"I don't know, really," replied the Captain. "It will all depend on the weather. You see, if a squally night, or even half a gale of wind were to come on, all I could do would be to keep out to sea, and then I am afraid your chance of getting to Bantry Bay will be small."

"What shall I do, then?"

"Why, in the morning, if the weather permits, I will creep in as close to the shore as I can, and put you on board the first craft I see that will land you on the coast, and, at all events, you cannot be then many miles from Bantry."

"That will do. I am used to a tramp on foot; so I can manage it very well."

"A-hoi!" cried the man on the look-out in the shrouds.

"Ay—ay!" shouted the Captain. "What is it?"

"A light on the starboard bow."

"Cape Clear, for a thousand pounds!" said the Captain. "Bring me my glass."

The Captain gave a steady look at the light, and then gave it as his decided opinion that it was the light at Cape Clear; so he gave orders to the man at the wheel accordingly, and the ship surged onwards under full sail through the sea.

The suspicious sort of lull, of which the Captain of the ship had expressed his dissatisfaction, soon subsided; for the vessel had not got well clear of the promontory which forms the extreme headland of Cape Clear, ere there came over the surface of the sea from the south-west a white ripple that, as it approached the ship, grew into an angry wave.

"Keep her head to it!" shouted the Captain. "A squall—a squall! Look to yourselves, men!"

The ship wore round to the south-west just in time to meet the squall, or else it would have been struck upon the starboard quarter, and in all probability foundered; but, as it was, the foresail was shivered to atoms, and tons of mad, seething water deluged the decks.

The ship shook like a living thing, and for the space in which you might have counted five, it seemed to settle deep in the trough of the sea.

The seamen and the young passenger, whom no one knew, held on by the taut cordage; but Captain Gay missed his hold, and but that he came in the way of the main hatchway, would have been swept overboard.

As it was, Captain Gay, to his mortification, was carried along with some tons of water down the hatchway into the inner cabin, and there he lay for some time in a state of complete exhaustion.

"She rights!" cried the Captain. "Hold on!"

"Ay, ay, sir!"

"Keep her head west-by-south."

"Ay, ay, sir!"

"That will do. The squall is over; and now, I suppose, for something like a gale of wind."

"There is very little doubt of that," said the mate; "and if it don't shift, there is very little doubt of something else."

"What is that?"

"Why, of our being driven, by wind and water, slap on to the rugged coast of Galway."

"You don't think that, Jenkinson?"

"Indeed, but I do, sir."

"Keep her head seaward, then, as much as you can, and keep a good look-out to see how she goes."

"Ay, sir, I'll keep a good look-out."

The ship's head was put from the shore, and the Captain went, as well as he could, along the deck to where the young passenger stood; and, amid the rapidly increasing howling of the storm, he said to him:

"How have you fared, sir?"

"Pretty well. I held on."

"That was your only chance; and where is your fellow-passenger, can you tell me?"

"I don't know. The last I saw of him was his going along the deck in a sea that struck the starboard quarter, and came down on the main deck, after reaching nearly to the topmast, I should say."

"Then he is gone!"

"Gone, say you?"

"Yes, overboard—for a guinea. Well, I didn't like the looks of his face, from the first moment I saw him."

"Perhaps you did him an injustice, Captain. I am sorry for him, for if he were a good man, he is a loss to the world; and if a bad one, it is a pity he had not time to repent and turn a good one."

"Well, sir, perhaps you are right," said the Captain; "and, at all events, this is no time to be speaking ill of anyone, while who knows what may happen to the best of us. But, as I said before, I do think he had a most villainous look about him, and was as ugly as sin."

"You don't say so?" said a hollow voice; and upon the Captain and his passenger starting round, they saw the pale and cadaverous face of Captain Gay just above the companion-hatchway, glaring at them.

"Good Heavens! it's a ghost!" said the Captain.

"No—no," said the young passenger. "Don't be foolish. It is our friend of whom we were speaking."

"Yes," said Captain Gay, "it is. I was not washed overboard, but I was washed into the cabin, which is now knee-deep in water, and I am very much obliged to you, Captain, for your candid opinion of my personal appearance."

"Well, I hope you don't take it amiss?"

"Not at all."

"I didn't mean any offence, you know—one of us may be ugly, and the other of us may be beautiful, and no harm meant, you see, for we none of us made ourselves, I take it."

"Certainly not ; but I hope you don't mean that you are the beautiful one?"

"Oh, no—no—I——"

"All hands hold on!" shouted the mate. "Another squall is coming."

This was sufficient for Captain Gay, who flung himself flat against the weather bulwarks, and held on by the foot of the shrouds, so that he was tolerably safe, and in another moment one of the most fearful seas that can be imagined struck the ship, and all but laid her upon her beam ends.

That the vessel righted at all really seemed little short of a miracle under the circumstances, but she did do so ; and although one of her masts had sprung, and she lay deep in the water in consequence of the quantity she had shipped, she was still seaworthy.

CHAPTER XXIX.

CAPTAIN GAY SAVES HIS FELLOW-PASSENGER FROM DEATH.

LET the reader now imagine that six long and weary hours have passed away since that last squall struck the ill-fated ship, *The Shannon.*

It is midnight, and there is not a star in the vault of heaven. Black and angry clouds, from out of which flash at times streams of lightning, are all around. The sea is covered with foam, and the huge billows each instant threaten destruction to the ship.

The coast is near at hand.

A chain of rocks, jutting out from the headland, to which, in spite of anchors and rudder, the ship drifted, was discernible as the forked lightning for a moment now and then lit up the sea with an awful brilliance, only to make it all the darker by contrast the succeeding minute.

The Captain was lashed to the helm, and two of the crew had been washed overboard, entangled in the tackle of the main-mast, which had gone by the board some hour or so before.

The two passengers clung convulsively, for they were both benumbed by cold, to the main shrouds on the starboard side of the labouring ship.

The remainder of the crew worked at the only pump that would act.

Clank! clank! came the monotonous sound of the pump amid the howling and shrieking of the wind, and the hoarse roar of the waves.

The sound suddenly ceased.

"Pump for your lives !" roared the Captain.

"It is of no use. The pump is broke. All is over now."

A cry of despair burst from the lips of the Captain; and, folding his arms across his chest, he let the ship drift at the entire mercy of the winds and the waves.

"Lost—all lost !" shouted the mate.

"Lost !" muttered the Captain; and he let himself hang by the cord that was wound round his waist, and which tied him to the rudder. "Yes, all is lost !"

Captain Gay's face was pale as death, and his dark, snaky hair was dashed from his cheeks by the roaring wind. His eyes were bleared and bloodshot, for he thought that he looked death in the face.

The younger passenger was pale, too ; but he looked calm and firm, and only now and then he muttered a name—that name was Millicent.

Yes, this younger passenger was George Drayton, the husband of Millicent Ardent, and it was of her and her sad widowed state that he thought, as there appeared no chance of life for him on that terrible night at sea.

Captain Gay did not speak.

It was now quite evident that the ship was settling in the sea, for the motion of it upon the waves was not nearly so violent as it had been, and it was only at long intervals that it lost, even for a moment, now, its horizontal position. So far, it was not so bad to stand upon the deck; and if the cause of the improvement in that respect had not been so truly terrible a one, all would have been well.

"Captain !" cried the young husband of Millicent. "Captain, tell me where we are ?"

The Captain uttered not a word. He seemed to be past all interest in everything human ; but the mate cried out in a hoarse voice :

"It doesn't matter much where you are, youngster. You will soon find out where you will be, and that is at the bottom of the sea."

"I trust not."

"You may trust not ; but you will be there for all that, I rather think. We are lost, and nothing can save us now."

"The boats ?"

"All staved."

"Swimming ?"

"What! in such a sea ? Oh, no—no!—there it comes again. Don't you hear it ?"

"What—oh, what ?"

"Another squall."

"God help us !"

"Amen !"

With a deafening roar over the wild waste

of waters came the squall again, and striking the ship nearly broadside, over she went, till her starboard bulwarks were under the sea; but this had an effect that was not quite looked for. She did not actually capsize, and so by being, as it were, lurched over, she got rid of a great quantity of water that was in her cabins and hold, and when she righted, she was higher out of the water than she had been for the last hour.

George Drayton dashed the water from his face and eyes, and hardly knowing whether he was above or below the surface of the sea, he called out the name of God!

"Dead—dead!" said a voice close to him.

This was the voice of Captain Gay; but George Drayton now found what had happened, and hope sprang up in his breast again, as he cried out:

"Why, she rides out the gale yet. She rights—she rights!"

There was no reply.

The mate, with the only remaining three men on deck, had been swept into the raging sea; and the Captain of the *Shannon*, insensible, and lashed to the wheel, Captain Gay and George Drayton, were the only living persons on board the lost ship.

A dull, red glare now lit up a portion of the sky, and by intently looking in that direction, as the ship rose and fell with the waves, George Drayton saw that it was a large fire kindled on the shore, no doubt as a beacon to them as regarded the direction in which it lay.

"Yes—yes," cried George Drayton. "There is hope yet. Why, the shore is close at hand. Can you swim, fellow-passenger—can you swim?"

"Swim?" gasped Captain Gay.

"Yes: for if you can, there is hope yet."

"Hope? Oh, no—no!"

"You can't swim?"

"Yes, I can swim; but where is the hope?"

"Everywhere. All around us. When next the ship goes over as she did awhile ago, shorewards, leave her, and strike out for yonder light. It is our only chance."

"I am tied here."

"Tied! How mean you?"

"Literally, I mean. I tied my arm to the shrouds, and I am too cold to undo the knot."

"I will undo it."

George Drayton was cold, too; but his blood was younger than that of Captain Gay, and the prospect of safety had made it flow still more freely, so he succeeded in releasing Captain Gay's arm from the shrouds to which he had tied it.

"There, now you are free. Why, you would have gone down with the vessel, without a chance."

"I should—I should. If I live over this night, I shall owe my life to you."

"Oh, don't mention that; but look out for the next squall, that is all."

The ship steadied itself wonderfully. The water had again found its way into the cabins and the hold, and now the bulwarks were

scarcely six inches from the surface of the angry mass.

"She is settling!" cried Captain Gay. "Don't you feel a strange motion in the ship?"

"I do—I do."

"We shall be sucked down with her into the water."

"You never spoke a truer sentence than that, my friend, in all your life," cried George Drayton; "so here goes. Follow me, if you ever wish and hope to see the sun of another day."

The sea was rushing over the deck, so that the young man had only to throw himself forward to be right into it; and as he did so a large wave caught him, and carried him far towards the shore.

Captain Gay followed his example, and swam strongly and steadily, and with much greater calmness and self-possession than from his former conduct might have been expected of him; and so they both went towards the coast, to which the lurid red glow of a huge bonfire gleamed to welcome them.

The once good ship *Shannon* settled lower still in the sea. It shook from stem to stern, and was still for a moment; and then, stern foremost, down it went.

There was one shriek that rose above the roar of the waters and the wind. It came from the Captain, as the water touched his lips, and he felt himself going with the ship.

Another moment, and all that remained of the *Shannon* were a few broken spars and casks floating on the surface of the sea.

George Drayton found that the distance to the shore was, although far from being great, yet much greater than he had thought; but, still:

> "Like a strong swimmer,
> The foam at his lip,"

he pressed on, and it was fortunate that the set of the tide, as well as the fury of the storm, were both landwards, and rather aided than impeded him.

As he rose at times upon the crest of the waves, he could see the fire on the shore, and figures moving before it occasionally; and it was a world of strength to him to be quite sure each time that he did so see the fire and the figures, to feel quite certain that he beheld them more and more distinctly.

On—on he went, till he found, suddenly, that he could touch the ground with his feet, and then he thought himself safe; but a great wave caught him at the moment, and, whirling him over like a cork, cast him, high and dry, upon the stony beach, but in a state of insensibility, for he had struck his head against a rock; and what the wind and the waves had spared, the first touch of the shore seemed as if it had sacrificed.

Where George Drayton was cast by the sea was not above twenty yards from the fire that had been kindled on the beach, and one of the two men who tended the flame cried out:

"Arragh, then, Mike! bedad, there's a something on the beach. Let's come and see to it."

"See to it yourself, Paddy, whiles I look to the fire; an', if any ship thinks proper to come into this bit of a creek, it's to pieces she'll go mighty quick entirely, I take it."

"True for you, Mike; and what for did we light the fire for, and go for to waste the turf and the sticks, I'd be liking to know, if it wasn't for that same?"

"To be sure, Paddy; and what with the fine weather, and one thing and another, trade hasn't been nowise brisk of late. Yes, beyant the little bit of a yacht that we took a month ago, and cut the throats of the owner and the crew of as they came to the rocks, we have had no luck at all, at all."

"Bedad, not a bit."

"But the saints are good to us now, Mike."

"True for you, they iz; so be off, Paddy, and take your knife wid you, my boy, while I attend to the fire, anyway."

Paddy, with a long knife in his hand, which was used indiscriminately for killing pigs and cutting the throats of any unfortunate persons who happened to be wrecked upon that coast, and who might put in an inconvenient claim to property washed on shore, ran along the rocks towards where poor George Drayton lay.

The fact was, that at the point where the *Shannon* had been wrecked, there existed a few wretches, whose subsistence consisted in taking advantage of such calamities.

Wreckers, without one spark of humanity in their dispositions, there inhabited a few squalid huts; and when a ship was seen in the offing in distress, a fire was kindled upon a point of the coast, which, if she made any attempt to reach, would be certain to be her speedy and effectual destruction.

Death, then, without a hope, seemed to be the fate of George Drayton.

CHAPTER XXX.

CAPTAIN GAY, FOR ONCE IN HIS LIFE, DOES A GOOD DEED.

NOTHING on earth, it appeared, could save the young husband of Millicent now from the fearful death that awaited him at the hands of the murderous wrecker.

The villain crept on over the rocks towards the prostrate young man with slowness and deliberation, for the low rocks were covered with sea-weed, and very slippery, and the wind still blew so fiercely, that that alone made it rather difficult to preserve a good foothold.

The knife gleamed and sparkled as the devious light of the huge fire fell upon its well-shaped blade.

What must have been the thoughts of the cold-blooded scoundrel who at that moment crept on beneath the heaven above him, and with the eye of his Maker upon him, to commit one of the greatest crimes it is in the power of humanity to be guilty of? Could it be possible that he believed anything of the great Author of heaven and of earth, or that there was such a thing as justice here or hereafter? Well, it is a strange thing that human nature can be so utterly stultified and blinded to its own common, and, one would think, combined interests, as to commit any crime at all; but so it is, and so it ever was. This miserable wretch crept onwards to take the life of a fellow-creature, not for the certainty of some great good to himself—not for the motive of doing something that would have a lasting, beneficial effect upon his fortune or condition—but merely upon the vague hope of finding something in his pockets that might satisfy the wishes or the caprice of the passing moment.

But what must have been the sensations of poor George Drayton at this moment, who, having partially recovered from the swoon he had fallen into, had just opened his eyes; but had not the strength to move hand or foot, and yet saw the murderer stealing towards him with such undisguised intentions to slay him!

The few moments that ensued of horrible suspense seemed to be a lifetime to George Drayton.

"Paddy, my boy!" cried the man by the fire. "Paddy, my boy, where is you!"

"It's here I am, Mike. What's the shindy now?"

"Have you put him out of his pain, Paddy?"

"Not yet."

"Be quick then."

"Yes—yes."

"Help! Oh, God, no!" cried George Drayton. "Murder! You cannot be such a fiend!"

"Bedad, then! you are able to cry out, are you? I'll soon stop the tongue of you!"

The villain made a spring from a piece of rock upon which he was, to another close to George Drayton, and then he lifted the knife, and, shaking back the long, shaggy hair from his eyes with his other hand, cried:

"Tell me now, afore you go off, who and what are you when you is at home?"

"Help—help!"

Crash came something against the head of the wrecker, and he fell a corpse on George Drayton; so coming by a far easier death than such a cold-blooded and remorseless villain deserved for his manifold offences.

"Saved—saved!" cried George Drayton.

"Yes," said a voice. "I was only just in time, though, it appears; but it is done effectually, I think."

The voice was that of Captain Gay.

By what fortunate accident Captain Gay got to that spot at so opportune a moment is soon told.

When the vessel turned over in the way we have stated, and when George Drayton felt the full danger of staying by it any longer, and took to the water in preference, Captain Gay did the same, and after swimming for some distance, the wave that had dashed

George Drayton to the shore did something for him, but not enough, for as he was further from the beach, it had not force sufficient to take him clear of the surf, so on its recoil it carried him out again to sea.

This might have proved fatal to Captain Gay, as he was getting very much exhausted, indeed; but chance threw in his way a long broken piece of the topmast, and he clung to it with renewed hope of deliverance from death.

The piece of floating spar not only supported him in the water, and rendered swimming much more easy to him; but, by inspiring him with fresh hopes of saving himself, it gave to him renewed strength to battle with the wind and the rain.

The consequences of all this was that he just succeeded in scrambling on to the beach at the moment when the wrecker lifted his knife to give the quietus to poor George Drayton.

With wonderful thought at the moment, Captain Gay seized the spar upon which he had floated to shore, and with one blow of it rescued George Drayton, thus putting the wrecker completely out of the way of doing further mischief.

"You have saved me," said George Drayton, "and I think that even in the obscurity of this terrible night I recognize in you my fellow-passenger on board the *Shannon*."

"The same," said Gay. "Are you hurt?"

"I think not. What's that?"

The man by the fire called to his companion to come back to him, not knowing what had happened.

"Paddy! Arragh, there, Paddy, fair play, you spalpeen. It's yourself that is taking all you can get, and leaving me here to mind the fire. Come back, Paddy; bad cess to you."

"Who is that?" said Gay.

"The companion in crime of the rascal whose murderous knife you saved me from."

"Ah, indeed. Then he may as well join his companion. I have not been so long from old Ireland but that I can speak its vernacular pretty well."

Captain Gay, upon this, called out with the most admirable imitation of Irish:

"Bedad, then, why doesn't yourself come this-a-ways?"

"I'm a coming. Is there anything to be got, Paddy?"

"All galore, anyway," said Captain Gay.

"You don't say so! Arragh! then, Paddy, as sure as my name is Mike, you're a mighty clever sort of a chap. Is he dead, anyway?"

"Dead as nothing," cried Gay.

Upon this assurance, the other one came running along the beach towards the spot with all the speed he could; and Captain Gay stooped down, so that he should not see who it was that was there, until too close to avoid him.

"Where are you, Paddy?"

"Here-away."

"How mighty queer you speak, Paddy!"

"Do I?" said Captain Gay, suddenly springing to his feet, and confronting the rascal. "I'll make you speak mighty queer, soon, my fine fellow, or I am much mistaken."

The wrecker recoiled for a moment in dismay; and then, suddenly drawing a large horse-pistol from a pocket of his shaggy overcoat, he levelled it at the head of Captain Gay, saying as he did so:

"Take that, and go where you like."

Bang! went the pistol; but it was no wonder that, in the uncertain light that the flame from the flashing fire cast on the beach and on the rocks, the fellow missed his mark, and that a couple of bullets with which the pistol was loaded, flew past Captain Gay's head.

With more courage, then, than one would have been inclined to give Gay credit for, he darted in upon the fellow, and grappled him by the throat.

"You villain!" he said, "one or both of us shall not live five minutes longer!"

"Then it's you, bedad, that will die!" said the wrecker, as he strove to fling his adversary to the ground. But Captain Gay was strong and active, and well versed in wrestling; so down they both went together, only Gay was uppermost.

The pistol fell from the grasp of the wrecker, and Captain Gay just happened to lay his hand upon the barrel of it. The stock of the weapon was heavily loaded with metal, and the pistol was a good twelve inches long altogether.

The use that could be made of such a weapon, although it had been discharged, at once occurred to Captain Gay, and with one blow of the stock he fractured the wrecker's skull.

The fellow's hands released their hold of Gay's throat, and he gasped out something that was unintelligible.

Gay was up, and kneeling on his chest in another moment, and with two more blows he placed it out of the power of all the surgery the world ever saw, or is ever likely to see, to put one spark of life in that inanimate form again.

"That's settled," said Captain Gay, as he flung the pistol from him, and rose to his feet.

"Where are you?" cried George Drayton, as he staggered forward with the very same bit of spar in his hands with which Captain Gay had swam on shore. "Where are you? Help—help!"

"All is well."

"Thank Heaven!"

George fell on the beach; for, to tell the truth, he was by far too weak from the loss of blood consequent upon the wound he had got upon the head against the rocks, to have been of any real assistance to Captain Gay, and it was only the strong will to try to aid him, that had enabled him to rise to his feet, and grasp the bit of broken spar in the way he had done.

CHAPTER XXXI.

CAPTAIN GAY AND GEORGE DRAYTON HAVE
AN IMPORTANT CONSULTATION.

THE wind was now each moment abating in its violence, and the waves, subsiding rapidly, were leaving the beach, for the tide ebbed quickly.

The cold gray light of the coming dawn was spreading itself over the eastern sky.

Captain Gay climbed up on a little heap of rock which was about six feet above the level of the sand, and looked about him with a long and wistful glance.

"I should know this spot," he said, "well enough. Ah, yes! how confusing it is to be thrown into a place that you know ever so well, when you don't expect to see it. Yes—yes! I know this bay well. It has rather a bad name for being the resort of wreckers; but it is not five miles from Lorton Castle, the estate of my worthy employer, the Duke of Lorton, and father of the late Marquis of Dalewood. Well, it is a mercy that, amid all the wrecking, and swimming, and fighting, I have kept the will safe and sound in my possession. If I had not, before starting on this somewhat perilous voyage, taken good care to wrap it up in the oiled silk that holds it so well, it might have suffered, or been lost entirely; but, as it is, all is as it should be, and I shall get my reward of the old Duke."

"My friend," said George Drayton, as he sat upon the sands, "is there light enough for you to tell me whether all this moisture about my head be blood, or salt water?"

"Oh, yes!" said the Captain, approaching him.

"Well, which is it?"

"A little of both; or rather, I should say, a good deal of both. You have had a knock on the head, I see."

"I have, indeed."

"Did the wrecker give it to you?"

"No. It was against a rock, when I was cast on the shore by a wave, I rather think."

"Likely enough; let me bind it up for you with this handkerchief; and, for your consolation, I can tell you that it is a physiological fact that the air of Ireland is peculiarly good for the renovation of broken heads, for if it were not, the population would be decimated from that cause alone in a short time."

George Drayton smiled faintly.

"My good friend," he said, "I owe you my life; and although, now, I am poor and friendless, yet the day may come when I may be able to show my gratitude."

"Gratitude?"

"Yes. It is a feeling that lies deeper than mere words; but it is one that will last for ever."

"Well, I feel quite strange. This is about the first time in my life that anybody has ever promised me anything for gratitude; but never mind. What I did is of little consequence, after all, and I did it from the impulse of the moment. It is a deed, too, that cannot bring with it any regret, for it is doing a good service to society, at all events, to put out of the world a wrecker."

"It is indeed."

"Come, now, can you walk, do you think?"

"I will try."

"Do so; and in order to encourage you to try, I may observe that, before long, the families and the neighbours of these two rascals of whom we have so happily got rid, will be down here on the beach to see what good fortune has attended them, and it will be just as well that we are gone before they arrive."

"Yes—oh, yes. But do you know where we are?"

"Oh, yes. On the coast of Galway."

"But the precise spot you know not?"

"Yes, perfectly. You may make yourself quite easy upon that score. Fortune has cast us upon a part of the shore that is familiar to me, and I can guide you through a chasm or gully in the rocks to the mainland, and, as I hope, out of the way of the wreckers, whose coming may be momentarily expected. Don't you see how the day is dawning?"

"I do, indeed."

Yes, the day was dawning over the deep sea, and in long soft lines of light was dancing upon the still agitated billows; but as if actuated by the calming and gentle voice of nature, the storm that even up to that moment had blown in fitful gusts over the waters, subsided; and, in a few minutes more, one of the loveliest days that the season of the year could possibly present began to give a fair promise of its existence.

"How charming, and how beautiful!" said George Drayton. "I feel a thousand times better already for the looks of this fair morning."

"Yes," said Captain Gay, "it does look promising. But come along. Recollect what I told you of the dangers of this place."

"I do—I do."

"Then take my arm, and let me lead you from it."

George Drayton had no wish, after his escape from death by the sea, and from the knife of the assassin wrecker, to run the same danger, and to think twice; so he took the arm of Captain Gay, and they together slowly ascended the slope of the shore.

To Gay the place was, as he had said, perfectly familiar, and his object now was to reach the gully, or opening in the cliffs, and so proceed to the mainland, before any of the connections of the wreckers should come down to the beach.

Just as Captain Gay and George Drayton got round an angle of rock, they heard a loud scream, and then a woman's voice shouted out something in the Irish language.

"What is that?" said George Drayton.

"It means," said Captain Gay, "that some woman has come down to the beach, and found one of the sweet creatures, with whom I had a tussle, dead, that is all."

"One of their wives, I presume?"

"Some delightful piece of feminine humanity of that sort, no doubt."

"It was a stern necessity."

"What was?"

"The killing of the two men."

"I rather think it was. When a couple of rascals come to cut a man's throat, there is no great difficulty in coming to the conclusion that it is a stern necessity to knock them on the head. But come on, I beg of you, as quickly as you can, for I hear other voices on the beach, and the wailing cries of that woman will soon give warning to the whole clan that something is amiss, and they will hurry to the spot."

Thus urged, George Drayton, feeling his great danger, hurried on with as much speed as he could up the narrow ravine, which had a most wild and romantic aspect about it. After they had proceeded a short distance it became much lighter, and then they all at once emerged upon some green sward, that had a most beautiful colour, although it only grew upon a depth of about six inches of loam that was upon the surface of the chalk formation beneath it.

They had now, however, got to the mainland, and although, take it for all in all, that part of the coast of Galway is decidedly rugged, yet it abounded in wild and natural beauties.

George paused to look about him.

"Well," said the Captain, "what do you think of old Ireland?"

"I admire this scenery."

"Ah, there is scarcely a kind of scenery in all the world but you will find specimens of it in this unhappy land. But come on, we may yet find it worth while to be nearer to aid than we are at present."

"Those wretches on the beach would surely not have the boldness to follow us?"

"Would they not! You don't know them. They would follow us as long as they could with safety."

"Hark!"

"What do you near?"

"The tramp of feet."

"Ah, and so do I. That is not the peasantry. Ah, I have it. The nearest station of military has sent a party to the beach to see what the wreckers are about, and here they come. Dismounted dragoons, too, as I'm a sinner. How awkward these fellows always are on foot."

As George Drayton and Captain Gay paused, they saw advancing towards them a party of about twenty-five dismounted troopers, with a couple of officers at their head, in undress; but the soldiers were fully equipped.

"Halt!" cried the commanding officer. And then, advancing towards Captain Gay and George Drayton, he said: "Who and what are you?"

"Passengers, sir," said Captain Gay, "in the ship *Shannon*, which now lies at the bottom of the bay."

"In truth then, gentlemen, I am glad to see you are safe of the rocks. Are any others saved besides yourselves?"

"Not one."

"Humph! We received orders to go down to the beach, and take care of both goods and people, if needs were; for the peasantry upon this coast have an ugly reputation for wrecking, as it is called, which seems in Ireland to translate itself into appropriating all the goods washed on shore, and cutting the throats of all the people who arrive in life, in order to put an end to all disputes as to the right of property."

"Ugly, sir, as the reputation is," said George Drayton, "it borrows no features from the imagination to make it so, for that was the precise course they adopted towards me; and but for the timely aid of my fellow-passenger here, they would have murdered me!"

"Indeed?"

"Yes; it was a miracle I escaped one fellow, with a knife in his hand for the express purpose."

"I should like to catch him."

"Why, he lies upon the beach, dead," said Captain Gay; "for the fact was, that the danger was so imminent, I had not time to be particular about the sort of knock on the head I gave him."

The officer smiled.

"And," added Captain Gay, "when a friend of his came to his aid, I was compelled to oblige him in the same manner."

"Well, sir," said the officer, "no doubt you will be requested by the local magistracy to give an account of the transaction. As for me, I think you have done good service, and if you will oblige me with your name and address, it will suffice."

"I am *en route* for Lorton Castle, and am a friend of the Duke's."

"That will suffice. And your friend here?"

"My name is George Drayton, and my destination is Bantry, where I hope to find a relation of whom I am in search, and to find whom is my object in coming to Ireland at all."

"Good morning, gentlemen. I must go down to the beach; but shall probably see you both again. By-the-by, they say that the old Duke of Lorton is on his death-bed."

"His death-bed!" exclaimed Gay, with astonishment.

"Yes. He was thrown from his horse only the day before yesterday, and much hurt."

"Then I have no time to lose, for I bring him news from England of the first importance."

"You had better be quick, then."

"I will. Good day, sir, and many thanks for your courtesy and for your intelligence. Come on, Mr. Drayton; I can promise you a hearty welcome at Lorton Castle. But as we go, if you do not think the question impertinent, will you tell me who and what you are, and anything further concerning yourself that may enable me to know well one to whom I have a feeling now of attraction, after what has happened to both of us?"

"Willingly," said George Drayton. "I am the husband of a young girl named Millicent, and I came to Ireland with the hope of finding a wealthy relative. I was bred up at college by some humane benefactor; and, in good truth, I know not if the name I bear be my own or not."

CHAPTER XXXII.

LORTON CASTLE IS IN A STATE OF WORSE CONFUSION THAN USUAL.

As George Drayton spoke, Captain Gay appeared to become still more and more interested in what he said.

"Pray," he said, "what is your age?"

"I am ridiculously young."

"Nay, not so; and yet the bloom of youth was upon your cheek yesterday, although it is a little washed out of it to-day. How old are you?"

"What do you guess me?"

"Humph! About twenty-two."

"I am not quite twenty."

"Indeed! You are young, and a married man, too."

"Yes," said George, with a sigh.

"Well, you have certainly got all the world before you, my young friend, and you have made up your mind that you will have its troubles in full bloom about you."

"What do you mean?"

"Simply that you are a married man."

"Oh! you don't know my Millicent!"

"No, I certainly do not; but, perhaps, some day I may have that pleasure."

"I should rejoice at the opportunity of introducing to her the gallant soul that had saved her husband's life."

"Thank you. Don't mention that, I beg. It was, after all, but a mere trifle. But what makes you doubtful of your identity?"

"Doubtful of my identity?"

"Yes. You said you were not sure that you were entitled to the name you bore."

"Oh, yes, I did; and, as you say, I am doubtful of my identity. It appears that I was reared by an old woman, who was paid largely for her attention to me, until I got to be of an age to be sent to school, where I was accordingly sent, and from there to college; and, having a kind of taste for the fine arts, I studied drawing in all my leisure time, and attained a certain degree of proficiency; but I never knew who paid for my keep and my education."

"Do you mean to say that you have no relation?"

"Not one."

"That's odd."

"Money was sent to me, and those who had to be paid for my education were paid; but, although I questioned them closely, I believe they could tell me nothing, but that a certain sum arrived in a blank envelope for the use of George Drayton."

"It's a strange story."

"It is; but the strangest part of it remains. These supplies suddenly all stopped."

"What did you do then?"

"Why, I got a living by my talent, such as it was, as an artist; and recollecting that my old nurse had told me that my mother had a rich relation near to Bantry Bay, I have come on the hope of finding him out."

"And what is the name of the relation?"

"Drayton, I suppose."

"Humph! It strikes me, my friend, that you have come on rather a wild-goose chase."

"It may be so; but, if this hope should prove fallacious, I can, and I will, work for Millicent while I have strength left me so to do. She deserves all that I can do for her, and Heaven will aid me, I hope, to do my duty."

"Ah, well! perhaps it may. But, here we are, not far from the old castle of Lorton, and since you have in so frank and easy a manner told me who and what you are not—for that seems to be the sum and substance of your communication—I think I ought to tell you who I am."

"As you please."

"Well, then, I am a sort of secretary, or man-of-all-work, to the Duke of Lorton. I think I am distantly related to the family; but, be that as it may, I am the right-hand man of the Duke, and I have been in London upon business of his, and am now returning with its result. My name is Gay. I have been in the army, and so am often called Captain Gay; and that's about all I have to say of the past and the present of your humble servant."

"You are a brave man, sir."

"Thank you!"

"And I, for one, shall always feel for you the greatest regard."

"You don't mean it?"

"Why not? What makes you say that?"

"Oh—why—I don't know exactly; but it is so odd to find anybody have any regard for one for doing a civil thing; that's all. Nevertheless, I believe you."

"I can well premise that you have a bad opinion of human nature, Captain Gay."

"A bad opinion? I rather think I have."

"I am sorry for it."

"Do you mean to say that you have a good one?"

"I do."

"Then I am much more sorry for you than you need be for me, I can tell you; but this is a subject upon which two men with different natures will never agree; so we will say no more about it; and here is Lorton Castle."

Turning rather abruptly round a clump of trees, they came in sight of a ruinous, dilapidated old building, of a castellated character. Some portions of it were covered with ivy, and others seemed to be in the last stage of decay. One wing only, from what could be seen at the windows, appeared to be inhabited; and the large, straggling half-park, half-wilderness that was in front of the building was the resort of pigs, donkeys, a cow, and several horses.

A stream of water ran at the foot of what might be called a lawn, under the windows of the place; and some half-dozen ragged urchins, and some others certainly not ragged, for they were in a state of nature completely, were amusing themselves by fishing in the stream.

As George Drayton looked upon the scene of waste, and decay, and litter, there walked up to him and Captain Gay a stout peasant, with a faggot of wood upon his shoulder, consisting of about as many pieces of wood as you might have clasped with your hand, but of which he evidently chose to make a burthen.

The man was without shoes or stockings; a ragged kind of coat was fastened by a skewer in front of him, and his hat, which looked as if it had been kicked through all the kennels in the world, had a pipe stuck through a hole in the remains of its rim.

As he came along, this specimen of the "finest peasantry in the world" trolled a song.

"The pastor came on a nag so tall,
    Ambling—ambling—ambling."

"Dennis!" cried Captain Gay. "Dennis, I say!"

"Bedad, then! Who's that, maybe?"

"Stop, you rascal!"

"Oh, then, good luck and showers of it to your honour; and it's yourself has come back, Captain Gay? The top of the morning to you, sir, and many of 'em."

"You are as idle as ever."

"Your honour?"

"I say, you are as idle as ever."

"Ah, I see your honour is as fond of a joke as ever. I'm just about carrying home these logs, your honour."

"Do you call them logs? Why, what is the use of carrying home a few miserable sticks like those?"

"It's to the castle I'm after taking them, Captain; and if they ain't enough, bedad, there's lots more where they came from, a mile down by the wood yonder."

"A mile! and this man will go a mile, and come a mile again and again," said George Drayton, "with such a miserable burden as this?"

"Yes," said Captain Gay, "he will; and that is the curse of this country—idleness; that it is that consumes health, wealth, and morals. But tell me, Dennis, how are all at the castle?"

"Mighty well, sir, barring the master, and he's as well as a four-year-old, sir, barring the ugly rap on the head, and the broken ribs, sir, and the dislocating, I think they call it, sir, of the backward bone of his body, sir; but he's mighty well, no doubt, barring that, sir."

"Trifles, indeed. But where did this happen, Dennis?"

"Why, sir, you know kicking Jenny, sir?"

"Yes—yes, the mare that he bought of Short, the gauger, you mean, Dennis?"

"True for you, sir, I do. Well, sir, the master took a gallop with her, sir, and she didn't like it, sir, so she tuke the bit in her teeth, and went on till she came to what she thought was the hardest bit of rock in the country, and there she laid the master, sir."

"Threw him?"

"True for you, sir; and an ugly throw it was, Captain, for since he has come home he hasn't tasted a drop of whiskey, sir, nor any of the quare stuff that he brought from town wid him, sir."

"Claret, you mean?"

"Faith, sir, an it's a witch you are. It is claret, sir, I mean, small blows to me, too, sir."

"This is bad news," said Captain Gay to George Drayton, "and I must make for the house directly.—Dennis?"

"Yes, sir."

"Go to the house as quickly as you can, and say that an English gentleman is coming, who will require change of clothes, a warm bath, and a room to himself, do you hear?"

"Yes, Captain. Change of rooms, clothes to himself, and something warm. Yes, Captain, it's myself as will give the message."

Off set Dennis; and Captain Gay, with a look of anxiety upon his face, hurried on so fast, that George Drayton, in his exhausted state, found it no easy matter to keep up with him.

"It is very unlucky, this," said the Captain. "He ought not at such a juncture as the present to have been so foolish."

"But he couldn't help it, I suppose," said George Drayton.

"Perhaps not; but he was sure to break his neck some day in hunting, for that is the usual end of your fine old Irish gentlemen. Only I complain of his doing it at this juncture, that is all."

"Is he an estimable man?"

"A what?"

"A good man."

"Humph! Well, I hardly know what to say. He drinks hard—rides hard—lives hard—has fought several duels—and, in fact, he is in every respect an old Irish gentleman, for he never pays his debts—borrows of anybody who will lend him any money—never goes to bed sober—has mortgaged his estates as far as he can—does nothing for his tenantry, and never thinks of the comforts, the rights, or the conveniences of any but one person."

"And what favoured person may that be?"

"Himself."

George Drayton laughed.

"I suppose you are jesting, Captain Gay," he said, "with me, because I am an Englishman?"

"Not at all. What I tell you is the plain, sober, and candid truth. As for me, although I am Irish born, I am a citizen of the world; and, therefore, I do not scruple to proclaim the faults of my own countrymen. But here we are at the entrance to the castle, and you see that there is not much state kept up in it. Mind that sow—she is going to make a dart out of the hall, I can see."

George Drayton had just time to get out of the way, as an immense old sow made a dart out at the doorway, followed by about ten or twelve of her progeny, and they all went grunting and squeaking along the lawn.

"But, goodness gracious!" said George Drayton, "do you mean to say that they let the pigs into the house here?"

"Oh, yes. I have often hunted one out from under my bed of a night—it is quite common; and then, overhead, you will see poultry roosting on a chandelier, that in its time, no doubt, cost a hundred guineas in Dublin."

"So I see. Well, this is strange, indeed, to the eyes of an Englishman."

At this moment several people came down the grand staircase into the hall, talking together as they descended.

CHAPTER XXXIII.

THE DUKE OF LORTON BIDS THE GREAT WORLD AND HIS CASTLE ADIEU.

"HE cannot live the day out," said one of the persons who descended the grand staircase of Lorton Castle to the hall.

The air of confusion, so to speak, appeared to increase each moment in Lorton Castle. The slamming of doors, the hurried footsteps of people passing to and fro, executing orders in all sorts of voices, and the howling of dogs, all made up a jumble of sounds that George Drayton thought strange indeed in such a house.

But if, under any circumstances, this conglomeration of sounds was strange in such a house, how much stranger was it that at such a time there should be such confusion! For had it not been, by some one, only a few moments before, announced that the noble owner of that palatial mansion—noble, we will admit, only by courtesy—was about to breathe his last?

It is impossible that we can bespeak anything in the shape of sympathy on the part of the reader for the Earl of Lorton—that must be taken for granted. But, still, those who had eaten of his bread, and regaled themselves upon his wine, ought, at least, to have had the common decency not to disturb his death-bed.

But this was a hundred years ago.

Now, Captain Gay looked wildly savage, and a strange expression came over his face as he stood upon the first step of the grand staircase.

A servant man came clattering down as if nothing at all were the matter above.

Captain Gay made a dart forward, and caught him by the arm with a grasp of iron.

"Scoundrel!"

"Oh, murder and blazes!"

"You know me?"

"Yes, yer honour."

"Who am I?"

"The dev—no, I mean the Captain."

"Good. Now, where is the Duke?"

"Oh, bedad, Captain, and it's going he is."

"Dying?"

"Yes, sure. The doctor says he's going quick to blazes, and Father Connor, too, is with him, and is giving him consolation."

"Indeed?"

"Yes, Captain, that's it. And Jack Maguire has been here to beg for the dogs; and Nick Walsh has gone off with the gray mare, he has."

"Indeed? Ha!"

"You may say that, Captain, wid your own ug—I mean, swate mouth, and never a bit of a lie."

"Silence!"

"Yes, Captain."

"Take care of this gentleman. He is a particular friend of mine; and, mind, I leave you the charge of seeing to his wants."

"Yes, Captain."

"Be careful, now, or you will rue it."

Captain Gay then turned to George Drayton, saying to him, with an air of courtesy:

"May I beg, sir, that you will consider this house as your own? I will be with you as soon as I conveniently can. There is even more disorder here than usual. But as I don't believe all I hear, why, I do not quite give credence to everything that is stated of the condition of the Duke of Lorton."

"I am afraid," said George Drayton, "that upon such an occasion as this I am very much in the way."

"Oh, not at all."

"For, if so, I will, of course, go at once, and try to find something like rest and shelter in some of the huts of the peasantry that I saw as we came along. I beg, sir, that in this matter you will deal frankly with me."

Before Captain Gay could make any reply to this, there came down the grand staircase, at rather a quick pace, a little bald-headed man, regaling his nose as he came with a pinch of snuff.

When this individual saw Captain Gay, he called out:

"Ah! Captain, is that you?"

"It is, Doctor Rowley. How is the Duke?"

"Farther on the gallop."

"Dying?"

"Yes. He is nearly in at the death. I have done all that skill can do to save him, and, as I can do no more, I didn't see the good of sitting by the bedside to watch him."

"Certainly not. Who is with him?"

"Father Connor, Mrs. Daly, Tim the huntsman, and a few others, that I don't know. I think they are trying to get a will out of him, too."

"Ah, indeed! Who is trying?"

"Why, there is a Mr. John South. I think they call him, from London. I don't know him, but——"

Without waiting to hear another word from the doctor, Captain Gay bounded up the ancient grand staircase three stairs at a time, for he began to entertain an idea that something might possibly be going on in the chamber of the dying Duke that was not quite to his interest.

At the top of the grand staircase there was

a long gallery, the walls of which were covered with pictures, many of them costly and well-executed portraits of the family.

Traversing this gallery with rapid steps, and not casting a single glance to the right or to the left of him, Captain Gay reached about two-thirds of its length, and then he came to a door, covered with crimson cloth.

There was no fastening to the door, so that he easily pushed it open. Another door just within it was ajar, and Captain Gay at once stepped into a very handsome apartment.

There were abundant evidences of the greatest neglect in this room. Chairs over-turned, broken wine-glasses on the floor, hunting-whips, swords, pistols, a saddle on the table, and all the conglomeration of articles that could possibly be conceived.

To all this Captain Gay paid no regard; but, striding across the room, pushed open another door.

That door conducted him to a smaller apartment, which was evidently a dressing-room. It was elegantly fitted, or, rather, it bore the traces of having been so at one time.

As soon as he got into this room, Captain Gay heard the sound of voices, and that those voices came from the Duke's bed-chamber beyond, he was perfectly sure.

Captain Gay paused to listen.

The door of the bed-chamber was but partially closed, so that by placing his ear to the small opening, he could catch everything that was said within the room.

It was the rich, oily voice of Father Connor that was speaking. Captain Gay knew that voice in a moment.

"Well, Lorton," said the priest, "if you do as Mr. South wants you, and he seems to be a very sensible, right sort of man, I think that your end will be peace in this world, and you will go to glory in the world that is to come. —Amen!"

"There is no doubt of that," said another voice that Captain Gay did not know.

"None in the least," added the priest.

The voice that Captain Gay did not know was, no doubt, that of Mr. South, from London; but what he did there, was to Gay, at that moment, the greatest mystery in the world.

The Captain was exceedingly anxious to hear the voice of the Duke of Lorton, and he had not long to wait.

"Curses on you all!" growled the dying man. "Away with you! Curses on you all!"

"Amen!" said Gay to himself.

There was now a silence of a few moments' duration; but it was then interrupted by a couple of voices in the room, in loud dispute, in which the words, "Thief—blackguard!" and such like phrases of eloquence were freely used.

Father Connor then cried out:

"Faith, then! you ought to be ashamed of yourselves, to be disputing here about dogs and hares, and the Duke's soul on the high road to everlasting glory!"

"Ha, ha!" laughed someone.

"Gay!" cried the dying Duke, with sudden energy, and in a startling voice. "I want Gay!"

"Oh, then, don't you know," said Father Connor, "that you sent him to England?"

"Yes—oh, yes, yes! Where is he now?"

"Far enough off, I'll warrant," said the priest.

"I cannot die till he comes! I cannot—I cannot!"

"Oh, yes, you will die content enough, if you will only sign the will that this good gentleman lays before you."

"I have no doubt about that," said Mr. South, in oily accents. "The Lady Bridget is your Grace's own sister, and who so proper to inherit your Grace's personal property as she?"

"Ah! who, indeed?" said Father Connor.

"So—so," muttered Captain Gay, "that is how the cat jumps, is it? This Mr. South is an agent of Lady Bridget, is he? And by some means she has found out that the Duke is dying, and wants a will made in her favour. Ha! well, that will not take place, I think."

"Peace—peace! all of you," cried the Duke, in an impatient tone. I cannot die without Gay. I cannot—I cannot! The blood of my own kindred is upon my head!"

"He's going to confess!" cried Father Connor. "He is going to confess, and make his peace with the church! Get out of the room all of you—get out! He is going to confess!"

Captain Gay thought it quite time to interfere; so, suddenly pushing the door open, he entered the room, saying:

"Your Grace, I have returned from London, and am here at your Grace's service!"

The effect of this sudden appearance of Captain Gay, whom everybody present thought far off, was most astounding.

The two or three people who were in the room, for the purpose of trying to possess themselves of some of the moveables in the shape of horses and dogs of the dying man, shuffled to another door in a moment, and stood at it ready to get away as soon as they possibly could, for they had rather a lively idea, apparently, of the possible sort of violence that Captain Gay might resort to in order to get rid of them.

The gentleman from London—Mr. South, as he had been named—rose from a chair by the bedside of the dying man, and looked calmly and coolly at Captain Gay, as if he really thought his presence was a nuisance at that moment, and no doubt he did so.

Father Connor, the priest, elevated his eyebrows a little, and that was all the notice he took of the unexpected return of Gay.

But the effect upon the Duke of Lorton was rather different. The moment he heard Gay's voice he uttered a shriek, and sat up in his bed.

"Who is that?" he cried. "Who is it? No—no! it cannot be Gay."

"It is Gay, your Grace," said the Captain. The Duke uttered an exclamation, and then

CAPTAIN GAY PAYS A VISIT TO MALONEY'S CABIN.

fell back upon his pillow again, and appeared to be suffering from some fearful convulsion.

"He is going now," said Mr. South. "I think, sir, whoever you are, you had better have stayed away; or, at all events, have let him be prepared for your presence in some way before you made your appearance here."

"Sir," said Captain Gay, "when I want your advice, which is not at all likely to be, I will ask for it."

"You are impertinent, sir."

"I intend to be so."

"Silence!" said the priest. "Is this a time or a place for any quarrelling, gentlemen? For shame!"

Mr. South sank back into his seat again; and Captain Gay, with a slight bow to the priest, said:

"I hope I see you quite well, Father Connor?"

The priest made only an impatient gesture in reply; and then Gay stepped close up to the bed, and bending over the Duke, he said: "Your Grace sent me on a mission. I have the result of it to tell to you."

"You speak to one past hearing you, I think," said Father Connor.

As if in direct contradiction to this opinion, there was a rustling of the bedclothes, and to the surprise of them all, the Duke slid out at the side of his bed, and stood at his full height upon the floor.

"Speak!" he cried. "Speak, Gay! speak!"

Captain Gay started back, and looked confounded at this address, and the Duke staggering across the room, sat down in an old, massive easy-chair that was against one of the walls.

"He is mad," said Gay.

"No!" said the Duke, "I am not mad. Heaven help me! I was mad; but as my death is near, I am sane again."

CHAPTER XXXIV.

THE DUKE OF LORTON DIES WITHOUT THE BENEFIT OF CLERGY.

A SHUDDER passed over the form of the Duke, and Father Connor took a blanket from the bed, and threw it round him, saying, as he did so:

"You may recover yet."

"No—no," said the Duke, faintly. "I thank you. Heaven help me! Will you all pray for me?"

"Yes," said the priest.

Mr. South and Captain Gay did not speak, but the persons near the other door of the room cried out, clamorously, that they would pray for him as long as they lived, and after, too; and one of them then said:

"Please, your Grace, perhaps I may have the pair of bay cobs?"

"Be off with you," said the priest. "I will curse you if you stay here another moment. By bell, book, and candle, with the greater curse, I here curse Tim Hogan, and——"

By the time he had got thus far, the superstitious fears of the cormorants were awakened, and they precipitately rushed from the room to avoid hearing the remainder of the malediction that the priest was pronouncing upon them.

"A good riddance," said Father Connor, quietly.

"Gay!" cried the Duke, fighting with his hands in the air. "Where is he, or is it all a dream?"

"I am here," said Captain Gay, doggedly.

"No—no! Oh, where?"

"Here!"

"I cannot see. There is a cloud before my eyes. Oh, Heavens, let me see!"

"His sight has gone," said Mr. South, "and death is near."

"Hush!" said the priest.

"Yes, your Grace," added Captain Gay, in a softer tone, "I am here at your pleasure. I have been upon your business."

The Duke now made several efforts to speak, but could not. He clutched his throat then with his long, bony fingers; and, strange to say, that seemed to give him the power to articulate, for he said:

"My son—my son! Oh, where is he? My poor boy—my son—my son!"

"Dead!" said Captain Gay.

The head of the Duke dropped upon his breast for a moment, and his hands moved convulsively. Then he said:

"Fiend! demon! You killed him!"

"Not so. He fell a sacrifice to an accident at a fire in London. His death was no man's doing."

"Swear it!"

"I do swear it!"

"The oath is nothing—nothing! You killed him! Will you jeopardize your soul by saying, by all your hopes here and hereafter you did not?"

"By all my hopes here and hereafter, I did not kill him. I did not injure, or seek to injure, a hair of his head. Are you satisfied?"

"I think I am. He is dead?"

"Yes, dead. And now, my lord, I have something for your private ear, which no one should listen to but yourself. May I approach you, and whisper my tidings to you?"

"Yes—oh, yes!"

Captain Gay stepped up to the side of the large chair upon which the Duke sat, and, bending his head forward, whispered to him in such tones that only he could hear:

"Your Grace sent me to London on rather a delicate mission, and I may take upon myself to say, that I performed it tolerably well. Your son, the Marquis, is no more; but he, too, had a son. He left a will providing for that son to the extent of his possible means, and acknowledging his marriage, and that son's perfect legitimacy. I have that will now in my possession, your Grace. You will recollect that you promised me an ample reward, and I do hope that now, notwithstanding I find your Grace rather indisposed, that you will recollect I have done the service you sent me upon, and give me my reward."

Captain Gay paused.

The Duke took no notice of him; but with his head sunk upon his chest, continued apparently to listen.

"With regard to the Marquis's son," added Gay, "I regret to say that I have not been able to find him; but I can inform Your Grace that he is living in obscurity in London, somewhere, and that, from all the evidence I have been able to get together concerning him and his position, I am inclined to think he does not even know his own name. Do you hear me, my lord?"

The Duke said nothing.

"I have further to add," said Captain Gay, "that the Marchioness—that is to say, your son's wife—I beg to apologize for calling a person in such a rank of life as she was, the Marchioness—I have, however, the pleasure to inform you that she, too, is dead. I hope you are gratified at this news?"

Captain Gay paused, and listened for a reply.

"This is folly," said the priest. "What on earth are you going on with all that whispering about, Captain?"

"Private affairs, holy father," said the Captain.

The priest stepped up to the Duke, and

peered in his face for a moment; and then, turning to Captain Gay, he said:

"Have you said your say, man?"

"I have."

"Then you have had it all to yourself, for the Duke is dead."

"Dead?"

"Yes, and has been for some minutes, I should say. Only look at him, and convince yourself."

"Confusion!" cried Captain Gay.

At that moment the corpse of the Duke, for he was, indeed, no more, slipped from the chair, and fell with a dead weight upon the floor of the room.

Everyone in the apartment was startled at this but the priest, and he preserved his equanimity pretty well. Captain Gay then called out in a loud voice:

"Where's the Duke's will? Of course the Duke made a will. Who has it? It is quite necessary that I, as the nearest and best friend of the deceased, should know. I say, where is the Duke's will?"

"You need not trouble yourself, Captain Gay," said the priest, quietly, "for I can tell you the Duke declared that he had made no will at all."

"No will?"

"So, indeed," said Mr. South, "he did declare, and I suppose it is the truth. I attended here on behalf of the Lady Bridget Lorton, to whom he might naturally have left his vast property."

"Oh, indeed?" sneered Gay.

"Yes; but my mission here is over. I shall now leave Lorton Castle at once, for my firm impression is, that there is no will; but yet I presume the Lady Bridget is the next of kin to the late Duke, now."

"Indeed, sir? There is the Marquis of Dalewood," said Gay. "Pray, how do you dispose of him?"

"You have disposed of him."

"I, sir?"

"Yes. Surely you have a very short memory to forget that in this very room, only a short time since, you declared that the Marquis of Dalewood was dead."

"You did," said Father Connor, who was, by a glance, appealed to by Mr. South.

"I was a fool, then; but—but there is the Marquis's son. He was married."

"But I heard you whisper to the Duke," added the priest, "that you could not find him, and that he did not even know his own name."

"In that case, then," said Mr. South, with decision, "I will go to London, and advise the Lady Bridget to put in a claim to the whole of the property, as custodian for the young Duke."

"The young who?" roared Captain Gay.

"The young Duke of Lorton, sir. The son of the deceased Marquis of Dalewood, who now, by the decease of his father and his grandfather, is Duke of Lorton, and heir-at-law to the whole of the vast properties of the Lorton family."

Captain Gay actually gasped again at this. For a moment or two he could not speak; and then, only by an evidently violent effort recovering from the state into which the speaker had thrown him, he said:

"Sir, you—you are right."

"I know I am."

"I cordially concur with you in this—a—this matter. I will do all I can to aid you. The—the estate owes me some few thousands, which, no doubt, the Lady Bridget will be very well prepared to pay to me."

"I don't know, sir, anything about that. I am the Lady Bridget's man of business, sir; and if you send in your bill, it will be submitted to me."

"My what?"

"Your bill, sir."

"You are mad, Mr. South! I have no bill. My services were of a private and confidential nature to the late Duke, and do not come under such a category as will allow of a bill being made about them."

"Then, sir, you must look to the late Duke for payment."

"Indeed?"

"Yes," added Mr. South, as he buttoned up his coat, "yes, sir. I can assure you, too, that in my account of what has transpired here this day, I shall not forget that his Grace the Duke of Lorton accused you of the murder of his son, the Marquis, and had to get your oath that you had not killed him. Of course that point is easily ascertained in London; but it shows what he thought of you."

Before Captain Gay could reply to this very imprudent speech of the London lawyer—imprudent to a degree, considering where he was—there came such a clap of thunder, that Lorton Castle seemed to shake to its very foundations.

All conversation was put a stop to, and one of those fearful storms to which the west coast of Ireland is subject, took place, and lasted for the space of half-an-hour in all its intensity.

Mr. South, who had never seen anything like such a confusion of the elements, was really alarmed, and yielded to the wish of the priest that he should remain at the castle till the latter part of the day.

"You can easily, then," said Father Connor, "get a guide to the nearest port, and there, perhaps, you will find some vessel for England."

"I have my horse," was the reply; "all I shall want will be one of the peasantry to show me my way."

Of course the chamber of death had been left. Captain Gay had disappeared somewhere in the house—no one knew exactly where; but, as the storm subsided, he entered the apartment in which Mr. South was; and, with a frank and easy manner, which he had the art of assuming at his pleasure, he said:

"Mr. South, I hope that you will forgive any little disagreement which may have arisen between us; and, upon reflection, I feel that the first wish of Lady Bridget must be to find out her nephew, the now young

Duke of Lorton. I think I ought, before you leave the castle, to give you all the information in my power."

"Sir, I thank you," said the lawyer.

"Don't mention it. The fact is, I have recently come from London, and accident has placed in my power much information of consequence, in my search for the lad."

"Any information, sir," said Mr. South, "that you can give will be very thankfully received by me on behalf of the Lady Bridget. I may say that I am not wholly without some sort of clue to the history of the young Duke and his mother, the Marchioness; but probably what you tell me will tally with what I do know, and clear up some of its obscurities."

"I hope so, sir."

From the words that Mr. South had uttered, Captain Gay felt that any trumped-up story would be a failure; so he sat down by him, and, strange to say, told him the truth.

But the reader must not suppose that, because Captain Gay told Mr. South the truth, he told him the whole truth. On the contrary, he suppressed a great deal of it.

He told him how the Marquis had perished in the fire at the Opera House, and how the Marchioness had died of grief upon seeing his dead body, and how the Ardent family were friends of hers, and would aid in any way to find the young Duke; and, in fact, what he told, so well tallied with what Mr. South knew, that that person said, at the conclusion of the Captain's narrative:

"I am quite convinced, sir, that whatever may have been your peculiar position with the late Duke, you have dealt honestly with me, for I know enough to be able to come to that conclusion, and what you have told me will very materially aid me in London."

"Sir, I thank you. Will you give me a note saying so much, and recommending me to the notice of Lady Bridget Lorton?"

"With pleasure; and you can, likewise, call upon me in London."

CHAPTER XXXV.

CAPTAIN GAY CLEARS THE WAY FOR A GRAND STROKE OF DIPLOMACY.

Mr. South there and then sat down, and wrote for Captain Gay a brief note of recommendation to the Lady Bridget, in which he stated that he had received reliable information from him, and that, no doubt, he would be of great service in tracing the young Duke.

That note was the death-warrant of the London lawyer.

The rest of the day was so unsettled, in consequence of the storm, that no one ventured out of the castle. There was a gloom over the spirits of everyone, too, in consequence of death being in the house; and the whole place wore an aspect very different from any that it had borne previously.

The body of the Duke had been placed on the state-bed, and a pall of velvet thrown over it. The shutters of that wing of the huge establishment were all closed; and as now and then the rain dashed against the casements, the servants tremblingly crept along the wide, dull corridor, and spoke to each other in whispers, as though too loud a voice could possibly disturb him who slept the sleep of death beneath that roof.

It was within about an hour of sunset, when Captain Gay stealthily took his way to a room upon the same floor as that upon which the Duke had died.

This room into which he went, and the door of which he very carefully locked behind him, was one of great antiquity and rich magnificence. The walls were all of old oak, enriched by carvings executed by no mean hand; and the ceiling was painted in some allegorical subject, that time had rendered more obscure—if that, indeed, were possible—than it had been originally.

Captain Gay stood now in this room, and drew a long breath of seeming relief. It was that kind of relief that a man feels when he is sure he is alone, who, for some time, has felt the necessity of playing a part, in consequence of the eyes of other people being upon him.

"Once again," he said, in a low tone of voice, "once again I am here in this room, the secrets of which I only, by mere chance, one day discovered. It is possible, now, that I may be able to unearth something that may forward my views."

Before he proceeded to leave this room again, which he had the means of doing by a very different mode from that by which he had entered it, Captain Gay went to the door, and listened intently.

The long picture gallery, from which the room opened, was as silent as the grave.

A grim kind of smile came across the face of Captain Gay, as he said:

"I will warrant there is not a soul in all Lorton Castle who, now that the shadows of the coming night are upon the old pile, will venture half so near as the gallery would be to the room in which the Duke sleeps the sleep of death."

Captain Gay was right enough in this supposition, for superstition, at all times a prevalent feature in the human character, was in Ireland cultivated, if we may so express ourselves, to a vast extent.

"Yes," added Gay, "all is well—all is well."

He now went to a portion of the wall of the room upon which hung a life-sized portrait of some ancestor of the Lorton family.

By the dim light of the twilight that was now fast fading away, the Captain searched narrowly along the moulding of the once richly-gilt, but now terribly tarnished frame in which the portrait hung.

One would have supposed that he was intent upon finding out if any of the enrichments of that frame happened to be missing; but he had an object of more importance in view.

After a time, he placed his thumb upon a

little gilt knob, or button, among the ornaments of the frame, which was so well shaped like the others, that had no significance or secret at all been connected with them, it was quite out of the question chance could ever have induced anyone to pay more attention to it than to any other trifling salient point of the frame.

By exerting a pressure, however, upon this little button in the moulding, Captain Gay produced rather a surprising effect.

A spring was released, which had the result of causing the portrait to turn upon a centre, so as to present a clear opening in the wall of about two feet in width.

All looked dark within that opening.

It did not require a conjurer to come to the conclusion that it had been a long time since that secret panel in the wall had been opened. The black dust that was disturbed, and which fell at the feet of Captain Gay, was sufficient evidence upon that point.

"It is strange," said the Captain; "but, in good truth, I seem to have had this secret all to myself. I doubt if even the Duke knew of it."

Gay was right so far, for the fact was, that the Duke of Lorton, who now lay in death in a chamber contiguous to the room in which he (Gay) was, did not know of any such secret panel in the wall.

It had been the fate of several Dukes of Lorton to be upon anything but good terms with their successors, and the heirs to their titles and estates, and thus it was that many little family secrets that otherwise would have been duly transmitted from one generation to another, had died with the last holders of them.

Thus, then, the late Duke's father had known of the secret panel in what was called the scroll-chamber; but the Duke who was known to Captain Gay did not.

How he (Gay) had found out the secret, matters not; but if it was by accident, it must have been a very rare one indeed.

There was no difficulty for a man of Captain Gay's slim and agile figure to pass through the opening in the wall, so he did so at once; and then, taking about six steps along a singularly narrow passage to his right, he, by touching some other spring, opened another panel, which led him right into the bedroom of the defunct Duke.

This panel was likewise concealed by a picture and its frame, so that it had escaped observation, as the other had.

What had been the motive for constructing such a secret mode of getting from the principal bedrooms of Lorton Castle may easily be conjectured from the disturbed condition of Ireland for some centuries—a disturbed condition which is so very evidently indigenous to the soil, that it seems likely to continue to the end of the world.

There was a solemn and complete darkness in the chamber of the dead Duke.

Even the daring and reckless Captain Gay could not help feeling something in the shape of a slight terror as he stepped into the room which contained the dead, whose evil passions he had known so well, and ministered to, to the utmost of his ability, while in life.

He paused a moment, as if in trepidation, and then he strode over the floor, saying as he did so:

"Tush! Am I to begin now to entertain feelings that I have scoffed at since I was an urchin?"

He found his way to one of the windows, and very carefully opened one of the shutters about an inch. He was afraid to open it further, for fear some servant or follower of the house should by chance look up from the courtyard.

The evening, though, was much too far advanced for Captain Gay to rely for light on the illumination which might make its way through the partially opened shutter. All he wanted was a little of that twilight, that he might see to procure an artificial light.

By the aid of a phosphorus match, Gay now lit a taper, and then a tall wax candle that stood upon a bracket in the room, with a plaster cast of the Virgin Mary in a niche behind it.

Captain Gay then closed the shutter carefully.

The wax candle took some three or four minutes to get thoroughly into a condition to give its maximum amount of light, and then it shed a tolerably defined lustre through the room, the most noticeable object in which was the state bed, with its feathers at the corners, and the black pall—the same that had been used for some generations in the family—covering the body of the deceased Duke.

This pall was a kind of heirloom in the Lorton family; and as it was not a very agreeable object of contemplation, nor pregnant with any very pleasant reminiscences or suggestions, it was never looked at or disturbed during the lifetime of any Duke of Lorton; but, after the funeral, was placed away in an old wardrobe, there to rest till it was again wanted.

The consequence of this was, that the damp and the moths had had it all their own way; and as Captain Gay now looked at the pall, he could see shining, crawling things twinkling in the light upon its surface, and here and there a large hole where a portion of it had been fairly eaten away.

With a shudder, he turned away from the bed.

By the bed's head there appeared an antique cabinet, evidently, from the meretricious character of its ornamental work, of French manufacture; and it was to this article of furniture that Gay now paid every attention.

Well he knew that it was there where the Duke was wont to keep his private papers, and that if there should be anything likely to be of service to him (Gay) in his proceedings contingent upon the death of his patron it was in that cabinet he should find it.

The door was locked.

This was an obstacle that Captain Gay had provided against, so far as he could, for he had brought with him some skeleton keys, in the use of which he was a tolerable adept.

The lock, however, foiled him.

"Curses on the antique piece of lumber," he said. "I must force it, after all." •

With these words, Gay produced a small crowbar, and placing the end of it between the doors of the cabinet, he with an effort burst them open, at the expense of the lo k and a large piece of the carved moulding upon the edge of one of the doors.

Of course it would have suited Gay better to have left no evidence of the presence of anyone with violent intentions at the cabinet; but he could not do otherwise than he did, unless he chose to abandon his designs, and that he was the very last person to think of doing.

The cabinet being now fairly open, disclosed a number of drawers of all sorts and sizes, and Captain Gay began his search and examination of them in a very systematic manner indeed, by taking them just as they came.

"Humph!" he said; "antique pistols, some coins, all good for something. Ah, some jewels! Yes, the star that my Lord Duke wore upon state occasions. The gold hilt of a sword—good!"

All these articles Captain Gay placed in the ample pockets of his broad-skirted coat.

Continuing the search, then, he came to some bundles of papers, which he carefully looked at exteriorly; and then in a drawer he found a folded paper with the ominous words upon it of:

"*Memoranda for the last Will and Testament of the Duke of Lorton.*"

"Ha!" said Gay, as he opened the paper. "This may be worth knowing. Let me see."

The paper contained a disposition of the Lorton estates, so far as they were in the gift of the Duke, to one Morton Gravanie, of the Court of Rome; and truly now was Captain Gay puzzled to know what could be the meaning of that; but he put the paper in his pocket after reading it, and then, taking it out again, he said:

"It is better destroyed—much better destroyed. It would but interfere with my plans, and can never forward them."

Captain Gay held the paper in the flame of the candle till it was burnt to the last piece he held in his fingers.

CHAPTER XXXVI.

CAPTAIN GAY MEETS WITH A SLIGHT SHOCK.

"I DO not know," said Gay—as he looked about him, after finishing his searching of the drawers in the deceased Duke's cabinet— "I do not know that I need stay here any longer, for I am pretty well satisfied that there is no actual will to interfere with me and my projects."

A deep sigh came upon the still air of the room.

Captain Gay turned completely round upon his heel, and he felt a cold perspiration break out upon his brow, as this sound met his ears in the chamber of death.

"What is that?" he gasped.

His eyes were riveted upon the old pall.

The sigh came again.

For a moment, then, Captain Gay thought his senses were going to leave him, and he reeled back till he came to a chair, into which he sank, keeping his eyes still upon the pall.

There was a slight movement of the old faded covering of velvet that rested upon the dead Duke.

Captain Gay recovered from the dimness and confusion that had come over his senses, and all his faculties were concentrated in watching the bed and its terrible occupant.

The velvet shook violently, and a half stifled cry came from beneath it.

"By Heaven, he lives!" said Gay, in a voice of terror. "He lives! It was but a swoon!"

The Duke of Lorton dashed the velvet pall from off his face; and, in stifling accents, cried:

"Help!—help!—help!"

Gay, notwithstanding he had a pretty good appreciation of what really was the state of the case, namely, that a deep and death-like swoon upon the part of the Duke had been mistaken for death itself, was yet so terrified, that he made a rush to reach the secret panel, and escape from the room.

The last energies of expiring life were in the Duke of Lorton still; and with a yell of anguish, both of mind and body, he threw himself from the bed, and pursued Captain Gay.

Another moment, and Captain Gay would have escaped through the panel, and dashed it shut in the face of the Duke; but he was just too late. With the circling arms of madness, the Duke laid hold of him, and essayed to drag him to the floor.

All strength for about twenty seconds or so seemed to desert Gay, and he felt himself upon the point of swooning with terror; but, by a great effort, he recovered his presence of mind, and, turning, he grappled with his assailant.

That contest was truly a fearful one. The Duke and Captain Gay, twined in each others arms, fell to the floor together. The Duke tried to fix his teeth in Gay's throat, and it was only by dashing his head from side to side that Gay avoided the bites of the dying madman.

They rolled over twice, and then Gay was uppermost. There were upon the ancient hearth of the room what are called iron dogs, for burning peat fuel and logs of wood. They were close to one of those thick iron supports, and with the desperation of the moment, Captain Gay clutched the Duke's head by the scanty hair on each side of the temples; and lifting it by main force about a foot from the ground, dashed it against the iron dogs.

The crash was sickening, and the blow

seemed to be effectual. The long, bony fingers of the Duke relaxed their hold of the throat of Captain Gay, and once again the Lord of Lorton lay an inert mass in his chamber.

A violent knocking at the door of the room at this moment sounded to Gay as if it had been at his own heart.

"What's that?" he gasped; "what's that?"

The knocking continued.

Such an access of trembling now came over Captain Gay, that, although twice he made an effort to rise from the floor by the side of the now unquestionably dead body of the Duke of Lorton, he as often found he had not the requisite strength to enable him to do so.

The sound of voices confusedly talking to each other at the door now struck upon his ears. One said:

"Send for Father Connor. Perhaps he has the key of the room."

"Yes—yes!" cried several.

This awakened Captain Gay to the fact that he was liable at any moment to be burst in upon by the ordinary door of the Duke's bedroom, which, of course, had been locked on the outside.

The fear of being caught there had all its effect upon him, and he rose to his feet, and made a rush to the secret panel in the wall.

Captain Gay was just in time. He got through the panel, and closed it at the moment when the key of the chamber-door, having been found somewhere, was rattling in the lock.

Another moment, and the door was opened.

Captain Gay stayed just long enough on the other side of the panel to hear the cry of horror which arose from the persons who penetrated the chamber of the dead, and saw the body of the Duke lying upon the floor, and the pall which had covered him, in confusion, half off the bed; and then he crept along the narrow passage between the walls, and got into the scroll chamber.

"An escape!" said Gay, as he sank into the first seat that presented itself to him. "An escape!"

He was right. It was an escape, and a very narrow one, too, for the fact is, he, by his tyrannical behaviour at Lorton Castle, was anything but a favourite with the servants and retainers of the ancient house, and had he been found accidentally in the Duke's chamber in the act of rifling the dead, so to speak, it is more than likely that his life would have at once paid the penalty of an offence which would, to the superstitious minds of his foes, have appeared to be doubly atrocious.

He wiped the perspiration of intense fear from his brow, and tried to get up a smile; but it was a faint and sickly one.

"I would give something now," he said, "for a good glass of brandy; but, as it is not to be had in this part of the earth, I must sit awhile and recover myself, as best I may, without it. What is this?"

He had dived his hand into his pocket, and found something cold and sharp. It was the brilliant star that he had found in one of the drawers of the Duke's cabinet. He took it out, and looked at it, and shook his head, while a sardonic smile played upon his lips.

"Who will ever wear this again?" he said. "Who has the right to wear it? The son of the Marquis is of course, now Duke of Lorton, and possessor in right, though not in fact, of his vast properties. He has a right to place this glittering bauble on his breast, and to wear it in the face of all the world; but will he ever?"

That was, indeed, the question.

The star rested in the hand of Captain Gay, and he seemed to fall into a deep reverie as he sat there with it in his hand.

That reverie was an important one to many innocent, and to some guilty people, for it was during it that the daring and unscrupulous Gay made up his mind to the course of action he should pursue now that the Duke of Lorton was no more.

After a time, he spoke in a low voice.

"It ought to go hard," he said, "if now, with what I know, and out of the confusion and the clash of interest in this high and noble family, I do not contrive to carve my own fortune. I ought to do it."

This was the proposition that seized hold of the imagination of Captain Gay, and which carried him very far in his thoughts beyond the sum of money which he had expected to get from the Duke for the will of his son, the Marquis of Dalewood, which he (Gay) had so cleverly, and so audaciously, contrived in London to get possession of.

When he came to Ireland, there is no doubt but that he had no ideas beyond the enhancing as far as possible the price he expected for that document; but the death of the Duke, and other events, opened to him a new prospect.

Of one thing, too, the reader may rest perfectly assured, and that is, that no human feeling—no movement of holy compassion—no regret for the infliction of any amount of misery upon others—would for a moment turn aside Captain Gay from his purpose.

"Yes," he exclaimed, after a silence of a few minutes, "I think I begin to see my way now."

He rose, and paced the small chamber to and fro, and his countenance as he did so took many shifting and strange expressions.

Villainy, though, was at the bottom of them all, and shone like a baneful light through every other emotion of that man's soul.

"Yes," he added, "I see my way. I must first get rid of this Mr. South, or he will be in my way. Then I will myself carry the tidings of what has occurred here to Lady Bridget, and I think I can possibly find an heir to the estates of Lorton, who, owing all to me, shall pay me like a prince, and for ever be in my power, at the same time that I draw largely upon the gratitude of Lady Bridget, who possibly may be well enough pleased, when she knows that the Marquis of Dalewood was really married, to find the honours and the titles of the family fairly perpetuated. I must think—yes, I must think; but the death of this London lawyer is quite settled."

Captain Gay, no doubt, went upon the judicious system of doing one thing at a time; so, now, without vexing himself about ulterior matters, he turned his attention to the best way of disposing of Mr. South.

In the conversation he had had with the London lawyer, some short time before he went to the chamber of the dead Duke, Gay had for once in his life told the truth, and no doubt the reader thought such a course most incompatible with the conduct of the Captain, as usually displayed; but even then the idea of preventing South from reaching London in life was in the mind of Captain Gay; so that the truth that he (Gay) told him, may be considered to have been, to some extent, his absolute and unconditional condemnation.

The lawyer little dreamt that Lorton Castle was to be so fatal to him.

Unlocking the door of the small chamber now, Captain Gay left it, and walked across the gallery, and down the grand staircase, and then he soon became aware of the state of excitement that the whole house was in.

Servants were hurrying to and fro, or conversing in hurried and anxious whispers. Father Connor had been sent for, as well as the surgeon of the neighbourhood; in fact, all was terror and confusion, contingent upon what had met their gaze in the Duke's chamber.

Captain Gay put on an admirable look of surprise as the singular events, with many additions, were told to him.

The relation was that, with many howls and shrieks, the whole wing of the castle in which the Duke's rooms were situated, was alarmed, and that upon opening the door, a large apparition, with extended wings, was seen crouching down by the side of the dead body of the Duke on the floor.

From this it was evident that the Evil One himself had made an attempt to carry off the body; but had been foiled by the appearance of those who came to the room just in time to stop him.

CHAPTER XXXVII.

MR. SOUTH FINDS HUMAN LIFE CHEAP IN IRELAND.

CAPTAIN GAY was well enough pleased to let this version of the story gain credit; so all he remarked about it was rather what tended to confirm its possibility, than otherwise.

Mr. South made his appearance in the hall while Gay was talking to some of the servants, and, with a smile of incredulity, he said to the Captain:

"You do not really, sir, give any credence to this absurd story?"

"I don't know anything about it."

"Oh, but," said George Drayton, stepping forward, "it is really too ridiculous, my dear sir."

"Ah, my young friend," said the Captain, "are you there?"

"Yes, Captain. I feel very much moved now, and only hope I am not in the way in this house of mourning, and, I may truly add, confusion?"

"Not at all," said Gay, with rather an equivocal smile. "Do you, Mr. South, still purpose leaving us to-night?"

"Yes, if I can get a guide to Bantry, which, I suppose, you can find for me with ease?"

"I can, sir."

"Then I shall, I assure you, be much beholden to you to do so as soon as possible, for the night is coming."

"Trust to me, sir."

Captain Gay then took George Drayton aside, and said to him:

"Will you do me a favour?"

"Certainly I will. I owe you too much to refuse you one. What is it?"

"Nothing particular; but will you remain until to-morrow morning in the castle?"

"Oh, yes!"

"Be it so, then. I will take every care of your comfort here, and I have something of importance to say to you in the morning."

"I shall expect your communication with impatience. I am, as you know, most completely a waiter upon fortune, and but that I still feel very anxious to discover if, indeed, I have a relation in Ireland at all, I should wish myself in London, with those who I know will welcome me for the sake of one who is dear to them."

"Humph!" said the Captain, "they are rather—low, are they not?"

"Low, sir?"

"Nay, my young friend, I do not want to offend you. I did not mean to use the word invidiously; I merely meant that they were in but poor circumstances."

"That is true; but it is impossible that they can be low. I beg of you to disburse your mind of that idea. She whom I love, and who bears my name, is fit to grace any station."

"Indeed?"

"I assure you of the fact."

"Well, Mr. Drayton, you ought to be the best judge of that, as a matter of course; and all I am anxious about is, that you should not gather any offence from what I have carelessly said."

"Not the least."

"That is well."

George Drayton, who could not divest himself of the strong feeling of gratitude to the man who had snatched him from death, held out his hand in token of complete sincerity, and Gay shook it cordially, and then left him.

"Where is Dennis Ryan?" said Gay, to one of the servants.

"Faith, Captain, and there he is!"

"Oh, I see him."

Captain Gay made his way to old Dennis Ryan, who was a sort of major-domo, or house-steward, to Lorton Castle; and, addressing him at the same time that he pointed out to his notice George Drayton, he said:

"Dennis, I beg that you will pay all the

attention you possibly can to the comforts of that young gentleman. He will stay the night here, and in time you will find out so much about him, that you will rejoice at any attention you have paid him."

"Faith, then, Captain, it's meself that will serve him; and it's a good-looking boy he is, to be sure."

"He is so."

"Faith, and that's true, Captain. Lave him to me, sir, and it's the best in the castle that he'll get, any way."

"Thank you, Dennis."

"Small thanks to me, sir; and it's only the right thing, you know, to look to the stranger."

Captain Gay bowed, and left Dennis, who immediately went up to George Drayton, and set about accommodating him to the utmost extent he possibly could in the castle.

"So far, so good," said the Captain to himself. "My projects go on well. And now for Mr. South. He was rather anxious for the Duke to make his will. I wonder if he has made his own? Ha—ha!"

Mr. South was still in the hall, and as Gay came up to him, he said, in quite a friendly tone of voice:

"Sir, if you will walk into the library, which is lighted, I perceive, and wait for me, I will now go and get you a guide to Bantry. I think you said you had a horse here?"

"I have, sir."

"Then trust to me."

Mr. South expressed his acknowledgments, and quietly sat down in the library, while Captain Gay went out of the castle. What for? Why, to find an assassin!

Alas! that it should be so; but he had not to look far for what he required.

Captain Gay, when he got to the great hall-door of the castle, and stepped out into the open air through a narrow wicket gate, almost recoiled before the dash of rain and wind that met him.

"Curses on the weather!" he exclaimed; "that English lawyer will be frightened at it, and not venture forth to-night, I fear."

The night was not a very dark one, for the clouds were thin, and scudded across the sky at a terrible rate. It was only now and then that the south-west gale brought over a densely-loaded rain cloud, which scattered a flood over the surrounding country, and then was off again.

The dash of rain that had come into the face of the Captain on stepping into the open air, was over before he got six paces from the hall door.

"It is not so bad as I thought it, after all," he said. "Perhaps I can succeed in persuading him to leave the place."

Gay took his route now to the left, and scrambling through the grounds of the castle, which in that direction did not extend to any great distance, he got to a miserable sort of highway, and about half-a-mile from the commencement of that he came to a point in the road at which he paused, for there was a deep and dangerous quarry close to that spot.

Captain Gay knew that the edge of this quarry was left quite bare of all protection. To be sure, half a day's work, and half a load of timber, would have made a good and complete fence along the edge of the quarry; but it was in Ireland, and so how could such a thing be expected to be done?

"Curses on the idleness of the thieves!" said Gay, as he moved cautiously along. "I have more than half-a-dozen times very nearly fallen into the quarry."

By the dim night light, after proceeding a little way from the high road, Gay came to a straggling path, which he knew would lead him to the most dangerous part of the quarry, and in the direction of a miserable collection of peasants' huts close at hand.

A few lights twinkled in the windows of the huts, if windows they could be called, which were only rude holes in the wall, with a piece of paper pasted over them.

Captain Gay paused for a few moments, and looked about him. An ash tree of rather gigantic proportions grew close to the spot, and as he glanced up at its branches, dashed about in wild confusion as they were by the wind, he said:

"Yes, this shall be the spot. I will take good care that it is well known. This will do."

Advancing, then, to one of the huts which was at some distance from the rest, and from which there came no light at all, Captain Gay took a large-sized horse pistol from his pocket, and with the butt-end of it knocked rather loudly at the wretched door.

The whole hut, so miserable and crazy was it, seemed to shake under the influence of the blow that Gay gave to the door of it.

There was no reply.

Captain Gay was not a man very easy to repulse; so, after waiting for a few seconds, he dealt the door another blow, and then a voice from within growled out:

"Who are you? Be off wid you, and don't be disturbing a fellow at this time o' night. Be off wid you, I say, or, by the saints, I'll send a pair of slugs through you!"

"Maloney!" cried Captain Gay.

"Oh, bedad, it's the Captain."

"Maloney, I say!"

"Yez—yez. Coming it is I am.—By the holy Virgin, but there's some mischief afloat, for the Captain is about."

The door of the hut was flung open, and a dim shadow appeared in the doorway.

"Get a light," said Gay.

"Oh, yez, Captain; and it's meself is mighty glad to see you. Leastways, see your honour, I don't be after pretending to say that I can just this-a-ways; but your honour's voice is good for the ears, any way."

"Pshaw! get the light."

"Perhaps your honour will walk in?"

"Yes. Are you alone?"

"Bedad, yes."

Gay entered the hut, and Maloney knelt

before a turf fire; and, placing a piece of paper in the reddest part of it, began blowing it to induce it to light.

In a few moments the paper burnt into a blaze, and then Maloney lit a miserable kind of rush candle that was stuck in a lump of clay against the wall.

The candle in a few seconds gave all the light it was capable of emitting; and then Captain Gay got a good look at Mr. Maloney, and Mr. Maloney got a good look at Captain Gay.

The reader is acquainted already with the latter of the two personages, but not the former; so we may say that Mr. Maloney was, to all appearance, the *beau ideal* of a ruffian.

Coarse featured—short and thick in stature—projecting brows, retreating forehead, huge jaws and a bullet-shaped head, and an awful squint, completed Mr. Maloney's attractions. He was attired in a long kind of coat, fastened down the front by several pieces of string, and it is probable that the nether garments of Mr. Maloney were not of the best description.

With a fawning aspect and manner, which sat upon him something with the grace that a compliment would come from a bear, he brought a three-legged stool to the front of the turf fire, and giving it a wipe down with the skirt of his coat, he said:

"Oh, then, it's a blessed night when the likes of yer honour comes a visiting to a poor sowl like me. Long life to yer honour, and many of them."

"Silence!" said Gay; "listen to me."

"An it's meself that will do that same."

"Maloney!"

"Yes, yer honour?"

"You once had a tidy holding of land?"

"I had; bad cess to them as took it from me."

"You were dispossessed by Mr. Hope's agent, and I let you have this bit of a cot to sleep in?"

"True for you, sir."

"Till I could get you a holding on the Lorton estate."

"The saints be good to yer honour!"

"And, I believe, I protected you from the hunt that was made after you, when they said you shot Mr. Hope's agent?"

"Amen!" said Mr. Maloney. "Vartue is its own reward."

Captain Gay smiled.

"Maloney, there is at the castle an English lawyer. He will pass this way on horseback—hem! I think I can find you a holding of five acres to-morrow, on easy terms."

Mr. Maloney's eyes twinkled, and stepping close to Captain Gay, he said, with a screeching sort of laugh:

"The English lawyer's bones will whiten at the bottom of the old quarry, Mr. Gay. He—he! The ould firelock will do its work. Ha—ha! Is it that what you mane, Captain? Is it that same?"

CHAPTER XXXVIII.

CAPTAIN GAY GETS RID OF ONE OBSTACLE TO HIS PROGRESS.

"KEEP off, curse you!" said Captain Gay, as he pushed Mr. Maloney from him.

"But is it that?"

"It is."

"Bedad, then, it's done, Captain," returned the ruffian.

"Listen to me. He will ride his own horse. He wants a guide to Bantry. You will be the guide as far as here."

"It's myself that will do that, sure. Oh, good luck to you, Captain, for throwing a honest penny in the way of a poor boy. You might have gone to anybody else, and got the job done, so it's mighty obliged to you I am for thinking of me."

"Don't mention it," said Gay, ironically. "There is a seven-shilling piece for you as earnest; and if you come to the castle to-morrow morning, and tell me it's done, I will give you a flagon of whisky."

"Long life to yer honour!"

"Follow me!"

"Bedad, then, I will."

Captain Gay stalked from the hut.

Making his way with what speed he could to the castle, followed by Mr. Maloney, the Captain soon reached the wicket-gate again.

Turning to Maloney, he then said:

"You will wait here till I come out with the Englishman, and then I leave him to your custody. Do you comprehend?"

"Exactly, Captain."

"Very good. You will be here at eight in the morning?"

"Bedad, then, it's meself that will. Hooroh!"

"Silence, idiot! Be quiet!"

Mr. Maloney was quiet, accordingly, and waited outside the castle gate, while Captain Gay went in to seek the victim.

Mr. South was in the library; and the Captain, as he entered, got up quite a pleasant smile, as he said:

"I have found you a guide, sir, whom you can really trust, which I am sorry to say cannot be done so far as regards all our peasantry upon this estate."

"Well," said Mr. South, "I have heard strange things of some of your peasantry."

"No doubt, sir. There are good and bad among them."

"Oh, of course. We ought not to condemn all. I shall communicate to the Lady Bridget the information I have received from you, and I daresay that any expense you have been at she will authorize me to pay to you. I think you had better send me in a little account."

"You are very kind, sir."

"Of course, you can charge for your time, and your money out of pocket, in going to London."

"You are too good, sir."

"And all I can say is, that if I can be of

any service to you with the Lady Bridget, who will at once now lay claim to be custodian of the Lorton property——"

"Of course she will. Your horse is quite ready, and I wish you a pleasant journey, Mr. South. Is Lady Bridget an amiable lady?"

"Oh, yes. She is an old client of our house."

"Then that speaks volumes for her, sir."

"Not at all—not at all; but, of course, we do the best we can for our old friends. Good evening, Captain Gay—good evening. You may rely upon my favourable report of you, for I have reason to believe you have told me the exact truth."

"Indeed I have, sir."

What a patronizing air the London lawyer gave himself to Captain Gay! He thought that, as he was going, he might as well leave an impression behind him that he was, indeed, somebody. Poor man! With his professionally circumscribed mind, how little he appreciated the fiendish spirit he was addressing.

"Here is your guide," said Gay, pointing to Mr. Maloney, at the door of the castle, as the lawyer mounted his horse.

"Thank you!—Oh, so you know the road to Bantry, my man?"

"Yes, yer honour."

"Very well. I will make it worth your while to be civil and attentive. I hope I may trust you?"

"Yer honour may be sure of that."

"Very good. Now lead the way, and keep to the high road, my good man; for I have heard that some of the peasantry hereabouts are but a lawless set."

"There's all sorts, yer honour."

"No doubt—no doubt!"

Mr. Maloney trotted on a few paces before, and Mr. South followed him, feeling very important as he did so, and enjoying the thoughts of what a story he would have to tell of his peregrinations in the wilds of Galway, to his friends in London.

"It's mighty dark, yer honour," said Mr. Maloney, when they got near to the tall tree.

"It is so. I can hardly see you as you go."

"Suppose I get a lantern, your honour, and then your honour can see me mighty well."

"A lantern, my good man! Where on earth in such a place as this can you get a lantern?"

"There's an honest man, sir, in a cottage hereaway that will lend me one, if yer honour will wait a minute."

"Well—well! Don't be long."

"Not a minute, yer honour."

Mr. Maloney went to his own hut, and from a snug hole in the thatch he took an old gun, that he kept in prime condition: and, with all the unconcern in the world, he sallied out again, keeping the tree between him and the lawyer.

"Hilloa!" he then said. "Is yer honour there?"

"Yes—yes!"

"Take that, then, and the divil fly away wid you."

Bang went the gun; and, with a cry, Mr. Maloney himself fell backwards. The barrel had burst, and a piece of the jagged iron had plunged into his skull.

Half-a-dozen slugs, with which the gun had been loaded, seemed all to fly into the face of Mr. South, and, like a corpse, he fell from his horse. The animal, terrified by the noise, fled maddened along the rough road, and the deed was done.

"What's that?" cried a voice from one of the hovels close to the spot. "Arragh, there! what's that?"

"Somebody kilt entirely," said another.

"I shouldn't wonder," said the first speaker, as he closed his door again, and took no further notice of the little transaction.

Captain Gay emerged from the shadow of a hedge not far from the brink of the quarry. His anxiety to see Mr. South put out of the way had induced him to follow Maloney and his victim.

"Maloney?" he said. "Maloney?"

There was no reply.

"Maloney, I say?"

A deep groan came upon his ears.

"What can be the matter with him?" said Gay. "I will soon see."

He took from his pocket a dark lantern, and removing the slide from before the lens, he was enabled to cast a stream of light upon the ground, and so, moving it about, he crept on till the light fell upon the dead body of Mr. South.

One look was sufficient to let him see that the skull of the lawyer was battered in by the shots.

"It is done!" he said. "Good-night, Mr. South. Much obliged to you for your kind offer of patronage, sir. Maloney, where are you?"

A strange bubbling noise, like someone drowning, came upon his ears.

"What on earth is that?" he said.

The noise continued, and then the ray of light from the bull's-eye of the lantern discovered to him Mr. Maloney lying on his back, with the fragments of the gun in his hand. The wretch was alive.

"So—so!" said Gay. "That's it, is it?"

His practised eye saw in a moment what had happened to Mr. Maloney, and well enough pleased he was at it. A piece of the barrel of the gun actually projected from the villain's head, and yet he lived.

"Why, Maloney, what is this?"

"Mercy! Oh, holy—saints!"

"Oh, indeed!" said Gay. "I'm very much afraid, my dear friend, that the saints will not pay the remotest attention to you. You seem to be in rather an ugly fix, Mr. Maloney."

The eyes of the mortally wounded man glared upon Captain Gay.

"Save me! Oh, save me!" he exclaimed, hoarsely.

"Upon my word," said Gay, "I don't see how. But if you wait a minute, I will attend to you. I am now going to throw the body of the lawyer over the brink of the quarry."

"No—no—mercy!"

"Oh, Mr. Maloney, I beg that you will not doubt it; but, if you do, you will have every opportunity of satisfying yourself, for I intend, after disposing of Mr. South, to throw you after him!"

The wretch tried to utter a yell of dismay, but the blood that came up into his throat, from a gash in the neck, that another portion of the broken barrel of the gun had given him, nearly choked him, and he could only make the odd noise that Captain Gay had heard before, and which resembled someone in the agony of drowning.

Another minute, and over went the body of Mr. South to the bottom of the old stone quarry. Then Captain Gay approached Mr. Maloney, who, strange to say, had risen to his feet, and appeared to be in a perfect state of convalescence.

"Well, my good friend?"

"Bedad, sir, an' it is well, is it not any way?"

"It is indeed."

"Yes, Captain. It's a heretic, too, that he was any way?"

"He was."

"And a Saxon, too, sir!"

"A Saxon, too."

"Oh, then, Captain, it's yourself that will always do a good turn to the Maloneys for this same?"

"I will, indeed. I am one, Mr. Maloney, who is ever of opinion that one good turn deserves another. Can you see anything of our late friend down the quarry?"

"Bedad, sir, and it would be a hard thing to see anything of him all the way down there, sir; but it's himself that won't trouble anyone in this world again."

CHAPTER XXXIX.

CAPTAIN GAY MAKES A GREAT CHANGE IN THE POSITION AND PROSPECTS OF GEORGE DRAYTON.

ONE thing was quite clear, and that was, that Mr. Maloney considered he had done rather a good deed, than otherwise, in shooting the English lawyer.

After the pause of a few seconds, the Captain added, in a very bland tone of voice, to Mr. Maloney:

"My eyes may possibly deceive me, old friend; but it seems to me really as if I saw at the bottom of the old quarry, a something like a spark of light."

"The saints be good to us, sir! What can that be?"

"I cannot imagine, Maloney. Just try if you can see it. A little this way, if you please. There, just look as far over the edge as you can."

"Yes, sir."

Mr. Maloney, with bated breath, and his eyes preternaturally wide open with the hope of being able to see the spark of light that Captain Gay spoke of, leant over the edge of the quarry, as he replied:

"Bedad, no, sir. I can't say that I do see that same."

"Look again."

"I am looking again, sir."

"And you don't see it?"

"I can't say that I see anything in the world, but lots of nothing at all at all."

"Then go and look for it."

With one vigorous kick, the Captain sent Mr. Maloney headlong over the precipitous verge of the quarry, and down he went.

There was a smothered shriek—a wild exertion—a sickening sort of crash, as the wretched man struck against a ledge of rock, that in an instant scattered his brains to the night air, and then all was still as the grave.

Captain Gay shook for a moment.

"That is over," he said.

With hasty steps he turned away from the brink of the old quarry. More than once, though, he crouched low to the ground, and listened intently, for the echo of the dying cry of his own suborned assassin was in his ears, and again and again he thought he heard it.

Imagination was making a coward, after all, of the Captain.

"Pho!" he said, as he reached the regular bit of roadway that led direct to Lorton Castle. "Pho! I am a fool. The fellow is well rid of. He would have been a pest to me about this night's work, if he had lived."

Captain Gay dashed the heavy drops of perspiration from his brow as he spoke, and strode on.

But once more he paused to listen, for some sound came upon the night air. It was the cry of some bird disturbed from its nest; but it seemed to the fancy of the Captain as if it shaped itself into the cry of—

"Murder!—murder!"

The cheek of the ruffian blanched as he heard it, and he was compelled to lean for a few minutes against the trunk of a tree for support.

"What is the meaning of all this?" he said. "Am I getting old, or are my faculties falling from me? Is that bugbear, that they call conscience, really a thing that I have yet to find a reality? Pho! no—I am myself again. I laugh at everything that others call sacred. I pursue my own course, and I defy——"

What Captain Gay was going to say he defied, Heaven only knows, for he did not utter the words; but, at a quickened pace, he hurried on towards the castle.

Such a double murder as that which had been committed on that night could hardly have escaped the most searching judicial investigation in England; but in Ireland, when it was once done, why, there was an end of it.

As for the English lawyer, of course there would be no sort of inquiry about him at all, for nobody felt in the least degree interested in him; and as regarded Mr. Maloney, why, after a few days he, too, would be forgotten.

Captain Gay, however, had now a game to

CAPTAIN GAY MAKES AN ASTOUNDING REVELATION TO GEORGE DRAYTON.

play that he had scarcely as yet well considered in his mind; but he did mature it, and that thoroughly, too, before the morning.

As he sat in his solitary room in the castle, with a couple of lights burning on the table before him, and a bottle of the old claret, for which the Irish nobility were so famous, on the table, he concocted a scheme that had its effect not only upon him in after life, but upon every one of the *dramatis personæ* of our tale.

That scheme was as follows:

It was quite clear that, by the death of the old Duke of Lorton, the titles and estates of both the dukedom and the marquisate were vested in the son of the Marquis of Dalewood —that son who could not be found, either by the love of the Ardent family, or the hate of Captain Gay.

Lady Bridget Lorton, the sister of the deceased Duke, was the only important relation living.

"Now," said Captain Gay to himself, "if I can persuade this young man, George Drayton, who has told me that there is a mystery about who he really is, to fancy he is the son of the Marquis of Dalewood, I can put him in possession of all the property, and of the titles of the family, and impose him, no doubt, upon Lady Bridget, and get him, as the price of all that, to pay some enormous sum of money, with which I can get safely away to the Continent before the bubble bursts."

This, then, was the precious plan of Captain Gay, and his only doubt for a little time was whether to take George Drayton into the plan confidentially, or to make him one of the dupes of it.

After some consideration, the Captain decided upon the latter course, for he had seen enough of the young man to doubt, at all events, whether he would lend himself to such a fraud, with the full knowledge that it was such.

Having possession of some papers of the Duke's, and being well acquainted with his handwriting, Captain Gay now set to work to forge a document, which he thought would silence all the scruples, and put an end to all the doubts of George Drayton.

That document, which the villain wrote in a capital imitation of the hand of the Duke, ran as follows :

"Lorton Castle.

"I feel that my health is gradually breaking up, and therefore I think I ought to put upon paper certain facts concerning my son, the Marquis of Dalewood, and his family, which have come to my ears.

"In the first place, I have found that he has a son, and that he had that son placed with a woman of the name of Drayton, to nurse, and that the boy goes by the name of George Drayton. If, then, I should die suddenly, and my son, the Marquis of Dalewood, should likewise die, this George Drayton, whenever he can be found, is the Duke of Lorton, without a doubt. His father has neglected him, I understand, owing to his separation from his wife. Well, that may be—at all events, I understand that the young man has been educated and provided for in some way. The only risk is that, not knowing who he is, he may form some low alliance, and so tarnish the coronet he will one day have to wear."

This document, when completed, Captain Gay carefully rubbed and creased, so as to give it the appearance of having been written for some time; and then, as the morning light was peeping in at the casement of the room in which he sat, he threw himself, dressed as he was, upon the bed, and fell asleep.

It was pure exhaustion that alone enabled that perturbed spirit to find repose.

*　　*　　*　　*　　*

Captain Gay was awakened early in the morning by a loud knocking at his chamber door. Springing to his feet, he called out, in a tone of alarm :

"Who is there?"

"Only me, sir," said one of the domestics of the castle. "The breakfast is ready, sir; and, as we couldn't make you hear, we were afraid you were ill, sir."

"No—no. I am coming."

"Yes, sir."

"Is Mr. Drayton—that is to say, is the young gentleman who came to the castle with me last night, downstairs yet?"

"Oh, yes, Captain, and waiting for you."

"Very good ; say I will be with him shortly.

The few minutes that it took the Captain to make his toilet, and to reflect upon the proceedings of the night before, by no means brought about any alteration in his views or feelings. He was still resolved to carry out the nefarious scheme he had set on foot.

"There can be neither difficulty nor danger," he said, "in the matter ; and while all this is going on, if the real young Duke should happen to come in my way, let him look out—that is all. I will soon dispose of him, for the sake of his mother and his father, both of whom I detested in life, and still detest, even in death."

Lorton Castle presented a strange and melancholy appearance on the descent of Captain Gay to the breakfast-table, which was laid in a hall capable of accommodating some forty or fifty people, so that to find only George Drayton there, of all who had thronged the place the day before, gave it a very vacant look.

There was quite an over-politeness of manner about Captain Gay as he returned the morning salutation of George Drayton.

"Things look but cold and dreary here now, sir," said the Captain ; "but death in a house makes a strange alteration."

"It does, indeed. But I cannot understand the cause of the disturbance last night."

"Nor I."

"Oh, I thought, perhaps, you would be able to tell me more about it."

"Not I, sir. There was a disturbance, and that is all I know about it."

"But is it usual the moment almost that a gentleman of the rank and distinction of the Duke of Lorton is dead, for the house to be deserted in this manner?"

"It is here, sir. In the first place, the Duke has died without a will, and, therefore, everybody knows that all goes to the heir-at-law ; and so, as there is nothing to expect, why, people don't see the profit of staying."

"That is very heartless, indeed."

"It is. Well, there is another reason for the sudden departure, too, of many others."

"What may that be, sir? Superstition?"

"Oh, dear, no. Robbery."

"Robbery, say you?"

"In good truth, I am sorry to say I do. The fact is, that many who have left the castle with precipitation, have left it in company with every little portable article of value they could carry with them, in the hope that the heir, when he does appear, not knowing what there was here, will not miss what has been stolen, and then they will come back again to try and live upon him."

"This is atrocious!"

"It is atrocious ; but it is the way of the world, sir, not merely in Ireland, but everywhere else. When did you find human nature otherwise, I should like to know?"

CHAPTER XL.

GEORGE DRAYTON IS AMAZED AT THE PROSPECT BEFORE HIM.

YOUNG Drayton did not like this cold and sterile philosophy of Captain Gay, and he was silent for some little time; and then the Captain, who found that he had made rather an unfavourable impression, said:

"Come, sir, you must not believe that everybody is as bad as I say in my rather sweeping condemnation of society. Of course, all general rules have their exceptions."

"I hope so, indeed."

"You may be sure of that."

"Well, Captain, I think that I should like to make an exception of the man who, at the risk of his own life, saved me from death on this most rugged and fearful coast."

"Sir, I am obliged to you," said the Captain, with a look of gratification; for he thought the conversation was tending towards the very point he wished to bring it to.

"I speak no more than what I think," said George Drayton, "and I hope you do justice to my sincerity. There is one thing, though, that it distresses me to think of."

"What is that, sir?"

"It is the idea that the sudden death of the Duke of Lorton will affect your position and prospects, for you informed me that you were a sort of factotum to him, did you not?"

"I did; and you, if I did not dream, informed me that you were a dependant upon fortune, and that you were indebted for your education to some humane benefactor, and that you have always had a doubt about who you really are."

"I did so state it, and such is my position."

"Indeed?"

"You speak, sir, as if you doubted."

"I do doubt."

"Sir!"

"Nay, Mr. Drayton, do not be angry. I do not doubt you, or your story, in the least; but I do doubt if your position is at all dependent, or if you are in a position to wait upon fortune in any shape or way. I think I have a little surprise for you."

"For me, Captain?"

"Yes. The ways of Providence are inscrutable."

"So I have heard often; but I do not see how that phrase applies at all to me in my present position, sir."

"You shall see, though. Your name, you fancy, is George Drayton?"

"I do, and I do not."

"That is, you have been called by that name; but you have some doubt as to your title to it?"

"I have."

"And you were educated by some mysterious means, that you never knew anything about?"

"It is true."

"And you are married, you tell me, to the daughter of a poor, but honest man in London?"

"Yes; but it was in Devonshire where I was married."

"I know that; and you came to Ireland upon the doubt and the hope of finding some relation?"

"I did. The fact is, the person who passed as my mother, whether she was such or not, always hinted that I had a relation in Ireland, who was well able to befriend me, if he would do so."

"She was right."

"Right, sir? Do you know anything of me or of my family? Oh, Captain Gay, it will indeed be strange if, in addition to saving my life, you are able to put me in the way of clearing up the mystery of my birth."

"Strange, but true."

"True, sir? True is it? Heaven be thanked!"

Poor George Drayton was in such a state of excitement that his colour went and came like the sunshine of an April day, and he was quite incapable of paying any further attention to the well-spread breakfast-table before him.

"Let me implore you," he added, with emotion, "not to keep me in suspense; but to tell me, sir, all you know."

Captain Gay rose from the table.

"Follow me, Mr. Drayton," he said. "This apartment is by far too public a one for our further conversation. We are likely to be at any moment interrupted by the entrance of the servants, on any, or on no pretext. Follow me, if you please, and I will make a revelation to you which will fill your mind with wonder."

George Drayton sprang to his feet.

"I will follow you, Captain Gay, to the end of the world, if you only promise, when we get there, that you can, and that you will, put an end to the suspense which your words have created."

"I will do so."

"Lead on, then, sir."

Captain Gay smiled.

"Not to the end of the world, though, but only to a private room, where I can make sure of our not being interrupted in the most important conversation that you can ever have with mortal man, sir. This way, if you please."

The Captain made for the door; and George Drayton followed him, in that frame of mind that a man feels in when he cannot be sure that what is passing is real, or whether he is only walking in his sleep.

Captain Gay crossed the hall, and entered the old library of the castle. It was not often that either the Duke of Lorton, or his guests, ever troubled the worm-eaten and dusty volumes that had reposed for years upon the shelves of that room. The Captain closed the door; and, motioning George Drayton to a seat in a high-backed and richly-carved chair, he said:

"Pray be seated there, sir. It is your right."

"My right? You are mad!"

"No, your Grace, I am not, I hope."

"What?"

"Your Grace!"

"Sir, this is mockery. Why on earth do you call me by such a title? Why is it that, presuming upon the service you have done me, you now try to turn my brain? It is ungenerous, sir!"

"It would be, if what you say were correct; but when I call a man 'your Grace,' I have pretty well made up my mind that he is well entitled to the title before I give it to him."

"I dream! I dream!"

"No, you are wide awake. Listen to me?"

"I will; yes—yes!"

"Let every word that I say to you sink deeply into your mind, for they all concern your welfare in this world."

"Yes—yes!" gasped George Drayton, as he gazed in the face of Captain Gay, as though fascinated. "Yes, I will listen. Go on—oh, go on! Do not let me expire in the agony of suspense, sir?"

"You shall not."

George Drayton, with his hands clasped, and his head a little inclined forward, listened to the, to him, strange and wonderful words that came from the lips of the Captain.

"You must know then, Mr. Drayton—as it will be more convenient to call you for the present—that there has been much dissension in the family of the Duke of Lorton."

"Yes—yes."

"That dissension in a great degree arose from one little circumstance, which was, that in the opinion of the Duke, who has just died in this house, his son, the Marquis of Dalewood, disgraced himself by an alliance with a person in a very inferior station of life indeed."

"Go on—oh, go on!"

Captain Gay spoke with such excess of deliberation, that it almost sent poor George Drayton mad to listen to him.

"I will proceed as quickly as I can. That marriage, then, had the effect of completely estranging the Marquis and his father, the Duke, from each other, and they had not seen each other for nearly twenty years. They are now both of them dead."

"I understand."

"'Tis well. The Marquis soon parted from his wife, and that wife soon died; but, thinking that the anger of the grandfather—that is, the late Duke—was so great against the marriage, that he might do a mischief to her son, she preferred that he should be brought up in obscurity, not knowing who and what he was, than that he should have to trust to the tender mercies of his grandfather, or the neglect of his own father."

"It was weak on the mother's part."

"It was; and it was quite a mistake, for I know that the old Duke had no such sanguinary notions regarding his own grandson. If he had had such, it is not to me he would have looked for aid."

"No; you would at once have shrunk from such wickedness."

"Of course I would."

"I know it. Pray go on, sir."

"Well, they are both now dead, and the only heir to the large estate and the title of Lorton, is the son of the Marquis of Dalewood, who was brought up in obscurity somewhere, and kept by the fears of his mother in ignorance of his real rank and position in life."

George Drayton breathed with difficulty.

"That mystery, by, as I have said, the inscrutable decree of an all-gracious and a mysterious Providence, is about to be solved."

"Solved, say you?"

"I do."

"But you do not mean to say—that is, you —you—Oh, no, it is too wild a dream! It is impossible!"

"Stop! What would you say ought to be the reward of the man who, under these circumstances, could restore the heir to his title and estate?"

"Anything."

"Indeed! But what should be his reward if, in addition to all that, he actually snatched from death that heir? If, instead of leaving him to rot in a pauper's grave, he not only saved his life, but placed him in the proud position of a Duke, with an income of sixty thousand pounds per annum?"

"Anything—oh, anything!"

"What say you to one of those year's income? What say you, in round numbers, to one hundred thousand pounds?"

"I should say it was no more than he amply deserved, if, indeed, it could be fairly considered sufficient."

Captain Gay rose, and made a low bow.

"Your Grace, then, will learn from me that you are the lost heir of Lorton—that you are the long hidden son of the Marquis of Dalewood, and that I have it in my power, by documentary evidence, to prove as much."

"You—you can prove that?"

"Without the shadow of a doubt."

"Let me breathe a moment. No—no! It cannot be! Oh, what a change is this!—if it be true. No—no! Oh, no! I cannot think it—I cannot for one moment believe it. It is all a wild vision, and I am mad—mad!"

George Drayton clasped his hands over his face, and rested his head upon the table in front of the old chair upon which he sat.

Captain Gay let the tide of feeling have its way for a few moments, and then said, calmly:

"It cannot at all be wondered at that your Grace should, in truth, be most incredulous upon this matter. It does, in truth, appear most extraordinary."

George looked up.

"But when I tell you that I can prove every word I have said, to your satisfaction, and to the satisfaction of all who have any right to know the proof, I hope you will believe that I am not a madman, and raving."

"Then is this my house? Am I a Duke—Duke of Lorton? And is my wife—whom I wedded in poverty and doubt—a Duchess?—A Duchess! This is indeed a change!"

"Humph!" said Captain Gay. "Did you say wife?"

CHAPTER XLI.

GEORGE DRAYTON PROMISES TO DO ALL THAT
THE CAPTAIN REQUIRES OF HIM.

GEORGE DRAYTON looked in the face of the
Captain for a few moments in silence, and
then said:

"Yes, sir, I said wife."

"Then, my dear sir, don't say it again."

"Not say it again?"

"Decidedly not."

"And may I ask why not, seeing that I
have a wife?"

"Because you are the Duke of Lorton, and
it was George Drayton who married the
bouquet-maker's daughter, of Covent Garden,
in London. Bethink yourself, your Grace!
Would you like to introduce your old father-
in-law, the waterman-fireman, in his coat and
badge, to the dazzling circle of the Court of
St. James's?"

George sank into his chair with a groan.

"Pho—pho, your Grace!" added the Captain. "You were plain George Drayton,
trying to get a precarious living by the arts.
You can now patronize the arts to any extent
you like, by-the-by; but it won't do to make a
Duchess of a flower-girl."

"A flower-girl?"

"Yes. The discrepancy is too apparent,
and, besides, the marriage is all nonsense.
You did not know who and what you were."

"But I——"

"There, your Grace, I find you begin to see
this in its proper light. Only fancy your
mother-in-law! Ha—ha! Good old soul!
I daresay she is, in her way—supplying the
folks with cabbages and peas, while you, with
the Duchess, her daughter, occupy a foremost place in the rank and fashion of the
metropolis."

"It would be base——"

"It would—it would."

"To desert her who loved me, and who
consented to share my poverty with me!"

The Captain bit his lips.

"Hark you, sir," he said. "Here we two
are, man to man. Now, the proofs of who
and what you are, are wholly and solely in
my keeping. There they remain, if I find
that the person I can enrich and ennoble, has
such ignoble ideas."

"But it can't matter to you."

"Oh, but it does, though, matter to me
much. I have the interest of your family at
heart; and, besides, look you here, my lord,
you may rank with the highest and the
noblest now, and you will recollect that
George Drayton may be supposed to be lost
in the wreck of yesterday."

"Ah!"

"It is so; and your wife that is, will be a
widow. She is young, and, no doubt, not bad
looking—someone in her own class of life
will comfort her; and, forgetting you, she
will be much happier as the wife of some
grocer or cheesemonger, or something of that
sort, than she could ever be as a Duchess.
Bah! a Duchess is made, I rather think, of
different materials. You may, as Duke of
Lorton, lead to the altar some high born and
delicately-nurtured and beautiful girl, who
will shed a lustre upon your coronet."

"If I—thought——"

"What, my Lord Duke?"

"That she would forget me, and be happy."

"Be assured she will."

"I am tempted, surely. The papers you
speak of that will prove my rights—where
are they?"

"In my keeping, but——"

"But what? What do you mean by this
hesitation? Are they not mine? Why do
you keep them from me?"

"Hark you, my lord. When you have
written me your bond for the sum of one
hundred thousand pounds, and empowered
me to report and to prove the death of
George Drayton, I will assemble the whole of
the tenantry of the estate, and proclaim and
prove you Duke of Lorton."

"I consent—I consent. I will write the
bond now; and as for the death of George
Drayton—he is dead, and in his place lives
the Duke of Lorton."

"That is the way in which to view the
matter, my lord. I shall advise that you
proceed to London, then, soon, and be introduced to your aunt, the Lady Bridget. You
can then raise money at once on the estates,
if you do not find that the late Duke has left
enough to fairly start you in the fashionable
world. Oh, my lord, what a career is before
you!"

"There is, indeed! I gasp when I think of
it."

"Sixty-thousand pounds per annum."

"Yes—yes!"

"An ancient and honourable title."

"Oh, yes!"

"Immense estates in both countries. The
Marquisate of Dalewood becomes yours till
you have a son to take it."

"Yes, oh yes!"

"Why, at your age, too, and with your
appearance, which, you will forgive me for
saying, is truly distinguished, and at once
points you out as of noble blood, there is no
saying what career you may not aspire to."

"Yes," cried George Drayton. "I consent
to all your conditions. You have the power
to make me what I shall be, and I can give
a consent to your terms, surely."

"You can, your Grace. And now for the
bond!"

"Oh, yes. I promise to pay you one hundred thousand pounds on demand. I give you
a letter to the effect that I will execute any
legal claim you may have upon me. Will
that do?"

"Perfectly. And now about George Drayton?"

"Ha! ha! He is dead."

"He is. Just write a few lines, saying
that he is dead, and was buried upon your
estates?"

"I will. There, will that do?"

"Perfectly, your Grace; and now you are master of Lorton. I have the honour to place in your hands the will of your father, the Marquis, in which he leaves you all he had, and there is a memorandum written by the late Duke, which proves your identity."

George Drayton read with surprise both the documents that the wily Captain handed to him. It is needless to say that the will which the Captain produced, was not the real one he had robbed the Marquis's house of in London, but such a colourable copy of it as tallied with the forged letter of the Duke.

To George Drayton, though, the two papers seemed to be beyond all possibility of dispute, and he looked around him when he had read them, with the full conviction that he was indeed the Duke of Lorton.

How truly strange must have been the state of mind in which George Drayton was now. How different everything in the world must appear to him. Did any thoughts then obtrude themselves concerning his wife—the young and gentle being who had linked her fate to his, while his fate was one full of uncertainty? It is to be feared, that if now and then such a thought did occur to him, it was soon, too soon, forgotten amid the conflict of new feelings, and submerged in the glitter of his new condition.

Captain Gay was as good as his word.

By twelve o'clock on that day, everybody who lived at all within reasonable distance had been summoned to the castle. The tenantry thronged the great hall, and the neighbouring nobility and gentry were specially asked to be witnesses to a great family inauguration.

The Captain walked into the hall, followed by George Drayton, who, to the surprise of the assembled company, was in a full suit of the deepest mourning, with a diamond star glittering upon his breast.

"Ladies and gentlemen," said the Captain, "Allow me to introduce to you the Duke of Lorton."

Surprise was on every face, but the Captain did not give anyone time to say anything, but added—

"This is the son of the Marquis of Dalewood, who is no more, having come by his death by accident, in London, at a fire, only a short time ago. Here are documents to prove this gentleman's position, and the family solicitor has been written to, to come here and manage everything for him. He became most anxious that it should be known that the Lorton family had still a head, and so, he has authorized me to say this much."

"Yes," said George, stepping forward, "and I make all here welcome to Lorton Castle. The obsequies of my lately deceased grandfather will, of course, for some time, occupy my attention, as, in duty bound, they ought to do; but, afterwards, I hope to be able to prove that the race of Lorton has not degenerated."

There was a natural kind of grace of manner about George Drayton, that always pre-possessed strangers in his favour; and now, as no one was in a condition to dispute his claims, or at all inclined to do so, he was received with acclamation as the new Lord of Lorton.

"Captain Gay," he said, "you will be so good as to see that the best of everything the castle affords is at the service of the friends of my family. Let nothing be spared."

"Your Grace's orders shall be obeyed."

If anything had been wanting to set at rest all questions regarding George Drayton's right to the Dukedom and the estates, this liberal use of the cellars and the larder, would have at once put an end to it, and "all went merry as a marriage bell."

The presence of the deceased Duke in the house did not seem to have the slightest effect upon the depth of the potations that were that day drunk to the long life and happiness of the living one; and George Drayton could not but be a little shocked at the wild character of the orgies going on in the house where his grandfather, as he fully believed him to be, lay still unburied.

George mentioned as much to the Captain, who replied:

"Oh, your Grace, it is nothing. You are not in England, you know, where there is a kind of quiet decorum in society that you must not look for among my more impulsive countrymen."

"True. Yet if they had only waited till after the funeral, it would have looked better."

"Believe me, it is nothing. Let me strongly advise you not to interfere with them, your Grace."

"I certainly will not. That would be very ungenerous of me, after I had myself asked them here."

"It would, indeed."

"But there is one thing, Captain Gay, that I want to know."

"I am ready to give your Grace any information."

"How am I to get money?"

"Ready money, your Grace, of course, means? That is easily settled. I have written to the Dublin bankers to tell them how you are situated, and took upon myself to ask them to send one of their firm here, to speak to you about money."

"You have done well. I, of course, have money at the bankers?"

"I expect so."

In the course of the next day a gentlemanly-looking man arrived at Lorton Castle, and announced himself as chief clerk of the banking house of the late Duke.

Upon being introduced to George Drayton, this gentleman said:

"Your Grace, perhaps, is not aware that we have standing to the credit of your noble grandfather the sum of five hundred thousand pounds?"

George nearly gasped for breath at this; but he managed to look calm, and merely bowed.

"But," added the cashier, "I am afraid we cannot put your Grace into possession of that sum till certain legal forms confirming your Grace in your title and estates are gone through."

This was a disappointment.

"What am I to do for money in the meantime?" said George.

"Oh, that is easily managed."

"Is it so?"

"Yes, your Grace. I am empowered by the firm to lend your Grace to the extent of one hundred thousand pounds upon your note-of-hand, at a legal rate of interest, for we have no doubt of your Grace's true position."

"That will do perfectly well," said George Drayton.

The transaction was quickly concluded, and in another half-hour the poor, the penniless, the struggling George Drayton, had in his pocket five thousand pounds in bank-notes to begin with.

Captain Gay joined him with a smile.

"All is well, my lord, with the banker, is it not?"

"Oh, yes, perfectly well. Do you want any money?"

"Why, a thousand pounds would not be amiss. There are some little things to settle."

"Don't mention it. There is a thousand-pound note, my good friend."

CHAPTER XLII.

THE NEW DUKE ARRIVES IN LONDON IN GREAT STATE.

THE old Duke of Lorton was within one brief week interred in the tomb of his ancestors. George Drayton was chief mourner. The funeral was truly gorgeous; and no one could possibly have thought—to see the barbaric magnificence of the old Castle of Lorton upon the occasion—that it was to herald its last master to the grave, that everyone thought proper to appear in such array.

As for George Drayton, he, in the affair, may be considered as a mere cipher. He placed himself entirely in the hands of the nefarious Captain Gay, and whatever that individual told him was right and proper, or usual to do under such circumstances, that George Drayton did.

To be sure, there may be found some excuses for this young man's conduct, under the peculiar circumstances in which he was placed, if we look at them with anything like an unprejudiced eye.

In the first place, his very intellect was intoxicated by his sudden and marvellous change of fortune. To find himself raised at once from a poor, and even nameless artist, to the height that he now occupied, was enough, indeed, to dazzle and to turn any brain.

Then, he could not be expected to have very much feeling in the way of regret for the old Duke.

What had his grandfather been to him?

George Drayton knew very well that all the nonsense that is tattled about relationship is nothing, and that it is to association alone that all those feelings are to be ascribed which people are fond of attributing to the natural, as they call it, ties of blood.

Hence, then, the utter indifference he felt towards his noble family; and the complete composure with which he attended the funeral of the old man—whom he firmly believed to have been his grandfather—had scarcely a parallel.

It was an immense relief to George Drayton when the funeral was over, and when he was able to leave the guests feasting by themselves in the old halls of Lorton, and retire to the peaceful shadows of the old library, to think a little by himself.

But there was a busy friend, who was not likely to leave him long alone.

That friend was his great guide and counsellor, Captain Gay.

George had not been a quarter of an hour in the library alone, when Captain Gay entered it.

"Your Grace is fatigued," he said, "I fear."

"I am indeed, Gay."

"No wonder. Your Grace's feelings have been tried to-day. I have to congratulate your Grace upon the great presence of mind and calmness with which you got through the funeral."

"Don't give me more credit than I deserve, Gay."

"Nay; but it is rather one of the characteristics of the Lorton family that they have the art of concealing their feelings."

"Perhaps one of their characteristics is rather that they don't feel," said George; "for, to tell the truth, it cost me no effort to be quite cool and calm at the funeral of my grandfather, whom I really never knew. If I had exhibited any feeling upon the occasion, I assure you, Gay, that that would have been the acting, and not the absence of it."

Scarcely a perceptible smile lit up the face of Captain Gay, as he replied:

"Well—well, be it as it may, your Grace, I can assure you that your guests think highly of you for it, and call you one of the real old stock of the Lortons, in consequence."

"Ah! my guests are very kind; but, tell me, Captain, how is it possible that they can drink in the awful way that they do, and are doing?"

"Drink, your Grace, did you say?"

"Yes; they drink more at a sitting, each man of them, than would last me a month."

"Oh, they are used to it. They will sit there as long as they can possibly see a bottle of wine on the table."

"And then?"

"Why, then, when they are half-blind with drink, they will yet feel for the wine."

"But does it not kill them?"

"Oh, dear, no. The next stage of the business is to fall under the table, and there, in some way or another, they sleep off the excess;

and in the morning they don't seem much the worse for the overnight's debauch."

"It is surprising. A third part of what they take would make me seriously ill for I don't know how long."

"Ah, yes, no doubt; and so it would them."

"How do you mean?"

"Why, that a third part of what they take would make them ill, but the other two-thirds put them all to rights again. There are many things that, in a limited dose, do much mischief, but which, carried out, cease to be noxious."

"It is a strange thing; but it does not matter to me. I start for England to-morrow."

"As your Grace pleases."

"You will go with me, Gay?"

"Of course, your Grace. As your personal attendant."

"Attendant? Oh, no! you will go as my friend."

"Yes, your Grace, as your friend and attendant. I have thought that part of the affair over, and I have come to the conclusion, for many reasons, that my best way of being of continued service to you, is to appear as your valet. By that means, nobody will be jealous of me, or question my right to be about you. By that means, too, I shall hear and see much more of what is passing, than as if I made an appearance in a higher capacity."

"You are a strange fellow."

"I am, your Grace; but I beg that you will, in this little matter, allow me to please myself."

"Oh, of course."

"Then that is settled."

"There is another thing, too, Gay, that I want settled," said the Duke (for we may as well, as everybody calls George Drayton the Duke, now call him such, likewise). "There is one thing else that I want some attention paid to."

"What is it, your Grace?"

"My wife."

"Humph! No doubt somebody or another will pay some attention to her without your Grace troubling yourself about her."

"You misunderstand me. She is poor. Her friends are poor. I am rich: and if it be a settled thing that I must, now that I am a Duke, forget that she is my wife, I should yet like that she shared, to some extent, my good fortune."

"It is a good thought. Shall I send her some money?"

"Oh, yes—yes."

"How much?"

"A thousand pounds."

Captain Gay shook his head.

"Excuse me, your Grace, but that would be very imprudent. It would drive the Ardent family quite mad, I assure you, such a sum! and very likely they would become so completely public by their extravagances, that you would be in continual fear of them.

Let me manage this little affair for you. I will take care to raise them above all want, and, indeed, to let them have enough, from time to time, to give them every comfort in life. Pray leave it all to me."

"Be it so. You can let me know how you arrange it."

"Certainly, my lord."

"That, then, is off my mind," said George, with a deep sigh, that showed it was anything but off his mind. "Get everything ready for my going to-morrow to England. I can't bear this place. It is in London where you tell me I have a handsome house, that I must occupy."

"Yes, my lord, there is your father, the late Marquis's, mansion close to Montagu House, in the most fashionable part of London, waiting for your reception. To be sure, it was but a gloomy-looking place when last I saw it, and it will want expended upon it some twenty or thirty thousand pounds, to make it what it ought to be for you; but that can be done."

"Oh, yes, of course."

How strangely indifferent George Drayton was to the now comparatively trifling expenditure of twenty or thirty thousand pounds! To be sure, the sound of such sums of money hardly brought with them a real appreciation of their amount; but it was curious to hear one talk in such a way who had never in all his life held fifty gold pieces in his hand to call his own.

But such is the world.

The following morning all was bustle and excitement at the old Castle of Lorton. The family carriage, with four good horses, stood at the gate to take the Duke to Bantry, where a ship would be in waiting to carry him to England. Much of the old plate, and all the jewels that could be collected, were packed up to take to London; and Captain Gay was in his glory.

Strange to say, though, that since his elevation to the peerage, and since he had become so rich, George Drayton had gone down in his looks. He seemed thinner, paler, and decidedly much older looking than before.

Had he already begun to find out that a coronet was not the easiest thing to wear, and that riches did not cause happiness? Probably he had.

Poor Duke!

Well, he left the castle of his ancestors, as he called it, and as he really thought it, for in the midst of all his follies and all his vices, if we may use so harsh a term to some of his acts, let it always be remembered that George Drayton really and truly did think himself the Duke of Lorton, and not that he was the victim of the villain Gay, who, for his own purely selfish purposes had set up such a puppet as George was.

Before starting for London, however, Captain Gay had written the following letter to the Ardent family in London. It will best explain itself:

"Galway, Ireland.
"Barony of Kilbush.

"MADAM,—I am directed to write to you by one, concerning whose welfare, no doubt, you are anxious. Some weeks or so ago, a large ship was wrecked on this coast, and every soul on board perished; but some few lived an hour or two after being cast ashore.

"Among the few who so lived, there was a young man, named George Drayton, and before he died, he placed in my hands the sum of fifty pounds, which he requested might be sent to you for the use of his wife, who he stated was your daughter. He then breathed his last. I inclose you a draft on a London banker for the fifty pounds, and a certificate of the young man's death and burial here in the barony.

"I am, madam, with sincere condolence for the loss you sustain in the death of your son-in-law,   "JONATHAN BURKE,
"Magistrate of the county.
"To Mrs. Ardent, Covent Garden, London."

This letter, Captain Gay thought, would just do for the Ardents, and settle the question with them of the death of George Drayton. There was a magistrate of the county, of the name of Burke, so if they ever went so far as to make that inquiry, they would, probably, be quite satisfied about the correctness of the statement.

The manner of the wreck of the ship, too, could easily be authenticated; so that, upon the whole, Captain Gay really considered that he had very cleverly severed George Drayton from any connection with the Ardent family in Covent Garden.

CHAPTER XLIII.

RETURNS TO THE ARDENT FAMILY AND THEIR SITUATION AND PROSPECTS.

THE cleverest and deepest laid scheme will, at times, miscarry, and by the simplest possible means, too; so we shall see how the villainy of Captain Gay in the end recoiled upon himself.

Let the reader now recall how the Ardent family were left, which will be quickly done by a reference to the point at which we left the honest and amicable people.

Jane and the tailor, Peter Bolt, it will be found, are on very good terms indeed, and the tailor's suit prospers exceedingly; and, perhaps, all the more so that Mrs. Ardent was employing him to wait for her money in the lottery.

Alas! that money was coming from the little secret receptacle in the floor of the kitchen, where old Jacob Ardent had hidden the late Marquis of Dalewood's gold.

Well, it was very wrong, to be sure, of poor Mrs. Ardent to interfere with that gold; for, after all, she knew it was not hers; but then it was very wrong, or, at all events, very foolish, if not very wrong, of old Ardent not

to trust her with the secret of the possession of it, for this to her could have been done.

Mrs. Ardent was like Cæsar's wife—very good indeed when she was trusted.

Millicent, too, was at home, and waiting hopefully for the return of her dear husband, George Drayton, for whom she had the most unbounded admiration, and in whom she had the most unbounded confidence, as the little conversation she had had concerning him with her friends will sufficiently testify.

Alas, poor Millicent!

Such, then, was the state of affairs at the bouquet-makers in Covent Garden, on the very day when George Drayton, with a diamond star glittering upon his breast, was attending as chief mourner at the obsequies of the great Duke of Lorton.

Corporal Budd was rather in an awkward position now, and if there was an unhappy man in London, it was certainly that gallant and rather extensive individual.

It will be remembered that one, and perhaps, after all, the principal reason why Jane had refused to dignify his military existence by becoming Mrs. Corporal Budd, had been that before Millicent went to Devonshire, the Corporal had professed the most unbounded admiration for her charms.

The ladies admire constancy in a lover more than anything else; and so it was that Jane, when she found the Corporal transfer his attentions to her—had no faith in him.

But there must, after all, be something in first love, notwithstanding all that has been written and said to the contrary; for, to let the reader into a secret, the moment the Corporal saw Millicent again, all his old affection returned for her in tenfold force.

Poor Corporal! Yes, he loved—he adored Millicent; but she was now another's, and to look or speak as though he loved her at all was now an insult. What could he do but pass the remainder of his days in bitterness and anguish, envying the man who possessed the happiness of calling Millicent his own?

This, then, was the exact position of the Ardent family, and their immediate connections, at the period when George Drayton was undergoing such important alterations in his condition.

We will now, with the reader's permission, step into Mrs. Ardent's flower shop at half-past ten o'clock on a Tuesday morning, some three weeks after George Drayton had first set his foot upon the Irish coast.

The sun was shining, and the bouquets looked charming. Old Ardent had gone to his avocation by the river, Jane was away on some message in another part of the market, and Millicent was in the kitchen, superintending some culinary affairs for the dinner of the family.

There was upon the face of Mrs. Ardent a look of fidget and of anxiety, and every footfall that came near the door caused her to start up with a jerk, that set her heart beating for five minutes afterwards.

She was waiting for Peter Bolt, who was

to bring her news of the lottery, that had been drawn the evening before.

"Oh, dear—oh, dear!" she said. "I do, indeed, begin to feel that it's hardly worth the thirty thousand pound prize to be in such a fidget as I am now. I wish—I——. Oh—oh! don't!"

"Why, mother," said Millicent, "what is the matter? I only laid my hand upon your arm."

"Then, don't do it again. You did give me such a turn. Oh, how cruel of you!"

"Cruel, mother?"

"Yes, you know it was. You know how nervous I am."

"Of late I do think you are; but what did you say, dear mother, about the thirty thousand pound prize?"

"Nothing at all."

"I thought you did."

"Then you thought wrong."

"Nay, dear mother, do not be cross with me, or scold me to-day, I beg of you, for I am unusually happy. I have had pleasant dreams all the night long; and, do you know, I seem to have a sort of presentiment——"

"A presentiment?"

"Yes, mother."

"Oh, of what? The—a—the—a—prize?"

"What prize?"

"Nothing—nothing. Oh, how foolish I am. But you said you had a presentiment. What is it about, Milly?"

"About dear, dear George."

"Oh, indeed!"

"Yes. I seem as if I were quite certain we should hear some news of him to-day. My heart is so light, and I am in such good spirits. There, now, do you not think, mother, that that is a presentiment worth the knowing?"

"Oh, yes—yes, I daresay it is."

"You only daresay? Oh, how coldly you speak, mother. But you do not know him as I know him. He is so handsome, and so good, and so kind, and so——"

"There—there, I don't want to hear any more about him. You will never have done, Milly, about your George's handsomes and kindnesses. Upon my word, you are quite a worry."

With tears starting to her eyes, poor Millicent went into the kitchen again, and sat down to think alone of George Drayton.

"I'm a wretch," said Mrs. Ardent, when she was alone, "I'm a wretch, and I know it! I am unkind to everybody, and all on account of the lottery. Oh, if I should lose again this time, what a thing it will be! Let me see. I have taken half the money that Jacob hid in the kitchen, and I shall have to take the other half for the purpose of winning it back again; and as soon as I do, what a relief to me it will be to replace it! Oh, yes, that will be joy, and then I will never try the lottery again while I live, for I am so wretched, and so cross, and so——Oh, gracious, there is Peter Bolt!"

Peter popped his head in at the door of the shop.

"How do you do, missus?"

"Come in—oh, come in."

"Yes, mum, I'm coming. Ain't it a nice day?"

"No—that is, yes. Well?"

"Pretty well, thank you, mum."

"Oh, you fool!"

"Well, that's civil, at all events, Mrs. A. I know as I ain't a conjuror; but, for a person to cry out 'Oh, you fool!' is rather too bad."

"Silence!"

"Yes, mum. How is Janey?"

"You wretch! Answer me at once. Is it 4747?"

"Oh, the lottery?"

"Yes—yes! Tell me at once."

"A blank, mum, in course."

"A blank—in course?"

"Yes. Didn't I tell you so?"

Mrs. Ardent clasped her hands over her face, and rocked to and fro in silent anguish for some minutes, and then Peter Bolt's sympathy was fully and energetically awakened, and he said:

"Come—come, Mrs. A., don't you take on about that now. There's lots of people get blanks as well as you; and if you'd seen some of their looks, you'd say to yourself: 'I'll never, while I live, try the lottery again,' that you would. Now, you have lost a goodish bit of money."

"Oh, silence—silence!"

"Yes, mum. You have lost a goodish bit of money, as I was a-saying, and so, if I was you, mum——"

"If you say another word, I will kill you!"

"Oh, lor!"

"Yes, I will kill you! I know I have lost much money—I know that better than you can tell me; but I tell you, Peter, that win I must—I must win, and I shall, or I shall go mad!"

"Oh, gracious!"

"I shall lose more money, perhaps; but some day I must win. Peter, you must go, and, at any cost, no matter what, buy another ticket."

"Another, mum?"

"Yes, another. Hush! It is for my life's sake now. There is the money. Go at once, Peter. I must win—I tell you I will win! I shall go quite mad if I do not soon. Oh, Peter, pity me!"

"I does, mum."

"Oh, you villain! Hold your tongue, do!"

"Lor, Mrs. A., and mother-in-law that is to be, didn't you go for to ask me to pity you?"

"No, booby!"

"Oh, I begs your pardon, I'm sure. I thought——"

"You have no business to think at all; so don't aggravate me by doing it."

"Oh, lor!"

"There—there! take these five guineas, and get another ticket as soon as you can, and mind this time that the numbers are 3838. Don't forget them, on your life!"

"I won't mum."

"Well, then, what are they?"

"Oh, I know—9687."

"Oh, you stupid dolt! But I ought not to trust to your memory, and yet, who knows—oh, who knows——?"

"What, Mrs. A.?"

"Why, there may be luck in it."

"Luck in what, mum?"

"In your accidental pronunciation of those numbers. Yes, there is luck in them. I see that they will win the great prize. I make no doubt in the world but that I shall dream of those very numbers to-night. I won't have 3838; but I will have what you have said, Peter."

"I would, mum, if you have any at all; or I would have any other that came uppermost, for they will be all the same."

"How do you mean by all the same?"

"Blanks, mum."

"Oh—oh! you take my breath away! I tell you, Peter Bolt, that if I don't win this time, I am a dead woman, and you will never marry Jane."

"Never marry Jane?"

"Never—never! while Covent Garden is a market."

"But I don't want to win Jane, mum, in a lottery—that I don't. Why, scissors and thimbles, what has your losing in the lottery to do with my marrying Jane, I should like to know?"

"It's on the cards."

"On the what?"

"On the cards. I understand how to tell fortunes by the cards, and I can assure you, Peter, that what I say is just what fate disposes. So now be off, and mind you watch the drawing all next week; and if the prize should come to my number—oh! then, fly here in a moment!"

"I will," said Peter, as he left the shop; "but she is as mad as possible."

CHAPTER XLIV.

DREADFUL NEWS REACHES POOR MILLICENT.

"YES," said Mrs. Ardent, as she sat alone in her shop, after Peter Bolt had left her, "yes, I shall and I must win this time in the lottery. I feel a sort of presentiment that I shall; and, indeed, if there is any truth in the cards—which, of course, there is, or how would so many people believe in them?—there is a great sum of money coming, and a letter."

Poor Mrs. Ardent! What a world of unhappiness she had brought upon herself by thus tampering with her own conscience in the matter of the hidden money in the kitchen!

Well she knew the inflexible character of old Jacob Ardent, and that, let her say what she would, he would look upon the abstraction of the gold as a robbery.

Then she dreaded what a maze of difficulty it might lead her into if he should find out

the gold was gone, and happen to suspect some innocent person of stealing it. What should she do then? Would she be compelled to be her own accuser? Yes, for after all she could not see an innocent person suffer. That would, in truth, be very terrible to her.

No prize in any lottery could possibly have compensated Mrs. Ardent for the pangs she suffered in her own mind.

Millicent all this time sat in the kitchen; and although she had certainly more than once heard her mother's voice raised to rather a high pitch, she knew that Peter Bolt was there, and she thought that, as usual, her mother was exercising the sort of authority over him, which the good lady was so fond of exercising over anybody and everybody who would permit her.

This was one of the little social faults of Mrs. Ardent—a slight love of domineering over people who could not help themselves; but, if they let her do so, they were sure in the end to reap some solid advantage from her good feelings towards them, for she was particularly fond always of anyone she was in the habit of scolding.

But a change was about to take place in the position of affairs at the Ardents' home.

The postman came with a hurried step to the door of the shop.

"Mrs. Ardent," he said, "one-and-eight-pence, if you please, mum."

"Lor a mercy! One-and-eight-pence, did you say?"

"Yes, ma'am, a letter from Ireland."

"Ireland?"

"Yes, Mrs. Ardent, and very nearly a double one, too. Be quick, please, ma'am."

"Yes, yes—there. Oh, gracious! a black seal! Yes—yes! It is—some death—some——"

"Mother," said Millicent, looking from the kitchen, through the door, and holding it a little way open as she spoke, "was that the postman?"

Mrs. Ardent hid the letter beneath her apron, as she replied:

"No—that is, yes. He wanted a direction, that is all, my dear, that is all."

"Ah, what a disappointment! Do you know, whenever I hear the postman, I say to myself, 'Ah, there will be some news of my dear George.'"

"Yes—yes, I—say so, too."

"Do you, indeed, mother?"

"Of course I do, my dear. But, there, go away now—go away do, for I am busy, I tell you. Go away, my dear, and don't trouble me."

"Yes, mother."

Millicent went into the kitchen again, and, closing the door, sat down to some work, and after a little time her mother heard her singing in a calm and serene tone of voice.

Slowly poor Mrs. Ardent took the letter with the huge black seal from under her apron, and looked at it. Her hands trembled as she did so.

"She expects news of George Drayton," gasped Mrs. Ardent, "and my heart tells me that here is news—black news. Alas—alas! if he is no more, it will kill her—yes, it will kill my poor child! Oh, Heaven! omit such a blow!"

The market was unusually dull and silent just then; there was not a footfall near the house of the Ardents. A death-like silence seemed to fall upon the very air. It appeared as if all nature paused while the agitated woman opened that letter.

She did open it.

Something fell to the floor from it. There were two papers. One she picked up, and she saw upon it the words:

"Pay to the bearer the sum of fifty pounds on sight of this."

The note was signed by a Dublin banker, and it was addressed to one in London.

The other paper contained the following words:

"This is to certify the death and burial of George Drayton, in the barony of Kilbush, on the coast of Galway, this 21st day of February."

Mrs. Ardent uttered a cry of despair.

The kitchen-door was opened suddenly.

"What was that?" said Millicent.

"Nothing. Oh, nothing—nothing!"

"But I thought I heard a cry."

"No—no! Go away—oh, go away."

"But mother—dear mother—you are ill—you look agitated. There are tears in your eyes. Oh, mother, what is it?"

"Nothing—nothing! Leave me—oh, leave me! If you love me, leave me."

Millicent shuddered at the vehemence of her mother, and retreated to the kitchen again, where she sat silent and terrified.

Mrs. Ardent, then, with trembling fingers, lifted the letter, and read it word for word as we have presented it to the reader in the handwriting of the villainous Captain Gay. Yes, there it was—the base account, in its cold, official sort of form, of the death of poor George Drayton, and of the sending the fifty pounds, which was stated to be his property.

The good woman sat like a statue, with the papers crumpled up in her hands, and her eyes fixed on vacancy.

Then a burst of tears came to her relief, and she sobbed:

"My child—my child! My Millicent!"

There was a slight noise from the kitchen.

In a moment, as if by magic, the sobs of Mrs. Ardent ceased, and she stifled her tears. She thrust the letter and its inclosure into a drawer, which she closed and locked.

"It is my duty to tell her," she said. "I must tell her all. It is my place to stand between my child and the despair of her soul. I am her mother, and I alone can speak to her at such a time as this. Yes, I must comfort her—I must bid her rely on heaven. I cannot meet her without telling her. She must know all now, and at once. Oh, Millicent

—Millicent—my child—my child—widowed so soon! Heaven help her!"

Jane came in at this moment.

"Oh, Aunt, do you know there are such great doings in the street up by Montague House, and they say——"

"Hush! Oh, don't—don't!"

"Don't what, Aunt?"

"Don't speak to me, Jane, but without asking any questions, now, do as I bid you."

"Yes, dear aunt, I will—I will, but——"

"Ask nothing. All I require of you is to mind the shop here, and to take care, until I call to you, that no one interrupts me and Millicent in the kitchen, for I have something to say to her."

"Yes, dear aunt, I will obey you; but I am sure that it is something dreadful you have to say to her."

"It is."

The young girl's heart was melted at once; and, sitting down upon a little low fruit-basket, she began to cry.

"My dear, don't cry," said Mrs. Ardent. "I will tell you what it is, Jane."

"I know—I know."

"You know, do you say?"

"Yes, Aunt; there is but one thing that could make you look as you now look—there is but one thing that you can possibly wish to tell poor Millicent alone."

"And—and that is—is——"

"That her husband is dead."

"Jane, you are right. George Drayton is no more. There, my dear girl, read this while I go to her. Hush!"

Millicent was singing again:

"How happy, how happy the young wife will be,
   As she smiles on her husband—a babe on her
      knee;
The sunshine shall gleam through the sweet
      cottage door,
And——"

"Millicent!" cried Mrs. Ardent, as she went into the kitchen, "do not break my heart—oh, do not! Oh, no—no—no!"

"Oh, Heaven! What is the matter, mother?"

"Nothing. I—only—that is, I feel a little flurried, and so, hearing you sing, you see, I thought that—that——Shut the door."

"Yes, mother."

"Bolt it."

"Yes—yes."

"We are alone?"

"Oh, yes; but why all this secrecy? What is it? Something has happened. Oh, mother—mother, tell me!"

"I—will—try."

"Yes—yes, dear mother. Come, now, do not weep."

"You are very happy?"

"Yes, so happy! If dear George were but here, I should, I do think, be the happiest girl in all the world; and to-day, too, I have felt so very light and cheerful, and so full of spirits; I feel as if I could sing and laugh——"

"Sing and laugh?"

OLD ARDENT SETTLES SCORES WITH PETER BOLT.

"Yes, mother, and why not? for, after all, you know, if George should be disappointed in getting aid from his relatives, why, he and I will toil and work for each other, and be happy, for all that."

"Yes—I—yes."

"Come, then, dear mother, tell me what distresses you?"

"I will. Do you know, I thought that it was possible—that is to say, I sat in the shop, and a letter—I thought a letter with, you see, a black seal—one-and-eightpence, you see—nearly a double letter—you see, I at first thought that—that——"

"Mother—mother! what is it?"

"Nothing—nothing! Millicent—Millicent —nothing, I tell you!"

"A dream, perhaps?"

"Yes, only a dream."

"Ha—ha—ha! Oh, yes. A dream, only a dream! You are telling me a dream, mother, that is all?"

Mrs. Ardent was nearly choked.

"That—is—all," she gasped. "A—a dreadful dream. My child—my child—I—no—no! It is sinful!"

"What is sinful?"

"To deceive you. It is real."

"Real! No—no—no! George—George! It is about George! Mother—mother!"

"My child—my own Milly! Do not—do not look upon me thus, my Milly! Help! No—no! God is with us! To my heart, my darling—to your mother's heart! Why do you not speak? Do not look at me this way! Speak—oh, speak to me! My child—my child! why do you not weep? for he is dead!"

Millicent fell like a corpse to the floor.

Mrs. Ardent ran out into the shop, screaming and wringing her hands, and crying out:

"Dead—dead—dead!"

CHAPTER XLV.

SHOWS HOW STRANGE IT IS THAT NATURAL AFFECTION SHOULD DIE.

Her young, fond heart is nearly broken.

Poor Millicent lies on a couch in the kitchen of the bouquet-maker's house. Her mother is bathing her temples with vinegar. The old man is upon his knees by her side, and poor Jane is weeping in a corner of the room.

Peter Bolt is minding the shop—that is to say, he is supposed to be minding it, for in the agitation of his spirits, poor fellow, he is selling anybody anything for the most ridiculous prices imaginable.

"Millicent, my child," sobs Mrs. Ardent. "Can you speak to me now? Oh, try if you can speak to me."

"Mother!"

"Thank God for that! Did you hear her, Jacob? She did speak to me."

"Yes—yes," said the old man. "Oh! but this is, indeed, a heavy blow for my poor girl. Far—far away, too. Alas—alas!"

"Mother," said Millicent, again making an effort to rise, "do you think I shall die soon?"

"Oh, no—no! Will you desert me, my darling? God has taken your husband from you; but it is for His good purposes. Why should you wish to leave me all alone?"

"I am very unkind."

"No—no, not that! But time will soften this blow."

"Will it?"

"Oh, yes—yes! Believe that it will."

"The letter—the letter, mother! There was a letter about this. Let me see it. It is my letter."

"Patience — patience, dear Milly! To-morrow, when you are better and stronger, dear, you shall have it."

"No—no! Now—now! Oh, give it to me, or I shall go quite mad. The letter!"

Terrified by the wild and frantic manner of her daughter, Mrs. Ardent presented the letter to her, and Millicent held it in both her hands, and read it through and through.

"Dead—dead!" she gasped; "and such a death, too!"

"My dear child," said her father, who had but a few moments before entered the shop, "death is but death, come it when it will, and

how it will. We must all die. Be comforted."

"Comforted? With what? How? Who says comfort and I will ever know each other again? No—no! I wish I were dead, too, for then I should see him again! Mother?"

"Yes, dear?"

"Don't you think I shall see him again?"

"Assuredly, my darling."

"There is great hope in that. Father, forgive me; there is comfort, after all, in that. I am better now. Mother, I must wear black—for ever black; my soul is in weeds. Heaven help me! What is that? What noise is that?"

A faint "Hurrah!" came upon the air.

"Something in the streets, dear. Heed it not."

Millicent rose from the couch, and stood in an attitude of listening.

"What is it—what is it? How strange!"

"What is strange, dear?"

"I don't know; but it seems as if those sounds in the street had each of them an echo in my heart. There, again. Do you hear them now? Who are they cheering in such a manner? Who is it? Is my George dead? Who says he is dead—who says it?"

"Alas—alas!" said old Ardent, "her poor wits are gone!"

Mrs. Ardent sank to the floor, and wept bitterly; for she, too, thought that grief had turned Millicent's brain.

"Hurrah, hurrah, hurrah!" came the sound of cheers from many throats in the street.

Millicent still stood in an attitude of listening. How dreadful she looked!

"There, again!" she said, wildly—"there, again!"

"Oh, my dear—dear child, do not listen to those sounds; they are nothing."

"Oh, but mother, I don't know that. Did you say George was dead?"

"Yes—yes—and the letter—you have the letter."

"'Tis false!"

She crumpled up the letter in her hand, and flung it to the floor with a look of indignation.

"'Tis false! I'll not believe it. Heaven in its goodness would not take him from me. Hush! Ah! The cheers again. Why do they come to me as if addressed to my broken heart in such a manner? What is it?"

Peter put his head in at the door of the kitchen.

"I say, Mrs. A., don't be alarmed. It's only something coming through the market."

"What is it?" said Millicent.

"Oh—oh!"

"What is it, I say?"

"Answer her, Peter," said Jane.

"Yes. It's a great lord—a Duke, they say, who has been ever so long away, or lost, or something of the sort, and he is coming through the market, you see, on his road home, with six cream-coloured horses and his valet is throwing money to the crowd, you see, and so, in course, they cry out: 'Hurrah!'"

"A great lord?"

"Yes, Mrs. Drayton."

"Oh, no—no! Don't call me that! And yet I am Mrs. Drayton—George is my husband."

"He used to were," said Peter, "afore he went dead."

"Silence!" said old Ardent; "don't say that, Peter. Do you not see what affliction is in this house? You must not speak of it so lightly as that, Peter."

"I won't."

"Hurrah—hurrah!" cried the mob at this moment. "Long life to the Duke! Hurrah! Clear the way! Clear a road there! Here's more money! Hurrah—hurrah!"

It was evident, from the sound of the voices, that the whole mob, with whoever it was escorting with such riotous and wild demonstration, was going by the door of old Ardent's house.

"This is very sad," said Mrs. Ardent. "We are but ill fitted for such disturbance now, Heaven knows! Close the door, Peter Bolt—close the door."

"Yes, mum."

"No—no!" cried Millicent. "Do not close the door. I am going to see what this is. I think I ought."

She placed her hand over her eyes for a moment, as if in deep thought, and then she said:

"Oh, Heaven! I hope I am not mad, indeed!"

"Alas—alas!" said old Ardent, in a low voice to his wife. "I fear that that is past praying for."

"I fear so, indeed. Shall we detain her, Jacob?"

"No. It is better to humour her. It is far better to let her do as she pleases; but we can go with her. Well, my dear Millicent, where is it you wish to go?"

"This way—this way."

With sudden energy, Millicent seized her bonnet that hung on the wall, and with it in her hand, she ran out of the kitchen, and through the shop to the door.

At the moment that she got there, the mob, which consisted of somewhere about three or four hundred people, raised another great shout, and she saw a magnificent carriage, drawn by six cream-coloured horses, coming slowly along. A number of market-carts at that moment got blocked up in some manner about the spot, and just opposite to the bouquet-maker's door the carriage came to a stop.

"Hurrah!" shouted the mob. "Long live his lordship."

"Move on there—move on!" cried several voices, to the owners of the carts.

They, to do them justice, made every possible exertion to get out of the way; but, just as they did so, the window of the carriage next to the bouquet-maker's shop was let down, and a gentleman in a powdered wig, and with a star upon his breast, and elegant lace ruffles at his wrists, looked out, and cried:

"This is insufferable! Cannot a nobleman's-carriage be permitted to take its way through the thoroughfares of London in peace? Drive on, there—drive on!"

The market-carts got out of the way; the six cream-coloured horses made a dash forward, and the carriage, with the elegant gentleman inside it, and the four footmen hanging on behind it, covered with gold lace, disappeared like a vision.

Poor Millicent uttered a shriek, and then, springing forward, she cried in a frantic voice:

"George—George Drayton! It is my George—my husband! 'Tis he!—oh, Heaven, 'tis he!"

She fell into the arms of Corporal Budd, who at that moment had pressed through the crowd, and just reached the door of the Ardents' house.

"What is all this about?" said the Corporal. "Millicent! Oh, what has happened to her?"

Mrs. Ardent was half frantic, and she could not speak; but Jane had presence of mind enough to beg of him to bring Millicent into the house, which the Corporal did in a moment, for to him the weight of Millicent was as nothing; and, besides, there was quite enough of his old affection for her remaining to make the carrying her anything but a task that he looked upon with disagreeable eyes.

The screams of the young woman, and the frantic cries she had uttered, had been too sudden and transient to have any effect upon the crowd that was following the carriage of the nobleman who had been so extremely liberal in his distribution of money on his route, so that in a few minutes the shop of the bouquet-maker, and its neighbourhood, was as quiet as before.

And George Drayton went home to his mansion close to Montague House.

Yes, it was no other than the new Duke of Lorton whose carriage had thus made its triumphant progress through London. It was the husband of Millicent who, with the powdered hair, and the star upon his breast, and the lace ruffles, and the elegant attire generally, had looked from the window of his state coach, and demanded to know why it was that a nobleman's carriage could not be permitted to go in peace on its way.

Did he know where he was? No. Did he hear the cry of his wife? No.

In the first place, George Drayton was very little, if at all, acquainted with London; and the worst fact was, that he did not know that his carriage was in Covent Garden market at all, at the time when such vociferous people surrounded it, and when it came to a stop so suddenly at, for him, so *malapropos* a place.

To be sure, at the moment that he drew up the window again, to shut out the noise of the people, he heard a scream; but that that scream came from the lips of his Millicent he had not the least notion.

And so, George Drayton, the Duke of Lorton, went to his house, as he called it, in some portions of which workmen of all descriptions still were busy refitting and redecorating it for the reception of so great and so wealthy a nobleman.

It may be supposed that the mind and imagination of George had become half crazy by this time with his new condition; but yet he was ill at ease, and it was only now in the society of Captain Gay, who furnished him with specious reasons for his neglect of his wife, that he could know a moment's peace.

The face of Millicent, as he last saw her when he took leave of her in Devonshire, haunted him. He could see the tears in her eyes, struggling with the joy of hearing him disclose how dear she was to him, and that nothing but death should ever separate them.

Nothing but death!

Well, he had connived at the villainy of Captain Gay, so that by this time she thought him dead. So he told himself. But little did he imagine that before he had been six hours in London, he was doomed to give her the most practical refutation of the allegation possible.

CHAPTER XLVI.

NEW PERSONAGE APPEARS UPON THE SCENE.

THE shock which the mind of poor Millicent had received, first by the news of the death of her husband; and, secondly, by seeing him in life, was too great for her nervous system, and she remained in a state of insensibility for so long that, in alarm, medical aid was called in.

In about six hours she was entirely recovered, but something like brain fever appeared too likely, and the medical men shook their heads at the state of their patient.

They did not know, though, the mysterious influence that the mind exercises, in some extraordinary cases, over the body. The conviction was so strong upon the memory of Millicent, that George Drayton was yet alive, that she only waited for the system generally to rally before she acted upon it.

To be sure, she lay a week ill—much too ill to move from her bed; but as soon as she recovered sufficiently to have a will of her own, she adopted a determination which, no doubt, had the effect ultimately of saving her life.

She declined taking any more medicines.

"No, mother," she said, "I am weak, and my mind has received a very severe shock, but I am recovering now, and nature will do more for me than art. I will wait with what patience I can."

Of course the medical men were exceedingly disgusted, and left her, as they said, to her fate, which was, that she got better, and gathered strength each passing hour.

And now that old Jacob Ardent saw his dear Millicent, as he thought, recovering, he felt that he had something to do which he would no longer delay doing.

On the evening, then, of the seventh day after the passing of the Duke in his splendid carriage past the door of his house, the old man sat in his kitchen, with a more than usually thoughtful look; and he was about to address something important to his wife, when a footstep in the shop announced the approach of someone.

"Dear me," said Mrs. Ardent, "I daresay now it is that Peter. I will go to him, Jacob. —Oh, if he brings news of the lottery!" added Mrs. Ardent to herself, as she bustled out of the kitchen, but took good care to close the door, so that her husband should not be enlightened upon the subject of the lottery affair.

Mrs. Ardent was mistaken, though. It was not Peter, but a slim, tall, delicate-looking young man, very pale and haggard-looking, and who spoke in a feeble, though very sweet voice, as he said:

"Madam, I have called to ask a favour of you."

"Oh, dear me, I can't," said Mrs. Ardent —for she assumed that this was a genteel beggar—"I can't, indeed. We have so many pulls."

"I fear you misunderstand me, madam."

"What is it, then?"

"It is merely that you would permit this slip of paper to be exhibited in the window of your shop. I hear that many of the nobility and gentry come here for bouquets, and so I thought they might see it."

"Dear me, what is it about?"

"Will you please to look at it, madam?"

"Yes, to be sure."

The youth handed to Mrs. Ardent a slip of paper, on which was written the following words:

"The writer of this would be happy to give lessons, upon the most moderate terms, in Latin and in French, or in mathematics, to any young gentleman in want of such instruction."

"You don't say so?" said Mrs. Ardent. "Why, dear me, you are very young!"

"I am, indeed."

"And you have got to get your living?"

"I have."

"But, of course, your friends look after you?"

"No—no! Alas! I have none."

"Poor boy! No friends, and you don't look strong, either. Well, I'll put the bill in the window, and, what is more, too, I will take good care to draw attention to it. Mind you call soon, and who knows what good luck may be in store for you?"

"Madam, I thank you with all my heart. I am, as you say, not strong, and I fear—ah! this faintness again!"

The youth staggered, and would have fallen had he not contrived to reach a chair just in time, into which he sank, saying as he did so:

"I faint—I die! Oh, starvation is, indeed, a terrible death!"

"Starvation!" cried Mrs. Ardent, with a

shriek. "Oh, gracious! you don't mean that? Starvation!"

"Yes—yes! I think it is now two days since I tasted food; but I do not beg. Oh, no—no! I can die."

"Indeed! But you won't, though. Jacob—Jane—Millicent! Hilloa! bread and cheese—no, meat—dear me—no, the cherry brandy! Come here, all of you! Run for something to eat! Quick here! He is starving to death!"

The outcries of Mrs. Ardent soon brought the whole family into the shop, and, upon her explaining the cause of the alarm, some wine was procured and given, with difficulty, to the fainting youth, who was carried into the kitchen, and tenderly attended to.

In the course of half-an-hour, by the judicious mode in which old Ardent gave him nourishment, he was wonderfully recovered, so that he looked quite a different being.

"Heaven will reward you for your kindness," he said. "I can go now. I will pay you when I can."

"Nonsense!" said old Ardent. "Do you want to insult people after they have been kind to you?"

"Oh, no—no! not for worlds."

"Then don't talk of paying again, if you please, young man. I only wish I could recollect where I have seen your face before."

"Have you seen me, sir?"

"I am certain of it."

The old man and the youth now took a long look at each other, and then they both shook their heads, as it was evident they could neither of them call to mind any circumstance which tended to let them know that they had met before.

"I may be wrong," said old Ardent; "and I suppose I am, but I seem as if your face were familiar to me; but it can't be, or, if it is, I must have seen you in the street—that's all."

"It may be so."

"And what is your name, young sir?"

The youth hesitated, and then said, in a low tone:

"Frank Western."

"Well, Mr. Frank Western, I am sorry to see you in such a sad plight. What do you mean to do?"

"I don't know, indeed."

"Can you go home alone?"

"Home? Alas! I—I have no home but the streets. Who will shelter me? I have no money, but I hope soon to earn some, and then, if it be ever so humble a home, it will be my own."

"To be sure it will, my good lad; but you are wrong in one thing, however."

"Am I, indeed?"

"Yes. You said you had no home, and I can prove that you have. You shall stay here till you can turn yourself about a little. God forbid that I should close my doors upon you. What do you say, wife? Can we not knock up a little bed for him in the old lumber-room upstairs, eh?"

"To be sure we can."

"Then it is as good as done, Mr. Frank; and as for the little that you will eat and drink, why, there are a good many of us sit down every day to our humble table, and it won't be missed."

Poor Frank burst into tears. He could not thank those who had been so kind to him, for when he tried to do so, the words seemed as if they would choke him.

"Now be quiet, will you," said old Ardent, "and don't say a word more about it. Come, now, let us to supper, wife, and then you and Jane, and Milly, for it will amuse her mind a bit, perhaps, will set to work to make the spare room a little comfortable for this good youth, who will share what we have. Have you no mother or father, though, in good truth?"

"None, sir. My father I never knew, and I have lost my mother."

"Poor boy! Well—well, I see that these questions distress you, so we will not ask them. You are an honest and good youth, I think, or else you belie your looks very much. You will get quite strong again soon, I'll be bound. Why, you can help me, I've no doubt, with my boat on the Thames."

"I shall be delighted to do so."

"Yes," said Mrs. Ardent, "and I'll warrant he will be quite a Turk in making up a bouquet."

"I will do my best, madam, though I fear you will find me but very awkward at it."

Lights were now lit in the kitchen, and then the family of the bouquet-maker had a better look at their young guest, and they were quite charmed with the elegance of his appearance, and the positive beauty of his face. Mrs. Ardent seemed as if she could never make enough of him.

And now poor Millicent, who tried always to be as cheerful as she could, crept downstairs from her room, and the young stranger was introduced to her by her mother.

"You are very welcome," she said, softly. "I seem as if—as if I ought to know you well."

"It's very odd, but so do I," cried Jacob Ardent. "It's a mystery; but who knows it may not come to light some of these days?"

"It may father, indeed."

"My dear, you look much better, to-night," said Mrs. Ardent.

"I am better, mother. I want to speak about something to you all."

Frank Western rose to leave the room; but Millicent placed her hand upon his arm, saying:

"No—no. It is no secret. Pray stay. Father, there came in the letter from Ireland a note, or bill, for fifty pounds."

"Yes, my dear."

"Where is it?"

"Your mother has it, my child."

"Then, mother, let the money be got to-morrow. I may possibly want some of it soon. You, too, will find it of service. It, no doubt, of right, is mine to use as I like, and sent to me by George."

"Well—well, don't mention him now, my dear."

"Not mention him?"

"No. It will awaken your grief again."

"Oh, no. I have much anxiety, mother, but no grief now."

"No grief?"

"None. I had terrible grief when I thought he was dead—I thought my heart would truly break; but not now that I have seen him."

"Seen him?"

"Yes. I saw him look from that carriage that stopped for a moment at our door a week ago. Do not stare at me, all of you, in that way. You think me mad—you thought me mad then, and you have been glad that I have not mentioned it since, for you have calculated that the wild idea has gone from me; but it is not so. I have thought of it day and night. I tell you all, and I solemnly declare to you, that it was George, and no other, who looked from that carriage."

"Alas! alas!"

"Do not say alas, father, for I will find him."

"But, my dear girl, I can tell you who it was who looked from the carriage, for I have made inquiry."

Millicent smiled.

"I have told you, father, who it was. It was George Drayton!"

"Alas, no! It was the Duke of Lorton, the son of the late Marquis of Dalewood, my dear!"

"Gracious goodness!—is that possible?" cried Mrs. Ardent.

"Yes," added old Ardent. "Listen. I cannot myself tell you very well how it has come about; but it is the fact for all that. I heard the people pronounce his name. Blessings on his head! Oh, what a joy this is to me, indeed!"

"But, Jacob——"

"Oh, don't plague me, wife—don't plague me, I say; I have much to think of. Oh, that his poor mother were alive now! That would be something—would it not?"

"Oh, my poor heart!" said Mrs. Ardent. "I feel as if all the world, and the market, were going round and round with me."

"Come—come," added old Ardent. "I have such a story to tell you all, that you will be amazed at; and as for you, my own dear Millicent, I hope that the Lord will bring you your senses back again. Come, listen to me."

—

CHAPTER XLVII.

PETER BOLT GETS SOMETHING BY THE LOTTERY, THOUGH MRS. ARDENT DOES NOT.

THE little party at the bouquet-maker's looked at each other as if they thought old Jacob Ardent's senses were, at all events, on the go, for there was quite a flashing light in the eyes of the old man, and he seemed so pleased, that he could hardly contain himself.

"Why, Jacob," said Mrs. Ardent, "I feel as sure as sure can be, that you are a little out of your mind."

"No, wife—no."

"Yes; but what is the matter, then?"

"I will tell you. I have made all the inquiry I can, and I have come to a conclusion——"

"About what?"

"About the young Marquis of Dalewood. Oh, dear no, what am I saying? It is not about him that I am coming to any sort of conclusion at all."

"Oh, dear—oh, dear!" sighed Mrs. Ardent. "He will be obliged to have a strait waistcoat on, as sure as fate. What do you mean, Jacob, and what on earth and in Covent Garden are you talking about in this sort of way?"

"Pho! pho! wife. I am all right, I tell you; and the only reason why I say that I ought not to talk of the Marquis of Dalewood is just because there is no such person now in the world."

"Then the sweet young Marquis, whom we never saw, must be dead and gone, as sure as fate."

"No, he is not; but he is the Duke of Lorton now, I can tell you, which is all the better. I saw one of the footmen in the Duke's livery, and I took him to the corner house yonder, and gave him a glass of purl, and asked him all about it; and what do you think he said?"

"Oh, what?—what?"

"Tell us, father," said Millicent, stepping forward; "what did he say?"

"My dear child, you shall hear. He said that the old Duke of Lorton had died in Ireland, and that this young gentleman in the carriage was his grandson."

"His grandson?"

"Yes, the son of the late Marquis; and if so, who can he be but the son of our dear Marchioness?—Heaven rest her soul. And so, of course, the very youth we were so anxious to find, you see."

"Oh, Jacob, it must be so."

"No," said Millicent.

"No, my dear? Why do you say no?"

"It does not matter. Perhaps I am mad. It may be that I am mad. It is sometimes a great mercy of Heaven to drive its creatures mad, and it is indeed one in my case, for I feel very happy."

"Happy, my child?"

"Yes, father, happy."

"And with your loss, too?" sighed Mrs. Ardent.

"No, rather with my gain."

Millicent smiled as she said this, and went and sat down on a low seat by the window. It was quite clear that the load which the death, or the supposed death of George Drayton, had placed upon her soul, was removed.

The old couple looked after her with anguish in their looks, and then old Ardent just touched his forehead with his hand, as if to signify that she was quite mad.

Mrs. Ardent wept.

"Well—well," said the old man, "don't you cry about it, my dear. Who shall say, after all, that it is not, as the poor child says herself, a great mercy?"

"But it is very dreadful, for all that!"

"It is—it is."

"And it will be the death of me, Jacob."

"No—no! you must not say that, because that is about as foolish a thing as you can do, wife. Dry your eyes, now, and look as cheerful as you can, and attend to the poor child. I am going out."

"Where to, Jacob?"

"On business. I must make some inquiries; and then, if they are all answered, as I hope and expect to find that they will be, I have something to do that you know nothing about."

"Dear me—what?"

"Ah! you will be delighted."

"Shall I?"

"Of course you will. It is a kind of surprise that I have kept for you, my dear; but I knew it would come some day, for I said to myself: 'Heaven will not desert His own; and if a man wants to do a good deed, it isn't in reason that Heaven should not some day or another give him the opportunity of carrying it out.'"

With these words, old Jacob left his house.

The errand that he went upon was a specific one. It was by dint of yet further inquiry to make certain that the information he had of the arrival of the young Duke of Lorton was quite correct, and without doubt.

The flutter in the heart of the old man upon this occasion was very great. He still, as the reader will surmise, considered himself to be in full possession of the sum of money which had been intrusted to him by the late Marquis for his son. Beneath the floor of the kitchen of his humble house, old Jacob Ardent really thought that the considerable sum in gold reposed in safety, waiting for its owner.

It was to make quite sure that that owner was indeed at hand that the old man now went out.

We dread to contemplate the character of his feelings when he shall discover his secret receptacle broken open, and the money he had taken such care of, gone.

That poor Mrs. Ardent, in her wild hope to win a large sum in the lottery, had taken it all, guinea by guinea, the reader is well aware, and it may be surmised how much real wretchedness was in store for the Ardent family.

But we will not anticipate.

Hardly had old Ardent left his house, when the door of the shop was very gently opened, and Peter Bolt put in his head.

"Mrs. A.," he said, "are you here, mum?"

"Yes—oh, yes!"

"Oh, I'm glad of that. May I come in, mum?"

"Yes, Peter. Come in here. I think you had better go upstairs, my dear Millicent."

"Yes, mother."

Millicent rose, and obeyed her mother, for she always understood that a recommendation to go upstairs meant that her mother did not wish her to be below.

Peter Bolt did not come into the shop with his usual freedom of manner, and one hand was over his right eye as he entered.

"Dear me, Peter," said Mrs. Ardent, "what on earth is the matter?"

"Only my eye, mum."

"Your eye?"

"Yes, Mrs. Ardent. I don't think as you can get anything by the lottery, mum; but I have, I can tell you."

"Oh, Heavens! A prize?"

"No, mum, a decided blank."

"What on earth do you mean?"

"Look here, mum."

Peter took his hand off his eye, and exhibited it to Mrs. Ardent, who saw that it had received a blow, which had given it a decidedly purple tinge. In fact, Peter Bolt had what is called a black eye of the most unmistakable character.

"There, mum, what do you think of that?"

"Oh, Peter!"

"Yes, it is 'Oh, Peter;' and so, as I say, if you never got anything by the lottery, I have—that's all."

"But, Peter!"

"Mum?"

"The lottery didn't give you the black eye."

"No, but Timothy Buckle did."

"Timothy Buckle?"

"Yes; I'll tell you just how it all happened. When I went in to get my number, mum, who should I see there but Timothy Buckle; and when he see me lay down the money, he says, says he: 'Hilloa, Peter Bolt,' says he, 'how did you come by that?' 'What's that to you?' says I. 'Nothing,' says he; 'but you couldn't have come by it in the regular way,' says he; and so then I up with my right hand, and hit him on the nose, and he up with his left hand and returned the little compliment on my eye, and here it is."

"Oh, dear—oh, dear!"

"Yes, that's just what I said when I got it; but it don't much matter, mum, for it's very nearly all in the family, and when I marry Jane, it will be altogether so, you know."

"I am so sorry, Peter."

"Oh, it don't much matter, mum; only I do wish one thing with all my heart."

"What is that?"

"Why, that you would give up the lottery."

Mrs. Ardent sighed.

"Come now, mum, do!"

"I will—I must, Peter. If I don't get the prize this time, I will never try again, you may depend."

"I'm glad to hear it."

"But do you know why, Peter?"

"Because you have made up your mind to it."

"No. It will be because I have no more money to try with. Oh, Peter, it was not my own money!"

Peter Bolt fell flat to the floor, or rather he would have fallen flat to the floor had not a small market-basket of flowers received him, and there he sat, to their great destruction, looking wildly at Mrs. Ardent, as he gasped out:

"Not your own, mum? Oh!—oh!—oh!"

"No, Peter, no!"

"Oh, lor!—oh, lor! We shall all be hanged, and no sort of a doubt about it, and yet—and yet——"

"Yet what, Peter?"

"You don't look like a highwayman, mum."

"Oh, no—no! It is my husband's money."

"Your husband's? Oh, then, that alters the case. It's all, I see, all in the family."

CHAPTER XLVIII.

OLD ARDENT THINKS OF GIVING THE DUKE AN AGREEABLE SURPRISE.

PETER BOLT was so pleased to find that the only person Mrs. Ardent had robbed was her husband, that he vaulted himself out of the basket, and looked quite animated. Mrs. Ardent was weeping.

"Lor, mum," said Peter, "there ain't no sort of occasion to take on about it, I'm sure."

"You don't know."

"Yes, mum, I do. What's Mr. Ardent's, you know, is yours; and what is yours is all your own: so, you see, there can't be much harm done, except the losing the money, and that's bad enough, I'm sure."

"It is, indeed."

"Then don't cry, Mrs. A., for you don't know yet but you may get the great prize, and in that case, you know, all would be right."

"It would, indeed," said Mrs. Ardent, with sudden animation. "It would, indeed; and all I can say, is, that if it be not so, I shall go out of my mind at once. I feel I shall be much better dead."

"Oh, dear—oh, dear! Well, mum, don't say another word about it till the time comes. It's no use wishing for a misfortune to come, and making yourself as miserable about it beforehand as if it had come, you know."

"You are right there, Peter; and now you can go. I beg of you to keep the secret of my venture in the lottery, and to keep a good watch upon the drawing; and if you find that I have a prize, don't hesitate for a moment to call a sedan-chair, or a coach, or anything you can get hold of, and come here direct with the joyful news."

"I will, mum, and then I suppose—eh?"

"What—what?"

"I may look for an instant union with Janey?"

"You may, indeed; and, what is more, I will set you up in a shop in the Strand."

"Oh, then my fortune is as good as made, I can tell you, Mrs. A., and I shan't mind another black eye for that, I'm sure, though I hope yet to come across Master Timothy Buckle, and give him a something for himself."

Peter Bolt, with his black eye, and the promises of Mrs. Ardent in his favour, left the shop, and he had hardly been gone two minutes, when a servant in livery came in, and cried out:

"Is this Mrs. Ardent's?"

"Yes—yes."

"Oh, then there are five guineas, and you will be so good as to make up five bouquets, and send them to the Duke of Lorton's, this evening, just before dinner time."

"The Duke of Lorton's? Oh, gracious!"

"Yes, the Duke of Lorton's, at the back of Montague House. Why, what is the woman staring at?"

"Nothing—only—I—that is—oh, dear!"

"Upon my life, I think you are mad; but mind that the bouquets are brought before six o'clock."

"Yes—yes. But, my good man—oh, he is gone! The Duke of Lorton sends for no less than five bouquets at a guinea a-piece. What am I to think of it? How strange it is. Does he then, indeed, recollect that we were kind to his mother? Had she mentioned us to him? It must be so. Oh, yes—yes, and he will be now a good friend and patron to us, and all may yet go well. I have half a mind to put these five guineas beneath the tile in the kitchen floor, so that if Jacob should look for his money, he will not be able to say that it is all gone; but yet, alas! what are five guineas to two hundred? No—no, it is of no use attempting it, and—and I may get another small chance in the lottery with this money, too!"

Poor, unfortunate Mrs. Ardent!

While all this was going on at the Ardents' house, old Jacob himself had sallied forth for the express purpose of making such inquiries as should satisfy him that it was indeed the real and veritable grandson of the old Duke of Lorton, and the son of the Marquis, who was now in London.

In order to carry out these inquiries, he went to the neighbourhood of Montague House, and there he happened to see a servant in the Lorton livery.

This man, who had been engaged by Captain Gay, and told all that the Captain wished to be told to anyone else, informed old Ardent that it was indeed the son of the late Marquis of Dalewood who had come to the title of the Duke of Lorton by the death of his father and grandfather.

Old Ardent could no longer doubt the fact.

"Do you know," he said, "when the Duke is likely to be at home?"

"Oh, yes."

"When—oh, when?"

"To dinner at six."

"Oh, but he must not be disturbed at his dinner."

"Well, I should rather think not, old gentleman. But do you want to see his Grace?"

"I do, indeed."

"Then it will be very difficult, indeed."

"Difficult! How difficult?"

"Why, his right-hand man of business won't, if he can help it, let anyone see him."

"Indeed; and who is that?"

"Mr. Brand."

"Brand?—I don't know him."

"Oh, he came from Ireland with the Duke, and though he wears the Duke's livery, he ain't a servant, I can tell you; and the Duke talks to him quite familiarly. In fact, he is the Duke's grand adviser and confidential friend."

The reader will surmise that this Mr. Brand is no other than our old acquaintance, Captain Gay, who has thought proper to assume that name in his new capacity of major-domo to the Duke of Lorton in London.

Old Ardent sighed as he thought of the difficulty of getting an interview with the Duke; and then he smiled at the thought of what he had to say to him when he should be so fortunate as to see him at all.

"I tell you what, my good sir," said the footman, "I shall be in the hall at four o'clock, and the Duke, I daresay, will be at home. You come then, if you want to see him, and I will take good care that you are announced to him; that is all I can do."

"Thanks—thanks. I think he will see me, for something seems to tell me that he will recognize my name. There was one who loved him well, who could not, I should think, have failed to tell him there was such a person as Jacob Ardent in the world. I will be at the house at the time you mention, and many thanks to you for your kindness."

"Oh, don't mention that, old gentleman. The fact is, that Mr. Brand is such a tyrant, that if I thought it would provoke him for you to see the Duke, I would do anything to bring it about; so now, good-day, and mind you come."

"I will—I will."

Old Ardent hurried homewards, and as he went, he said to himself:

"Yes, I will go, and I will go with something in my possession, too, which will gladden the heart of the young Duke. It isn't the money that he will care so much about, I know, for to a rich man like him that cannot be much; but he will be glad to see the packet of papers, and the letter that his father left with me. Yes—yes, if he has any heart he will weep with joy to see them, and as the son of the dear Marchioness, he surely has a kind and good heart."

Jacob Ardent went home in a happy mood that day, and as he entered his house, he said with a smile to his wife:

"Come hither—come hither, I have something to say."

"Something to say?"

"Yes—yes. Why, what do you tremble at?"

"Tremble?"

"Yes, wife, you seem all of a shake."

"You—you said that—I—thought—that you had something to say. You said so."

"Yes; but what put it into your head that it was anything at all unpleasant—eh?"

"Oh, nothing—nothing, only I—I——"

"Tush—tush! Come, now, don't be foolish. Look at me now—look at me well."

Mrs. Ardent did look at him. There was joy in the old man's face, joy and pride.

"Oh, gracious!" she said, "what has happened?"

"Nothing."

"But you look so strange, Jacob—you look as if something had really happened."

"No, wife, nothing has happened, I can tell you; but something will happen. I am going to pay a grand visit."

"A grand visit?"

"Yes. Come into the kitchen, and shut the door."

"Oh, no—no!"

"No?"

"That is, I—Did you say the kitchen?"

"I did. Why, what on earth is the matter with the woman? Has anything happened? Has anything gone amiss in my absence? Oh, speak to me!"

"No—no!"

"Our child? M——cent?"

"She is upstairs. Indeed, there is nothing the matter, I assure you, Jacob."

"You—you frightened me. I thought there was. You gave me quite a fright, that you did."

"I did not intend to do so."

"No matter—no matter. I have something to do which would, I think, restore me if I were at the point of death. I have an act of justice to do—of merely plain, common justice: but I do feel pleased that it has fallen to me to do it. Come this way; I have a secret to tell you, wife. I have a little surprise for you that, for once in a way, you never even dreamt of. Ha—ha!"

CHAPTER XLIX.

JACOB ARDENT FINDS HIS FONDEST HOPES CRUSHED.

LIKE a criminal going to execution, Mrs. Ardent followed her husband into the kitchen.

"Shut the door. Ha—ha!"

She shut it.

"Oh, Jacob, do not laugh so."

"Not laugh? Why not laugh? Ha—ha! I am going to astonish you, old woman. I am going to tell you a grand secret—quite a grand secret, and you must not—no, indeed, you must not—take it amiss that I did not tell it you before."

"No," said Mrs. Ardent, faintly.

"Because, you see—ha—ha!—there were reasons."

"Yes."

"Such good reasons as you will approve of, I'm sure. Ha—ha! And you will say that your husband is an honest man, which is about the greatest thing to say of any man that I know of. Here, now, have we been married a matter of forty years, and in all that time, I will say it—yes, I feel that I can say it, and so I will—neither of us have ever done an act that we need be ashamed of telling to the other. Have we now, old woman?"

"N—n—no."

"Why, what on earth is the matter with you? Oh, wife, as I came along now—only just now I passed—where do you think?"

"I don't know, Jacob."

"The lottery-office."

"Oh!"

"Good gracious! what is the matter?"

"Nothing. I—only—felt a pain in my head—I mean, my side. It is gone—gone quite now. Oh, yes, it is gone quite."

Old Jacob Ardent looked at her in surprise for a few seconds; and then he said, as he drew a long breath:

"Wife, you alarm me. A pain that made you scream out in that way is a very bad thing."

"Yes, but it is gone now."

"Thank God!"

"So say I. But—but you were saying something—something about the—the—a—a lottery office!"

The words "lottery-office" nearly choked poor Mrs. Ardent in the effort to pronounce them.

"Yes, I was saying something about the lottery-office, wife. I was saying, that as I came by it, I saw a crowd of people—I saw boys with pale faces, and trembling hands—I saw haggard-looking men, with bleared and bloodshot eyes—I saw women with babes in their arms!"

"Oh, horror!"

"It is enough to make one cry out 'Oh, horror!' I said to myself, the woman who takes her husband's gold to this accursed shrine of Mammon, must be a bad wife—a bad mother."

"No—no!"

"Yes, it is so; and a curse and a desolation to all whose peace and happiness are bound up with hers."

Poor Mrs. Ardent felt faint, and likely to drop to the floor. It was only by a great effort that she kept her senses.

The old man continued:

"Yes, and I blessed God that my own home had been unpolluted by the presence of the demon avarice in the person of a lottery-ticket."

"Yes," gasped Mrs. Ardent.

"And that was one reason, but not all the reasons, why I felt so happy when I came in."

Little did Jacob Ardent dream that he was speaking daggers to his wife by what he said, and that each word struck upon her heart like a tangible blow, that turned her sick, even unto death.

"Come—come!" he said, suddenly, "we won't talk of such things any more. I have something more agreeable to say to you, old woman—so cheer up. All is well. Ah, it is the thought of our poor child, Millicent, that

makes you look so sad. Why did I say all is well, while she suffers?"

"Yes, Jacob, it is the thought of her, and—and—and——"

"And what?"

"I was going to say, that the thought of her should make us ever charitable and forgiving to each other."

"Surely, yes."

"And it will do so?"

"It ought, if it don't."

Mrs. Ardent did not like the words "if it don't," and she shook with conscious guilt—that guilt which her own heart told her was now upon the eve of being disclosed to her husband. Surely the agony that she then endured, in some degree expiated the crime of which she had been guilty.

"It is quite time," added old Ardent, "that we ought, indeed, to be kind and charitable to each other, old woman; but I think we have been, do you know."

"Oh, yes—yes."

"Well, then, get me out my Sunday coat, wife."

"Your Sunday coat, Jacob?"

"Yes; my Sunday coat; for, do you know, I am going to visit a great lord—a Duke, my dear, so I must go quite grand, do you see?"

"Yes, but——"

"Nay, now, don't vex me by making any words about it; for the real truth is, you don't know anything about it."

"Then tell me, I implore you, Jacob."

"Hey-day! Why, what a fright you seem to be in! Well—well! woman's curiosity, I suppose. The old story, since the days of Grandmother Eve, so I ought not to say anything against it, and, therefore, I will just tell you all about it."

"Oh, do—do!"

"Now, don't interrupt or plague me, wife, and then I shall get on capitally. You don't know now—that is to say, you don't suspect where you are."

"Where I am?"

"No."

"Why, in the kitchen, to be sure."

"Yes, so far, that is true enough, but you don't know at all what you are near?"

"I am near you Jacob."

"Oh, yes, that's true; but do you think now you are near a great treasure—such a treasure as you never saw in your life before; gold—gold!"

"Gold?"

"Yes, gold. But don't be frightened. It isn't ours. Oh, dear no. That's the beauty of it. I don't think I should like half so well to look at it if it was."

"Oh, Jacob!"

"Ha! ha! you may well say, 'Oh, Jacob,' and you will say, 'Oh, Jacob,' again, when you come to know all about it, I can tell you. Look at that table?"

"Yes—yes."

"You see it?"

"I do."

"Then look under it. What do you see?"

"The—a—the—a—tiles of the floor."

"Good. Look at this one, then, in particular, of the tiles of the floor, and tell me what you think of it?"

Old Jacob Ardent pushed the table on one side, and placed his foot on the very tile beneath which he had hidden the Marquis's money. He knew that tile well, and so did poor bewildered, terror-stricken Mrs. Ardent, for the matter of that.

Poor woman, she knew it too well.

The old man rubbed his hands together with glee as he now said, in a calm tone of voice:

"Wife, I have for some time now had a something on my mind which I intend this day to take off it, and I am quite sure that I shall sleep all the easier for so doing. Look you, wife; beneath this stone——"

Mrs. Ardent shook like an aspen leaf.

"Beneath this stone is a small bag with two hundred golden guineas in it. What think you of that?"

She could not speak.

"And now, wife, for the how and the why they came there. When the poor Marquis of Dalewood sought the shelter of this humble but honest roof on that awful night which saw the death of both him and his poor lady, he placed certain letters and other documents in my hands, and, said he: 'Jacob, here are papers which, if ever you see my son, I desire that you give to him, and here are two hundred pounds, which likewise you can give to him, Jacob, and I charge you for my sake, and for the sake of my poor wife and child, to take care of the money for them.'"

Mrs. Ardent swayed to and fro, as if she were upon the eve of going mad.

"You are affected," said old Ardent, as he wiped his own eyes with the sleeve of his coat—"you are affected, and so am I—I knew you would be."

She tried to speak, but she could not.

"Well—well, you shall see the money, and then you will believe it all. Oh, wife, what a sacred deposit that money was, and how large a sum, too, and all in bright and beautiful gold; but it was quite safe—quite, with us, you know. We would have wanted bread, and yet we would not have touched a single guinea of it—would we, wife?"

Mrs. Ardent uttered a cry of despair, and upon her knees she strove to get along the floor towards her husband, holding up her hands as she did so in an attitude of supplication that was terrible to see.

Old Ardent looked at her for a moment or two in silence, and then he passed his hand across his brow, as if to clear away some thoughts from his mind that were too terrible to be entertained for longer than a half minute of time.

"What is this?" he said. "Oh, Heaven, what is all this?"

———

CHAPTER L.

JACOB ARDENT THROWS HIMSELF ON THE MERCY OF THE DUKE.

SOME terrible suspicion of the truth, if not the absolute truth itself, began to dawn upon the mind of old Jacob Ardent, now that he saw how seemingly beyond all reason his wife was affected.

"What is it?" he cried, in a voice that rang through the room. And then he added, in a whisper: "No—no! It cannot be!"

"Jacob—husband!"

"Don't—oh, don't drive me mad! What have you to say to me? Nothing—say it is nothing?"

"Mercy!"

"Mercy? Why do you say that? Why do you ask of me mercy?"

"Mercy and forgiveness! Oh, kill me, if you cannot be merciful, and forgive!"

"Ah!"

"The gold—the money—the two hundred golden pieces—I thought them yours, Jacob—I thought them all yours! How could I think otherwise?"

"No—no—no! You did not—you could not——"

"Mercy—mercy!"

"Hold! Keep off! Not another word—not another word for a moment or two! Silence—silence! I say, silence!"

In an instant, Jacob Ardent had his large pocket clasp-knife in his hand. The thickest of the blades was opened, and by its aid he lifted the tile beneath which he had hidden the money. The empty bag was there only!

For the space in which you might have counted twelve, a kind of stupor seemed to have come over old Jacob Ardent. He knelt by the side of the tile with the empty bag in his hand, and looked about him like one half awake.

It was the voice of his wife that roused him.

"Jacob!—oh, Jacob!" she said; "speak to me, and have mercy upon me! Speak! Oh, speak!"

With a cry, partly of anguish and partly of rage, he sprang to his feet.

"Fiend!—devil!" he cried. "If I were to kill you, I——"

"Oh, lor!" cried a voice: and the face of Peter Bolt peered into the room. "Oh, lor!"

"What do you want?" roared Jacob Ardent.

"Hip—hip—hip—hurrah! Nine cheers for the girls that we love, who are fair in the heavens above. I—don't think I'm in the least—drunk."

"Villain!"

"Hurrah—hurrah! The prize—the prize! We have won! I tell you, and everybody would trust me—that is to say, I would trust everybody—no, that ain't it—everybody would——Hurrah! we have won the great prize! Hip—hip!——"

"Oh, no—no! Yet it may be," screamed Mrs. Ardent. "Oh, if it be so, it is a charm that bids me live again. Oh, joy—joy! The great prize did you say?"

"Yes, missis—yes! Hip!——"

"Silence! tell me all. Peter—Peter—good Peter! Oh, for the love of God, tell me at once!"

"Yes, I——"

"What is all this?" roared Jacob Ardent.

"Oh, fortune!" cried Mrs. Ardent. "The money will all come back again! All will yet be well! Peter, speak to me! You said that I had won, did you not? Oh, say so again!"

"Yes, missis—yes! Hip!——"

"Don't say that, but assure me that you have been to the drawing."

"What!" cried Jacob Ardent. "Is it of the accursed lottery you speak? Is it possible that you have taken this sacred gold for the unholy purpose of venturing soul and body in that awful gulf of iniquity?"

"No—no, husband! That is, yes. But bear with me for a moment. We have won! Speak to him, Peter Bolt, and tell him we have won!"

"Yes, Mr. A., we have won. I was there, and we have won, as the old lady says. Oh, my Janey is a darling, and I love her night and day, in spite of what all the corporals in all the world may say. Upon my life, I rather think that last line is what we call a foot or two too long."

"Villain!" cried old Ardent, springing at him, and seizing him by the collar. "Confess all, or I will be the death of you!"

"Confess—all—oh!"

"Yes, confess all."

"Well—I—a—Missis, we have won, at last. I tell you that's a good job. 74, you know."

"Yes—oh, yes!"

"Ha—ha! That's the time of day."

"I will shake the life out of you!" said old Ardent.

"Oh, spare him!" cried Mrs. Ardent. "I will tell all. But, Peter—Peter, answer me truly, or I shall go mad!"

"Yes, missis."

"Where you at the drawing of the lottery?"

"I were."

"Did you hear the number yourself, with your own ears?"

"Lor, missis! And how could I hear with anybody else's? I'll warrant my ears are long enough. 74——"

"Yes—yes! Go on."

"And 47——"

"No—no!"

"Yes, mum. 7447."

"Oh, Heaven!"

"What's the matter, missis? That was what won!"

"Lost—lost!" screamed Mrs. Ardent. "It was 7474. Oh, I am mad—mad—mad!"

She fell in a swoon on the floor; and old Ardent grappled Peter Bolt by the collar, and

they rolled over each other just as the parlour door was opened, and a man, accompanied by a couple of police-officers, looked in, saying:

"There he is; and I'll take my oath, before any justice in Christendom, he did not come by the money honestly. I have seen him half-a-dozen times, at least, at the lottery-office, and they say he has spent two hundred pounds there."

"Which is him?" said the constable, stepping forward.

"There he is. Peter Bolt, the tailor."

"I have him!" said old Ardent. "He is a robber! To prison with him! I'll have him hanged!"

"Oh, lor!" said Peter.

The constable laid hold of poor Bolt by one cuff, and then by the collar with the other hand, in that scientific manner which is supposed, or was then supposed, to be the best way of securing culprits, and thus he held him.

The uproar now in the house was sufficiently great to bring both Jane and Millicent to the kitchen, and it was with no small degree of surprise they saw what was going on.

Millicent flew to her mother, and raised her from the ground, and placed her in a chair, exclaiming, as she did so:

"Alas! was there not affliction enough in this house without this? Who has done this, father?"

"No one," said old Ardent, firmly; "no one. Jane, where are you, my dear?"

"Here uncle."

"Do you see that man?"

"Oh, yes, uncle; it is Peter—my Peter."

"Well, he is a thief!"

"A thief!"

"No!" roared Peter. "No—no—no!"

"But I say yes. Look at this empty bag, Jane. There were two hundred guineas in it. They have all gone through Peter Bolt's hands to the lottery-office. What say you, now?"

"Oh, Peter—Peter! you have broken my heart! I can never think of you again. Go, go! Oh, go from me! I can only pray, now, that I may forget you."

Poor Jane sobbed as if her heart would break.

Peter looked like a man in a dream. The shock of the events that had occurred, and were occurring about him, had had the effect of completely sobering him, and he was as white as a sheet. The faculty of speech seemed, too, to have deserted him.

"Away with him!" said old Ardent.

"Come, young fellow," said the officer; "I suspect this will turn out to be rather a serious job for you. Robbing in a dwelling house is hanging, as sure as fate."

"Hold!" cried Mrs. Ardent, rising from the chair on which poor Millicent had placed her, and looking like a ghost, so pale and wan was she. "Hold, I say!"

They all paused, and looked aghast at her.

"Peter Bolt is innocent. I alone am guilty."

OLD ARDENT OBTAINS AN INTERVIEW WITH THE MARQUIS.

"You, mother?" cried Millicent.

"You, aunt?" ejaculated Jane.

"Yes. I gave him the money to go to the lottery-office with. It was as my messenger he went. He thought it was my own money. I told him it was. He is innocent."

"Oh, Peter!" said Jane.

"Oh, Janey!"

"Why, good gracious!" said the officer, letting go his hold of Peter, "whose money was it, then?"

"Mine!" said old Ardent; "and that is my wife's."

"Oh, then, no felony has been committed after all?"

"None!"

"Then, Mr. Timothy Buckle, what the deuce did you bring me here for, all about nothing?"

"Well, I thought, you see——"

"Never mind what you thought," said Peter Bolt, suddenly putting down his head, and making use of it as a battering-ram right at the stomach of Timothy Buckle. "Never mind what you thought. You had no business to interfere in other folks' affairs, so get out, will you! There, now, how do you like that—eh?"

No. 9.—(Marquis.)

CHAPTER LI.

CAPTAIN GAY EXPLAINS HIS TRUE POSITION TO THE DUKE.

THIS strange and totally unexpected attack upon the part of Peter Bolt, so thoroughly took Timothy Buckle by surprise, that, although much the braver and stronger man, he succumbed to it, and found himself lying on his back in the middle of the street, in about half a second of time.

Peter Bolt came back to the kitchen with an air of triumph, saying:

"I rather think I have settled that; and now, Mr. Officers, you are not wanted here at all; so, good afternoon, or evening, if you please. There is the door."

"Go!" said Ardent.

The officers left the room, muttering that they would make this infernal Timothy Buckle pay them for their loss of time.

"Peter," said old Ardent, "you can go, too."

"Yes, Mr. A., but—but——"

"If you have anything to say to me, you can say it at some other time. I don't want to hear it now."

"Well, but, Mr. A., I merely wanted to say that I hoped you would forgive me for my share in this little affair. I'm quite sure that I didn't know——"

"Be off with you, or I will make you."

"Oh, lor!"

The menacing look of old Ardent induced Peter to make a very precipitate retreat; but, as he went, Jane gave him a look and a little nod, as much as to say, "I'll make it all right;" and so poor Peter felt very much comforted indeed.

When he was gone, old Ardent turned to Millicent and Jane, and said, in a low tone:

"Leave us alone for a while."

They felt that some explanation was wanted between the husband and wife, so without a word they left the kitchen. Old Ardent locked the door after them.

During the next half-hour there was heard the sound of weeping in the kitchen, and now and then of voices, and then old Ardent opened the door, and called upstairs:

"Milly—Milly!"

"Yes, father."

"You can come down, and so can you, Jane. I am going out, my dears, for an hour or so."

The two young women came downstairs gently. They saw the traces of tears upon the face of Mrs. Ardent, as well as upon that of Jacob Ardent; but the manner in which he said "Good-bye for the present," to his wife, showed them that whatever had been the cause of the strife and discussion, it was over.

The fact was, that Mrs. Ardent had freely and fully confessed all, and thrown herself upon the affection and the mercy of her husband. That affection, and that mercy, had been amply sufficient to respond to the appeal, and she was forgiven.

He had a noble heart, had that old man.

But now, on what errand was old Ardent going? He had no money to take to the Duke of Lorton. No; but he could tell him the whole story, and that was what he meant, in the pride of his honest old heart, to do.

But while old Jacob is—with slower steps than he would have made had he had the gold to place in the hands of the Duke—taking his way to the family mansion of the Lortons, it will be as well for us to take a glance at the situation of affairs between Captain Gay and the new Duke, and the position in which the Duke, alias George Drayton, found himself in London.

Where there are ample resources, in the shape of ready money, at command, things that otherwise would lag fearfully in their progress can be done quickly; and it was truly amazing to see what the genius of money had been able to accomplish towards the grandeur of the new Duke of Lorton.

Post letters had preceded the arrival of the new Duke, in London; and the old mansion at the back of Montague House was placed in a forward state of repair, and some of the most costly furniture that London could afford, on the spur of the moment, had been placed in it.

Splendid carriages were procured, and the stables were full of horses of the highest breed and beauty.

A couple of dozen servants were hastily placed in gorgeous liveries to attend upon the Duke, and the interior of the mansion really looked a blaze of magnificence.

The fact is, that the bankers of the family, completely deceived by the representations of Captain Gay, had advanced a very large sum at once, which sufficed, as Captain Gay said, to carry on the war with.

Immediately upon coming to London, Captain Gay had waited upon the Dowager Lady Bridget, the aunt of the pretended new Duke, and had told her so specious a tale, and exhibited to her the letter written by the murdered Mr. South, that she did not doubt George Drayton to be her real relation.

The old lady joyfully embraced him, and protested, as is usual with the dotage of age, that she did see a great likeness to the family in his features.

Old Lady Bridget Lorton belonged to a race of human beings who, it is to be hoped, are now extinct. She had but one idea, which was, that her family was the greatest, next to royalty, in all the world.

Pride of the most overbearing and ridiculous character was the one grand characteristic of her nature; and for the purpose of pandering to that pride, or of carrying out its foolish and, in many cases, wicked impulses, she was perfectly unscrupulous.

In so far, then, the old Lady Bridget was for a woman just about as wicked and as unprincipled as the Duke of Lorton, who had died at Lorton Castle, was for a man.

It is not very likely that George Drayton felt much inclined to bless fortune for introducing him to such a relation as this.

But there was no help for it. She and he seemed to be the last representatives of the noble family of Lorton, and as, with palsied head, she looked at him, he thought he had never dreamt even of such a thorough specimen of a haughty, bigoted old grandee as she.

Captain Gay had taken good care, though, to warn the young Duke of the vast importance of standing well with this ancient piece of superstition and old world pride; so he managed to receive the old lady with every appearance of respectful consideration, whatever might be his real feelings.

It was quite clear that Captain Gay was now playing such a game, that he considered nothing too mean and nothing too villainous for its accomplishment.

Hence he had chosen even to dress himself in the livery of the Duke, in order that his continual presence about his person might not excite wonder; and, besides, he thought that a valet's livery would be about the very best disguise he could be in.

Captain Gay had no wish in the world to cultivate just then the acquaintance of any of his old friends in London. They might have very materially interfered with his plans.

And now we hardly know how to excuse the conduct of George Drayton to the reader.

He ought, the moment he reached London, to have gone direct to the Ardents in search of his wife.

He did, however, no such thing.

We may suppose, then, that he was, so to speak, intoxicated with the novelty of his position, and that he dreaded to avow to the world that his father-in-law was a waterman-fireman—his mother-in-law a bouquet-maker, and his wife, his Duchess, the daughter of such humble people.

This false pride, from the impulses of which so many persons—from far less cause than George Drayton had—have fallen, was the rock on which he struck.

And yet he loved Millicent.

If he had remained plain George Drayton, not the force of worlds would have separated him from her. If he had, by the genius of his mind, or by the perseverance of his labour, raised himself to any position, it would have been his pride and pleasure to have raised her with him; but to find himself a Duke, when he had not known it, and then to find himself wedded so far beneath him, was too much for his nature.

A fearful struggle began in his mind between love and pride—a struggle that Captain Gay foresaw would come, and for which he was fully prepared, as will soon be shown.

At one moment the Duke thought that rank and wealth were as nothing compared with the love of Millicent; and then again he seemed to hear upon the very air around him the laugh of ridicule which Captain Gay had taken the pains to assure him would fol-

low the declaration of his marriage with the daughter of the bouquet-maker of Covent Garden.

Truly all is not gold that glitters, and the new Duke found already, so to speak, his coronet filled with thorns.

The plain fact was, that George Drayton in three weeks looked three years older than he had done before.

And yet he was the Duke—yet he had sixty thousand pounds per annum! But he was miserable despite all that.

The thought that he was in the same city with his Millicent—the reflection that a quarter of an hour of the many quarters of an hour of which the day and night consisted, would, if he so willed it, have taken him to her side, was nearly driving him mad, and the wear and tear of his soul was visible in his face.

The tempter watched him, and took good care never for more then a few minutes at a time to let him be out of his sight.

After all, then, George Drayton was but a splendid captive in a gilded cage.

It was evident to him, too, that there was a perfect, and capital, and complete understanding between Captain Gay and his old aunt—as he called her—the Lady Bridget. He felt that somehow he was, after all, very like a puppet in their hands, from the avarice of the one, and the insane pride of the other.

CHAPTER LII.

CAPTAIN GAY AND THE YOUNG DUKE HAVE THEIR FIRST QUARREL.

Such, then, was the state of affairs at the mansion of the young Duke of Lorton.

Here, though, it is necessary that we should again intimate that up to this time certainly not the smallest doubt had arisen in the mind of George Drayton with regard to the story that Captain Gay had told him.

George fully believed himself to be what it had suited Captain Gay to tell him he was—namely, the Duke of Lorton, and heir to the vast estates of the Lorton family.

Had he for a moment had any doubt upon the subject of his identity, it would have no doubt induced a very different line of conduct in him forthwith.

But he had no such doubt.

The time, however, was now at hand when his eyes were to be rather widely opened to the true position in which he stood, and we shall soon see what an effect that rough proceeding had upon him and his prospects.

The reader will now be so good as to accompany us to the splendid mansion of the new Duke of Lorton.

It has been before stated that, notwithstanding the small notice the London tradesmen had had in the matter, wonders had been done in the way of the adorning of the home of the young Duke.

The apartment to which we now wish to

introduce our readers was one of the most costly magnificence.

Hangings of satin, with varied flowers in gold and silver, depended from the tops of the casements. The walls, too, were richly gilt, and adorned in panels of the most elegant designs.

The floor was covered with a carpet, the flowers upon which looked like nature itself.

The furniture was of the most costly description. Crimson and gold were the colours that predominated in that truly magnificent saloon.

It is three o'clock in the afternoon, and a number of servants in the Duke's livery are passing in and out of the room, and now and then putting some of its costly contents to rights, while they occasionally conversed with each other.

"I say, William," said one, "this seems to be a rare good place we have got here."

"I believe you, Ben."

"High wages."

"Yes—yes!"

"Little to do."

"Yes—yes!"

"And plenty to eat and to drink."

"Yes, that's true."

"Well, but," said another, "there is a drawback to everything, you know. What a tyrant that valet, or major-domo, or gentleman-waiter, or whatever he calls himself to master, is."

"He is, indeed."

"Oh, he is a positive wretch."

"You may say that."

"The Duke himself don't want much waiting on—he is as mild and as quiet as a lamb; but as for his great man—oh, dear! there is no such thing as satisfying him."

"That's true, Stephen; but you know he it was who hired us."

"He did."

"Yes; and, what's more, he told us all that we must consider ourselves as here only during his good pleasure, for that the Duke left all such matters to him, and that he could discharge any of us at a minute's notice, if he pleased."

"He told me the same."

"And me—and me."

"Well then, it's quite clear that we may look upon ourselves as his servants more than the Duke's."

"That's true, and, in my opinion, I——"

"Well, and in your opinion?" said Captain Gay, suddenly appearing in the midst of the group of servants, who had been too intent upon their own gossiping to heed his stealthy approach."

"Oh, lor!"

"Oh, don't be afraid. I like to hear all sorts of opinions, my good fellow. Come, now, finish your speech."

"I—a—I—a——"

"No stammering. Go on."

"I—a—that is,—I was going to say, a——"

"Well, what?"

"That I hoped long to have the pleasure of seeing your honour, that was all, for it is a pleasure."

"Liar!"

"Oh, sir—oh!"

"Hark you all! When I hired you, I told you that if there was one thing more than another that for my own peace, and for the peace of this house, I feel bound to act upon, it was that there should be no gossiping. Now, don't let me hear any more of it. Be off."

"Yes, sir."

The servants ran off in different directions, and Captain Gay seated himself on a couch.

"I feel rather weary," he said, "and yet I don't know why, very well. The aspect of affairs doesn't please me. The Duke is not happy, that is clear."

A servant entered the room.

"What now?"

"Some letters, sir."

"Bring them here."

"For the Duke, sir."

"Bring them to me, I say, fool. Be off at once."

The servant handed Captain Gay several letters, the superscriptions of which he looked carefully at.

"Humph! nothing to be afraid of here. Invitations to assemblies, and dinner parties—solicitations for custom—Ah, they shall have enough of that. Well, here I am; but yet I am not satisfied. Old Lady Bridget, with all her influence, doesn't seem to be able to get the new Duke recognized at Court. They are confoundedly particular about his lineage, surely; but it is awkward rather."

Another servant appeared.

"What now, idiot?"

"A letter for the Duke, sir."

"Bring it here."

"Yes, sir."

"The salver, dolt! Is that the way to hand a letter? If you hand me a letter again, or anything else, without using the salver, I'll break your stupid skull, thick as it is."

"Yes, sir."

"Be off!"

"Yes, sir."

The terrified servant made haste from the room, and Captain Gay looked at the letter in silence for some few moments; then he said:

"Ah, from the Lady Bridget to her nephew, the Duke, as she thinks him. I wonder now what the old lady has got to say? She has written 'Immediate,' too, on the letter. Well, I daresay I can manage to seal it again, so here goes. It is highly necessary that I should know as much, if not a little more of the Duke's affairs, than he does himself."

Captain Gay broke the seal of the letter, and read as follows:

"MY DEAR NEPHEW,

"I have seen the Queen, and she thinks that His Majesty will require great proof of your real position; and I fear that more proof than we have (which really to me is quite satisfactory) is not to be had.

"I have, however, I think, got over the difficulty. The Prime Minister is rather anxious to get a noble and worthy husband for his daughter, the Lady Christina, and I have sufficiently managed the affair with her mother, that you may consider the matter as settled; and on the day that you lead the Lady Christina to the altar, you may depend that you will be received at Court, and no questions asked about your rights, which, although they might be, no doubt, well and fully proved, would, in such proving, involve the declaration that your mother had not belonged to the nobility.

"I will call upon you, my dear nephew, in the course of the evening—and am your loving aunt,   "BRIDGET LORTON."

"Oh, indeed," said Captain Gay, when he had finished the letter. "A match provided already for the Duke. This is rather rich. Ha—ha!"

The idea of George Drayton, he being already the husband of Millicent Ardent, being forced, or cajoled, into a marriage with the daughter of the Prime Minister, seemed to be, to the mind of Captain Gay, one of the richest of jokes.

"It will be capital," he said; "and if it smoothes other difficulties, what on earth can it matter to him? I cannot very well claim my money of him till he is fairly settled, by a reception at Court, in his dukedom; so everything and anything that will tend to expedite that desirable result will be to me right welcome, and will, as a matter of course, insure my support. He shall marry the Lady Christina, if I can make him do so."

Captain Gay now approached a table on which there were writing materials, and sealed up the letter again.

It was with a different seal, to be sure; but that did not matter, as it was impossible that the Duke could take upon himself to say what sort of seal his aunt had used.

It was well for Captain Gay that he was prompt about this proceeding, for he had no sooner finished, than a door opened communicating with the saloon, and George Drayton, the Duke of Lorton, as he really thought himself, hurriedly entered.

There was a look of disquietude about the Duke's face, which Captain Gay noticed at a glance.

The Captain bowed low with affected humility.

CHAPTER LIII.

CONTAINS SOME RATHER CURIOUS EXPLANATORY MATTER.

IT was quite clear that the Duke was very much out of sorts about something or other; and, as he threw himself into a chair, he gave utterance to a deep sigh.

"May I hope that your Grace is quite well?" said Captain Gay.

"No."

"No?"

"I mean that I am not quite well. I have no objection in life to your hoping I am; but I am very far from it."

"Indeed, your Grace! Shall I send for a physician?"

"Yes, if you can find one who can

"'Minister to a mind diseased,'

but not otherwise, Gay."

"I am sorry to hear your Grace say so. I did, indeed, and in truth, think that the brilliant destiny which appeared to be yours would have made your life one scene of gaiety and delight."

"Did you, indeed?"

"I did, indeed!"

"Then you were mistaken. I am miserable."

"Miserable?"

"Yes, quite miserable!"

"What, the great Duke of Lorton miserable? The owner of the vast estates of the Lorton family—the possessor of sixty thousand pounds a year—miserable? It really transcends all belief!"

"It may do so, and yet it is true."

"I am bound to believe my own ears; but yet I cannot help thinking that some little attack of the vapours, some trifling feeling of *ennui*, must be all that is the matter."

"Would it were—oh, would it were!"

"I hope nothing has happened to—to——"

"To what?"

"To discompose your Grace."

"Nothing new."

"Is there possibly, then, anything in the past that has the power to do that?"

"Yes, much."

"May my curiosity get the better of my respect so far as to allow me to ask what?"

"Yes, you may ask what," cried the Duke, rising, and pacing the room in agitation. "You may do so, for I am only mad, I tell you, Captain Gay. Am I not in London? Am I not here, in the very city, and breathing the same air as my wife—my poor—poor Millicent? Oh, I shall go quite mad!"

Captain Gay looked upon this sudden passion of the Duke with the most perfect calmness.

He took an elaborate pinch of snuff.

The poor Duke covered his face with his hands, and rocked to and fro upon the chair.

"Yes, I feel that my brain will not stand this constant wear and tear," he added. "Oh, why did this prospect open before me? Oh, why did not fate leave me what I was, instead of making me what I am? I am wretched!"

"Humph!" said Captain Gay.

"Must I surrender her whom I love, for the sake of the empty bauble of a coronet that is now in my grasp? Must I barter my very soul for all the parade and state for which, in good and honest truth, I care not?"

"Oh!" said the Captain.

"I tell you, Captain Gay, and I tell all the world through you, that one smile from Millicent Ardent is worth all the idle state of twenty Dukedoms."

"Indeed!"

"It is so."

"Well, your Grace, have you done?"

"Done what?"

"Your noble lamentations against fortune for making you a Duke, and giving you sixty thousand pounds a year."

"Have you no soul?"

"I don't know."

They looked at each other for a few minutes in silence; and then Captain Gay, with a low bow, handed the Duke the letter from Lady Bridget.

"Perhaps," he said, "this letter, which, from the superscription, I guess to be from your worthy and exemplary aunt, will contain something that may alter the current of these gloomy thoughts."

"No—no!"

"Yet take it and read it. It is but common courtesy to one who has received you well."

The Duke did take the letter, and listlessly opened it. The contents were soon perused, and with a pale face and flashing eyes, he rose to his feet.

"Captain Gay?"

"Yes, your Grace."

"Read this letter."

Gay pretended to read the letter for the first time, and looked quite calm as he folded it up, and said:

"Well, I am surprised. Why, your Grace is the very spoiled child of fortune."

"What do you mean?"

"What do I mean? Why, that not content with placing you in so high and noble a position as you now occupy, fortune is resolved upon smoothing the only difficulty in your way, by providing you with a handsome and a noble Duchess."

"You are mad!"

"Indeed, I hope not. The letter is plain enough, I take it."

"Yes, the letter; but you, and you only, know that it is an utter impossibility to comply with its conditions."

Captain Gay shrugged his shoulders.

"You know that I am already married."

"Oh!—ah!—that is, George Drayton was."

"I was."

"Pardon me. The Duke of Lorton is quite another person, I assure your Grace."

"My name may be altered, Captain Gay; but I am not. I am still the husband of Millicent Ardent."

"But permit me to observe that that very interesting young person considers herself a widow."

"A widow?"

"Oh, yes. I thought that to keep her in a state of suspense would be the height of cruelty; so, you see, I took good care to send her a certificate of your death and burial, with which, no doubt, she is quite content. A large sum of money, as you well know, was sent likewise; and so I would ask your Grace, in all sober and serious reason, what earthly obstacle is there to your marriage now with a lady in your own rank of life?"

"Oh, fiend—fiend!"

"Well, that is my thanks."

"Thanks? You have destroyed me, body and soul! But it is not yet too late."

"For what?"

"To declare my marriage."

"It is too late. Dread the consequences of such a step."

"What consequences?"

"The hostility of the Court—the non-recognition of your title—the enmity of your aunt—possibly the being branded as an impostor."

"I care not."

"Indeed?"

"No! I care for nothing, but that peace of soul, which I can never have unless I own to my marriage with Millicent, and claim her as my wife. What to me are titles—honours—wealth——"

"Well, there is another consequence."

"What is that?"

"The hulks!"

"The what?"

"The hulks! Have you never heard of them, my good sir? The hulks! What do you glare at so?"

"At the wonderful assurance of the man who dares to speak to me as you speak."

"Oh, is that all?"

"It is enough, I think."

"Well, perhaps it is; but now, your Grace, it is time, since you talk of owning your wife, and so putting an end to all prospect of the recognition of your title without inquiry, that you and I settled accounts together at once."

"Settled accounts?"

"Yes, your Grace: if you are prepared to pay me the sum of one hundred thousand pounds, you may go to the devil in your own way, for all I care."

"You know I cannot pay you until my position is sufficiently recognized to enable me to raise that sum on the Lorton estates."

"Very well, then, you are bound, not only to throw no sort of obstacle in the way of that pleasant little process, but, on the contrary, to do anything which can possibly facilitate it."

"Everything in honour; but I won't barter my soul for the sake of raising such a sum, even for you, my good friend, Captain Gay."

"Then you are resolved?"

"I am."

"To seek your wife, and avow your marriage with the bouquet-maker's daughter?"

"I am."

"Well, your Grace, you shall not have to say that you did not go with your eyes open upon such an errand. I now throw off the mask. It is time that we understood each other. Henceforth we change places.—You are not the Duke of Lorton!"

"Not the Duke?"

"Not at all. I don't know or care who you are; but I wanted a Duke, and you came handy in my way, so I made you one, that is all; and now you can reflect, if you like, upon your position."

CHAPTER LIV.

GEORGE DRAYTON FINDS HIMSELF IN THE TOILS OF THE TEMPTER.

GEORGE DRAYTON was so thoroughly astonished at this revelation of his true position by Captain Gay, that he staggered back as if he had been shot, and sank upon the sofa with a deep groan.

"Ah," added the Captain, "your Grace seems a little surprised. I thought you would be; but, after all, it is better that you should thoroughly understand your position. We can work better together."

"Villain! wretch! monster!"

"Oh, go on. I am used to hard names. They break no bones. Go on—go on!"

"Oh, Heaven, save me!"

"Pho! you can save yourself."

"I can—I will, and it shall be by at once denouncing this villainy to the law."

"Ha—ha!"

"You dare to laugh!"

"Yes, I do."

"Villain! Do you know the peril in which you stand?"

"*We* stand, if you please. The peril takes the plural number, if you please, in this case. We both stand in peril, if you are a fool; if you have the sense of a cat, we stand in none."

"Scoundrel! You cannot hope to compromise me in your acts?"

"Compromise you? Why, what do you suppose the law would call us?"

"The law call us?"

"Yes. Accomplices in crime; and, if you must confess all, it would only be evident that fright caused you to do so, at the eleventh hour; but you have gone too far. I don't know but your neck might be in danger for it. Yes, to be sure it would—of course. The signing bills and bonds to the bankers, in the name of the Duke of Lorton, is rank forgery, and you have done so."

"No—I—I——"

"Oh, yes! They hold the documents. Why, your Grace would be hanged, as sure as fate."

"No—no! Oh, Heaven!"

"Yes—yes! It is true."

George Drayton shook in every limb, and was compelled to sink into the chair again.

"Come—come!" said Gay, "this is folly. There is not merely my safety, but every success in the course seems to aid us. Nobody but you or I can blow this, our plot, to the winds. You may, if you please, live and die the Duke of Lorton, or you may be a convicted felon. Do you, for one moment, hesitate in your choice of situations? Come—come, be a man!"

"Oh, that I were dead!"

"Stuff! Dead, indeed! Time enough for that in years to come. Now, I tell you what you can do. You can wed this Lady Christina, and then you can pay me, and you can secretly, you know, so enrich the family of your late wife, and so, by implication, enrich her, that that weight will be off your mind; and when you find that she, as a young widow, is rather apt to comfort herself for your loss with some one of her own class as a second husband, you will no longer have a thought upon the subject."

"Do I dream?"

"You did when you thought of thrusting from you all the goods that fortune had cast into your lap."

At this moment a servant glided into the room.

"What now?" cried Captain Gay.

"The Lady Bridget!" announced the servant.

"Admit her ladyship, instantly."

"Yes, sir."

The servant left the room.

"Rouse yourself," said Captain Gay to George Drayton; "rouse yourself, and be a man. Here is the aunt. Don't put on that hang-dog sort of look!"

"Alas—alas!"

"Why do you cry, 'alas!' my lord?"

"Do not insult me by the utterance of that title, to which I have no just claim."

"I will call you what you please; but your claim, it strikes me, is as good, if not better, than that of many a lordling, who is neither doubted by others, nor doubts himself. But courage, caution, and silence. Here is your noble aunt."

"I cannot——"

"You cannot what?"

"Persevere in this deception."

"The hulks!"

"Ah! that dreadful word!"

"Hush!"

Lady Bridget Lorton entered the room.

"My dear nephew, allow me to hope that you are quite charming. Ah, me! I think I begin to get about middle-aged myself."

"Middle-aged?" muttered Captain Gay. "The old hag is sixty, at the very least."

"Oh, aunt!" said the Duke, "I—a—that is—pray be seated. I am not very well."

"He calls her aunt," said Captain Gay to himself. "Ha—ha! I am safe—I am safe!"

"Not well, my dear nephew? Fie! and at your age, too, and with your nobility. Think of your ancestors, my dear. Indeed, I do think that everything in the shape of indisposition ought to be confined entirely to the lower classes."

"So do I, my lady," said Gay.

"Silence!" said the Duke. "Pray excuse me, Lady Bridget; I feel an unusual oppression about the brain, to-day. I don't precisely know what it is—but—but——"

"Oh, we will send for the Court physician."

"No—no! It is nothing. It is gone. I am quite well pleased—nay, quite delighted to see you."

"Ah! now you are yourself again, and I have come to congratulate you upon the fact that you will be presented and received at Court on the first of the ensuing month, and you will, likewise, be congratulated on your marriage."

"On my marriage?"

"Yes, my dear nephew, your marriage."

"Why, how did they know? Who has told? How——"

"Silence!" whispered Gay. "Recollect yourself."

"Well, but——"

"The hulks!"

The Duke tottered back, and turned pale.

"Well, my dear nephew," added old Lady Bridget, who was now too intent upon applying the volatile salts in a small bottle to her nose, to notice the confusion of the Duke—"my dear nephew, I have succeeded in smoothing all difficulties as to your reception at Court."

"Indeed?"

"Yes; and in the simplest manner."

"Yes—yes. I am glad——"

"You ought to be, for I have, along with that desirable event, secured you a connection that cannot be otherwise than perfectly satisfactory. But you received my note?"

"Oh, yes—yes, I think—that is, yes."

"Then you know all about it?"

"I do."

"Well, and it has your entire concurrence, of course; and you feel that I have indeed worked well for you? But, then, you are the last of the family; and so, if I did not wish to see the Lortons extinct, it was natural that I should do all in my power for you, you know."

"Yes; but—but I have not the honour of knowing, even by sight, the lady you propose to me as a wife."

"I daresay not; but that does not in the least signify, my dear nephew."

"Oh, does it not?"

"No. You shall, however, be introduced to her, you may depend, in due course."

"I am much obliged, aunt, indeed. I could have surmised that it was likely I should be introduced to the lady who was to become my wife. But is it not possible that when so introduced, I may not like her?"

"Eh?"

"I say, when so introduced, I may not like her."

"Not like her?"

"No."

"And pray, nephew, I would beg to ask you, with all due and proper submission to your very superior talents, what that can possibly have to do with the question at issue?"

This was spoken in such a tone of haughty sarcasm, that it was in truth a very difficult thing to reply to the question, and George Drayton stared at the old withered piece of pride and antiquity in silence.

"Come—come," she added, with a toss of her head, "you are thinking of your former state, I suppose?"

"Indeed, I am."

"I have no doubt of it. Then I can tell you that, with men of the rank to which you have been called, your liking, or your not liking the lady, is of not the smallest account."

"Not the smallest," said Captain Gay.

"Silence, sir!" said the Duke.

"I am your Grace's very humble servant," added the Captain, as he bowed, and retired to the recess of a window in the room.

"That man of yours," said the old lady, "is, I have taken notice, a very sensible sort of person. He brought me a recommendation from Mr. South, who, by-the-by, ought to have called upon me long before this. Indeed, I cannot think what has become of him."

"It is to be sincerely hoped, madam," said Captain Gay, as he bowed again, "that he has met with no accident."

"I hope so, too."

"Well, aunt," said the Duke, with a sigh, "will you give me till to-morrow to think of this marriage?"

"Yes, you may think as long as you like; but it is quite settled."

CHAPTER LV.

JACOB ARDENT PAYS HIS PROJECTED VISIT TO THE DUKE.

As old Lady Bridget uttered these words, a servant opened a door leading into the saloon, and said, in a loud voice:

"Mr. Jacob Ardent."

The Duke sprang to his feet, Captain Gay uttered an oath, and the old lady looked from one to the other in amazement.

"What is all this?" she said.

"A low person, my lady," said Captain Gay, "who, no doubt, wishes to see the Duke, but who will not be admitted. Charles!"

"Yes, sir," said the servant.

"Tell the person that the Duke declines to see him."

"No!" cried George Drayton. "Admit him instantly."

"But, your Grace——"

"I command you, Charles, if that be your name, to admit him instantly. I am master here, it should appear."

"Yes, your Grace."

Captain Gay merely bit his lips, and with a low bow retired to the window again.

Charles, the footman, with secret glee at finding the great man snubbed, retired to show old Ardent to the Duke's presence.

Then George Drayton, turning to the old lady, said:

"Aunt, will you oblige me by retiring to another saloon for a short time? I have some business with this man who is announced to me."

"But, my dear nephew, if it is some low connection, allow me, if you please, to urge upon you the necessity of putting an end to it at once."

"Yes—yes! Pray go now."

"To oblige you, anything."

The old lady left the room, and the moment the door closed upon her, Captain Gay placed his hand upon the arm of the Duke, saying:

"Are you mad?"

"How, or why?"

"Do you know who was announced?"

"I do."

"The father of——"

"Of my wife—of my Millicent! The only being who ever possessed, or who ever will retain, my affections. Yes, I know the name well."

"Then I say you are mad to see him."

"Am I?"

"You are, indeed. You don't know the danger. What if he should know you?"

"He never saw me. I will see him, though, let the danger be what it may. In this respect the Duke that you have made will exercise the authority of one. Urge me no more. You have made me nearly desperate. Do not go too far. If you would still have me your tool, do not abuse me too much."

The tone in which this was spoken sufficiently convinced Captain Gay that all further opposition was useless, and might tend only to the production of an explosion, which might at once blow to pieces all the fine fabric of deceit which he had piled up for his own interest. He retired with a shrug of his shoulders, saying as he did so:

"Be it so, then. I will listen to what he says. I suppose I may do that?"

"I care not."

One half of a folding door was thrown open, and old Jacob Ardent, with his hat in his hand, and looking rather paler than usual, tottered into the room.

The Duke felt sick at heart at the part that he had to play, and he sank into a chair.

Captain Gay, who was fearful that the old waterman-fireman might recognize him, took good care to keep out of direct sight.

"My Lord Duke!" said old Ardent.

"Well?"

"Oh, my lord! let me look at you for your noble father's sake, and for your still nobler mother's, bless them both, and rest their souls in bliss!"

"You knew them?"

"I did—I did! Oh, my Lord Duke, I am but a poor old man, and my name is Jacob Ardent."

"Jacob Ardent?"

"Yes, my lord. Did you never hear that name before?"

"No—that is, yes, I have."

"Ah, and I'll warrant it was from lips that

loved you well, and that you loved well, too, that you heard it."

"Yes—oh, yes—yes. My poor——"

"Mother."

"Yes—yes; that is, my mother, as you say."

It had been from the lips of Millicent that George Drayton had often heard the name of her father.

"Ah, bless her!" added the old man—"bless her. She is a saint now in Heaven, my Lord Duke.'

"Amen!"

"Yes, and so say I 'Amen!' and God bless her. But—but——"

"Say on."

"Oh, my Lord Duke, I—don't know how to say what I have come to say to you; and yet you look good, and kind, and feeling."

"Say freely what you please."

"And you will be patient, and—and kind, and feeling to the poor old man, will you, my Lord Duke?"

"Oh, yes—yes. Believe me I will—I am."

"Then—then, I—a—that is, I—Oh, I cannot say it!"

"Take your time."

"What an old fool!" said Captain Gay, in a low tone; "what on earth has the old idiot got to say?"

"My Lord Duke, on the night that your noble father died, he placed in my hands certain papers."

"Ah!"

"Yes. They are here, and with them he likewise placed in my hands the sum of two hundred golden guineas, saying: 'Jacob Ardent, I give this gold into your honest keeping, to hand to my son when you shall see him, and I know that you will consider the money as sacred, for mine and for his sake.'"

"And you did?"

"I did, indeed, my Lord Duke."

"What an old fool!" said Captain Gay.

"Honest, worthy old man! And do you mean to tell me that, in your state of poverty, with those around you whom you loved, whom this money would have done so much for, you never touched it?"

"Never!—oh, never!"

"Well," muttered Captain Gay, "of all the stupid old pumps that ever I heard of, this beats them."

"You are a marvel!" said the Duke.

"Nay, my good lord, don't say that. Let me hope, and let me believe, too, that there are very many honest men in the world, as well as old Jacob Ardent."

"I will think so for your sake, Mr. Ardent. And you have come to me now, no doubt, as soon as you heard of my arrival in London, to perform my father's wishes?"

"I have intruded upon you, my Lord Duke, for that very purpose, and none other."

"Well," said Captain Gay, "of all the old fools that ever stepped, this is the worst. Why, he might have kept all the money, and not a soul have been the wiser."

"Honest, worthy man!" said the Duke, holding out his hand. "I do not know how to express to you my admiration."

"Oh, my good lord, there is something yet to tell, before I can take that honoured hand."

"Something!—what? Is it of—of——"

"The money."

"Oh, only the money?"

"Yes, my Lord Duke. Alas! I had the money, as I thought, quite safely hidden; but when I went, only a short time since, to look for it, woe to me, it was gone!"

"Gone?"

"Yes. Oh, yes, all—all gone!"

"Oh, of course," said Captain Gay. "Ha! ha! Why, what a fool I was, now, to be taken in by this old rascal's pretended honesty. Ha! ha! this is good, indeed. Gone, of course. Ha!"

"But how do you mean that it is gone?" said the Duke.

"I will tell you all. I came to tell all, and I will do so, let the consequences be what they may. I hid the money from all the world—I did not even tell my wife where I had hidden it; but she, it appears, when I did not suspect it, watched me, and found the gold. Her thought was that it was all my own, and that it was from her only that I, in my avarice, hid it. Alas! from time to time, being inflamed with a desire of gaining a sudden fortune in the lottery, she took it all."

"Ha! of course," said Captain Gay. "How devilish well he does tell the story, to be sure."

"Heed it not," said the Duke, who saw truth in the old man s face, and in every tone of his voice. "Heed it not, my good old friend. I hope and desire that you will not give yourself another moment's uneasiness upon the subject."

"Oh, but, my Lord Duke, it shall all be paid."

"I think I see it," said the Captain.

"Yes, it shall all be paid. It may be a long time, to be sure; but if old Jacob Ardent lives, it shall be paid, my Lord Duke, every farthing of it—every farthing."

"Stop a moment," said George Drayton, as he stepped to a table, and hastily wrote a few lines on a scrap of paper. "There, take that, old friend, and make your mind easy."

"Ah! my lord, this is an acquittance of the debt, but I cannot take it. No—no!"

"Not take it?"

"No, I cannot. I should be very unhappy, indeed, if I were to take it. I can work yet, and so can my wife, and so can our poor widowed child, Millicent!"

The Duke uttered a deep groan, and covered his face with his hands.

———

CHAPTER LVI.

MILLICENT RESOLVES TO SEE THE DUKE OF LORTON.

"There, now, you see," said Captain Gay, stepping forward, and speaking in an assumed voice, so that old Ardent should have the less chance of recollecting him. "There, you see, by talking about the deceased parents of His Grace, you have deeply affected him."

"Perhaps I have, Mr. Flunky," said old Ardent, who did not like the tone in which he was addressed by an apparent domestic; "but those tears are honest ones, and won't do His Grace any harm."

"You had better go away now."

"Why?"

"Because, you see, His Grace doesn't want you any longer."

Old Ardent looked at him steadily.

"I don't know where," he said; "but it seems to me as if I had seen you somewhere before, and didn't like you."

"You are mistaken, quite."

"Well, perhaps I am, and perhaps I am not. Good evening, my Lord Duke, and may Heaven bless you for your kind reception of a poor old man. The hearts of those at home will be all the lighter, when I tell them what a good, and kind, and truly noble soul you have. I bid you humbly farewell, my Lord Duke."

"Stay—oh, stay!"

"At your lordship's service."

"You said that—that you had a daughter?"

"Alas, yes, poor girl! She is a young widow, my lord. She married a good man, but he is dead—dead."

"Dead?"

"Yes, my Lord Duke. Ah! if he were not, he would help us all to repay the debt we owe to your noble lordship; but poor George Drayton is no more!"

"No more?"

"Yes, my lord—yes. I did not know the lad; but from all I can hear of him, he was of the order of nature's nobility, my lord—no disparagement to your lordship."

"Yes—yes; and your daughter—is she well —is she happy? Is Millicent pale and thin? Does she weep? Oh, tell me if my——"

"The hulks!" whispered Captain Gay.

The Duke sank back into his seat again.

"Go—go!" he gasped. "I—I have nothing more to say to you, old man. Go now. Farewell! I am done—done!"

"His Grace is not very well," said Captain Gay, "and by your presence here, Mr. What's-your-name, you are only aggravating his indisposition, so if you really have any regard for him, you will go at once."

"That is sufficient," said old Ardent, "God bless and preserve him! I am going at once."

He turned and left the saloon, full of wonder at the strange manner in which the Duke had questioned him about his daughter Millicent.

No sooner was the old man gone, than Captain Gay, in a voice of terrible, but yet suppressed bitterness, spoke to George Drayton.

"Are you mad?" he said. "What in the name of all that is infernal, induced you to speak to him of his daughter?"

"Peace—oh, peace!"

"Peace, indeed! You are taking the best steps you can to destroy your own peace. What peace can you ever hope for, while you allow such follies to possess you?"

"None—none."

"None, indeed; but rouse yourself, I beg of you. You will ruin all by this folly. Think of the abyss on the brink of which you stand."

"There is an abyss either way."

"How do you mean?"

"I mean, that it is to plunge into an abyss to persevere in this wretched deception, and it is an abyss to escape from it; but which is the deeper, I know not."

"Oh, pho—pho! This is but childish folly. You can do so much for the Ardents, that they will sing with joy. You can give them your custom, you know. You can send there for your bouquets."

"Ah, yes, that reminds me; ring for a servant."

"With pleasure."

A footman answered the summons, and the Duke said:

"Send hither the man I sent for the bouquets to Covent Garden."

"Yes, your Grace."

Captain Gay's face flushed, as he said in a low tone:

"What! Have you then sent there already?"

"I have."

"It was imprudent."

"I care not. I sent a man with five guineas to order five bouquets, and I want to know whom he saw."

"Well, there is, perhaps, no harm in it. Here he is."

"Now, sir," said the Duke, "did you go for the bouquets?"

"Yes, your Grace."

"Whom saw you at the shop?"

"An old lady, sir."

"And—and—a—younger one in widow's weeds?"

"No, your Grace, I did not."

The Duke sank back on the couch on which he had seated himself, and with a deep sigh, he said:

"You may go."

The servant left the room.

"This is all very romantic, indeed," said Captain Gay; "but let me tell you that if it is persevered in, it will be fatal to you. If you really will and must have information of your amiable widow, I will get it for you, and get it, too, with so much discretion, that it shall not in the least degree compromise you, and yet it shall be complete and full. You ought by this time to have a respectable notion of my talents, I should say."

"Go, then—oh, go then at once!"

"I will; but, in the meantime, let me beg of you to speak fairly to the old Lady Bridget. This marriage of yours with the Lady Christina she has set her heart upon, and if you resist it, she will desert you and your cause, and then you are lost."

"Listen to me, Gay."

"I am all attention."

"You must, if I comply with your wishes for the present, find out some mode of ultimately putting off the match."

"I cannot."

"Then I will tell Lady Bridget at once that I defy her, and that I will not countenance the arrangement."

"You are mad!"

"I care not. Such is my determination!"

Captain Gay reflected for a moment.

"Well, then, I consent. You may depend upon me. Even at the eleventh hour—ay, if the bride were ready in the church, if the service were begun, I will find a means of breaking off the match."

"You swear it?"

"I do, so help me——Well, I don't like oaths: they come to nothing, after all. But I will keep my word, you may depend; and you have seen enough of me to know that I can do pretty well what I please. Is it a bargain?"

"It is—it is!"

"And you will seem to consent?"

"I will. I am in the toils, and I see no way of escape. I will consent, and I trust to you; but I do so, because I have in my own hands the means of fulfilling your promise; for even at the altar I can refuse to speak the words which would make me a perjurer and a bigamist, for I am the husband of another."

"All will be right," said the Captain; "and now, farewell. I will soon bring you some news from Covent Garden market, you may depend. All you have got to do is to have patience."

Captain Gay seemed to leave the house, and then the Duke went to his aunt, to whom he said:

"I consent to your wishes, dear aunt, in all things."

"My charming nephew! you do not know what pleasure you give me; but I can only see that, after all, you are a true member of the Lorton family."

This, under the circumstances, was rather an equivocal compliment—at least, George Drayton felt it to be such, and he only bowed in reply to it.

"I will set the lawyers to work at once about the marriage settlements," said the old lady. "The fact is, you see, that Lady Christina Harrowby only dates from Anne."

"Oh, indeed."

"Yes, while we came in with the Conqueror."

"Ah!"

"You understand, therefore, that that circumstance gives us a very great advantage over the Harrowbys."

"Yes—oh, yes !"

"You see that, my dear, quite clearly ?"

"Nothing can be clearer," said poor George, in a distracted kind of manner. "Nothing can be possibly clearer than that."

"I knew you would say so."

"Yes, and even now, perchance, she weeps for me."

"Oh, dear, no."

"Yes, yes, she loves my memory."

"Good gracious, what are you talking about ? I can assure you that the Lady Christina Harrowby, though she does only date from Anne, is too well bred to weep for anybody or anything in all the world."

George Drayton started. His thoughts had been with his own poor, neglected Millicent.

"My dear aunt," he said, "will you excuse me ? My head is rather in a bad way just now. I think I have over-fatigued myself to-day, and I require rest."

"Then, good-bye. You had better lie down a little. I heard that your carriage could hardly get through that low Covent Garden. market. I wonder that the wretches who live in such places have the impudence to dare to look at a Duke. I should like to have them all built up within brick walls in some low part of the town, and not allowed to come out after a certain hour of the day when the aristocracy have risen, and are about to appear."

With this amiable speech, the old Lady Bridget, after embracing her supposed nephew affectionately, left the room, and, ordering her carriage, she soon afterwards left the house, and went home.

Happy old lady !

George Drayton flung himself upon a couch, and gave himself up to despairing thoughts. Never could he have believed it possible that any train of circumstances could have entailed upon him so much misery; but then he had never contemplated even the amount of guilt that he felt he was committing.

CHAPTER LVII.

CONTAINS SOME PARTICULARS CONCERNING THE REAL DUKE OF LORTON.

THERE were, no doubt, very many people on that day when the Duke of Lorton sat upon a sofa, and felt so wretched, who were to the full as miserable as he; but certainly no one could be much more so.

Poverty has its pangs—destitution and want may strew the path of some men with thorns; but all that is nothing to the agony that must be his who finds that he has yielded to some most unworthy impulse, and that by so yielding he has involved himself in the meshes of an intrigue, from which he sees no way of escape.

Yes, there was one way.

That way was the route to a jail—the route to the dock of a criminal court—to a felon's cell.

George Drayton had not come so far as to say that he dared encounter all that as yet. It was too terrible to think of, and he told himself, too, that if he did make up his mind to denounce himself, he would by so doing bring disgrace and ruin upon poor Millicent as well.

"Oh, Heaven !" he said. "What shall I do ?"

"Nothing," said a voice.

He started to his feet. The evil genius of his destiny—Captain Gay, *alias* Mr. Brand—stood by his side.

"You here ?"

"Yes, your Grace, I am here."

"Leave me—oh, leave me! Do not mock me by that title, to which I feel I have no right."

"Oh, indeed ! Well, I only came to congratulate you upon the favourable condition of your affairs."

"Favourable ?"

"Oh, yes; highly so. The marriage that the Lady Bridget has brought so nearly to a conclusion for you, will install you in your position without the likelihood of a dispute. The family of your wife will find that they are as much interested with your Dukedom as yourself; and if ever at some future time any strange accident should cast a doubt upon your title, why they will smother it up."

"Indeed !"

"Oh, yes ! You don't suppose, do you, that everything goes quite smoothly with what we call the old families of this, or of any other country ?"

"I do not understand you."

"You don't ?"

"Indeed I do not."

"Then I will tell you. Very many of the noble families of England, what with the interpolation of changelings, in lieu of the right heirs, the intrigues of the females, and the profligacy of all parties, are in such a position, that the present holders of the titles, and the lords of them, have about as much right to such as you or I."

"Can this be so ?"

"Oh, yes, it is true. Have you not heard of eccentric and odd noblemen ?"

"Yes."

"Of one, for instance, whose whole delight is in having an imitation stage-coach made, and dressing himself like a coachman, and driving it. You have heard of that ?"

"Often."

"Well. His noble mother, no doubt, admired his noble father's coachman. That little preference fully accounts for the bias in the young nobleman's mind. Do you see that ?"

"I see what you mean. If what you say be true, one half of the English nobility must be in such a situation, for they are celebrated for the most brutal and degrading tastes."

"Just so; but you put it at quite a low estimate when you say one half."

"It may be so."

"Well, my lord, that is how the world wags. But now to look more at home, and to

MILLICENT MAKES A LAST APPEAL TO GEORGE DRAYTON.

consider your own affairs, I say, I feel that I can and ought to congratulate you."

"Good Heavens, upon what?"

"Your prospects, and your position."

"My misery, you mean."

"Oh, dear, no. You have the reins in your own hands now. You have nothing to do but to marry the lady provided for you by your aunt, and all objections to your title, and to your reception at Court, vanish at once. You see, you are not as if you were in the position of a man contesting a right with another, for there is no opponent to you in the field at all."

George groaned.

No. 10.—(MARQUIS).

"Yes," added Captain Gay, "all is well."

"Well? Oh, no—no."

"No?"

"No; I say all is anything but well. Do you know what I was considering about just before you came in?"

"No. What?"

"About the propriety of going before a magistrate, and giving him a detail of all that has taken place, and giving myself up to justice."

"Up to a fiddlestick! Upon my life you are quite a droll fellow—you are indeed. Give yourself up to justice! Justice? Ho! ho! As if, now, there was such a thing at all to give yourself up to."

"There is such a thing."

"Now, my good friend, don't—don't speak in that sort of way. You have signed cheques upon the bankers in the name of the Duke of Lorton."

"I have, but——"

"Nay, hear me out. That is forgery—and forgery, under the maternal and fraternal laws of this country, is hanging, without a hope or a chance of mercy."

"It is—it is."

"Well, I'm sure no man in his senses will put his neck into a noose when he can keep it out. But come, come, I did think that we had quite settled all this, upon my life I did. The fact is, that it is too late now to stop; you are so far committed in this matter, that your very life, as you see quite plainly, depends upon your carrying it out; and, I tell you, you shall carry it out."

"Shall?"

"Yes, shall. It is quite time that we comprehend each other now. You and I change places. You have something to do that is essential to my views; and now that you have gone so far, I tell you, you shall do it."

George Drayton gazed in the face of Captain Gay in silence for a time, and then he said:

"Are you the fiend himself?"

"As you like to think me!"

"Or am I mad?"

"No; but it is I who keep you in your senses. Come now, enjoy what fate has so singularly placed in your possession, I beg of you, and don't be so foolish as to cast it from you, just to be the prey of all sorts of harpies. Now, for we must consider it, what good do you do by giving up this affair, and going and cutting yourself to pieces about it?"

"Good?"

"Yes, what good, now?"

"Alas, I know not."

"No, nor anybody else. You don't restore the title and the estate to the right owner, for there is none. You don't restore yourself to your wife, Millicent, for you will be hanged. What then on earth do you propose to yourself to do?"

George was silent.

"Come now, your Grace, just go on as you have begun, and by so doing you place yourself in a position to do no end of good with the large fortune at your disposal. You can relieve distress—you can make your wife's family quite comfortable—you can even embark in the search for the real lost heir to the Dukedom of Lorton, and if you find him, you can place him in such easy circumstances that he will not miss his footing."

"Oh, do not tempt me!"

"Tempt you? Well, that is a good one. But, however, you are in a better frame of mind now, and so I leave you. I have important business in hand. Good-day."

Captain Gay left the room, and George Drayton was alone again.

"I don't half like the humour he is in," thought Gay, "and I have a fancy that the people in the cursed bouquet-shop might be very dangerous. If I could but think of some way of getting them out of the way now, what a capital idea it would be. I wonder, if I were to pay a visit to the place, if they would know me in my new dress, any of them? I should think not. I wore moustaches when I was last there, and now I have shaved them off. I was in such a very different costume, too; and I rather think I have the art of altering my voice. Yes, I will pay a visit to the Ardents, and pick up what news I possibly can there."

With this determination, Captain Gay left the house of the Duke of Lorton, and made his way direct towards Covent Garden market.

It did not take him very long to get there, and he walked twice past the shop of the Ardents before he ventured to go to the door of it.

In the shop he saw Mrs. Ardent, and he thought that there was an air of great seriousness upon the good woman's face, which he had not seen before.

"Can it be possible now," he said, "that these people have any suspicions of the truth?"

This was an idea which, even in passing, gave to Captain Gay a pang of alarm; but before he left the Ardents he was doomed to experience a much greater shock than that passing thought of danger could possibly give him.

"Pho—pho!" he said. "How is it possible they can suspect anything? It is quite out of the question. I will go in, and speak to the old woman, and try if I can dexterously lead the conversation to family affairs. These common people generally have their stupid heads so full of their abominable family concerns, that you may easily get them to talk about them for an hour, and the difficulty is to stop them at such an exercise when once they begin."

CHAPTER LVIII.

CAPTAIN GAY SEES AND RECOGNIZES MRS. ARDENT'S LODGER.

CAPTAIN GAY, with all the assurance in the world, opened the door of the shop, and walked in.

Mrs. Ardent looked up.

"Any fruit?" said Gay.

"No, we don't sell it."

"Oh, I really beg your pardon, madam, I thought you did; and seeing that this looked to my mind the most respectable shop in the whole market, why, you see, without much further consideration, I opened the door, and intruded upon you."

"You are very good, sir. But we only sell flowers and bouquets."

"Oh, yes—to be sure; and upon my life, very beautiful ones you have. Really—very fine. Your own growing, I suppose?"

"Oh, lor, no! We have them sent from the country to us."

"Indeed? Well, I declare! I never did see such taste in the selection of colours in making up bouquets. I feel perfectly confident, madam, that it is you who preside over the making of these very exquisite and skilfully put together bouquets."

"Yes," said the gratified Mrs. Ardent, for flattery is ever welcome. "Yes; but my daughter, Mrs. Drayton, and my niece, Jane, aid me very much in getting them up, and are both very clever, I assure you, sir."

"If they take after their mother, they are clever, indeed."

"Oh, you are too good, sir."

"Not at all—not at all. So your daughter, Mrs. Clayton, then, resides with you?"

"Drayton, sir."

"Oh, I beg your pardon—Drayton. Yes, you did say Drayton; but I am so bad at names, and always was. I hope Mr. Drayton is quite well."

"Alas! sir, my poor child is a widow."

"A—widow?"

"Yes, sir."

"Why, gracious goodness, she must be a very young widow, then, for I was, to tell the truth, rather surprised to hear you say that you had a daughter old enough at all to be a Mrs. Anybody, considering that you are only in the prime of life yourself."

"Oh, dear, sir, I am older than I look."

"Are you, though?"

"Yes; now, sir, what should you suppose my age to be?"

"Thirty-eight."

"Believe me, sir, I am forty-four."

"You don't say so? Confound it," thought Captain Gay to himself, "she is fifty-four, if she is any age at all.—You don't say so, ma'am? Well, now, you do surprise me. And so Mr. What's-his-name is dead?"

"Alas! yes."

"Well, but so young a widow should get over her grief, and soon marry again. If she is at all like her mother, I am quite sure she need not look far for offers."

"Well, sir, that is as it may be; but I don't think my poor girl will marry again. Her mind is affected."

"Mad?"

"Oh, no—no, not that quite; but the shock of her poor husband's death—he was drowned, sir, in a wreck—has just a little touched her brain."

"What a good—hem! I mean, what a dreadful thing, to be sure. Then you take care of her, I suppose; and she is not in a state to be allowed to go about at all, I fancy? Hadn't you better put her into an asylum?"

"Oh, dear me, no; she is so kind and good and affectionate, that there is no occasion at all for that; but between you and me, sir, and the post, she thinks her husband is not dead yet."

"Oh!"

"Yes, sir; she will have it that he was never drowned, and that it is all a delusion."

"Oh!"

"And she goes so far as to say that she has seen him."

"The deuce!"

"Sir?"

"Bless me, I mean."

"Yes, sir; and that she is satisfied there is some villainy going on about him somewhere."

"Why, you don't mean that?"

"I do—that is, she does; but, lor! bless you, sir, it is quite a delusion. Now, who do you think she thinks, and in fact says her husband is now?"

The colour faded from the cheeks of Captain Gay, and even his great presence of mind and self-possession forsook him for a moment, so that he could not reply to Mrs. Ardent till she had repeated her question.

"Who do you think, sir, she says is one and the same with her husband, sir?" said Mrs. Ardent.

"I don't know," he just managed to gasp out. "I really can't say, madam. Who?—who?"

"Why, sir, a great nobleman."

"A—a—great nobleman?"

"Yes, sir; a Duke!"

"No!"

"Yes. The Duke of Lorton."

"The deuce!"

Captain Gay had seated himself on a chair in the shop; but now he sprang to his feet with a vague idea that he was, all along, instead of taking in Mrs. Ardent, being taken in himself, and that the plot upon which he so much prided himself was on the very verge of being blown up. He glanced around him even, not without a dread that a police-officer might pop his head in at the door, and say to him:

"Captain Gay, you are wanted."

Mrs. Ardent looked at him in surprise.

"Dear me, sir! ain't you well?"

"Well—well?"

"Yes, sir."

"I—that is—you—no—yes—I am only so very much surprised at what you say. I am so full of sympathy always with every disaster that I hear of, that it affects me quite as much, do you know, as if I had something personally to do with it; and your truly pathetic description of your daughter's mania touched me to the heart."

"Oh, sir, you are very kind."

"Good! she knows nothing," thought Gay, "and it was a false alarm, then, after all. She could not play such a part with such a face. I am a tolerable actor, but she would beat me all to nothing. No—no; there is no more danger than what may come of what she tells me. There is no discovery yet."

It was an immense relief to Captain Gay to be able so soon to come to this conclusion in the matter, and he sat down again in the chair, determined to get all the news he possibly could while he was there, and while Mrs. Ardent was in the communicative mood in which he had found her.

"I don't know," he said, "how to apologize to you, madam, for my seemingly odd conduct; but it is my way. It is nothing in the world but from my excess of sympathy."

"Oh, sir, that is not a fault."

"You are very good to say so."

"All the world would say so, sir."

"Then, my dear madam, before I go, let me ask of you one question. Is there anything that I can do, having, as I can tell you I have, ample means to remedy in any way, or to alleviate in any way your distress of mind?"

"Alas! no."

"Money? Is that of any service?"

"Oh, sir, no. I don't know how it is; but it seems as if Heaven had looked down upon us, and taken care that, in addition to our other miseries, we should not have that one; so that we have done better in our business lately, sir, than we have done for a long time past."

"I am delighted to hear it."

"Oh, but, sir——"

"Yes, madam?"

"Look at this."

Mrs. Ardent took the bill from the window that the destitute youth, Frank Western, had there placed, and showed it to him, saying:

"If, sir, you can in any way aid the writer of this, it will be doing a real goodness, sir."

"I will, with pleasure. And—so—your daughter thinks that the Duke of Lorton and her husband are one and the same person?"

"Yes—alas! yes."

"But you have tried to reason her out of the folly?"

"I have—I have; but it is all in vain. She only smiles, and says: 'Dear mother, you do not know what I know.'"

Captain Gay bit his lips, as he thought:

"What does that mean?—what can she know? Has George Drayton himself, after all, doubled upon me, and played me false, and let her know all, under some pledge or promise of secrecy? If he has, all is lost at once and for ever."

This was anything but an idea calculated to improve the equanimity of Captain Gay, which, from the whole interview, had been very seriously shaken; and he said, in rather a nervous sort of way, to Mrs. Ardent:

"Have you no idea of what she means by that?"

"None, sir—none at all."

"Humph! It is odd."

"It is, indeed, sir; but I should think that, after all, such a strange idea will not last long. Time does wonders, you know, sir; and soon she will become reconciled to the news of her husband's death, and with that feeling will vanish the strange idea that he and a great nobleman are one and the same person."

"When did she first get the idea, and how?"

"Oh, you see, sir, the Duke of Lorton's carriage came through the market, and was stopped by the market-carts just by our door, and Millicent happened to look out, and the Duke looked from the carriage window at the same time."

"Ah, yes, I see it all."

"Sir?"

"I mean that I can easily see how upon a disordered brain some accidental likeness may have told. Who is this, madam?"

Frank Western entered the shop at this moment, and bowed to Mrs. Ardent with a smile of great gratitude and affection.

CHAPTER LIX.

THE YOUNG DUKE KNOWS NOT HIS FATHER'S FOE.

As Captain Gay rose from his chair, he looked hard at the young man, whose appearance now was very much improved from what it had been when he was first introduced to the reader. A little kindness and a little food had done wonders for the famishing youth, and his eyes had brightened, the colour had come back to his cheeks, and he, in fact, looked quite a different being from what he had done when he came into the shop in so perishing a condition, and asked leave of Mrs. Ardent to put up the written paper in her window.

"This is the young man, sir," said Mrs. Ardent to Captain Gay, "that I was speaking of."

"'Tis he!" gasped Gay.

"Sir?"

"Nothing—I—I—that is, am a little faint, that is all. Nothing. Oh, so this is the young man?"

"Yes, sir."

The youth made a very elegant bow, as he said:

"You were speaking of me, then, to this person, Mrs. Ardent, I presume, and in your own kind way, of course, I may be quite sure of that?"

"And why not?" said Mrs. Ardent. "I'm sure I have nothing but kind things to say to you, and of you."

"Oh, you are too partial to me."

"Not at all."

This little refined dialogue let Captain Gay hear the voice of the youth perfectly. By the light that was in the shop, too, he saw his face quite well.

From that moment Captain Gay made up his mind that he had found the son of the Marquis and Marchioness of Dalewood, and the veritable owner of the dukedom and estates of Lorton.

Yes, reader, this famishing youth was that person; and it may have been chance, or it may have been—as we are more inclined to think—the directing hand of Heaven that brought him to the shop of the Ardents on the occasion before described, when from that time he became a much-loved inmate of their home.

Captain Gay was so much struck by this incident, that it really was a relief to him to have to say nothing for two or three minutes, during which Mrs. Ardent and the real young Duke spoke to each other so kindly.

But Gay had always looked forward to the probability, however remote, of obstructions to his views rising up before he had secured the money from George Drayton, which he was to be paid for his share in the fraud; but, to tell the truth, he hardly could, in the most imaginative moments of his existence, have supposed that he was to meet with the real Duke of Lorton at the bouquet-maker's shop in Covent Garden.

But he did not now entertain a doubt upon the subject.

After the lapse of two or three minutes, then, which were in reality such a relief to him, he made a desperate effort to recover his composure, and spoke.

"I am quite delighted," he said, "to make the acquaintance of this young gentleman."

The youth bowed.

"And I am sure it will give to me the greatest possible satisfaction to forward his views in any way that I possibly can, and as quickly as I can."

"I have, sir, but one view," said the youth, "and that is, to be able, by such few talents and acquirements as I have, to get my own living, so as not to be a burthen to those whom Heaven will surely reward for providing me in my destitution with a home."

"Come, now," said Mrs. Ardent, "you must not say anything about that, because the real truth is, you see, sir," turning to Captain Gay, "we would rather have him here than not, we are all so fond of him."

"I don't wonder at it."

"You want to spoil me, Mrs. Ardent," said the youth.

"No, I don't; and I don't think I could if I did want to do so."

"I have been thinking," said Captain Gay, "that I might get him something lucrative to do."

"Oh, sir, if you can."

"I will try. Will you call upon me this evening after eight o'clock, at the address I will give to you?"

"With pleasure, sir."

"Then give me a piece of paper and a pen or pencil, and I will write it down for you. There, can you find it?"

Captain Gay handed the paper to the youth, who read upon it the words:

"'Dalewood House, at the back of Montague House.'

"Dalewood House?" he said.

"Yes. Well?" cried Gay, who had written that address for the express purpose of testing the knowledge that the youth might have of who and what he was. "Yes—yes. Do you know it?"

"I have heard of it."

"When, and where?"

"Mrs. Ardent has mentioned it to me in connection with some very strange and romantic incidents that happened some time ago, in which she and her family were much mixed up."

"Oh, indeed; and—and—you know nothing further of it?"

"How should I?"

The look of ingenuous truth of the youth as he looked in the face of Captain Gay while he uttered these words, could not have been put on, and Gay was at once satisfied that he knew nothing that it was at all dangerous for him to know, and that when the Marchioness, before her death, had said that from fear of compromising, in the eyes of his son, the Marquis of Dalewood, she had kept that son in total ignorance of who and what he was, she had spoken the exact truth.

"This will do," thought Gay. "I must get rid of him."

It was rather a suspicious remark for Captain Gay to make concerning anybody—that he must get rid of them. It might mean almost anything in the way of criminality, as the reader, from the previous career of that notable villain, is well aware.

Turning, then, to the youth, he said, with an air of unconcern that, now his mind was more at ease about the extent of knowledge that the youth had of his own history, he found it easy enough to put on:

"I shall expect you, then, about the hour of eight to-night, if you please; and between this and then I perhaps will think of some plan of proceeding for your welfare."

"You are very good, sir. I will be there."

"Do so. Good-day, Mrs. Ardent. I shall, I hope, be, in time to come, a good customer for your admirable bouquets."

So saying, Captain Gay left the shop.

He had, indeed, got information with a vengeance, by his visit there—much more information than poor Mrs. Ardent dreamed there was to be got at all in her house.

"What is to be done now?" said Gay, to himself. "The boy has turned up at once. He is, without in my mind the shadow of a doubt, the veritable young Duke. What can I—what ought I to do? Tell him all? Oh, no—no! That will do no good. It may obtain me a pardon for the present; but that is all that my seeming tardy repentance will get for me, and that I despise. What can I —what ought I to do?"

He hurried on, for Captain Gay could walk at a good round pace, and still think deeply.

"If George Drayton has but the least inkling of this, it will blow the whole plot. Let him have but a notion that the real young Duke is to be found, and he will no longer hesitate about his course to pursue; but will at once, let the consequences to him and me be what they may, tell all. Curses on him!"

Captain Gay reached the pathway by the side of Montague House, leading to Dalewood House. Then he paused, and leaned against the gate before he proceeded farther, in order that he might thoroughly make up his mind to the course he was to pursue before going into the mansion.

"Yes, I see it all," he said. "Let but George Drayton know what I now know, and he goes and tells all, and I am the only victim in the whole business. The real Duke is on such capital terms with the Ardents, that he will, of course, put an end at once to any repentance of George Drayton, and the affair will end in him and the Ardents all arranging matters to their mutual satisfaction, and hauling me off to prison. Ha—ha!"

It was not very likely that Captain Gay, with all his natural firmness and feelings, would quietly sit down, even with such a very discouraging prospect as this before him.

Clenching his fist, he shook it in the air as he said, in a voice of deep and concentrated rage:

"Fate seems to be fighting against me; but I can settle very much of the danger by taking the life of the young Duke. I can kill him, and then how will they all look?"

Captain Gay thought he had only to determine to kill the young Duke. It is possible that a higher power than Captain Gay had already determined that he should not do so.

But it was with a determination that, rather than suffer himself to live in dread of the youth, he would murder him, that Captain Gay now betook himself to Dalewood House.

The unhappy George Drayton was at home.

"Is he alone?" said Captain Gay, sharply, to the servants who opened the hall-door for him.

"No, sir."

"No? Who is with him?"

"A young woman, sir."

"A young what?"

"A young woman, sir, with some bouquets from Covent Garden market, sir."

Captain Gay staggered back, as though he had been shot, and was glad to sit on one of the hall chairs. He glanced at the footman like a maniac, as he gasped out:

"Tell me! Was—was she—was she in mourning?"

"She wore a widow's cap, sir, and she said that she must see the Duke, on business of the very first private importance, sir; so we let her."

CHAPTER LX.

CAPTAIN GAY FINDS THE PLOT THICKENING AROUND HIM.

IT was with a frantic yell of rage that Captain Gay sprang from his seat, and seized the footman by the throat.

"Villain!" he said. "Did I not leave orders that no one was to see the Duke, till they had seen me first?"

"Ye—e—s, sir."

"Then, confound you! why did you let this woman get at him? Tell me that. But, no! I don't care about it. It is done now—it is done!"

Captain Gay pushed the affrighted footman from him, and paced the hall in evident agitation. Then suddenly he cried out:

"How long has she been here?"

"Half-an-hour, Mr. Brand."

"Half-an-hour? Time to win a kingdom! Half-an-hour, and I gossiping at the shop in the market! Oh, fool—fool!"

He darted upstairs three stairs at a time.

"Well, that's funny," said the footman. "I wonder whether he meant, now, himself or me, by 'fool—fool?'"

Captain Gay could not, when he rapidly put all the circumstances together, for one moment doubt that it was actually and truly Millicent herself who had brought the flowers, and who, despite his precaution, had got an interview with her husband, and of course claimed him.

He felt like a man standing upon a mine that he knew to be fired, and from the proximity of which he had no means of retiring.

The idea struck him for a moment that the wisest thing he could do was to lay hold of what valuables and money he could, and quit the house there and then at once and for ever.

For the space of about a minute this idea found favour in the mind of Captain Gay, and then he gave it up.

"No," he said, "I will not fly like a frightened cur. I will see it out—I will see the end of it, if it be my death to do so. I will not fly!"

The villain had courage.

But was it indeed true that Millicent was with George Drayton? Millicent, the faithful and the true, actually once again with him who seemed so far removed from her, and was yet so near?

Yes, she was with him. She had been with him for half-an-hour, or, indeed, rather more.

The information of the footman was quite correct, and the inferences of Captain Gay as to the identity of the visitor were quite correct also. She was there.

Captain Gay reached the first floor of the house, and entered a large and exquisitely-furnished room, called the yellow drawing-room. There were folding doors opening from this room into another, as richly furnished, but all in crimson. He thought that it would be in this inner room that he should find George Drayton and Millicent.

Now, there were two large folding doors separating these two rooms, and Captain Gay had an idea that it would not be at all difficult to open them a little way—an inch or so, and listen to what was passing, and, indeed, to look in.

No scruple of any sort was likely to stand in the way of Captain Gay doing this; and so with a stealthy step he entered the yellow drawing-room.

Even with the folding-doors closed, he heard the sound of voices in the adjoining apartment.

"They are there!" he said, in a whisper.

But he was not satisfied by hearing merely the sound of the voices—he wanted to hear exactly what was said, in order that he might come to some definite conclusion regarding his own position; so with the greatest care he turned the lock of the folding doors, and parted one of them an inch from the other.

This opened a long slit from the very floor to the ceiling, so that Captain Gay had no sort of difficulty in peeping into the room.

George Drayton sat on a couch with his face hidden in his hands, and Millicent, his wife, in her dress of mourning, but with her widow's cap thrown on to the floor, stood a few paces from him with her hands clasped, and in silence.

She was apparently awaiting the effect of some appeal that she had made to him. Her face was flushed, and joy sparkled in her eyes, for she knew that the seeming dead was in life.

Captain Gay uttered an awful imprecation.

* * * * *

Leaving the villain Gay to listen to the latter part of the interview between George Drayton and his young and fair wife, Millicent, it is necessary, for the reader's satisfaction, that we should relate what took place at that interview from its commencement.

When Millicent had declared that she would take the bouquets to the Duke of Lorton's, her mother did not think that, upon more mature reflection, it was a determination she would carry out.

But her mother even did not know the depth of feeling nor the womanly courage that was at the bottom of the heart of Millicent.

She had made up her mind to see the man whom she thought, notwithstanding the rank and the very different circumstances by which he was surrounded, was her husband.

It is difficult to say what power, except actual force, could have prevented her from so doing.

Hence, then, about the time that Captain Gay started from Dalewood House on his very cunning errand to the bouquet-maker's, Millicent had started to go to Dalewood.

They must have crossed each other on the road.

Now, the servants knew perfectly well that Mr. Brand, as the Captain called himself, was particularly anxious that no one should get at the Duke but through him; but they hated the tyranny of this Mr. Brand, and they were ever ready to thwart him in any way that it appeared at all possible so to do.

Hence, when Millicent reached the door of Dalewood House, and asked to see the Duke, they felt all the inclination in the world to let her do so.

"What do you want with him?" was the question.

"To speak to him alone."

"Indeed! And who are you?"

"A friend of his."

"Did Mr. Brand tell you to come?"

"I never heard of such a person."

The result with the servants was, as far as Millicent was concerned, in her favour, and they agreed that the Duke should be told that some one wanted to see him with some

bouquets, and that he should be allowed, in the absence of Brand, to decide for himself the question of to be seen, or not to be seen.

George Drayton was lying upon a sofa, in no very enviable frame of mind, when a servant approached him.

"Your Grace?"

George Drayton started.

"What is it?"

"A young person desires to see your Grace."

"Who? who? I won't see anyone—I think I won't. Who is it?"

"She comes with some bouquets, she says, that have been ordered."

"Ah?"

"Yes, your Grace, and she most earnestly desires, she says, to see your Grace alone, if your Grace pleases."

George felt faint and sick at heart. Something too well told him who it was. He sank back on the sofa, and the colour, for a moment or two, left his very lips.

"Shall I ring for assistance? Is your Grace ill?"

"No—no. I—no."

The servant looked amazed and terrified.

"It is nothing—nothing," said George Drayton. "You will take no notice of it—you will not mention it?"

"Certainly not, your Grace."

"That is well. Is—he—here—in the house?"

"He?"

"Yes, Gay—I mean Brand."

"Mr. Brand is not within, your Grace."

"Well—well—and—the—a—a—lady—the person, I mean the lady—I will see her; yes, I will see her. Let her come here. I will—I ought to see her."

"Yes, your Grace. Shall I show her into a reception room?"

"No,—here! here!"

The footman left the room.

"It is my Millicent!" cried George. "It is the dear one whom I loved, and love still. It is my own very much injured, suffering Millicent! Oh, grant me courage now to see her—to speak to her; and yet to—to—to deny her!—I must! I must! It has come to this, that I must deny her, and my soul at the same time, for that denial will weigh against me on the day of eternal judgment like a load of lead!"

He covered his face with his hands, and rocked to and fro in the agony of his despair.

The door creaked open.

George dared not look up.

The footman spoke.

"The young person with the bouquets, your Grace, if your Grace pleases."

The door was closed again.

George Drayton knew that Millicent was in the same room with him, but he dared not yet look up. He heard her light footstep on the silken carpet, and yet he dared not look up. The face he had so longed to see—that he had dreamed of in his poverty and in his prosperity as the most welcome sight on earth to him, he knew was there; but yet he dared not lift his eyes to it.

Oh, what agony was that!

He heard her footstep again—nearer—nearer, till it came to him; but yet he had not courage to look up to her, for guilt was in his heart.

It was that which made him so weak, and so full of pain, in the presence of her whom he ought to have hailed with joy, and placed next his heart.

And poor, poor Millicent, too. What must have been her feelings at that time?

Truly, in a different way, she was to be to the full as much, if not, indeed, much more pitied than George Drayton, for she had done no wrong—she had yielded to no temptation. There she was, what she had ever been—his true and constant wife.

Oh, yes, Millicent was to be pitied much more than George Drayton, for she was utterly and completely blameless.

CHAPTER LXI.

LOVE AND TRUTH TRIUMPH OVER ALL OBSTACLES AT LAST.

THIS was a state of things that could not possibly last very long.

Millicent spoke.

Oh, how her first words thrilled through the heart of George Drayton! They were the first words he had heard from her since he had left her to go to Ireland. That seemed to him as if it were a very, very long time ago. The very sound of her voice sank upon his heart, in the so well-known and so well-remembered tones, with a gush of joy, and yet of pain.

"I understand," she said, "that I am speaking to the Duke of Lorton? Is it so, sir?"

"It—it—is!" he just managed to say.

"Oh, Heaven, yes, the voice, too!" cried Millicent.

George Drayton shook like an aspen leaf; but he was in the toils of the tempter, and he made an effort to do as he was bidden to do on pain of death—death on a scaffold by the hands of the hangman! Since that image had been presented to the terrified imagination of George Drayton, it had been ever present to him; so he, as one may say, managed to look at Millicent by turning his head round towards her with what appeared to be something like a violent spasmodic effort.

Their eyes met.

"George—George!" she shouted.

"Madam!"

That one word, pronounced with frigid coldness, struck her as if a knife had reached her heart. Even in the very act of springing towards him, she seemed arrested as if struck by some fiat of Providence, and turned to marble.

"Well?" he said again.

She drew slowly back.

"No—no—no! He could not say that! No—no! I am mad—I am mad!"

"Your business with me?"

"My business, sir—with you!" She passed her hand over her eyebrows, as though by that action she could clear away some mist that obscured her faculties. "My business with you, sir, did you ask of me?"

"Ay."

"Sir—your Grace—Oh, pardon me that I do not always use your proper title."

"It does not matter."

"I would beg—implore you to look at me!"

He did look at her.

"Do you not know me?"

He shook his head.

"I know you not."

Millicent uttered a faint cry, and nearly fell to the floor. She clasped her hands, and a look of perfectly indescribable woe covered her face, as she said:

"It is not so, then, and they are right. Oh, Heaven! it was still left to me to be able to see by their looks and whispers, and their tears, that at times they thought me mad, and now I feel that I am mad—quite mad!"

George sank back on to the sofa again, from which he had risen, and uttered a low moan.

"What was that?" she said.

"What?"

"I heard a moan, as of some heart in great agony, that would fain hide its grief, but could not."

"You moaned."

"I?"

"Yes, I heard you. Have you aught else to say to me?"

He strove to look at her; but he was compelled to turn away his head from that cold, colourless, despairing face.

It was too terrible for him to look upon. She gathered strength in a few moments to answer him, and then she said, in a low, choking tone of voice:

"Sir, have you a brother?"

"No."

"A brother very like you, I meant?"

"No."

"Then you—you are not my George?"

"Madam?"

"Pardon me—oh, pardon me! I know—I feel that this visit here needs all the apologies I can make to you, and all the pardon you can give to me. I entreat your forgiveness. I am widowed, as you see. My heart is on the wild seashore, where I know now that my poor dead George—my beloved—lies buried. Oh, your Grace! nature, for some reason, has made you so like him—in tone—in look—in form and features—that my heart cried out when first I saw you pass our door in the market, that you were my husband—my once much-loved George!"

He turned completely round, and sobbed.

"But you will pardon me, sir. It seemed as if the blight that had fallen upon my heart from the moment that I had heard of my husband's death, cleared off, and sunshine was there again. I looked at them all at home, and smiled, and told them that he lived; and then they thought me mad—mad! You hear, sir?"

"I—I—do."

"But I thought that I was right, and they told me then that the great lord who had passed through the market was no other than you, sir, the Duke of Lorton; and then there came orders for bouquets for you, and it seemed as if some good angel had whispered to me: 'Millicent, take the fair flowers, and go and see your husband.'"

George's head sank on his hands.

"You feel for me, sir?"

He could only sob.

"Well, sir, I came; but—but you do not know me. You can only pity me, sir. You never saw me before, and you have no brother so like you, that my George may be he—and I am desolate again, sir. Oh, sir!"

"Yes—I—hear."

"You pardon this freak of weakness?"

"I—do."

"Farewell, sir. God bless you for your likeness to one who is so dear to me. Oh, Heaven, I am indeed now desolate!"

George in an instant sprang to his feet, and in a voice that rang through the saloon, called out to her:

"Millicent! my Millicent! to my arms! to my heart once more! My own, my wife—my only love! To your own George's heart again!"

With a shriek of joy, she flew towards him. She flung her arms around him, and between tears and laughter, she clung to him with frantic energy.

"It is—it is my only lost one! my husband! Oh, yes, God is good yet to me. It is George! George! Oh, joy! joy! joy!"

"Yes, dearest and best, I am your own George Drayton."

Their tears choked their utterance now for a time, and it was some minutes before she could look him in the face, and then she said:

"My George, and could you—could you say you did not know me? Could you say so to me?"

He only wept.

"Did you really not know me, George?"

"I knew you well. My heart knew you."

"Oh, yes; let me look at you again and again, to be quite sure that this is you."

"Oh, Millicent—Millicent, you ought to curse me!"

"I? Oh, no. I am no widow now. There—there, I am now a wife again—a happy wife."

She tore the widow's cap from her head, and flung it on the floor; and then, as the long tresses of her hair fell freely once again down her neck and shoulders, she flung herself into his arms, and wept aloud.

"Oh, dear," said Captain Gay, who had just seen this last portion of the interview, "that is very fine indeed. It appears that I am just in time for the denouement."

"Millicent," said George, after a pause, and speaking in a voice that was broken by sobs, "I know not what to say to you. How can I ever hope for your forgiveness?"

"Do not hope; you have it. All is past—all is forgiven. You are my own again."

"For ever and ever, Millicent!"

"Yes, George, that is well; but oh, tell me, if I do not in truth really dream, how all this came about? Are you what you seem, dear George? Are you a Duke?"

"No. Oh, no!"

"No? and yet——"

"And yet, you would say, I call myself one, and take upon myself the state of one. Oh, Millicent, as you see me I am a Duke; but there is a mystery in my Dukedom."

"Indeed!"

"Yes, which neither you nor I can fathom yet. I know not what to say to you, Millicent."

"Say that I am your wife."

"You are—you are."

"Your Duchess?"

"Oh, no—no!"

"No! And why not? I am your wife, you know, George, and the wife of a Duke is his Duchess. Is not that the rule, dear George?"

"It is, but——"

"Ah, you would say how much dearer a title it is to feel and to know that I am your love, and that you still feel for me all that you did when you were poor and friendless. But, George?"

"Yes, dear?"

"How could you say you did not know me? How my mind recurs to that again and yet again."

"Alas! alas!"

"Well, I will not speak of it, although it hurts me, and makes me think that either you do not love me, or that I am mad. How much better to be mad than that! But what a stately house this is, George. What luxury—what troops of servants. Oh, indeed, this at least must be all real."

"It is Millicent; but now sit down by me, and let me tell you something that you must do for the sake of the dear love you bear to me. I know and feel that you will do it, dear, dear Millicent."

CHAPTER LXII.

CAPTAIN GAY DISTURBS A GOOD UNDERSTANDING.

GEORGE DRAYTON drew Millicent to the sofa, and made her sit by his side, and then he said to her:

"My Millicent, you see me here, apparently the lord and master of all the grandeur that you see around you."

"Yes—yes, you are."

"No—no. I am its slave—its very worst slave. There is not time to tell you all now; but I must trust to you, you see, to trust in me."

"Oh, yes—yes, for ever and ever."

"I knew you would. Then, Millicent, in

order that I may be clearly and safely enabled to come to your father's house, and claim you as my own before all the world, you must consent to say nothing of me, nor of my existence, for at least three days from this one."

"Three days!"

"Yes, dear Millicent, it will take me that time to make some arrangements that are most essential. I have no time to tell you what they are, for even now I dread that your presence here, with the knowledge of who you are, should be known to one by whose villainy we are for awhile so cruelly separated, and who will still try the utmost of his diabolical cunning to prevent our reunion. Do you comprehend me?"

"Yes, oh, yes, I do. What is it you would wish me to do then, dear George? I will obey you in all things."

"I wish you to say nothing of this interview with me. I wish you to go home as if it had never taken place, and there, in perfect reliance upon my truth and my love, to wait for me."

"I will."

"You promise me this?"

"With my whole heart. And you will come to me soon?"

"Each minute will seem an age of agonized suspense till I can so come to you, Millicent."

"In three days?"

"At the latest."

"Then I will be content. I have a peace of mind now that will lift me above all sorrows. I have found my lost treasure, and all is joy again. I shall now be able to look gleeful at home; but they will still merely think that I am mad, as they thought before, so it does not matter. In three days I shall see you again."

"Yes, dear one."

"Three whole days! Well, it must be, so there's an end of it. And now you want me to go, George?"

"It is necessary that you should, my Millicent, in order that our meeting soon again may be for ever."

"Ah, that is a hint to go, indeed!"

She rose from the couch on which she had been sitting with him; but there was a smile on her face, and there was joy in her heart. She was no longer widowed; but the young husband of her girlish desires lived—and lived, too, for her. In three days he would be able to own her as his wife for ever.

What did the listening Captain Gay think of all this?

We shall soon see.

Millicent put on her widow's cap again.

"It is only for three days," she said, with a sigh, "and then farewell to it for ever, I hope. I am going, George."

"May Heaven's blessing go with you!"

"And your blessing, too."

"Yes, dear Millicent, my blessing, and my prayers. Stay, though; here is money. Take this purse."

"George!"

"Yes, dear, what would you say?"

"Is it yours?"

He dropped the purse, and staggered back. The question was quite sufficient to put him in mind that it was not his, and that, in fact, he had been now for some time living with large sums of money advanced to him by the bankers of the Lorton family, under the supposition that he was the Duke.

"Millicent," he said, "I swear to you by Heaven, that when this money was placed in my hands I thought it mine; and I have but the bare word of a villain that it is not now. I may be yet the victim of a double plot, for all I know to the contrary; so, take the money."

"No—no!"

"Yes, Millicent. It is honourably come by, so far as I am concerned, I assure you, dear one."

"No—no. Do not ask me; I dread to touch it. In three days, love, we shall meet again, and then you will tell me all; but until that happy hour shall come—a very happy hour, as you tell me—when we do meet again, and part no more, I would rather take no money."

"As you will, Millicent. Perhaps you are right, after all; but if I am a Duke, you are my Duchess."

"Ah, did I not say so, George?"

"You did, and when you said so, you spoke the honest truth. I will, in the time that is to elapse before we meet again, take such steps as shall prove me to be what I seem to be, or I will return to you as the plain George Drayton that you thought me."

"Do so, and all will yet be well."

"Yes—yes. They can't make me the victim when I have been so much deceived. It must be the deceiver surely, and not the dupe, who must suffer."

"What mean you, George?"

"Nothing—nothing. My mind is full, dear one, of what I have to do; but it is useless to attempt to make you comprehend, in a few short words, a long and a most eventful history, such as I have to tell you. Go now, I implore you, and trust in me as you would trust in Heaven, for now the one will be as likely to deceive you as the other."

"Oh, what joyful words!"

She still clung to him. She could not yet find it in her heart to tear herself from his arms. It was so long since she had seen him, and such an awful shock had the news of his presumed death given to her, that he seemed even now a something scarcely real, and she felt half inclined to think, that if she once more parted from him, some fresh train of strange mysterious circumstances would intervene to try to snatch him from her.

"I am weak and foolish, George," she said, "for I cannot tear myself away from you, although I wish to do so."

George Drayton was far from not appreciating the feeling with which his young wife spoke; but the danger of her presence there struck him forcibly. He had a lively sense of the daring recklessness of the character of Captain Gay.

Little did he imagine that that very person was now listening to every word that was uttered in that interview, which ought to have been a secret one.

George looked full of anxiety.

"I will go," she said. "I will. Farewell."

"Farewell, dear Millicent."

She tore herself from him, and at the moment that she did, a door was opened leading from the grand corridor without, and a servant made a hesitating appearance.

"What now?" cried the Duke.

"Pardon me, your Grace. I did not know your Grace had anyone with you, or I should not have intruded."

"Your errand, sir. What is it?"

"Your Grace's aunt, the Lady Bridget Lorton, has sent to say, that at twelve tomorrow, the solicitors on both sides will be here to see the signing of your Grace's marriage contract with the Lady Christina Harrowby!"

George staggered back as if a blow had been struck him by some invisible hand.

Millicent clasped her hands over her heart, as if she feared it would burst its bonds.

The footman turned and left the room, closing the door carefully after him.

"Ha! ha!" said Captain Gay, as he pushed the folding doors open an inch further, "that will do."

It took Millicent a few moments to recover from the shock of surprise which this speech of the footman had occasioned her. It was a speech which in an instant upset all her faith in George Drayton, and which appeared positively to give the lie to every one of his protestations. No wonder that it all but took away her breath, so to speak, and left her stranded on the wide ocean of doubt and perplexity.

The silence was truly awful.

George Drayton could not but feel all the construction that Millicent might, and could put upon what she had heard. It represented him in the most odious and unprincipled light possible, and yet how at such a moment to explain to her that, notwithstanding what she had heard, he would and could keep his word with her, was what puzzled him.

She spoke first.

"Oh, Heaven!" she said. "Can baseness such as this exist in the heart of one whom I have loved, and whom I thought was all that honour could make him? Can this be really possible?"

"Millicent!"

"No—no! Do not speak to me. Only answer me one thing, as you hope for peace here, and mercy hereafter."

"I will. What is it?"

"Did that menial allude to your marriage?"

"He did; but——"

"Enough—enough! Oh, do not burthen your soul with more false vows and protestations! I now see it all. First, neglected, and a forged report of your death sent me; then repudiated, till you found you could do so no longer—when chance brought me into your presence; and then attempted to be basely deceived by a three days' reliance upon your word, while during that interval you would be wedded to another!"

"No, no!—I swear——"

"I say, no. Swear nothing, George. It is but too apparent; but the law shall decide between us. I would have lived for your love; but I will now live for my own honour! I will not hear another word!"

She darted from the room, and left the house before the bewildered George Drayton could interfere to stop her, or issue any orders to detain her.

Captain Gay, rubbing his hands together, came out of the next room.

CHAPTER LXIII.

CAPTAIN GAY GIVES HIS DISINTERESTED ADVICE TO GEORGE DRAYTON.

"Bravo! bravo! bravo!" cried Captain Gay, gently patting his hands together, as if he were quite graciously applauding some scene at a theatre.

George Drayton turned and faced him.

"You here?"

"Yes."

"Fiend! villain!"

"Oh, go on. You have of late found some foolish sort of gratification in calling me names; but I do not see how that little splenetic exercise can advance either your views or mine in the least degree, my good friend."

"Call me not friend—wretch that you are!"

"Go on—go on!"

"No—no, I will put an end to this at once! Better any fate than to be the plaything and the toy of such a fiend as you are. Better perish in body, than in body and soul together. I may not make my peace with man; but I think I can with Heaven!"

"Go on—go on. Bravo! Upon my life, I never heard a better speech than that in all my life; nor better delivered, too. It has the true sentimental flavour about it, and I give you immense credit for it."

George looked at him, confounded.

"Do you think I cannot kill you?" he said.

Gay smiled.

"You must think so."

"Why, may I ask?"

"Because you take such pains to tempt me to do it."

"I don't think so; you are not a fool. Pray, would the little additional crime of my murder tend in any way to clear your prospects, or add to the facilities of getting out of the little difficulties you are now in?"

The reasonableness of what the rascal said struck George forcibly, and he sat down in the nearest chair with a groan.

Captain Gay felt that the paroxysm was

over, and that, for the time, he had his victim again in his power.

"Come, come," he said, "you are so violent and so abusive, that you will not stop to hear what one has to say to you till you have exhausted yourself."

"Say on. I think I can hear anything now. I am a coward to you because I am guil "

"Pho! don't talk nonsense."

"What would you have me say?"

"Nothing till you have heard me out. I see, what I was very doubtful of before, because this is the first time I have had any experience of such a very odd thing, that you really are attached to your wife."

"Really attached to her?"

"Yes."

"I loved her once—I shall love her ever!"

"Hem! Well, that, of course, is your own affair; but the fact that you think very much of her now has, I must confess, rather staggered me in my belief, and I begin to feel that it will be necessary to take some steps to unite her to you, and to free you from your embarrassment.

"What do you tell me?"

"I say, I find that you never will be happy in your present position; and that, therefore, the next best thing will be to relieve you from it with safety, and, as far as the world will hear anything of it, with honour."

"Is this some new delusion?"

"No. I want to bring the affair to an end, if I can by any possibility do so."

"How?—oh, how?"

"Suppose, now, I find the real Duke—eh? What would you say to that, my good friend?"

"In the name of Heaven! am I, or am I not, the real Duke? Do tell me that, I implore you?"

"I thought I had told you."

"You did say something of it, but how can I believe what you say?"

"Then what—on earth! if that is the charitable sort of light in which you happen to view me, is the use of your asking me any questions at all?"

"You speak truth there, at all events. It is no use."

"None in the least; but when I give information, it is generally correct. You are tired of this life?"

"Most heartily."

"You would be glad to see an end to it, provided you could get out of it with honour and with impunity?"

"Oh, most glad."

"Then leave it to me, and you shall only give me, if you please, a couple of days to do it in, and I flatter myself that I can as safely undo the meshes in which I have wrapped you as I did them up about you."

"But this marriage?"

"I will put it off."

"You will—you can?"

"I both can and will. If you like to trust me this once, I will serve you in your own way, though, mind you, I don't think it is

serving you; but that is a matter of taste. However, if you trust me, you must do so implicitly. You cannot be in a worse position than you are, and you will soon find out if I play you false or not."

"I will trust you."

"Your hand upon it."

"No—no, I cannot shake hands with you; but I give you my word of honour."

"Well, that will do. Now, all I ask of you is to be quiet—to do nothing—to write nothing, and to see no one for two days, except as I shall direct you. Do you agree to these terms now?"

"I must, perforce."

"Then it is all settled; and as far as regards your extrication from all the complication that is around you, and that has given you so much disquietude, you may go to bed, for I will do it all for you."

"Be it so," said George Drayton. "You have brought me to the state in which I now find myself by your arts and your intrigues, and it is your duty to release me from it; but beware, sir: you are now tampering with a desperate man. Beware! I say, of any treacherous conduct towards me, or you will tempt me to add to all other complications the one particular offence of your death."

The Duke left the room.

"Ha!" said Gay, "good, that. As if, now, I could not take care of myself against him! But things grow a little critical, and what I do must be done with tact. I have gained time, and that is one very great thing. If I had not made this arrangement with him, I do think he would have started off after that wife of his that he is so unaccountably fond of. The idea, now, of anybody caring one brass button about his wife! It is the most preposterous thing I ever heard of!"

A footman appeared at the door.

"What now?"

"A young gentleman, sir, who gives the name of Frank Western, desires to see you."

"Ah, yes. Bring him here."

"Yes, sir."

"Well, who says I am not a bold fellow? Here is the real Duke of Lorton I bring to his own house, for the purpose of holding a communication with him, the result of which shall be to dispossess him for ever of it. Ha—ha! A timid man, now, would not have dreamt of that. Oh, dear, no. But he comes. Now for an experiment to know if he is aware of his real Christian name."

The youth entered the apartment with a low bow, for he was a little surprised at the costly character of the mansion.

"Oh, how do you do, Mr. Gerald?" said Captain Gay.

"Sir?"

"How do you do?"

"But you called me Gerald. How came you to know that name, sir, I beg to ask?"

"Oh, then, Gerald is your name, is it?"

"It is, sir; but I adopted the name of Frank, because I have often heard my mother say she had enemies, and I thought they

MILLICENT MYSTIFIES CORPORAL BUDD.

might still be enemies to me; but how you came to know that my name was Gerald, is to me quite a mystery, sir."

"It is easily explained."

"Is it so, sir?"

"Yes, my good young friend, I didn't know it at all; but I have been speaking to a gentleman, an old friend of mine, whose Christian name is Gerald, and so it came off my tongue quite at unawares when I saw you."

"That is very strange."

"Very; is it not? In fact, it is so strange that, if you did not know it, you would hardly believe it, would you now?"

"I confess I should doubt it."

"Of course you would. But now, Mr. Western, I have taken a great fancy to you, and I have spoken to the Duke of Lorton about you, and he has given me power to provide for you."

"Indeed, sir?"

"Have you any objection to go to Ireland?"

"None in the least, sir."

"Then you can go there to the Lorton estate, in quite a confidential capacity, with a salary of—of two hundred pounds a year, we will say; but you must set off to-morrow at the very latest, or you will be too late. Will that do?"

"Oh, yes—yes. I cannot express to you my thanks, dear sir, for this most unexpected and undeserved kindness."

"Oh, don't mention it. I said I would provide for you, and you may depend upon it that I mean to keep my word. When I say such a thing as that of anyone, it is generally to be depended upon, if my ability should serve me to do it, as I think it does in this instance."

CHAPTER LXIV.

MILLICENT ADVISES FRANK WESTERN NOT TO LEAVE LONDON.

THE gratitude of young Frank Western, as he called himself, was very great indeed towards the Mr. Brand—as he thought Captain Gay to be—for taking so much interest in his welfare.

Indeed, the youth, with all that ingenuous feeling and absence of guile, which is a characteristic of the better order of minds, found it difficult to say anything that, to his own perception, should be sufficiently expressive of the feelings he had in the matter.

Captain Gay was not at all moved by such feelings, although one would have thought that if anything could possibly have moved him, they would.

"Don't say another word about it, I beg," he said. "I pass all my life in trying to do good; and if I succeed in any instance, I am only too well repaid by the feelings of my own heart. Sometimes, in spite of all I can do, I fail; but when that is the case, I assure you it is not from the want of any wish or inclination to succeed."

"Of that, sir," said Frank Western, "I am quite sure. I will attend on you, sir, at any time and place you may be pleased to appoint."

"Oh, I will settle it all at once."

"Indeed, sir?"

"Yes; you will go to-night to Liverpool, if you like, so that you will be that far on your journey. You will, when there, look out for some vessel going to Galway, in Ireland; and when you get there, all you have to do is to repair to the Castle Lorton, and there wait further instructions from me as to what you have to do on the estate."

"Yes, sir, I will—I will."

"All is well, then; and you will find, I suspect, that you are provided for for life."

"Yes, sir; but—but——"

"Well?"

"Alas! sir, I feel ashamed to say that I have no means of going to Liverpool or to Galway. I have no money; and although the kind and good people who have afforded me a shelter, I have no doubt, would do all in their power to aid me, I feel a kind of dread at the idea of asking them for money."

"Your feelings are quite proper, young sir, and do you great honour. Do not suppose, though, that I overlooked such a very critical part of the affair. Here is a twenty pound note of the Bank of England. That will suffice, I dare say."

"Oh, yes—yes."

"Take it, then, and with it my sincere advice to you to be off as soon as you can."

"I will, sir—I will. At some other time, when my mind is calmer, I shall, perhaps, be better able to thank you for all this goodness."

Captain Gay smiled very graciously; and poor Frank Western left the house, quite elated at what he could not help considering to be his good fortune.

Now, while this interview was taking place between him and Captain Gay, Millicent, the wife of George Drayton, had gone home with her mind full of all that she had seen and heard at the house of the Duke.

She could not have any doubt at all but that George fully intended to play her false; and so heated was her imagination upon this point, that she hardly saw the route she took, and it was a wonder that she did not go out of her way.

She asked herself one question, though, as she got near to the old and well-remembered house in Covent Garden market, and that was as to what course she should now adopt in the strange situation in which she was placed.

"Shall I at once tell them all at home about it?" she said. "Or, shall I wait to give the matter some consideration first?"

She decided upon the latter course; so, as soon as she got into the shop and saw her mother there, she spoke in much her usual manner to her, saying:

"Did you think me long gone, mother?"

"Yes, my dear, I did; but, oh, tell me now, will you, what has passed? You could not see the Duke, I am quite sure, whom you went to see?"

"Mother, do not ask me anything just yet. You know that I never tell falsehoods; and, therefore, as I do not wish to tell the truth just yet, pray excuse me."

"Yes, my dear; but you are cured of the idea of thinking that the great grand Duke of Lorton and your poor George Drayton are one and the same person?"

"No, mother."

"No?"

"Certainly not; and now I implore you to ask me no more about it till to-morrow."

With these words, Millicent was about to leave the shop to go upstairs, but her mother stopped her, saying:

"Well—well, my dear, I have news of another sort for you."

"What news?"

"Our poor young friend, Frank Western, is likely to get a situation."

"I am glad to hear it."

"I knew you would be; and what is very strange, too, is, that the gentleman who is going to befriend him gives his address at Dalewood House."

"Ah!"

"Yes, my dear, it is so; and by his dress and appearance he is someone in the household of the Duke of Lorton."

Millicent pressed her hands upon her brow,

and remained for some few moments in deep thought. Then she felt that although there was a something to unravel in this intelligence, it for the time defied her, and she said :

"Mother, things are happening now that are to me but as a confused dream at present. But where is Frank Western, dear mother? Where is he?"

"Oh, he has gone to Dalewood House to meet the gentleman."

"To meet him? What sort of gentleman is he, mother—can you tell me?"

"Rather tall, and with black brows that nearly meet; and he had a very odd look about the eyes."

Millicent breathed more freely. It was not George.

"Mother," she said, "when Frank Western comes in, will you send him upstairs to me, for I wish to speak to him most particularly?"

"Oh, yes, my dear. But how strange you look! There is a flush upon your face, and your eyes are so bright."

"Mother—mother, I implore you not to question me, or even to look at me with curious eyes. I am nearly mad as it is."

She hastened upstairs, and shut herself in one of the small rooms of the dwelling.

"Alas—alas!" sighed Mrs. Ardent, "she need not say that she is nearly mad, poor thing, for I am afraid she is quite so. This is the worst affliction, after all."

It was in about half-an-hour when Frank Western entered the shop, and the moment he did so, he cried out :

"Oh, Mrs. Ardent, I have got a good situation at last, I think, and am going to leave you."

"Leave us?"

"Yes; and I am so happy!"

"Happy to leave us?"

"Oh, no—no, I did not think of that—no—no. I shall be anything but happy to leave you, for you have been so very—very kind to me. Ah! in the midst of my joy and exultation at having got something to do, I did not think of that."

"But what is it you have got to do?"

"Oh, I am going to be something or another, I don't know what, on the estate of a nobleman in Ireland."

"In Ireland?"

"Yes, the Duke of Lorton's estate."

"You don't say so?"

"I do, indeed; and I will soon convince you of it. Only look at this. Here is a twenty pound note to pay my expenses to Galway, where the estate is, you see."

"Is it possible?"

"Oh, it is indeed."

"Frank—Frank!" called Millicent from the stairs, "I think I hear your voice."

"Yes, Mrs. Drayton—yes. It is I."

"Come upstairs, I wish to speak to you."

"Dear me!" said Mrs. Ardent, "I ought to have told you as soon as you came in, but you were so full of your situation, and I was so full of listening to you, that I quite forgot.

Oh, my dear young friend, she is very bad—very bad, indeed!"

"Bad, is she?"

"Yes, in her poor brain."

"Alas, that is very sad!"

"It is, indeed; so mind what you say to her. The best way is to agree with her in whatever she may say."

"Yes—yes. I will go and try to soothe her, if I can."

Frank Western went upstairs at once, and when he reached the room in which Millicent was, she closed the door and placed a chair for him next to her, and then looking in his face, she said :

"They think here that I am mad, or nearly so; but let me beg of you not to answer what I am going to ask of you with any such idea, for it is not so, I assure you; and I will soon convince you that whatever has seemed to favour such a supposition, by appearing to be too romantic for belief, is true."

Frank looked at her in amazement. If this was madness, he thought, there was plenty of method in it.

Millicent having thus bespoken his attention, told him her whole story from the beginning to the end, to which he listened in the most unfeigned amazement.

She concluded, by saying :

"And so, Frank, you see that I am not so mad as to mistake a Duke for my lost husband, since he is such in reality."

CHAPTER LXV.

MILLICENT HAS HER SUSPICIONS OF A VERY IMPORTANT FACT.

"WHY, then," said Frank, "you are the Duchess of Lorton yourself?"

"If he be the Duke."

"Oh, yes—yes! How very odd this is, to be sure. I cannot at all make it out, and I am in a kind of maze."

"Perhaps we shall both of us better understand if you tell me your story now from first to last."

"Oh, yes, I will."

"I am all attention."

"Well, then, you see, my name is Gerald something, and not Frank at all. My mother always told me that there was a very great secret connected with my birth, which was to be found detailed among some papers that she always carried about with her, along with a portrait of my father, and one of myself, too, and of herself, so that I expect that with the papers there are three portraits somewhere, and my real name along with them."

"That is very strange!"

"It is, indeed. Well, we lived in great poverty together—that is, my mother and I, but still in great happiness, for we were all the world to one another; but one day she went out, and never came back to me, and the people where we lived said that they could not let me stay there any longer, so I was, so to speak, turned into the street at the time when I came here to ask your good mother to let the written paper I had drawn up, offering to give lessons, be placed in the shop-window."

"Then, in fact, you do not know who you really are?"

"Indeed I do not."

"But you are sure your Christian name is Gerald?"

"Oh, yes. My mother always called me Gerald; so I am quite sure of that."

"And so you have been given twenty pounds, and told to go off to Ireland at once by someone at the house of the Duke of Lorton?"

"Yes."

"And you think of going?"

"Oh, yes—yes."

"You must not."

"Must not go?"

"Certainly not. Hear me, Gerald. By the memory of your mother—by all your dearest hopes—by your love and reverence for Heaven, and for all that you most admire and love, I implore you not to go!"

"You amaze me!"

"Yes, I see that I do; but I have reasons —I have suspicions, Gerald, which only a day may convert into realities: but I beg of you, as you love truth, honour, and justice, not to go."

"I will not go."

"Oh, Gerald, you have made me happy by saying that."

"You have almost taken my breath away. Oh, tell me—do you know who I am?"

"I do not know, but I have some suspicions, which I beg of you not to ask me just now to describe; but I can see quite enough to be certain that if you went to Ireland you would not live long."

"Not live long?"

"No. It is your life that is sought."

"My life?"

"Even so. Was there no expression used to lead you to such a supposition?"

"Good Heavens! now I think of it, the man who called himself Mr. Brand, in some mysterious way knew that my name was Gerald; and he smiled so oddly when he said he meant to provide for me for life, that I felt my blood run cold."

"Just so. You were doomed."

"Can it be possible?"

"I am sure of it, Gerald; but by not going —by staying here in perfect quietness, you will baffle your foes, and you may end in doing great acts of justice and of mercy; so I have your word that you will stay?"

"Oh, yes—my word of honour."

"I am content. This is a weight off my heart. I have now much to do; but you will say to my mother that I have given you reasons for delaying your journey for a time, and that will satisfy her for the present."

"Yes, and I will send him back his money."

"No—no. That would be to let him know at once that you were not going. He must suppose you gone."

"Oh, yes, I see. Well, will you take charge of the twenty pounds?"

"Yes, if you like."

"Oh, yes, I cannot bear to have the note in my possession. It appears to me now as if there were some sort of enchantment in the touch of it. There, I am glad to get rid of it; and if I can do anything in the world that can aid you in any way in the procuring justice to be done to you, you know well that there is not a more faithful heart at your disposal than mine."

"I know it; and I want you to do something now at once before you go to rest to-night."

"Oh, what is it?"

"Do you know the barracks by the Birdcage Walk in St. James's Park?"

"Yes, yes."

"Then I want you to go there, and to find out Corporal Budd, and tell him I want him as soon as he can come to me."

"Corporal Budd?"

"Yes; you have heard of him?"

"Oh, yes. Mrs. Ardent told me that he once loved you very much indeed; but that you preferred George Drayton to him. Do you think it is right and prudent to send for a discarded lover?"

"Yes; in this matter I have too few friends to be over-choice; and, besides, I know that the Corporal has a good heart, and that nothing will give him so much pleasure as to do me a service, and I know that he will— when I explain to him that it must be so—do it in the most disinterested manner that it is possible to think of."

"Then he is a fine fellow."

"He is. So go now at once; and, oh! do be careful of your own safety! And, if by any chance you should again encounter that man who calls himself Brand, do not for one moment lead him to suppose that you suspect him, or that you have any notion of not carrying out your engagement with him."

"I will be very careful of that. After what you have told me, I feel as if I had had a very great escape from death."

"You have, indeed."

"Oh, I am sure of it now. I did not feel satisfied from first to last; and yet I could not tell why I was dissatisfied. That was the puzzle to me all along. But now I seem as if the mist had cleared from before my gaze, and as if I saw all my danger. Why or wherefore he should seek my life—is to me a mystery; but I suppose, that, too, will be cleared up some day."

"It will—it will."

"Then I am off at once to the Corporal."

Frank Western left the house immediately, and as he did not meet anyone, he had no occasion to say anything at all about his change of determination just then. He soon found the Corporal.

"Oh, Corporal Budd," he said, "I have come from Mrs. Drayton to you."

"To me?"

"Yes. She says that you can do her a service, and that as she knows you will do it, she has no hesitation in sending to you."

"Of course I will. With all my heart. What is it?"

"That I don't know."

"Well, I will go back with you. What a lucky thing it is that I am just off guard to-night. Upon my life, I am quite delighted at the idea of her sending for me. But stop!"

"What is it?"

"This is not a joke?"

"A joke?"

"No. It is no joke of yours, young sir, I hope—no boy's trick upon me, I hope—eh?"

"Upon my word it is not."

"Very well; then come on."

Corporal Budd and Frank Western went quickly back again to the bouquet-maker's, and Mrs. Ardent was quite surprised to see them come in together.

"Why—Corporal!" she said, "is that you?"

"Yes, ma'am."

"Well, I declare! And with our young friend Frank Western, too, who is going off to leave us this very night."

"No, Mrs. Ardent," said Frank, "I have thought better of it. I won't leave you in such a hurry, ma'am; so I will put it off for a day or two longer, I think."

"But can you?"

"Oh, yes. I have done so."

"Well, I am very glad to hear it; and it is very kind and indulgent of the good gentleman who has found you the situation, to let you put it off in this kind of way."

Frank saw the view that Mrs. Ardent took of the matter; and as that view put a stop to all further discussion about it, he let her remain in her error, and went upstairs to tell Millicent that the Corporal had arrived.

"Tell him I will come down to him directly," said Millicent, "and speak to him. Is there anyone in the kitchen, Frank?"

"No. Jane has gone out with Peter."

"And my father?"

"He, too, is out; and your mother is in the shop."

"Then I will come down to the Corporal, and speak to him in the kitchen, at once, Frank; and you may be there, too, and hear what I say to him, for it will be no secret from you."

Frank thought from her manner that she wished him to be present at her interview with the Corporal on account of the singular character of it, and considering that he had been an old suitor of hers, and that she had herself sent for him; so he made no opposition to the request.

The honest Corporal was in a great state of amazement at the whole affair, and could not for the life of him think what Millicent could have to say to him.

Of course, he looked upon her as a widow; and it is just possible that some passing thought that he might yet have a chance of making her Mrs. Corporal Budd passed through his mind.

———

CHAPTER LXVI.

MILLICENT TERRIBLY MYSTIFIES CORPORAL BUDD.

CORPORAL BUDD was by the fireside in the kitchen when Millicent came down to speak to him.

"Oh, Millicent," he said, as she entered the kitchen, "it is good of you."

"Good of me?"

"Yes, to think of me, when you wanted anybody to fight, or to go anywhere for you, or, in fact, to do you any service."

"No, Corporal Budd, it is good of you, after all the past, to be so ready to do me a service; but I knew you had a kind heart, and so I sent for you."

"You did quite right."

"I am sure of it. And now listen to me, if you please, very intently, for I am going to say something most important to you."

"Oh, lor!"

"Corporal Budd——"

"Yes, Millicent. I beg your pardon—I mean Mrs. Drayton."

That name—Drayton—seemed to stick in the Corporal's throat always, and to be pronounced with the greatest possible difficulty.

"Call me Millicent, if you like, Corporal," she said. "From an old friend like you it is quite an allowable piece of familiarity."

"Thank you, Millicent. It is the old name that I am used to, and I must confess I like it best."

"Well, then, Corporal Budd, I am going to-night, at the hour of eleven, to Dalewood House, the residence of the Duke of Lorton."

"Indeed!"

"Yes. Hear me out. I want you to go with me to the door of that house, so as to see me go in —I want you to watch for my return; and if in two hours I do not come out again, I want you to knock at the door, and demand to see the Duchess of Lorton."

"The who?"

"The Duchess of Lorton."

"Oh, lor! who is she? I don't know her a bit."

"You do know her well."

"I—I know a Duchess?"

"Yes; I am that Duchess."

The Corporal started back, and trod upon the cat, who gave him a good scratch in return.

"You a Duchess? You—you? Oh—oh!"

"Corporal Budd, my husband, George Drayton, is the Duke of Lorton; so, I, his wife, am the Duchess of Lorton. More I cannot explain to you just now; but I ask you at once, will you do what I ask of you?"

"Of course I will."

"That is enough, then."

"But—but——"

"But what? What would you say?"

"If they should tell me that there is no such person there, provided you don't come out, and I have to knock at the door?"

"Then you will go to the nearest magistrate, and say that you have reason to believe that the Duchess of Lorton has been foully murdered."

"Murdered!"

"Yes; and that evidence of the recent crime will be found in Dalewood House."

"You—you take my breath away."

"Will you do it?"

"I will—I will! But why—oh, why go there at all, if you have any suspicion of such foul play? Why rush there at what you evidently consider the risk of your life? Oh, Millicent, do not go!"

"I must. It is my duty—it is my fate."

"No—no! You must be taking some wrong view of the matter altogether. You must be—be——"

"I know what you were going to say, Corporal Budd. 'Mad' was the word you paused at."

The Corporal looked down, confused.

"I have but one reply to make," added Millicent. "Will you, upon your oath, do as I ask you?"

"I will, so help me Heaven!"

"And will you keep it secret?"

"I will—I will."

Millicent held out her hand to the Corporal, and he shook it with fervour in his.

"Now," she said, "I know you again, and I feel that in sending for you I did right."

"You did, indeed, Millicent, if you required one who would with his life defend you, and one who would obey your slightest wish, at peril of that life. Depend upon me, I shall not now be far from here for the rest of this night, till you are ready to go to Dalewood House, with me to escort you."

"I know it. Now leave me."

The Corporal left the house; and, in fact, he was in such a state of bewilderment altogether, that he was rather glad to get away without seeing anyone who might ask him troublesome questions, to which he would find it very difficult to reply.

The Corporal did not now intend to leave the immediate vicinity of the bouquet-shop. Although he did not quite comprehend all that was going on, he did comprehend quite enough to know and feel that Millicent was in some extraordinary danger, and that she had called upon him to aid her.

The Corporal was by far too much flattered by the trust that was reposed in him not to pay the most abundant attention to what he had to do.

And Frank Western, too, was very nearly as much puzzled at it all as the Corporal, only his closer habits of thought, and extensive reading, enabled him to catch better glimmerings of the truth through the mist of events, than the honest soldier could hope at all to do.

But, although Frank Western thought he saw pretty clearly how Millicent was situated, he had as yet no sort of suspicion as to who he in reality was himself.

Not the shadow of a thought crossed his mind that Dalewood House, and all that it contained, was his, and that he was the real Duke of Lorton.

That information, though, was coming to him, and not the less surely that it came rather slowly.

The intention of Millicent now will be tolerably apparent, from the arrangements she was making to carry it out.

It was her intention to make another call upon George Drayton, and, duke or no duke, to make such another appeal to his heart as should, in its result, one way or another, put an end to all question as to whether he meant to acknowledge her or not.

She considered that if he was deaf to such an appeal from her, that anything in the world might follow in the train of such a denial, and that even her life might not be safe.

Hence was it that she had resolved to secure some sort of evidence of her visit to Dalewood House, if it should so happen that she disappeared there.

This was, then, the mission of the Corporal; and among the acquaintance of Millicent, she knew no one who, from power to do it and from the will to do it, owing to personal attachment to herself, was likely to carry out such a matter as well as the honest Corporal.

"Yes," she said, "I will see George again—I will yet make an appeal to that heart which cannot be altogether vitiated by the gold that is around it, and by the situation in which its owner is placed. He may yet repudiate the attempted second marriage, and he may yet cling to me, and then all will be well; but if the evil advisers he has about him have greater power over him than I, then I will not be silenced but with my life. I will have justice—simple justice."

That in the mere principles of the project she was right, there can be no doubt.

The only mistake she made was in attributing too bad a course of action to George Drayton.

George was weak, but he was not wicked.

It is true that weakness leads to wickedness, and that it is difficult in many cases to say where the one ends and the other begins; but that difficulty scarcely existed in his case.

He never meant for one moment to marry the Lady Christina Harrowby, even granting that nothing had opened his eyes to the fact that he was not in reality the Duke of Lorton.

The great mistake he made was in trusting to the word of a man whom he knew so well as he knew Captain Gay, after the interview he had had with Millicent.

That was an error that might have been fatal; but it was quite matched by Millicent's fancying for one moment that her life might not be safe at Dalewood House from her own husband, George, who in reality loved her as well as ever.

Thus, then, these two people were rather at cross-purposes, and all owing to the false complexion that the villain Gay had managed to give to affairs in general that were between them.

The state of mind of George Drayton was truly pitiable, and he suffered such pangs of agony and remorse, that his appearance began very materially to suffer, and the servants at Dalewood House saw the fading colour and the sunken cheek of their young lord with the greatest surprise.

"Surely," they thought, "a duke, and the possessor of such a mansion as the Lorton estates furnish, ought to be happy, if anybody can be."

But dukedoms and estates do not produce happiness in this world any more than struggles and difficulties necessarily produce misery.

But it is to Captain Gay that we must now for a brief space turn our attention. He had a difficult game to play.

That wily villain felt that a very little might upset his plans altogether, and so he determined upon a very bold stroke indeed to rid himself of what he thought was a very great obstacle.

That great obstacle was Millicent.

Captain Gay flattered himself that for the sum of twenty pounds he had got rid of the real young Duke, and he knew that a note to some of the unscrupulous tenants on the Lorton estates would at any time prove his death; so he turned all his attention politely to Millicent.

CHAPTER LXVII.

CAPTAIN GAY AND LADY BRIDGET AGREE MOST WONDERFULLY.

It was a bold stroke that Captain Gay meditated. It was no other than to make a confidant of the Lady Bridget, the old aristocratic aunt of the Duke of Lorton.

The reader has seen quite enough of the old lady to be well aware of some of her little amiable peculiarities.

Captain Gay has seen much more of her mind and conduct and prejudices than the reader; so he felt pretty confident of the effect upon her of what he meant to say.

Within a quarter of an hour of his last interview, then, with George Drayton, Captain Gay was on the doorstep of the town-house of the Lady Bridget Lorton.

Her ladyship was at home.

The message to her that the secretary (for such Gay called himself to her) of the Duke of Lorton wished to speak to her, procured his instant admission.

The old lady received Captain Gay in her own boudoir, and looked as gracious as she ever looked upon what she considered to be one of the inferior class.

Captain Gay took quite a delight in flattering her foibles, and in adding as much as he could to the mass of pride, ignorance, and prejudice that made up what this old woman called her mind.

"I hope your ladyship," he said, "has recovered from the fatigues of the visit to Dalewood House to-day?"

"Yes, we have," said the old lady.

She often affected the style royal, and spoke of herself as "we," which mightily amused Captain Gay.

"That is a mercy," he said.

The old lady inclined her head.

"Your ladyship, I hope, will have the extreme goodness and condescension to listen to rather an important communication that I shall now have the honour to lay before your ladyship."

She inclined her head again.

"Your ladyship, no doubt, has noticed that at times the Duke, your nephew, has not appeared so fully to enter into the just and family views of your ladyship as he ought, and that fits of abstraction have come over him; and that, in fact, he has behaved like a man who, so to speak, had a something on his mind."

"We have noticed all that."

"I am glad we have."

"But we attributed it to the novelty of his situation."

"Oh!"

"In which, no doubt, we are right, as usual."

"I beg pardon, my lady, but for once we are wrong."

"Wrong?"

"Yes; very wrong indeed."

"You amaze me, sir!"

"I expected I should, my lady; but your ladyship, no doubt, has observed that it is more particularly since this intended marriage with the Lady Christina Harrowby has been on the *tapis* that the Duke has exhibited these freaks of temper."

"True."

"Then, your ladyship, I can inform you why he is in such a state of mind, and why his mind is so distracted, and why he views this marriage with such great aversion."

"And pray, sir, why is it then?"

"Because he is married already."

The old lady gave a slight start, and shook a little.

"Married—already?"

"Yes, my lady. Before he had the slightest idea that he belonged to the nobility, when he thought himself merely the child of fortune—or, rather, of misfortune—he fell in love with a pretty face, and he married the owner of it; so that is the cause of all the fidgety uneasiness that your ladyship has seen him exhibit, and that is the cause of the horror with which he seems to look forward to his nuptials with the Lady Christina Harrowby."

"Good gracious!"

"Yes, my lady."

"You surprise even us."

"So I expected, my lady."

"I feel quite—quite ill. Really—I—Hand me that ottar of roses—No, the—Cologne-water. Thank you. We are really very much shocked!"

"So am I; and really, my lady, I do think

that when a member of the nobility is in such a situation, it is one of the most calamitous things that can be."

"It is—it is. And pray, sir, in what station of life is the—the—a—individual?"

"Station of life? Oh, she is a greengrocer's daughter, in Covent Garden market."

The old lady dropped the bottle of Cologne-water with a smash, and glaring at Captain Gay, she said:

"A greengrocer's daughter! Oh, Heavens! A green—oh—oh!—a grocer! Oh, I shall die! The Lortons associated with a green—oh—oh! This is too much—too much! It is truly terrible! Why, all the low people in London will be claiming kindred with us."

"They will. They have all sorts of friends. One, I understand, sells coals and wood; another deals in 'hot pies, all hot!' at the corner of the street; another hawks about pussy's meat in a barrow—cat's meat!"

"Oh, for mercy's sake, be quiet!"

"Yes, my lady."

"You will kill me!"

"No, my lady."

"You will, I say—you will. Oh, what can be done? This is too dreadful to bear!"

"It is; and it is because I consider that something ought to be done, and that at once, too, that I came to throw myself upon the better judgment of your ladyship."

"Yes—yes."

"The greengrocer wife must be got rid of."

"Of course. The wretch must be got rid of."

"By fair means, or——"

"Otherwise."

"Just so. I perceive that we quite understand each other, my lady, upon that point!"

"We do; and I can only say that I think you take a very proper view of it, and I think very highly of you on that account—I do, indeed."

"Oh, my lady, your approval of my humble conduct is worth anything in the world, my lady."

"Well, you have it. Of course, as a common person yourself, you might have thought quite different. I don't say so to—to—hurt your little feelings at all. Oh, no."

"You are too good, madam."

"Well—well, let us think of what can be done. Do you recommend any course to adopt in the matter?"

"Yes, my lady. In the first place, I think an offer might be made to the low people, of a large sum of money, if they will, within the next twenty-four hours, take themselves off out of England altogether."

"Exactly."

"Then, if they accept it, they all disappear, and the marriage with Lady Christina, I think, may be easily consummated."

"To be sure. Of course."

"But if they refuse?"

"Refuse?"

"Yes, as they may; for low people are dreadfully obstinate, my lady, about what they call their rights. If they refuse, a something else must be done."

"Yes."

"A something that shall put the low wife out of the way."

"Yes."

"And that something must be a warrant from the Secretary of State for her private arrest, on a charge of corresponding with the Jacobites in France, you see, your ladyship, and her committal to the Tower, where no one will know who or what she is, and where, you see, she can be kept till she agrees to a divorce from the Duke."

"Excellent."

"Your ladyship likes the plan?"

"It is capital."

"And does your ladyship think you can get a warrant from my Lord Harrowby for her arrest?"

"Directly. His lordship is only too zealous in the new order of things in this country. He is quite delighted to grant warrants to arrest Jacobite people; because, you see, he was once a Jacobite himself, and he wants now to show the zeal of his conversion."

"Exactly."

"Then to a person of my rank he will refuse nothing. What is the imprisonment of a dozen of low, common people, in comparison to the fame of a noble family?"

"Oh, nothing at all."

"Nothing, indeed."

"Or even their existence?"

"Or even, as you say, Mr. What's-your-name, their existence. Oh, I wish our solicitor was in London. Do you know, he never came back, they say, from his visit to Galway."

"Indeed!"

"No."

"Well, it is possible that he is rusticating in some place there yet, my lady, surrounded by romantic scenery; but, however, I think I can manage this little affair as well as he."

"How will it be done?"

"Will your ladyship, at ten o'clock, have the warrant ready, in case of the horrid obstinacy of the low female?"

"Yes—yes."

"Then I will take care to have a coach ready to take her off, and three or four fellows to aid and assist. You will make the offer we spoke of, to the low people, and if they accept it: well and good; if they reject, away she goes to the Tower."

"And very proper, too. Dear me, what a trouble the common people are, to be sure. I don't know what is the good of them, for my part. They only make the streets look bad with their horrid looks. Faugh! I do hate them with all my heart. You may rely upon me being ready at ten o'clock, Mr. What's-your-name."

CHAPTER LXVIII.

CAPTAIN GAY FLATTERS HIMSELF HE IS ARRANGING MATTERS ADMIRABLY.

TEN o'clock, in the age of which we write, was quite a late hour in London. Now, with very many people it is considered to be only the beginning of the evening. But as that hour of the evening approached, the streets of the metropolis—when those whose varied and chequered fortunes we are recording existed— were beginning to assume quite a dull and sombre aspect, as if the night had begun.

About Covent Garden market, too, especially, there was a sort of dull and heavy aspect by that hour, for the folks in and about that neighbourhood were very early risers.

They had to meet the carts and the waggons of the market-gardeners, that came lumbering into London by the break of day, and so they could not afford to rise at fashionable late hours, but lived a very primitive sort of existence in that respect.

The shop of the Ardents was rather an exception, though, to the general rule of early closing. The character of the wares for sale necessitated the keeping open rather later than others.

Then the sale of the bouquets was the most profitable; and it often happened that quite late in the evening some gallant would come and offer any price for such a bouquet as he would like to present to some capricious fair one.

Then, again, some messenger had arrived frequently from the opera, or from some one of the theatres, in hot haste to purchase a bouquet for some young spendthrift, who sought by that means to propitiate the favour of a pretty actress.

For these reasons, then, the bouquet-shop often showed a light amid its floral beauties for a good time after the neighbouring shops had been closed.

But this was not the case, on this most strange and eventful night to the Ardents.

The circumstances of deep and absorbing interest that had occurred in their family— and that seemed to be only in progress—had so far disturbed their minds, that they did not pay that great attention to their ordinary business they were in the habit of paying.

It was a great relief to them when, without the charge of unwarrantable neglect attaching to the act, they could close the shutters of the bouquet-shop.

They did so, therefore, at an earlier hour than usual; and then Millicent descended from the room above, and peeped into the closed shop.

Her mother was there.

"Mother," she said—"mother?"

Mrs. Ardent started, for there was a strangeness of tone about Millicent that she had not noticed before in her, and which alarmed her.

"Oh, my dear," she said, "what is amiss?"

"Nothing I hope, mother."

"Thank Heaven! I thought, my dear, you spoke as though you were not well."

"Oh, yes, I am quite well. I think, mother, that I am too well to suit some people."

"Too well?"

"Yes, mother. I am in the way, and so my health is offensive. But where is my father?"

"He is coming. There he is at the door now."

"I am glad of that. I am going out; but before I go, I have something to say to him, and to you, and to Jane, too; for it is proper that another person besides you two should know it; and there is no one who, from her close relationship, and her love for us all, is more fit, or so fit, as she."

The calm air of reasoning with which Millicent spoke astonished poor Mrs. Ardent. She felt, if she could so have expressed herself, that by some means her daughter's mind had become expanded and peaceful suddenly like the bursting of a flower from its bud.

There are circumstances and events in life which produce on rare occasions such effects.

The interview that Millicent had had with her husband at Dalewood House had been to her one of the circumstances, and she felt that she thought and acted now differently from what she had done before that interview.

Mrs. Ardent called to her husband:

"Jacob—Jacob! Is that you?"

"Yes, my dear, it is."

"Come in, then. Millicent has something to say to us."

"Yes—yes."

"But why are you waiting there? Who are you looking at, at the door?"

"It's very odd!"

"What is very odd?"

"Why, Corporal Budd is in the market, and it seems to me that he takes good care he won't remove his eyes from this door, but why I don't know, nor will he tell me."

"Dear me, how strange!"

Millicent stepped forward.

"Did you say Corporal Budd, father?"

"Yes, my child."

"That is well. Now come in, for I have something to say to you both that it is necessary you should hear now and at once, or I may not be able to say it at all. Come in, both of you, to the kitchen, and let me not be interrupted by anyone."

Jane was in the kitchen at her knitting; and old Jacob Ardent and his wife followed Millicent in wondering silence. The door was closed, and then Millicent looked at them all, and, with a faint smile, she said:

"Do not look upon what I am about to say as a freak of madness, for I tell you all, and tell you truly, that I am not mad. I shall be able to give you quite sufficient reason to know that I am not."

"Oh, my child," said Mrs. Ardent, "do not think that we suppose you other than our darling Millicent. You have ever been dear to us, and you ever will."

"Yes," said the old man, "and I think that wish will be the very best thing for you, my dear."

Millicent shook her head.

"Still," she said, "I see that you have the same idea. You think that the news of the death of my husband, George Drayton, has turned my brain."

Old Ardent coughed slightly, and Mrs. Ardent said not a word. Jane looked full of interest and anxiety into the face of Millicent.

"Do I look mad?" added Millicent. "Do I speak as though I were distracted? But this is idle talking. I have that to tell you which will put this question at rest at once. The only reason why you think me mad is, that I recognized, or thought I recognized, in the Duke of Lorton, as he looked from his carriage-window, my husband. Is it not so?"

"Yes, my dear," said Jacob Ardent.

"Well, I took the bouquets that were ordered to Dalewood House this day."

"She did?" cried Jacob, turning to his wife.

"I think she did," said Mrs. Ardent, "and I thought she came home looking very calm, and so much better."

"Yes, mother, I saw the Duke."

"You saw—the—Duke?"

"I did."

"Oh, my child, what would he think of such an intrusion? How came it that they let you have an interview with the great Duke of Lorton?"

"Oh, but," said Jacob, "I, too, have seen him, and he is everything that we could wish him. Nature has made him noble. Did he not wish to give me a receipt in full for the money that——"

"There—there! Jacob," sobbed Mrs. Ardent, "fling that in my face, do! That is like you!"

"Well, I only——"

"Oh, go on, do!"

"Peace—peace!" said Millicent. "This is of no sort of consequence. I tell you that being determined to discover whether this resemblance between the Duke and George Drayton was a mere coinage of the over-burdened brain or not, I went to Dalewood House, and I saw the Duke; so that I can now tell you that he is my husband."

"He—your husband?"

"Yes."

"Oh, my dear child, you surely did not go the length of telling him that?"

"I did."

"What must he have thought?"

"God can only fathom his thoughts. He strove to deny me; but his heart at length spoke for me, and he acknowledged me as his wife. He only asked me to wait a short time ere he could acknowledge me before the whole world as such; but I will not wait. I found that he was on the eve of a marriage with another, and this night I go again to his house to stay in it as his Duchess."

Mrs. Ardent looked as though the end of the world had just been announced to her, and old Jacob sank into a chair in a state of very great bewilderment indeed.

Jane walked up to Millicent and looked her in the face, saying as she did so:

"This is not madness. It is the truth."

"Thanks, dear Jane," said Millicent—"thanks. It is the truth, and it is a truth that the whole world shall know before long. Father and mother, do you still believe, or do you still think that I am mad?"

CHAPTER LXIX.

CAPTAIN GAY AND THE LADY BRIDGET ARRIVE AT THE MARKET.

AFTER this testimony, and after the calm and collected way in which Millicent had spoken, there was, in good truth, very little room for any doubt upon the subject. Staggered and astonished by what they had heard already, the old couple pressed her for further and more minute particulars of her interview with the Duke, and this led to a long conversation, in which she recounted the circumstances of mystery, so far as she knew them, of the early part of George Drayton's life; so that everything seemed to favour the supposition that he and the Duke of Lorton were identical.

This was the first point that Millicent had to establish; and then, when she found it was so established in the minds of her friends that nothing could shake it, she said:

"Now listen to what further I am about to say. It is possible that George Drayton may not be the real Duke of Lorton, after all."

"Not the real Duke?"

"No. One of two things in that respect may have happened. First of all, he may fancy he is such from deceptive evidence, or he may have been persuaded that he is such from the machinations of other parties, who have made him the tool of their own projects."

"Good gracious!" cried Mrs. Ardent.

"Or he may know that he is not the real Duke, and may himself have joined in the general plot to take possession of the title and the properties of another. But—oh, Heaven! no! I do not—I must not—I will not yet think that!"

The feeling of desolation that appeared to sweep like a hurricane over the heart of Millicent at the mere supposition of George playing such a part as that, was truly dreadful, and she was compelled to seek a chair, upon which she sat, swaying to and fro and weeping, with her hands clasped over her face.

"My dear child," said Mrs. Ardent, "do not give way in this manner, I implore you."

"I will not, if I can help it, mother. God grant that he may be the deceived, and not the deceiver."

"Amen!" said old Ardent.

"But," said Jane, "he may be neither the one nor the other."

"How, Jane?"

"He may be really the Duke."

Millicent shuddered. She had the best reason in the world, as the reader knows, to doubt it, and very many concurrent pieces of testimony pointed out to her mind the young and apparently-destitute Frank Western as the real Duke of Lorton; but she did not feel that the time had come just yet to make that revelation.

The great experiment upon the heart of George Drayton had to be made first; and she had to ascertain that most important point of whether he was the deceived or the deceiver, before she moved farther in the matter.

"Let that rest," she said, "for the present —oh, let that rest! But what I am as the wife of George Drayton, and all that I may be as his wife, I am; and he and the supposed, or real Duke of Lorton, now at Dalewood House, are one and the same person."

"Of that I now entertain no doubt," said Jacob Ardent. "Oh, what a wonderful stroke of fortune is this!"

"It is, indeed," said Jane.

"And my daughter, then," said Mrs. Ardent, smoothing down her apron—"my daughter is an Empress."

"An Empress, wife?" cried old Ardent. "Whatever are you thinking of?"

"Of the dignity of the family, Mr. Ardent."

"The dignity of a fiddlestick! How can you make her out an Empress, when, after all, she can only be the wife of a Duke?"

"After all," thought Jane.

"And what of that, Mr. Ardent?" said the good woman, with a toss of her head.

"Why, then she is a Duchess, and not an Empress?"

"Well, sir, and I should very much like to know what is the difference?" said Mrs. Ardent, with a triumphant look, as though the question were a complete poser, and she had at once put an end to all argument upon the subject.

"The difference?"

"Yes, the difference."

"Oh, I——"

Bang—bang—bang! Rat—tat—tat! Bang —bang! came at the Ardents' shop-door.

Old Ardent sank into a seat, with his mouth wide open, Mrs. Ardent looked dreadfully flustered, and Jane made two steps to the door.

Millicent was very pale.

"Oh, good gracious!" said old Ardent, "it is the Duke come for our Millicent."

"Oh, Heavens, yes!" cried Millicent, clasping her hands. "He loves me still—he loves me still! Oh, gracious Heaven, this is joy— joy!"

Bang!—bang!—bang! came at the door again.

Jane flew to open it.

Poor Millicent, now that the idea that it was the Duke, her own George, come for her, had been put into her head, could think of nothing else, and, with a radiant flush upon her face, she stood ready to receive him. Poor Mrs. Ardent had hold of each side of her voluminous petticoats, in order to make her very grandest curtsey to him; and old Jacob stood on one side of the kitchen door, quite confounded at all that was going on.

There was the tread of feet—the rustling of silk, and then Jane opened the kitchen door wide, and announced:

"The Lady Bridget Lorton!"

The old Lady Bridget sailed into the kitchen most magnificently attired, and with her nose turned up at an angle of at least forty-five degrees, in consequence of the place she was walking into. She was followed by Captain Gay.

There was a look of blank disappointment on the faces of all there present.

Poor Mrs. Ardent, though, as she had been so fully prepared for it, made the elaborate curtsey, which Lady Bridget did not deign to take the least notice of.

Old Jacob jumped to the conclusion that she had come as a messenger from the Duke, her nephew, to take Millicent at once to his house as his Duchess. Jane had the same idea, and perhaps even Millicent herself had a thought of it.

"Brand!" cried Lady Bridget.

"Yes, my lady," said Captain Gay, advancing.

"Brand! A chair?"

"Yes, my lady."

Captain Gay seized a chair; and, after flapping the dust, or the supposed dust, off it with his pocket-handkerchief, he placed it for the Lady Bridget, who, with a look of the most unqualified disdain, sat down.

"Brand!"

"My lady."

"The vinaigrette."

"Yes, my lady."

Captain Gay handed her a vinaigrette, which she placed to her nose to counteract the supposed low air she was breathing in that place.

The Ardents looked on at all this in silent dismay and astonishment. A flush of colour, though, was slowly creeping over the face of Millicent, and old Jacob looked very earnestly at Captain Gay, as though he were trying to recollect him.

Brand, as Captain Gay now called himself, made up all sorts of faces to try and evade the scrutiny of the old man, at which he was excessively annoyed. Jane crept close to the side of Millicent, and whispered:

"Courage!"

"Yes, I shall need it."

"I think you will."

"I feel I shall."

"Brand!" cried Lady Bridget.

"Yes, my lady."

"Are these the—a—the a——" low people, Lady Bridget was going to say, but she thought it impolitic, so she said—"people you speak of, Brand?"

"Yes, my lady."

"Oh—ah, very good. My good people, I am the Lady Bridget Lorton, I may inform you."

"Thank you, my lady," said old Ardent. "Will you be so good as to inform me, too, who this flunkey is who came in with you?"

"Eh?"

"I say, who is this man?"

"Oh, that is a—a person—Brand is his name."

"Indeed. Well, Brand was not his name some time ago ; for, if I mistake not, I have had him in this house once before."

"Me ?" said Captain Gay. "Oh, dear, no. I can assure you, old gentleman, that you are very much mistaken, indeed. I have never had the honour of being here. Oh, dear, no—never !"

"I think you have."

"No—no—no !"

"That," said Lady Bridget, as she suddenly opened a large fan with such a jerk that it made poor Mrs. Ardent jump again, "that is of no sort of consequence at all ; and I don't want to hear anything about it. Brand !"

"Yes, my lady."

"Take the vinaigrette."

"Yes, my lady."

"And—a—Brand, you can explain to these a—a—low—I mean, you can explain to these common—that is, to these people, the reason of my presence here, Brand."

"I will do so, my lady, as well as I can. Hem ! that is to say, according to your ladyship's kind instructions in the matter. If I say anything that disagrees with your ladyship's kind and benevolent intentions, your ladyship will put me right."

CHAPTER LXX.

LADY BRIDGET AND CAPTAIN GAY FIND THEMSELVES IN THE MIDDLE OF THE MARKET.

IT took poor Mrs. Ardent till now to recover herself from the shock of all the events, but now she stepped before her husband, and, placing her arms a-kimbo, she said to the old Lady Bridget :

"And pray, ma'am, who do you call low people, and common people, I should like to know ?"

The old Lady Bridget looked at Mrs. Ardent for a moment or two in silence, and then she said :

"Female, go away."

"Female ? And pray, ma'am, who do you call a female ? What are you, I should like to know ? An Egyptian mummy, with a silk mercer's shop on its back !"

"Brand !"

"Yes, my lady."

"Take that wretch away."

Brand looked puzzled.

"I should like to see him try it," said Mrs. Ardent.

"Allow me," said Brand, then, in his most silky and oily tones, "allow me to suggest that you all hear what I have to say, by order of the Lady Bridget, before you fly into a passion, or begin quarrelling about it."

"Yes, mother," said Millicent. "Hear this man."

"Oh, very well. Female, indeed ! Wretch ! Hoity-toity ! Marry come up, indeed !"

"Peace, mother—oh, peace !"

"Brand !"

"Yes, my lady."

Lady Bridget pointed at Millicent with the end of her fan.

"Is this the—a—young person ?"

"Yes, my lady."

"Oh, you can go on, then, Brand."

"Hem ! My good people, the Lady Bridget Lorton has but one feeling in her bosom of any importance, and that is, the pleasure she derives from the diffusion of great happiness among all classes of society. It is in accordance with that feeling that she came here this evening to make a little proposal to you all—a proposal which I am quite sure the remotest good sense, aided by circumstances, of the Ardent family, will induce them at once to accept."

"Come to the point, sir," cried Jacob Ardent.

"Thank you ; you are very good. I will. The Lady Bridget brings with her a little document, which if this lady "—pointing to Millicent—" will sign, and you all witness, will put you in possession of a thousand pounds a year from the State, and the first year's annuity down at once."

Lady Bridget nodded graciously.

Captain Gay looked then about him, as much as to say : "Are you not astonished at this rather ?" And he took a piece of folded paper from his pocket, which was the document in question.

Millicent stepped forward.

"What are the other conditions of the document ?" she said.

"Oh, only one."

"Only one ?"

"That is all. It—it is just that Millicent Drayton renounces all claim to be the wife of the Duke of Lorton, and gives her consent to a divorce. Here is the document."

"Then," cried Mrs. Ardent, "you know, both of you, that my daughter is the Duke's real and lawful wife."

"Oh, yes," said Captain Gay, "I found it right, and so I thought it my duty to tell it. Having done so, my conscience was at rest. I have done my duty."

"Your what at rest ?" cried Jacob.

"My conscience, sir. Don't speak to me in that way. I have as much right, I hope, to a conscience as you have, I rather think."

Millicent, by taking two steps forward, seized the document from the hands of Captain Gay, and tearing it to pieces, she flung them all in the face of the Lady Bridget, exclaiming as she did so :

"There is my answer."

The Lady Bridget was so alarmed at this sudden and violent movement, that she flung herself back in her chair, and over it went with her, landing her on the floor in a very undignified manner indeed.

Captain Gay helped her up again as quickly as possible ; but her face looked demoniac with rage.

"Is this your reply," she cried, "you scum of the earth—you low, coarse wretch ? Is this the reply you dare to make to a proposal

CAPTAIN GAY RECEIVES AN UNWELCOME VISITOR.

that would have lifted you off the dunghill to which you cling?"

"Yes," said Millicent, "it is my reply. I am the wife of George Drayton. I care not if he be a Duke or not; but there is no power upon earth that shall induce me to forego my right to call him husband. We are solemnly wedded in the face of Heaven, and Heaven will aid me to keep the contract."

"Oh!" said Captain Gay.

"Yes," added Millicent, speaking with rapidity, her face flushing and her eyes twinkling as she so spoke, with a natural indignation which she could not control—"yes; and if there can be any character more

despicable than another, it is that of the woman who could come to another woman to make the proposal, madam, that has this day disgraced your lips."

"And," added Mrs. Ardent, "you may hear from me, you horrid old jezebel, that if we are poor, we are not so despicable as you, reasoning from a knowledge of yourself, choose to pretend to think us."

"I, too," cried Jacob, "have something to say. If it were not that you were such a poor, shaky old soul, I would turn you head-foremost out of my house."

"You are a horrid old woman!" said Jane, right in the face of Lady Bridget.

"To be sure she is," cried Mrs. Ardent, who had only stopped to gather breath—"to be sure she is; and, what is more, I am rather surprised that she should venture here within the market to insult us in this way. It isn't the safest thing in the world, I can tell her."

"No,". cried Millicent, "it is not."

"You odious, low, common, everyday-wretches!" screamed Lady Bridget, "I'll have you all hanged, I will!"

"You will have us hanged?"

"Yes, I will, you beasts!"

"Beasts, indeed! Who are you, you old she-baboon, I should like to know?"

"Hem!" said Captain Gay, as he indulged himself with a pinch of snuff, "we are in the middle of the market now, I rather think, with a vengeance."

Mrs. Ardent shook her clenched hand in the face of the old lady, and the old lady quivered with suppressed rage, and seemed very much inclined to try to scratch.

"Hear me!" suddenly said Millicent, and in a voice, too, that commanded attention—"hear me!"

Lady Bridget rose and looked daggers at her.

"Answer me one question, madam, before you go. Do you come here on your own part to make this disgraceful offer to me, or do you come as the emissary of him who, if he sent you, I shame to call my husband?"

"Go to the deuce, all of you!" said Lady Bridget.

"Oh, yes," said Captain Gay, "the Duke sent us."

"Then," cried old Ardent, springing forward, and seizing him by the collar, "you can go back to the Duke, and say that Jacob Ardent kicked you out of his house; and but that she may be a woman, he would serve this old she-dragon in the same fashion."

"Beware!" said Captain Gay.

"Oh, I know you—you came here before; and it was through you that the poor Lady Dalewood came by her death, you villain, you——"

"You had better take your hands off me, Mr. Ardent."

"No, I had not. You are a coward, sir."

Captain Gay placed his hand in his pocket to get at a pistol he had there; but Jane suddenly called out, in a loud, resolute voice:

"Hold, villain! We are not so helpless as you think us. Keep your head on one side, uncle, and I can hit him easily. That will do."

There had been from time immemorial an old fowling-piece hanging over the chimney-piece in the room, and Jane had sprung upon a chair and got it down, and had pointed it full at the head of Captain Gay.

It might or it might not be loaded; but the mere chance that it was gave Captain Gay such a turn that he disengaged himself from the grasp of old Ardent, and ran out of the room, and through the shop, leaving old Lady Bridget to fight her own battles all alone with the Ardent family.

"Now, ma'am," said Jane, "you go, too."

"Murder!"

"Be off with you."

"Murder! Fire! No, don't fire! I'm going—I'm going! Help—help! Police! Murder—oh!"

The door of the kitchen was suddenly flung open again, and Captain Gay cried out:

"Seize your prisoner!"

Three stout, active-looking men darted at once into the room, and seized upon Millicent.

"Oh, what is this?" said Mrs. Ardent.

"Help! Jane, help me!" said Millicent.

Jane pulled the trigger of the old gun, but all it made was a snapping noise.

"Ha—ha!" cried Captain Gay, "that is useless; but the intention to murder will be remembered, my girl, to-morrow. Officers, do your duty."

"Officers?" cried old Ardent. "What have officers to do here with my daughter?"

"We have a warrant," said one of the men, "from the Secretary of State, for the arrest of Millicent Ardent, *alias* Drayton, on a charge of high treason and Jacobinism. To resist us is death to whosoever may attempt it."

CHAPTER LXXI.

MILLICENT MEETS WITH AN ALLY AND PRESERVER IN THE MOMENT OF DANGER.

THIS announcement, made, too, in a voice of authority, and by a man whose resolute appearance confirmed the truth of what he said, struck dismay into the hearts of the assembled Ardents.

Poor Jane flung down the gun, and burst out crying; and as for poor Mrs. Ardent, all the spirit of opposition with which she had met the old Lady Bridget appeared to desert her.

Jacob Ardent felt at once how futile was anything they could do in the way of resistance to the law.

It was Millicent alone who in this sad strait seemed to preserve her presence of mind.

"Do not weep for me," she said. "If the law takes cognizance of aught that I have said or done, the law will likewise protect me against false charges."

"Oh, yes, that is quite correct," said Gay. "Now, gentlemen, if you please, off with her, unless——"

"Unless what?" cried Mrs. Ardent. "Oh, is there anything that can save my child?"

"Yes, madam."

"Oh, what—what?"

"If this lady," pointing to the Lady Bridget, "will become bound for your daughter's appearance, if called upon, she may be saved yet; and she will do so, provided you all agree to the terms proposed a while ago."

"Never!" cried Millicent.

"That will do. Away with her."

Millicent was hurried to the door; and then, while the Ardent family looked petrified by grief and astonishment, old Lady Bridget, with a strange, hysterical sound, cried out:

"He—he—he! Now, low wretches, you find that I have power to make you feel—yes, feel! He—he—he!"

She walked out of the kitchen.

"Ha—ha!" said Captain Gay. "You see now, my old friend Ardent, that you have been a little, just a little too hasty. You comprehend? Ha—ha! Oh!"

Jacob had facilitated his retreat by such a kick behind, that he blundered against old Lady Bridget, and nearly knocked her over.

"You wretch! What do you mean by that?" cried the old lady.

"Oh, my lady, a thousand pardons!"

"A thousand curses, sir. Mind what you are about, sir."

"Yes, my lady."

Millicent would fain have longed to say something yet, to her mother and friends; but the officers dragged her through the shop in another moment, despite her resistance.

A hackney-coach was drawn up quite close to the open door of the bouquet-shop.

There was no one with the coach; but one of the four men got up on the box, and took the reins; another sprang on to the footboard behind the vehicle; the other two forced Millicent into the coach, and sprang in after her.

"To the Tower!" cried the one who had got up behind the coach.

"Ha—ha!" laughed Captain Gay. "To the Tower!"

The hackney-coach drove off.

"Lady Lorton's carriage!" cried Captain Gay.

A dashing equipage drew up, and her ladyship got in. Captain Gay mounted the coach-box with the coachman, and off they went.

"That," thought Gay, "has been pretty well done, I take it; and now, if the Duke can be prevented from coming into contact with the Ardent people, and so from finding out what has become of his wife, there will be no great difficulty, I think, in arranging the whole affair very easily indeed—hem! We shall see—we shall see."

Captain Gay was quite right when he said, "We shall see;" for we shall, indeed, soon see how his fine-drawn schemes and villainous machinations failed, and recoiled upon himself.

The reader has not forgotten that Millicent had requested Corporal Budd to be in waiting in the neighbourhood of the bouquet-shop, to escort her to Dalewood House; nor has it been forgotten that when old Ardent came home, sometime before the old Lady Bridget and Captain Gay arrived, he had seen the Corporal dodging about the neighbourhood, but still keeping an eye upon the shop door.

Now the Corporal had seen all that had happened that there was to see on the outside. That is to say, he had seen the splendid carriage of old Lady Lorton draw up, and he saw her go into the bouquet-shop along with someone whom he did not know.

He saw the someone whom he did not know come out, and call out:

"Now—now!"

Then he saw an old hackney-coach come out of the shadow of some stands close by, and draw up close to the curbstone at the door of the Ardents.

All this was very mysterious to the Corporal.

In a few moments, then, he saw that there was some sort of bustle, and off drove the old hackney-coach.

"What on earth can all this mean?" said the Corporal, as he ran round the market, and met the coach just as it got opposite to the church.

It was at that moment that the glass of one of the windows was broken, and a voice called out:

"Help!—oh, help!"

Corporal Budd would have known that voice among a thousand. It was the voice of Millicent herself.

The fact was, that the Corporal stood close to one of the old oil-lamps which then disgraced London, and she happened to see him.

The attempt she made to let down the window of the coach-door was resisted, so she had broken the glass on the impulse of the moment, and called to him.

The Corporal felt every nerve in his body tingle, and as if the strength of ten men were in his arms at once.

"Stop!" he cried, as he flung himself in front of the coach, and seized the horses by their heads. "Stop, or it will be all the worse for some of you! Stop, I say!"

"Hold off, curse you!" cried the man who drove, as he made some slashes at the Corporal with his whip. "Hold off, or I'll strike your eyes out!"

The horses got restive, and began to plunge.

The Corporal had out a pocket-knife in a moment, and in another he had cut the traces, so that the horses dashed free of them, and galloped round the market, leaving the coach stranded like a wreck.

"Oh, that is it, is it?" cried the driver, as he rapidly descended. "I'll soon settle you, my fine fellow!"

He flung himself on the Corporal; but active and strong as he was, he had met with his match. The Corporal pitched him right over on to his head, and he lay insensible in the mud.

"Now for it!" cried the Corporal. "Now for you, old fellow! Just let me get hold of you!"

The man who had been behind the coach had, in the excitement of the moment, clambered up on to the roof; but the Corporal caught him by one leg, and had him down in a moment, and sent him with such a kick as an impetus, that he howled again, sprawling some twenty yards off, among a whole heap of decayed cabbage-leaves.

All this was done so rapidly, that neither Millicent nor the two men inside the coach knew very well what had happened, except that there was a deal of cursing and swearing, and a stoppage of some sort.

By the time one of the men opened the

door, the Corporal had gained a victory on the outside of the coach, and the moment the door was opened, he collared the man who appeared at it, and dragged him out, saying:

"Come out, you rascal!"

"Oh, Budd!" cried Millicent; "is it you, indeed?"

"Yes—yes!"

"Save me!—oh, save me!"

"Of course. I am doing it as fast as I can. There you go, I think, old fellow."

The man had tried to wrestle with the Corporal; but he was thrown with such a dab on his back that it seemed as if he would never get up again.

Millicent now sprang from the coach, and the man who still remained inside made an effort to get out at the opposite door; but before using the coach at all for the purpose it had been put to that night, they had taken the excessive precaution to fasten up that opposite door, so that he was compelled to escape out at the one at which stood the Corporal.

"Come out," cried Budd. "Come out."

"Yes, I—I am a coming. How are you? Eh? I had nothing to do with it, I assure you."

"Oh, indeed!"

"No, I am a poor fellow, sir, and they offered me something, as I felt a little dry. Something to drink."

"Oh, you are dry, are you? There, then, you will get a something!"

There was a large tank of water for the use of the market close by; and, seizing the fellow by the back of the neck and the waist, Corporal Budd, by such an exertion of strength as few men indeed would have been at all equal to, cast him right into it.

The splash the man made was prodigious, and it took him some minutes to escape; and when he did, he looked like a drowned rat.

"Is there any more of 'em?" said the Corporal.

"Oh, no—no," said Millicent; "you have saved me! You have saved me perhaps from death!"

"Have I, though?"

"You have—you have, indeed!"

"Then, I am the happiest fellow, I think, in all London at this present moment. But I don't understand what on earth it can be all about; and I don't suppose I am very likely to do so after all."

CHAPTER LXXII.

THE ARDENT FAMILY HOLD A CONSULTATION WITH A FRIEND.

POOR Millicent clung convulsively to the arm of the Corporal, for she could not yet believe that she was safe, and it was an immense relief to her over-charged heart to shed a flood of tears.

"Come—come!" said the Corporal, "don't you cry, Millicent. It is all over now, and you are safe."

"Am I so?"

"You are, indeed. Am I not with you?"

"Oh, yes, and to you, my good, and generous, and kind friend, I owe all. I shall never be able to thank you as I ought."

"I don't want any thanks. Lord love you, Millicent! the mere thought of itself—that I have been able to do you this good turn, will be grateful to me as long as I live. But what on earth does it all mean?"

"I hardly know."

"Who are these rascals?"

"Oh, I cannot tell you just now. It is too long a story. Take me home, I beg of you. No—oh, no—no!"

"No, do you say?"

"I do say no, for I have no home now that it is safe for me to go to."

"Not safe?"

"Oh, no—no! I have enemies so fearful and so unscrupulous, that this failure of their attempt at my destruction will but provoke another, when you may not be able to save me."

"Good Heavens! you don't mean that?"

"I do—I do! Is there nowhere you can take me to, where I can be safe and in shelter?"

"Yes—yes! Stop!—no—yes! To be sure, there is my old aunt, in George Street. She is poor, but she is honest, and she lives by me—you will be safe there."

"Yes! Oh, take me there at once; and then I have much, very much for you to do."

"Never mind about that. I will do it all were it ten times what it is. It is quite sufficient for me that you pay me the compliment of engaging me in your service, so don't scruple about how much work you give me. And now come on; I don't think anybody will like to meddle with you while you are under my care. No—no!"

The stalwart Corporal was right, for he was a match for any two or three ordinary men at any time; and with such an inducement to extra exertion as the protection of Millicent, there is no knowing what power he might be able to exert.

The distance to his poor old aunt in George Street, Westminster, was soon traversed, and Millicent found the house humble, but still neat and clean.

"Now, my dear friend," she said to the Corporal, when she had been duly welcomed by the old lady, who rejoiced in the name of Abigail Budd. "Now, my dear friend, will you go and bring here my father, and my mother, and Jane?"

"To be sure I will."

"And you will find a young gentleman in the house named Frank Western. Bring him, too."

"Oh, yes! I'm off."

"I shall await your coming with all the impatience in the world, for much must still be done to-night."

The Corporal at once started on his mission, and he made such good speed that he reached the bouquet-shop in quite an incredibly short space of time.

All was dark about the house.

The Corporal knocked.

After rather a long pause, the door was opened by no other than Jane, whose eyes showed that she had been weeping; and at the sight of the Corporal, she said:

"Oh, is that you? I don't think they can see you just now, Mr. Budd."

"Oh, yes, they can."

"But I tell you they are full of affliction. It is a very late hour; so pray call to-morrow."

"To-morrow won't do. I have just knocked over two fellows, and thrown a third on to a muck-heap, and a fourth into the market reservoir, and rescued Millicent out of a hackney-coach; and I intend to tell the old folks all about it."

"Oh! oh!"

"What is the matter?"

"You don't mean to say that you have rescued her?"

"I do, though!"

"Oh, Mr. Budd! God bless you! I am so grateful. We will all be so grateful to you. Will you forgive me for being surly with you?"

Jane, as she spoke, placed her hand on the Corporal's breast, and her face was so close to his that he screwed up his lips, and seemed on the point of going to kiss her.

"No," said Jane.

"Yes," said the Corporal, and he did kiss her.

"The first and the last," said Jane. "That is my gratitude for your business in the case of Millicent."

"I am paid a thousand times over," said the Corporal.

"And I," cried a voice, "am a mad tailor!"

Peter Bolt made but one spring from the open street right on to the Corporal's shoulders; and pulling off his cap, he flung it into the air, and then alighting as quickly as he had jumped up, he ran off like a maniac.

"Good Heavens!" said the Corporal, "what was that?"

"Oh, it was Peter," said Jane.

The Corporal looked up at the sky, for it was his impression that Peter Bolt must have dropped down upon his back from somewhere thereabouts.

"Goodness gracious!" he said, "where did he come from?"

"Oh, never mind."

"But it's very extraordinary."

"Yes—yes. Come in—oh, come in, and tell them the good news. But where is the dear Millicent?"

"In safety. She thought she had better go anywhere than home here, and she has sent me to fetch you all."

"Oh, what a welcome message!"

"And a welcome messenger, too?"

"Yes—yes. Quite welcome, ever and ever."

"Jane? Stop!—Oh, Jane!"

"What is it?"

"Won't you take a second thought, and, after all, get rid of that tailor that drops so oddly upon a fellow's back?"

"I can't."

"Hem! Well, if you can't, you can't. But, Jane?"

"Well?"

"Think again."

"No; it's too late."

The Corporal followed her into the kitchen as meekly as a lamb.

"Corporal Budd," said Jane, as she announced him.

"Yes," cried the Corporal, "Millicent is safe, and has sent me to bring you all to see her."

A shout of joy came from the Ardents, and the Corporal had about twenty questions asked him at once, so he replied to them all, by stating how he had rescued Millicent, and how he had taken her for safety to his aunt's humble abode.

This was news, indeed, for the desponding Ardents, and they nearly devoured the Corporal with their gratitude to him for it. They hastily got ready to go with him, and then he cried out:

"Oh, stop! I forgot."

"What—oh, what?"

"Why, she said I was to bring a young gentleman named Frank Western with me as well."

"Oh, yes—yes!"

"Is he here?"

"He is not within at present, and we don't know for the life of us what keeps him so late from home."

A modest tap at the door of the room at this moment announced someone, and Frank Western put in his head.

"Why, the outer door is open," he said.

"Is it so?" cried Jane. "Then it was my fault when I let in the Corporal just now."

"No, it was my fault," said the Corporal. "But, Mr. Frank Western, will you come with us all to see Millicent?"

"Oh, yes! But is she not here?"

"No. You can hear as we all go along why she is not here; but do not delay a moment."

They did not delay further than was just necessary to enable them to put on their things for the streets, and then they were soon on the road to George Street.

As they went along young Western said to the Corporal:

"There has been quite a disturbance in the market. The people told me that a man had been thrown into the tank."

"Indeed!"

"Yes; and he says it was an elephant, he thinks, that did it, for he is sure it was no man."

"Well, he is mistaken, for it was a man. I did it. And now, if you will walk alongside of me, I will tell you all about it, my young friend."

Frank Western listened in amazement to the details of an affair of which he knew nothing; and by the time he was master of the full particulars of all that had happened, the whole party had reached George Street, Westminster.

Imagine the joy of Millicent at seeing again so many dear friends.

CHAPTER LXXIII.

A GREAT PERSONAGE IS SENT FOR TO THE PARTY IN GEORGE STREET.

To be sure, the Ardent family could not help at times thinking that, after all, they were only going through the phases of some very strange and wayward dream, so rapid and so full of singular circumstances were the events of the last few days, and more particularly of the last few hours, to them.

Poor Mrs. Ardent was probably more really and thoroughly bewildered than anyone else, for that good lady always did get a little out of sorts when by any means she was taken from her own home ; a circumstance which so very seldom happened, that anyone who knew the family well would almost as soon have expected to see some of the fixtures of the bouquet-shop walking about the streets as to see her anywhere but in Covent Garden Market.

She flung herself upon the neck of Millicent, and had what she called a good cry.

"Now I am better," she said ; " but, oh, my child, what could they dare to pretend that you had done that you should be taken off to the horrid old Tower ?"

"Nothing, mother," said Millicent. "They know well that there is no charge against me in reality, and my arrest was but one of those wild exercises of power which the high and rich and titled of this and every other country are ever willing to attempt, but which, in the time that will soon come in free and happy England, will be impossible."

"Yes, my dear," said old Ardent ; " but what can we all do ? Alas! alas! we are poor, and but little able to cope with those who will spare no pains to persecute us."

"Who will persecute us ?"

"The Duke of Lorton, my child, who disowns you as his wife, and who, I cannot help thinking, is at the bottom of all this affair."

"It may be so, father ; but yet it is the Duke of Lorton who shall save us all."

"Save us ?"

"Yes, father. I know that in saying that to you all, I say what sounds very strange indeed ; but it is the truth for all that. I have now a revelation to make to you which will fill you with amazement and with joy."

"Indeed ?"

"Yes ; where is Mr. Frank Western ?"

"I am here, Mrs. Drayton, at your good service. I envy Corporal Budd that he alone was able to rescue you from your foes awhile ago."

"You, though," added Millicent, "will be able to rescue me, and those who love me, from worse foes."

"I ? Can it be so ?"

"It is so."

"Then I am only too happy."

They all now looked at Millicent, and a faint suspicion appeared to cross their minds that she was really wandering in her intellect ;

but she soon put such a supposition at rest by turning to her father, and saying :

"Father, on the night that the Marquis of Dalewood came by his death he left with you certain papers ?"

"He did, my child."

"Have you them still ?"

"I ought not to have any portion of them, and yet I have some of them for all that. I have a few papers that something seemed to whisper to me not to part with, although I took them to the present young Duke. I always carry them about me."

"Oh, father, have you them with you now ?"

"Yes, my dear, and with them a small portrait of the dear Marchioness, which I took out of the little gold locket frame in which it was, in order that I might carry it about me with the greater care."

Millicent looked much affected for a few moments, and then she said in a tone of deep emotion—

"Father, will you show that portrait and those papers to Mr. Frank Western ?"

"With all my heart, if he has any curiosity to see them. Here they are. Here is a letter in the handwriting of the Marchioness, and addressed—'To my dear son, Gerald.'"

"Gerald !" cried Frank Western. "Did you say Gerald ?"

"Oh, hush !" said Millicent. "Hear all before you speak. Let me do this in my own way."

The old man produced the letter and the miniature, and handed both to Frank Western, who, the moment he cast his eyes upon the portrait, sank into a chair, exclaiming—

"Good Heavens, it is my mother !"

"Your mother ?" cried old Jacob Ardent, as he sprang up to him. "Your mother ? Oh, yes—yes! In my dreams I ever thought I had seen your face before. You are her image! Why—why, good Heaven, how is this? Are you the young Duke? No—no! your name is Frank Western !"

"It is Gerald."

"Gerald ?"

"Yes—yes! Oh, Heaven, if this be a dream, let me not awaken from it yet. It is one of too much joy, and yet not unmingled with deep sorrow."

"Read the letter," said Millicent, faintly ; "read the poor Marchioness's letter."

Gerald Western motioned to Millicent to read it, and in a voice broken by sobs, in which the whole party participated, she read as follows—

"To my dear son, Gerald.—My son, something to-night prompts me to write this letter in case we should never meet again in this world. You fancy your name is Frank Western, the son of an officer in the army, who died fighting the battles of his country ; but your real name is Gerald, and you are the son of the Marquis of Dalewood, who is heir to the dukedom and estates of Lorton. I, your poor mother, am his Marchioness, and if you should find that I am only gone before you to that home which is beyond the skies, go at once to Dalewood House after opening the little silken bag which you wear at my request round your neck ever and next to your heart, and which now will reveal to you all that you ought to know respecting your title and real name and position.

"If I return to you this night, I will still let this letter exist, in the hope that it will yet reach your hands, in case chance or design of some enemy should, at any time, suddenly bring me to eternity.

"The blessings of your poor mother be with you, dear, dear Gerald, for ever and ever.

"Cecil, Marchioness of Dalewood."

To use a popular phrase, you might have heard a pin drop while this letter was being read, so profound was the silence in that humble house in which were collected those good people.

It seemed to take poor Gerald a minute or two thoroughly to feel his position, and then, with quite a burst of grief, he cried out :

"It is my mother's letter ! It is her hand ! Oh, God, why did she not live still for me ?"

"The hand of Heaven," said old Ardent, "is in all this."

"It is," said Millicent. "But now, Gerald, speak to me."

"Yes—yes !"

"Have you such a silken bag round your neck as is now made mention of in this letter ?"

The only reply that Gerald made was to produce it on the instant, and hand it to Millicent. With fingers that trembled so she could scarcely open it, she contrived to take from it a small folded paper.

Upon opening this paper, she turned to Gerald, saying:

"Shall I read it ?"

"Oh, yes—yes."

The paper contained the following words :

"My own dear son.—You are the son of the Marquis of Dalewood, and enclosed is the marriage certificate of your poor mother. Think as lightly of your father's crimes as you can; but claim your inheritance. This is from your fond mother,

"Cecil, Marchioness of Dalewood."

"This is conclusive," said Millicent.

"It is—it is !" cried old Ardent.

"I'm all of a heat," said Mrs. Ardent.

"The Marquis of Dalewood," said Millicent, turning to Gerald, "is no more, and, therefore, your Grace is the Duke of Lorton."

Gerald started.

That was the first time anyone had called him "Your Grace," and the title seemed to his ears like delicious music.

"Stop—stop !" he said, "you bewilder me by all this. I cannot as yet believe in its reality. It must be a delusion."

"It is no delusion, your Grace," added Millicent. "I know it to be the truth, and I

and all of us now throw ourselves upon your protection and your mercy."

"My protection ?"

"Yes—oh, yes! for your rank will be a shield, behind which we shall find safety."

"With my life !" cried Gerald, "I will stand between you and all harm. Are you not my dearest friends ?"

Millicent now went up to the real young Duke, and, looking in his face, she said :

"My husband, George Drayton, is deceiving, or deceived himself. If deceiving, will you be merciful to him ?"

"I merciful ?"

"Yes; he now sits in your house, and assumes your name. It is he who is by the great world presumed to be what you are in reality. How it has come about that such is the case, I know not just yet; but will you, if you know the very worst, be merciful to him for my sake ?"

"You distress me beyond reason, dear Millicent," said the young Duke. "You shall yourself dictate to me whatever you would have me do. I pledge you my word and honour to that."

"Then still he may be saved !" cried Millicent, as she began to weep hysterically.

It took some time to calm her; and then, as they all seemed to lean upon her for advice as to what to do, when she was again able to speak calmly, the young Duke asked her advice as to what should be his immediate action in the matter.

CHAPTER LXXIV.

MILLICENT GIVES GOOD ADVICE TO THE YOUNG DUKE.

After some few minutes' consideration, Millicent spoke.

"Your Grace," she said, "will consider exactly the present circumstances. One attempt, you see, has been made to send your Grace out of England."

"Oh, stop," said the young Duke; "I have a request to make you."

"A command to give, you should say."

"No—no! It is, that you would not call me by any other name than Gerald."

"Be it so, then. It does sound more pleasing ; so, Gerald, you have escaped being got rid of by being sent to Ireland, where, no doubt, you would soon have come by your death. It is, no doubt, too, believed at Dalewood House, that by this time I am safely bestowed in the Tower."

"Yes—yes !"

"Well, then, I think that it is the evil spirit in the shape of the man who was called Brand by old Lady Bridget, who either does all this without the knowledge of George Drayton, or who has such influence and power over him as to enforce his consent to it. In either case, this man, Brand, is the principal mover in all the iniquity that is being practised against you and against me."

"There can be no doubt of it. The fellow's

looks were to me truly demoniac, and I had to reason with myself upon what I thought a boyish prejudice to enable me to speak to him with common civility."

"Thus, then, you see," added Millicent, speaking with great and evident emotion, "in either case poor George Drayton wants some pity from us all."

"He does—he does! and something seems to tell me that he is as much the victim as anyone of us of that fearful and unscrupulous man, and that you will yet have many happy years with him."

"Blessings on you!" said Millicent, as the tears started to her eyes, "for the kind suggestion. But now I feel that we are all quite incompetent to act in this matter, and I advise that some legal aid be sought."

"What legal aid?"

"I advise that some lawyer of high standing be at once sent for, and that all be explained to him."

"There is the great lawyer, Mr. Mathew Coke," said the Corporal, "who lives at the corner of the Bird-cage Walk. I could run and get him, I daresay, directly."

"Do so, then, at once," cried the young Duke. "I will not sleep till I have put all the matter to rights."

The Corporal, without further bidding, at once started off in search of the lawyer, and he returned in the course of about a quarter-of-an-hour to say that he was coming.

"You will have him here pretty soon," he said, "I think. I saw his secretary, and when I told him without further explanation that it was the Duke of Lorton who wanted him, he said that he fully expected him from the House of Commons every passing minute, and that he would ask him to come right on to this place without getting out of his carriage."

"That is well," said the young Duke.

The sharp rattle of carriage wheels, and a loud knock at the street-door, now announced the arrival of the eminent lawyer, and he was soon, with some surprise on his face at the appearance of the place, in the room.

"It was the Duke of Lorton I was sent for to see," he said, in rather a dubious tone of voice.

"Yes, sir," said the young Duke, advancing, "and I am the Duke of Lorton."

"I had not the pleasure to know your Grace."

"I hope we shall be well acquainted for all that, sir." Be so good now as to take a seat while I tell you a very plain story."

The lawyer sat down, and with great rapidity and admirable lucidity and distinctness Gerald told him the whole story, and handed him the letters and miniature of the deceased Countess of Dalewood, his poor neglected mother.

He concluded by saying—

"Now, Mr. Coke, what do you think of all this?"

"Your Grace need hardly ask me the question."

"You have answered it, sir, by the title you have given to me. Will you accept the appointment of counsel to me, Duke of Lorton,

and become my friend and adviser in all respects?"

"With pleasure, your Grace."

"Then I place my affairs entirely in your hands, sir. What shall I do to get my inheritance?"

"Before twelve o'clock to-morrow your Grace shall be in Dalewood House as its master, and presented to the King, and received as the Duke of Lorton."

"Can you act so quickly?"

"Yes; there is nothing wanting in the way of proof. And now I will take the first step, if you will all come to my house, by going and fetching the Lord Chancellor to you and the Secretary of State, who are both at the House, and will be able to come upon what I shall say to them at once."

"Be it so," said Gerald.

It must not be supposed that Gerald took all this quite calmly. On the contrary, it was evident that it required a great effort on his part to control his feelings. The sudden change in his fortunes and prospects was enough to unhinge for a time any mind.

"Gerald," said Millicent, "I don't think we need trouble you any further just now."

"No," said old Ardent; "we will now go to our own humble home again."

"Not so," said Gerald. "I will have you all with me. Don't you think, Mr. Coke, they had better come?"

"Yes, your Grace; in fact, they are all necessary evidence upon the subject before me; and I can only say that I think my house honoured by the presence of such worthy persons."

After this there could be no hesitation about the matter, except as regarded the Corporal, and stepping up to the lawyer, he said, in his odd way—

"Beg pardon, sir, but I have nearly smashed four of the King's officers to-night. Pray, can you tell me if there is anything in the shape of an offence in that?"

"Offence?"

"Yes, sir. It was all in fair fight though, and I used no sort of weapon, I assure you."

"Well, I must confess, that to smash four of the King's officers seems to me something like an offence; but yet, under the circumstances, it may possibly admit of extenuation. How did you do it?"

The Corporal just told him how it happened, and Millicent added much to the narrative that the modesty of the Corporal omitted. The lawyer said then, with a smile—

"I think we can pull you through that, Mr. Budd, for I very much suspect they are not King's officers at all."

"You think not, sir?" inquired the Corporal.

"Certainly, that is my opinion, dear friend. There may have been a something in the shape of a warrant for prosecution on that sort of charge, that may mean anything or nothing, as you please to take it. However, all that can be set right, I have no doubt."

This was rather cheering intelligence for the Corporal, for however his own feelings might be pleased at what he had done, and however his own conscience might fully approve of the act, he could not shut his eyes to the fact that it might possibly be productive of rather serious consequences to him.

An assurance, though, from the high authority who gave that assurance that he might be safely seen through the matter, went a long way to quiet the mind of the worthy Corporal.

The whole party now went to the house of Mr. Coke, and there he left them, while he drove off in his carriage to the Chancellor's house, and to that of the Secretary of State.

Both of those personages were at home, and Mr. Coke lost no time in imparting his startling intelligence.

"Why, God bless me," said the Chancellor to himself, "I shall get a great deal of popularity by this affair, if I show myself as prompt and able in it as I am in doing bad actions just now in other respects."

"Dear me," thought the Secretary of State, "if I mind what I am about, this is an affair that will be as good as three or four votes in the House of Commons for me, for the Lorton family can manage as many."

For these reasons, then, both the Chancellor and the Secretary of State consented at once to accompany Mr. Coke to his house, to see the Duke of Lorton, and after only keeping the little party there assembled about one hour, he reappeared, introducing his illustrious friends with him.

The young Duke received them with great grace, and yet in a very dignified way.

On the route to the house, Mr. Coke had said quite enough to convince both of the illustrious official personages he brought with him of the real particulars of the case, so they were quite prepared to receive Gerald at once as the Duke of Lorton, without further questions as to his right and title.

In fact, his case was so very clear a one, that there could not be two opinions about it.

A consultation now commenced as to what was to be done, during which the clock in the room struck the hour of one.

"Gentlemen," said the young Duke, "I think that neither I nor any of my friends will sleep to-night. I have a very great favour, therefore, to ask of you."

"Name it, your Grace," said the Secretary.

"It is, that you will both, and you, too, Mr. Coke, accompany me and these kind friends to Dalewood House."

"Agreed. Be it so," said the Secretary. "And I will write a line to the officer on duty at the barracks to send a captain's-guard with us, for it strikes me that this Mr. Brand, who appears to be at the bottom of all this affair, will be a troublesome person to deal with."

CHAPTER LXXV.

CAPTAIN GAY FELICITATES HIMSELF UPON HIS GREAT SKILL.

WHILE all this was going on to the very serious detriment of the plans and projects of Captain Gay, that individual had never felt so much at his ease.

Captain Gay thought, in his own mind, that he had really managed matters with the greatest possible tact and precision; and he sat in one of the splendid rooms of Dalewood House, sipping his claret, and feeling quite happy.

"Ha!" he said. "I rather think I have got quite upon the weak side of old Lady Bridget. She promises me five hundred pounds for the way in which I have managed this little affair to-night, in getting rid of the wife. Ha! ha! If, now, she did but know of my scheme of getting rid of her real nephew by sending him to Ireland, what would she say?"

He poured himself out another glass.

"Upon my life, this old wine that has been stored for so long in the cellars of this house is first-rate—quite first-rate, I declare. Ha! ha! what a fool George Drayton must be not to drink more of it than he does. Since I told him he was no duke at all, but plain George Drayton, he seems to have been positively afraid to put a glass of the Lorton wine to his lips."

It was quite clear that Captain Gay, at the rate he was drinking it, had no such scruples to contend with.

"Well," he added, after a pause of some time, "the wife is got rid of. She is in the Tower, and there she will remain, until, by a private order from the King, she is sent out to the West India Colonies along with other suspected and disaffected persons, against whom positive legal charges cannot be openly brought; but who it is very desirable to be got rid of. Ha! ha!"

The Captain took another glass of wine.

"Let me see," he said. "I shall make, first and last now, I expect, a good fifty thousand pounds by this affair, and then I will go to Germany and get made a prince, and live there a very great man for the remainder of my days."

"Indeed?" said a voice.

Captain Gay started to his feet.

George Drayton, looking pale and haggard, stood before him, and gazed in his face.

"Oh, I thought your Grace had retired for the night."

"I had."

"Oh, but you—you——"

"Rose again. I cannot sleep. Conscience will not let me. I am going out, sir."

"Out, your Grace?"

"Yes. Brand or Gay, or whatever your name may be—devil included, perhaps—I am going out."

"You are serious?"

"I am."

"If he was not in earnest," thought Gay, "he would not have come to tell me of it. He has the notion of being honest and a fool, this fellow; but he wants discretion."

"Well, your Grace," added Captain Gay, "it is a very odd thing, but I had the same idea."

"You?"

"Yes, just the same idea; and if you sit down, I shall be able to tell you why I had it."

"No—no!"

"As you please; but as simply telling you why involves likewise the fact that I should impart to you some news that it is proper you should hear, I did hope that you would attend to me."

"Time is an object."

"Surely ten minutes cannot make much difference?"

"Well, well, I will listen to you; but do not tell me more lies, Gay. I have had enough of them already. What have you to say to me?"

"Well, I'm sure, considering the very polite way in which you put it, I might take offence; but I won't. I make every possible allowance for you. I know your feelings are hurt."

"They are, indeed."

"Well, according to my promise to you, I set about thinking of how I could get you safely and with honour out of the tangle of circumstances into which you have fallen."

"You should say into which you have dragged me."

"Well, as you please. Now, I felt that were it not that you regret your conduct towards your wife, Millicent, you would not be quite so ready to give up the good that fortune has placed in your hands—eh?"

"Tempter, I understand you; but I am willing to put it as you please in that respect. You and Lady Bridget have both convinced me that this deception of rank and state cannot be carried on without the renunciation of Millicent, and I will not pay that price for it."

"Hem! But if that price had not to be paid?"

"Then I might hold my position until I found the real duke, when, on the instant, I would give all up to him, and throw myself upon his mercy."

"Denouncing me, of course?"

"I would tell all the truth."

"Thank you. Well, then, as there is no real duke to be found, at all events, just now, I can relieve you of your other little regret."

"What?"

"Your wife has eloped!"

"Eloped?"

"Oh, yes. It sounds odd, doesn't it? These things always do to the husband. He never can believe it till it happens. But the fact is, she is off and away—Heaven only knows where by this time. There was a young fellow who had been making very violent love to her, and he and she concocted a nice little plot between them."

"No—no!"

"I say yes; it was agreed that he was to bring a hackney-coach to the door of the Ardent's bouquet-shop, and with some dissolute young friends of his pretend to arrest her for high treason. Ha! ha! that was to blind the Ardents, you see, for, after all, she did not want them to know what she was about; you comprehend—eh?"

George Drayton sprang to his feet, and his eyes appeared to flash with excitement as he looked in the face of Captain Gay for a moment in silence. Then he cried—

"Infamous calumniator! Dare you say this to my face?"

"Not if you don't wish to hear it: if it be one of those truths that are so very uncomfortable that people would rather shut their ears to, then say so and I am dumb."

"No—no! you are wrong. Tell me that you have concocted this infamous story, and I will yet forgive you."

"I wish I could; but if you will send to the Ardents anyone upon whom you can depend, you will ascertain that it is the exact truth. The fact is, she has jilted you upon finding that you were upon the point of marriage with another, and I expect that in a little time you will be asked for a settlement upon her, which you can, now that you know all, grant or refuse just as you feel inclined."

"It is false!"

"Very good."

"She could not. It is contrary to her nature!"

"As you please. But I merely tell you of it in order that you may feel free. And now for the conclusion of it. If you like to hold your title and let everything take its course for a time, I will join with you hand in hand in trying to find out the real heir to the dukedom, so that justice may be done."

"No—no! I see the plot."

"The plot?"

"Yes. This is to quiet me! This is to get me to do nothing—to make no movement—to remain a mere puppet in your hands. I see all that."

"Then you see much more than I do; and all I have got to say in reply to that is, do what you like, or——"

"Or what?"

"Pay me!"

"You know I cannot. You know I have not the means to settle with you."

"Then don't do anything to betray me, or to prevent yourself from having such means, that is all. After you have paid me, you can do as you please, you know."

"I can before that."

"Indeed?"

"Yes, I can submit to my fate."

"And even give yourself up to the law as one who has committed forgery, murder, and several other little matters too numerous to mention."

"Villain! Did you say murder?"

"I did."

"And forgery?"

"Oh, yes!"

"You know that I am innocent even of the most trivial of these offences; and, as regards murder, I never heard till this moment that it entered into the catalogue of your threats even."

"Oh! Ah, yes! Well, I will tell you just how it is."

"Oh, Heaven! Is it possible that I am, in truth, subject to the tortures of this fiend?"

"Come—come, Mr. Drayton, all this is nonsense. You are in for forgery, as you know perfectly well, by joining with me in concocting the certificate of your own death, and raising money of the bankers under the signature of Lorton."

"No! I say boldly—no!"

"Indeed!"

"In the first place, you did the act of forgery, as regards the certificate of my death, yourself."

"Yes; but who will believe it?"

"In the next place, when I signed papers in the name of Lorton, I believed it was my name. I have signed none since I knew that it was not."

"Yes; but who, I say, will believe that? It will be beyond credence, and I will take care to give every possible colour to the supposition that you and I in all things acted together; so we live together or die together."

CHAPTER LXXVI.

CAPTAIN GAY IS FOILED WITH HIS OWN WEAPONS.

THE poor Duke, or rather George Drayton, as we ought certainly to call him, now sank upon a couch with a deep sigh.

"I am quite delighted to find," said Captain Gay, "that you begin to see this affair in its right light. Ah!"

They both started. There was a slight noise upon the staircase outside the door.

Captain Gay stepped to the door, and looked out. All was still as the very grave.

"I thought I heard a noise," he said.

"And I, too," said George Drayton.

"It was nothing. Listen to me now. This is a crisis in your fate and mine."

"It is—it is! I want strength."

"For what?"

"To do right. To follow out the promptings of my own heart. I want strength. Oh, Heaven, grant it to me!"

"Pho! you mean to say that you have an idea of wildly rushing off and placing yourself in the hands of the police, just to suffer for what you really never did?"

"You admit that?"

"To you, of course I do; but I have woven such a web around you that, although I am the plotter, not you, you are as much involved in the consequences as I."

"But you spoke of murder?"

"I did."

"Surely it has not been at all necessary even for you to add that crime to your other villainies?"

"Your Grace uses rather harsh language; but I am not very particular on that ground; and so, with only the passing remark that you might be more polite, I will explain what I mean by murder in this case."

George Drayton looked into the calm, imperturbable face of the rascal with amazement.

"You recollect," continued Gay, "a Mr. South, who was at Lorton Castle?"

"Yes. He left for London?"

"He did in his own conceit, poor man!"

"In his own conceit?"

"Yes; but he was intercepted and murdered, as you seem to like to call things by their right names. His mangled body now lies in a stone quarry on the Lorton estate, and it will be difficult to convince a jury that you had not your part in the transaction."

"Villain! I cannot and I will not hear this language. You strive thus to intimidate me by mixing me up with deeds and crimes that from my soul I abhor. There is yet a Heaven above us, which will save me. I will fly from this house."

"Where to?"

"To the police."

"You are mad. What would you do there?"

"Denounce you, and the whole of this plot."

"To your own destruction!"

"I care not. Hark you, sir. Captain Gay, or Brand, or whatever name may really belong to you, you have risked your neck."

"As how?"

"In order to make sure of me, your victim, through my fears, you have gone too far. I cannot and I will not for one moment longer seem to have complicity with such a man as you."

"I tell you you are mad, then, and know not what you do."

"I do know that I run some danger from such a man as you. Out of my way, sir."

"No, wait till to-morrow; and then, if you feel as you do now—then, if you persevere in the same determination, I will no longer stay you."

"Now it shall be—now or never," said George Drayton.

"I am bound to stop you when you would rush upon your own destruction, and drag me with you in one common act of ruin."

"You dare not stay me."

"Indeed! I thought that you had a pretty good notion of what I dared do."

"Ah!"

"Yes, George Drayton, you shall not leave this house to-night. I have said it."

"And think you that you can prevent me?"

"I do."

Captain Gay drew from his breast a short poniard, and stood upon his guard. There was an expression of very great ferocity upon his face at this moment, and what might have resulted it is hard to say, had not there come a tap at the door of the apartment at this moment.

Captain Gay started.

"Who can that be?" he said.

"Come in," cried George Drayton.

The door was opened, and a servant said, in a clear, but not a very loud voice:

"Mr. Coke!"

The lawyer entered the apartment.

Now, we may state that this apartment was the very one in which George Drayton had had that terrible and anxious interview with Millicent, which interview had been overheard by Captain Gay, who, in order to do so, had stationed himself in the adjoining saloon.

Both of these saloons had doors going out upon the corridor, common to all the apartments upon the first floor of the house.

At the farther end of the other saloon to that in which Mr. Coke now stood there was a large bay window, that looked into the gardens of Dalewood House.

These little details the reader will find essentially necessary to the due comprehending of the veritable scenes that ensued in the house of the Duke of Lorton upon this deeply-interesting occasion.

The appearance of this Mr. Coke, unknown as he was both to George Drayton and to Captain Gay, was to both of them one of the most mysterious of circumstances, and they looked at him in mute surprise.

"Gentlemen," said the lawyer, in a quiet, calm kind of voice, "perhaps this is an intrusion?"

"It is, sir," said Gay.

"Is it to you, your Grace?" added the attorney, turning to George Drayton.

"Sir, I know not how to answer you till I learn the object of your visit here."

"Then I will explain it. There are suspicions abroad that you are not the Duke of Lorton; but that you and this man, who has sometimes called himself Captain Gay, and now, as I hear, calls himself Mr. Brand, are impostors."

"Ah!" said Gay.

"Lost!" said George Drayton, as he sank into a chair, and looked as pale as death.

"Pray, sir," said Gay, "in what capacity do you come here, then, to-night at such an hour?"

"Sir, I am a lawyer."

"A lawyer?"

"Yes; and I come here to see if the Duke has any arrangements that he wishes to make, as I am in possession of rather important information touching him and you."

"Oh, I see! Then your object is to effect some nice little arrangement of the affair?"

"It is."

"I thought so, sir; you are a sensible man. You were quite right to come alone."

"There you are mistaken, sir; I am not alone."

"Not alone?"

"No. There are friends of mine who are within call, if I think proper to call them, or if they fancy I am in any sort of danger."

"Oh, yes, I see; but if you can come to an arrangement with us, you will not call them?"

The attorney did not commit himself by any reply to this, and so satisfied was Captain Gay of his own astuteness, that he at once jumped to the conclusion that the lawyer had come to be bought off; so he stepped up to George Drayton and whispered to him—

"All is safe. He will take money. Offer him a thousand pounds at once and get rid of him."

"No!" cried George, starting to his feet.

"No?"

"No, I say again. I am sick to the very soul of my position, sir. You say that you are in the law, and that there are suspicions that I am not what I seem to be, and now I tell you that those suspicions are correct. I am not the Duke of Lorton, sir; but beyond being the victim of this man's most infamous plots, I am innocent of all wrong. This I declare in the outset; and now, sir, if you are armed with any authority to act, do your duty."

"Yes," said Captain Gay. "Take him away."

"I beg your pardon," said the lawyer; "but if anyone is to be taken away, it appears to me it ought to be you, sir."

"Me?"

"Yes—yes! I arrest you."

"You arrest me? Sir, it will take more than you to do that. Ah! what is this?"

The door opened, and a file of soldiers marched into the room.

CHAPTER LXXVII.

THE CONCLUSION.

THE soldiers, with their officer at their head, halted close to the door, and then Mr. Coke said:

"Are you satisfied?"

Captain Gay staggered back a pace or two, then summoning all his effrontery to his aid, he said:

"Of what am I accused?"

"Of forgery and murder."

"Then, there is my accomplice, if I have one. In fact, there is the man who got me to keep secret his crimes. There he is. His name, he tells me, is George Drayton: he imposed himself, though, upon me as the Duke of Lorton."

"It is false!" cried George. "False! False!"

"Have you any witnesses?" said Mr. Coke.

"No! Alas! not one."

"Ha!" said Captain Gay. "I have reason to think, too, from what has dropped from him to-night, that he has got rid in some way of a young man called Western; and that he, while in Ireland, committed or connived at the murder of a Mr. South, who, he found, stood in the way of the furtherance of his plans. Alas! gentlemen, I have been the

LADY BRIDGET MAKES HER LAST APPEARANCE.

victim of this artful and bad man; but I will appear as a principal witness against him."

"Silence!" said Mr. Coke.

"Certainly, sir."

"Is your name George Drayton, sir?" said Mr. Coke, addressing poor George.

"It is."

"Are you guilty of what this man asserts?"

"As Heaven is my judge—no!"

"But you have no witnesses?"

"Not one."

"Well, I will see if I can supply that deficiency in one respect. Mr. Western!"

"Here!" said the young Duke, appearing in the room, past the file of soldiers.

Captain Gay turned pale.

"Did this George Drayton try to send you to Ireland?"

"No; but that man, Brand, did."

"False!" cried Captain Gay. "Why, this very George Drayton got his wife put out of the way this very night."

"Indeed! Did you do so?"

"Oh, Heaven—no!"

"Millicent Drayton!"

Millicent glided into the room, and flew to her husband, whom she clasped in her arms, saying:

"George, I know your innocence! We have all been in the adjoining room for the last half-hour, and have heard all that has passed between you and that bold, bad man."

"My own dear Millicent!"

"Stop a bit," said Captain Gay. "Did you mean what you said, my dear madam?"

"I did, villain!"

"Thank you."

He took his hat from the table, and put it on his head, to the surprise of all present, and before anyone could stir to stop him, he said:

"Ladies and gentlemen, the game is up, and it strikes me now very forcibly that I am one too many here, and had much better go. Good-night."

He darted past the file of soldiers, and flinging open the folding-doors that led to the inner saloon, reached the bay window before anyone recovered sufficiently from the surprise of his movements to act.

It was the officer in command of the guard that recovered first, and he cried out:

"Do not follow him; he is safe."

"Oh, am I?" cried Gay, as he sprang upon the window-sill, and dashed one of the casements open.

"Make ready—present!" cried the officer.

"Good-night!" shouted Gay.

"Fire!"

A volley of musketry followed, and Captain Gay fell twenty feet to the ground, a mangled corpse, for the file of soldiers had so effectually executed the orders of their superior, to fire, that he was but one mass of fragments and tatters. The close of his career, though frightful to think of, was nothing more or less than he richly deserved. His course had been one of successful villainy for a long period, and but for the special interposition of Providence in bringing together the different members of our *dramatis personæ*, he might have ultimately triumphed in his chief plans, to the utter ruin of the peace and prospects of those whose only wish was to do well, and to live a quiet, peaceable, and virtuous life.

*   *   *   *

The young Duke advanced, and took the hand of George Drayton.

"Mr. Drayton," he said, "you and I will be friends, I hope. If you have committed any acts at all during your temporary occupation of my title, it is I whom the acts concern; and, for the sake of your wife and her dear friends, I forgive and forget all, and only ask for the continued kindly feeling of them and of yourself."

"Oh, is this possible?" said George.

"It is, dear George," said Millicent. "Once more, now, we are united, and happiness will be ours. How it was that we all this night happened to get together, and then determined to come to this house, will be fully explained to you in time to come; but, now, let it suffice to tell you that we had such authority that the servants could not resist, and that we all found our way to the next saloon, where we heard your own vindication and his own conviction from the lips of Gay himself."

"This is, indeed, the hand of Providence," said George.

"My dear son-in-law," said Mrs. Ardent, "let me embrace you. There! that has done me good."

"Welcome, my dear boy," said old Jacob Ardent. "A welcome to the heart of your Millicent's father."

"Dear friends," said George, "I am only too happy."

"Hear me, then," said the young Duke. "It is not for many hours that I have had in my hands the means of doing good; but it is a great gratification to me that my first ducal act shall be to appoint you, Mr. Drayton, if you will accept the office, my private secretary, at a salary of one thousand pounds per annum."

"Your Grace is too—too good."

"Then that is settled," added the young Duke; "and now you must all be my guests for a short time, till we have done talking over the strange, eventful history of the past."

But really it is quite out of the question that we should in so very summary a manner dismiss from the reader's kind consideration either Jane, or Millicent, or Peter Bolt; so we must say a few words about Jane's marriage.

The short stay that the real Duke of Lorton had made in the house of the Ardents had been sufficient to possess him fully of all the hopes, and all the fears, and all the affections of its family.

Well did he know the affection that subsisted between Peter Bolt and Jane.

It was, therefore, one of his great wishes, seeing that he had in reality secured the happiness of George and Millicent, to see Jane settled with the man whom she really loved.

Jane really did love Peter Bolt; and when she had said that there was nothing like a little tailor, after all, she meant it.

"Where is Jane?" said the Duke; and when Jane came forward, he said—"Where is Peter Bolt?"

"Here," said Peter, "I be, so frank and free. Jane is the darling of her Peter's heart, and never more from her will Peter part."

"That is right," said the Duke; "now, has anyone any possible or impossible objection to Jane and Peter Bolt being married to-morrow."

"Oh," said Peter, "as sure as fate, I'm patronised by the great. My Jane will be her Peter's wife, and make the joy of all his life."

"Stop," said Jane.

"Eh?"

"I don't think I will be married at all."

"Not mar—eh? Oh!"

"Till next week."

The Duke smiled.

"Fate," said Peter Bolt, striking an attitude. "Fate nearly knocked me on the nob, but now it's as good as a finished job. Jane is my own, I see it clear, and to Peter she will be ever dear."

"Upon my word," said the Duke, "I do think that your poetry is more exquisite than ever, Peter. But I hope Jane will have the wedding to-morrow, and the breakfast can be at Dalewood House."

"In that case, then,' said Jane, "I—a——"

"Yes, in that case she consents," said Mrs. Ardent, "don't you, Jane."

"If I am compelled."

"She is compelled," said Peter Bolt. "Oh, ye gods, and very small fishes, Peter is at the top of all his wishes! Oh, yes."

"Don't be a fool," said Jane, giving him a box on the ears.

"No, don't be a fool," added Mrs. Ardent, giving him a severe rap on the head with a thimble.

"And I tell you what," added Jane to Peter, "if you don't behave yourself, I say, as I said before, I will soon let you know where the broomstick hangs."

"Oh, there's a broomstick?"

"Yes," said Mrs. Ardent, "and very proper, too. She takes after her mother, poor dear, she does; and I can assure your Grace "—here Mrs. Ardent dropped a very low curtsy to the young Duke—"I can assure your Grace that I shall be only too proud to have the wedding breakfast of my daughter at your Grace's house. I have acted like a mother in the whole affair, I beg to say. I have thrown aside, as it was my duty as a mother to do, every obstacle in the way of the happiness of the young couple that I could think of."

The Duke smiled.

Well, the longest night will have an end, and at length the morrow came, and Peter Bolt and Jane Ardent were duly and truly married: the Duke of Lorton giving the bride away; and then the whole party went to Dalewood House, where a most magnificent breakfast awaited them in its grand saloon.

The young Duke drank to the health of the bride, and hardly had the cheers subsided when there came a thundering assault upon the knocker of the door, and several servants came into the saloon in rather a hurried manner.

"Who is it?" said the Duke.

"The Lady Bridget Lorton, your Grace," said one.

"Oh, our Aunt. Admit her."

The folding-doors were thrown open, and the Lady Bridget made her appearance. She looked about her like one in a dream.

The young Duke stepped up to her.

"I am informed, madam," he said, "that you are the sister of my grandfather; is it so?"

"Your grandfather? Oh—oh! Where is the Duke?"

"I am the Duke of Lorton."

"You?"

"Yes, madam," said George Drayton, stepping forward. "There was a great mistake and a great crime. I surrender to this gentleman, who is the real Duke of Lorton, all pretensions to that title. I am here as his guest and his servant."

"Then you—I—that is—oh, gracious! But——"

"Pray be seated, madam," said the young Duke. "Your claims as the sister of my father's father, and as a poor misguided, miserable old woman, are so great that you will not be refused entrance into this company."

"What!"

"Yes, said Peter, "I forgive you, you rum old guy, I do, with all my heart."

"Oh, dear me, where is that respectable person, Mr. Brand?"

"Dead, madam!"

"Dead?"

"Yes. Pray be seated."

"And, sir, you are the Duke of Lorton. What sort of company is this you have about you?"

"Oh, this is Mr. Ardent, a waterman-fireman—this is Mrs. Ardent, bouquet-maker, of Covent Garden—this is Mr. Drayton, my private secretary—this is his wife, Millicent Drayton—this is Corporal Budd, of His Majesty's guards—this is Peter Bolt, court tailor and costumier to the Duke of Lorton—this is Jane, his wife; this is——"

Old Lady Bridget uttered a shriek, and rushed from the room.

"My coach—my coach!" she cried out. "My coach, there, directly! The world is coming to an end. My coach, I say! Oh, this is too dreadful! What will happen next, I wonder? Oh, dear—oh, dear!"

The old lady was in such a violent state of agitation, that it was with great difficulty her two footmen could push her into her coach.

When the lumbering vehicle reached its destination, they opened the door, and presented their arms to help her out.

She did not move.

"My lady," said one; "we are at home."

Still there was no movement.

Lady Bridget was dead! Her own angry passions had brought on a fatal disease of the heart, and she sat in her carriage a corpse, surrounded by the finery that decked it, and the jewellery that glistened upon the cold clay.

The wedding party at the Duke's enjoyed themselves just as well, if not infinitely better, without Lady Bridget, than they would have done with her.

It was quite an affecting thing to hear the speech that Peter Bolt made upon this occasion. He indulged in all those witticisms for which the reader must long ere this have given him credit.

Really, on this occasion, Peter was more than himself; the little witty tailor was converted into a very sensible and well-informed man. He dwelt with such lucidity and brevity on the little episodes that had characterized his courtship, that he quite astonished the Ardents, and even the Duke, who had no idea that Peter could speak so clearly and so much to the purpose as he did on this occasion. He did not omit an iota, and did not forget to eulogize the good disposition of the Duke with the praise that was justly his due.

Mrs. Ardent, too, spoke, and she, in that speech, related all the story about the money that had been hidden in the kitchen by old Ardent. She told this as a sort of moral "Beware!" to the young folks, and ended by saying :

"And so, from all this, I beg of you, Jane, and I beg of you, Peter, never to have any secrets from one another, for they are the bane of all domestic happiness. Tell each other everything in the purest and most perfect confidence, I beg of you."

"We will," said Jane, "we will; and if Peter does not tell me everything, I'll soon make him."

"Yes," said Peter, "she will. I'll take care to keep no secrets from my Jane ; besides, it would be of no use if I did, for every night, when I am between sleep and wakefulness, before I get into my first nap, I talk aloud of everything that has transpired during the day; therefore, if I would keep anything to myself, I cannot, for that confounded habit. But I generally manage to keep out of harm's way, and not commit myself, so that I have never had any particular secrets to divulge ; and I never intend having any secrets of anybody else's, especially about lottery tickets, and such things."

Mrs. Ardent, on the mention of the "lottery ticket," would have boxed Peter's ears, had not the Duke interfered and pacified her rising choler, after which the harmony of the friends proceeded without interruption.

Who now could be so happy, or more happy, at all events, than the young Duke of Lorton? for he made happiness all around him. There can be no possible doubt but that the scenes of adversity he had gone through had done him a world of good, for they taught him that one lesson of life, in which it is very much to be feared the rich are more deficient than in any other.

The lesson is that of sympathy for the distress, the afflictions, and the feelings of the lowly.

* * * *

But little now remains to be told. Jane and Peter Bolt were set up in business by the Duke, and prospered well.

Corporal Budd was given a commission in the army, and rose to be a lieutenant-colonel in India ; and as for George Drayton and Millicent, they lived many years happily, and saw around them a smiling offspring.

Old Lady Bridget, as we have recorded, had died of chagrin and vexation upon finding how she had been taken in by Captain Gay ; and the young Duke himself was soon wedded to one whom he could love, for he wanted the favour of no high family to secure him in the possession of the titles and estates of his ancestors.

It was not long, then, after the marriage of the young Duke of Lorton, that George Drayton, his secretary, took the occasion to call to his mind much that had passed at Lorton Castle, while he, George, had been there along with Captain Gay.

The precise object of George Drayton in so calling to the mind of the young Duke these events, was to try to induce him to go to Ireland.

The Duke hesitated.

"I do not expect," said George Drayton, "that you will be likely to remain at Lorton Castle ; but I am quite certain that from the scenes of riot, waste, and rascality, you will there find that you will be anxious that the noble name you bear shall no longer, even by implication, bend to their association."

"That is a good argument," said the Duke.

"I hope it is."

"It is very good, friend, but I am quite certain that if I visit Lorton Castle it will give me no sort of pleasure, so will you take my commission to go there and thoroughly break up the whole establishment. I care not for it."

George took this commission, and in the course of a month's time Lorton Castle was dismantled and deserted, and it stands now on the coast of Galway, a melancholy ruin, and a sad example of the sort of feeling that an educated and satirical Englishman was likely to have concerning an Irish estate.

Long, then, and happily, did George Drayton and Millicent live, bequeathing to their children an honourable name, while by the fireside of a winter's night, when all was sleet and frost without, and when the keen wind swept past the well-constructed casements, they would tell their children the principal incidents of the most strange and remarkable story of their early lives and loves.

THE END.